THE SECRET SHE KEPT

By *Amelia Carr and available from* Headline Review

DANCE WITH WINGS
A SONG AT SUNSET
A WOMAN OF SECRETS
THE SECRET SHE KEPT

1	41	81	121	161	201	241	281	321	361	401	
2	42	82	122	162	202	242	282	322	362	402	
3	43	83	123	163	203	243	283	323	363	403	
4	44	84	124	164	204	244	284	324	364	404	
5	45	85	125	165	205	245	285	325	365	405	
6	46	86	126	166	206	246	286	326	366	406	
7	47	87	127	167	207	247	287	327	367	407	
8	48	88	128	168	208	248	288	328	368	408	
9	49	89	129	169	209	249	289	329	369	409	
10	50	90	130	170	210	250	290	330	370	410	
11	51	91	131	171	211	251	291	331	371	411	
12	52	92	132	172	212	252	292	332	372	412	
13	53	93	133	173	213	253	293	333	373	413	
14	54	94	134	174	214	254	294	334	374	414	
15	55	95	135	175	215	255	295	335	375	415	
16	56	96	136	176	216	256	296	336	376	416	
17	57	97	137	177	217	257	297	337	377	417	
18	58	98	138	178	218	258	298	338	378	418	
19	59	99	139	179	219	259	299	339	379	419	
20	60	100	140	180	220	260	300	340	380	420	
21	61	101	141	181	221	261	301	341	381	421	
22	62	102	142	182	222	262	302	342	382	422	
23	63	103	143	183	223	263	303	343	383	423	
24	64	104	144	184	224	264	304	344	384	424	
25	65	105	145	185	225	265	305	345	385	425	
26	66	106	146	186	226	266	306	346	386	426	
27	67	107	147	187	227	267	307	347	387	427	
28	68	108	148	188	228	268	308	348	388	428	
29	69	109	149	189	229	269	309	349	389	429	
30	70	110	150	190	230	270	310	350	390	430	
31	71	111	151	191	231	271	311	351	391	431	
32	72	112	152	192	232	272	312	352	392	432	
33	73	113	153	193	233	273	313	353	293	433	
34	74	114	154	194	234	274	314	354	394	434	
35	75	115	155	195	235	275	315	355	395	435	
36	76	116	156	196	236	276	316	356	396	436	
37	77	117	157	197	237	277	317	357	397	437	
38	78	118	158	198	238	278	318	358	398	438	
39	79	119	159	199	239	279	319	359	399	439	
40	80	120	160	200	240	280	320	360	400	440	

First published in 2012 by HEADLINE REVIEW
An imprint of HEADLINE PUBLISHING GROUP

1

Cataloguing in Publication Data is available from the British Library

ISBN 978 0 7553 8405 1

Typeset in Joanna MT by Palimpsest Book Production Limited,
Falkirk, Stirlingshire

Printed and bound by CPI Group (UK) Ltd, Croydon, CR0 4YY

Headline's policy is to use papers that are natural, renewable and
recyclable products and made from wood grown in
sustainable forests. The logging and manufacturing processes
are expected to conform to the environmental
regulations of the country of origin.

HEADLINE PUBLISHING GROUP
An Hachette UK Company
338 Euston Road
London NW1 3BH

www.headline.co.uk
www.hachette.co.uk

To Terry
aka Brit
with all my love

ACKNOWLEDGEMENTS

'You can't judge a book by its cover' they say, but it's the first thing you see when you're trawling the shelves. So the first person I'd like to thank is the jacket designer, Patrick Insole. When I first saw it, I was bowled over, and I just want to keep on looking at it!

As always, though, there are so many other people without whom *The Secret She Kept* would never have reached those shelves. Certainly I could never have written it without the help of people who know a great deal more about sailing than I do, and my grateful thanks goes to George Noden and also to my sister, Hazel Spence. I must emphasise that any blunders I've made are all my own. I'd also like to mention the Jubilee Sailing Trust who put up with me as a very inexperienced crew member on the *Lord Nelson* a couple of years ago. A fantastic experience that I'd like to repeat one day!

Another huge thank you goes to my agent, Sheila Crowley. Her lovely lilting Irish accent on the other end of the telephone always lifts my day. And a special mention for her assistant, Rebecca Ritchie, who gives me unfailing support.

More stars are the folk at Headline – Marion Donaldson and Kate Byrne, my editors, Jane Selley, my copy editor, Helena Towers, who generates wonderful publicity and is always just an email away when I'm trying (very inefficiently) to generate my own, and of course the wonderful sales team.

Someone else I simply couldn't manage without is Richard Spence, my lovely nephew, who looks after my website and is always there to advise me on the many problems I encounter in cyber space. Thanks, Rich – 'Auntie' really appreciates your help!

Last but not least I'd like to thank my husband, Terry, for putting up with the impossible person I become when I'm lost in the world of writing. And of course my daughters, Terri and Suzanne, my son-in-laws, Andy and Dominic, and my gorgeous grandchildren, Tabitha, Barnaby, Daniel and Amelia for all the happiness they bring me. Lots of love to you all!

AUTHOR'S NOTE

The Jubille Sailing Trust, which features in The Secret She Kept, is a real charity which owns and operates the Lord Nelson ship.

Although this setting is real, the characters are fictional and any resemblance to real persons, living or dead is purely coincidental.

For more information visit www.jst.org.uk

From The Falmouth Packet, July 1959

Local Yachtswoman Feared Lost

Well-known local yachtswoman Felicity Penrose is missing, feared lost at sea. Search and rescue helicopters from RNAS Culdrose have sighted her boat, the *Mermaid's Song*, adrift off the Cornish coast, but of Felicity there is no sign. Though the search is continuing, hopes of finding her alive are fading. 'We are not optimistic,' a spokesman said last night.

The loss of Felicity Penrose will be a tremendous shock to the sailing community. A highly respected and vastly experienced sailor, Felicity has competed in countless races and regattas. She and her long-time sailing partner Jo Best were due to compete in the bi-annual Fastnet Race in September.

'It is a terrible tragedy,' Jo Best told this newspaper. 'Fliss will be mourned and missed by so many people, both her friends in the world of sailing, and of course her family.'

Felicity, 25, is the wife of local businessman Martin Dunning and the mother of a two-year-old daughter, Emma, who was last night being cared for at home in Porthtowan by Felicity's sister, Maggie Penrose, whilst Martin, who refuses to give up hope, continues the search.

1

Part One
1989

ONE

EMMA

How can it be that life as you know it can be changed in an instant? That one moment things can be perfectly normal, mundane even, and the next a cloud of uncertainty hides the sun your little world revolves around, and everything has a different texture and colour and taste.

Until recently I thought I knew everything there was to know about myself, and it was all pretty straightforward.

My name is Emma Dunning and I'm a sports teacher at a school in north Cornwall. I was born in 1957, the only child of Martin and Felicity Dunning. My mother, whom everyone knew as 'Fliss', died in a sailing accident when I was two years old. I was brought up by my dad and Maggie, Fliss's sister, who became his second wife.

Maggie is like a mother to me; I barely remember Fliss at all. It's Maggie who has always been there for me, though of course she and Dad couldn't actually get married until seven years after Fliss disappeared and could be declared dead.

These simple facts are the building blocks for my life, the foundations on which everything else rests, and it has never, for one moment, occurred to me to question them.

Why would it?

But then I am confronted by a man who calls himself an 'investigative journalist'. A man who, with one little sentence, makes my world rock on its axis and sends me on a journey of discovery.

Nothing, but nothing, is the way I'd always thought it was.

Nothing will ever be the same again.

It happens, this cataclysm, on a Saturday in June, when I've been sailing. And though today began rather badly, by the time I get back to the Penryn River, I'm feeling in a much better mood.

Sailing can always lift my spirits – however stressed or gloomy I might be before I set sail, when I've had a few hours beyond the shelter of the Carrick Roads, with the wind brisk enough to send me skimming at an exhilarating speed and capricious enough to keep me on my toes, I'm at peace with the world. Today is no exception, though the barney I had last night with Philip, my boyfriend, is still unsolved, and I can't quite shake the nagging doubt that things are never going to work out between us. But strange as it might seem to someone who has never experienced the joy of sailing, I feel a whole lot better able to cope with it than I did when I left home this morning.

I'll try to explain.

Sailing at the weekend is a regular thing as far as I'm concerned, a ritual, really, and has been for as long as I can remember.

Sailing is in my blood. My grandfather, Bill Penrose, who was in the merchant navy until my grandmother, Greta, talked him into a shore-based job, confounded all her plans when he built his own boat, using a telegraph pole for a mast, and sailed it as far as South America before selling it and crewing his way home again.

My mother, Felicity, was practically a career sailor until I came along, and still sailed whenever she could until her death. And my father, Martin, has always kept a boat on the Penryn River. When I was a little girl he used to take me out every Sunday in the Silhouette he had in those days and I would spend the whole week looking forward to it. I learned the ropes from him, both literally and figuratively – how to hoist a mainsail, how to tack, how to run ashore or pick up a mooring. I memorised the Beaufort scale as I did my nine times table, and learned to recognise the different kinds of cloud formation. I knew the names of the sails and the parts of the boat long before I left primary school. I joined the Girls' Nautical Training Corps as soon as I was old enough and loved every moment. But it was still the weekend trip with Dad that I looked forward to most of all.

It's a habit I've kept up. Though I'm now thirty-two years old and have had a boat of my own since I was a teenager – Dad bought me a Laser for my eighteenth birthday – that weekly trip is practically sacrosanct. Trouble is, Philip has other ideas, and really, I can't blame him. He doesn't care for sailing. The few times he's ventured out with me, if the sea is choppy enough for me to get a buzz, he's turned decidedly green, which is not a great deal of fun for either of us. Plus, naturally enough, he would like me to be around so we can share the things he is interested in. I can see all that, but it doesn't alter the fact that I feel deprived if I can't get my fix of open water.

The row last night came about because Philip wanted me to go to Exeter with him today to look at a motorbike he is thinking of buying. And that appealed to me about as much as spending the day watching paint dry.

'Oh Philip – surely you don't want me tagging along?' I groaned.

'I thought it would be a nice day out. We could have a spot of lunch and you can pass your opinion on the bike . . .'

I snorted. 'My opinion wouldn't be repeatable! Anyway, I'm planning to go to Falmouth. And afterwards I want to pop over to Porthtowan to see Dad and Maggie. It's been a couple of weeks now.'

'You could do all that on Sunday. I think you'd enjoy a motorbike if only you'd give it a chance. It's a great feeling, all the freedom of the open road . . .'

'I get my freedom on the open sea. Look, Philip, if you want to go to Exeter, go. But I really don't want to spend the best part of my Saturday stuck in traffic on the A30 and in motorcycle showrooms.'

'OK — please yourself.' Philip said it offhandedly, but I knew he was hurt.

And I felt bad, because I do it all the time and it's just not fair on him. I know, for instance, that he would like us to move in together. He's suggested it, either obliquely or directly, more than once. But the thought of it makes me feel horribly trapped. I don't want to talk about it, think about it even. I like my own space too much. I like to make the decisions about my life without consulting anyone else — probably the reason why I prefer to sail single-handed.

Sometimes I wonder how I came to hook up with Philip in the first place; quite apart from the fact that I am so cussedly independent, we really don't have anything in common. In the beginning, that didn't seem to matter much. We fancied each other rotten and that was enough. Now, though, it's not. I'm irritated instead of flattered that he wants us to do everything together, and I feel horribly guilty because I can't be what he wants, but regretful and frustrated too. There's a part of me that would really like to settle down, get married, have a family. I was thirty-two in April, after all; if I don't get on with it, it will be too late. Philip is a really nice guy. A bit possessive, but kind. Generous. Totally dependable. He might be hankering after a motorbike right now, but deep down he's a pipe-and-slippers type. Give him a few years and he'll make the world's best husband and father. I'd be a fool to let him go. I know that, and yet it still doesn't really make any difference. I still baulk at the thought of being tied into a relationship.

Perhaps I take after my mother; she was a free spirit too, from what I've heard. Certainly I look like her. It's quite uncanny really. My hair is the same dark blond, my eyes the same greeny-blue, and my face more or less the same heart shape. Though I'm already seven years older than she was when she died, looking at photographs of her is still unsettlingly like looking into a mirror. And certainly we share the same love of the sea, inherited from Grandpa Bill Penrose, I suppose. So it would make sense if I'm like her in other ways.

Will I ever feel differently, I wonder? Is there someone out there for whom I'd willingly give up my independence? I'd like to think so. But to be honest, I'm not overly confident of it. No, I was feeling pretty frazzled this morning as I hitched the trailer with my dinghy aboard on to the tow bar of my Audi and headed for the coast.

My mood began to lift, though, the moment I turned into the lane leading down to the Penryn River.

Just as Saturday is my sacrosanct day for sailing, so the Penryn River is my special place. It's not snazzy, like the expensive yacht clubs; it's not even especially convenient, as it's tidal. But it feels like home to me. As I mentioned before, Dad has always kept his boats there and he still prefers to use it, though he could well afford to rent a berth in Falmouth. That's Dad all over. It's not that he's tight-fisted – though he does object to seeing money frittered away unnecessarily – it's just that he really doesn't like ostentation in any way, shape or form. He's happiest in an old sweater darned at the elbows and a pair of faded jeans or cords, and more often than not he drives a second-hand car that has come in as a part exchange – he has a dealership at his garage on the outskirts of St Agnes. Maggie once talked him into getting a flash new convertible, but he wasn't comfortable with it. It lasted less than six months.

He does have rather a nice boat, though, a nineteen-foot West Wight Potter, which, since it's summer, will be at the river. It was quite possible I'd run into him down there. If I didn't, as I told Philip, I planned to make a detour to Porthtowan on my way home to catch up with him and Maggie. If I timed it right, I might get one or two of Maggie's scones, fresh from the oven, or a rock bun, crunchy on the outside, soft and still warm in the middle. Maggie usually bakes on a Saturday, and the fruits of her efforts are to die for.

It was just after ten in the morning as I pulled off the road and into the lane leading down to the river. The turning is so well hidden by high hedges that you could easily miss it if you didn't know it was there. It's like a secret place for people with boats, the rabbit hole leading to Wonderland or the back of the wardrobe from which you can step into Narnia. Narrow and winding, it slopes gently down between banks thick with creamy clusters of cow parsley, spikes of purple foxgloves and spreading bouquets of pink campion. Much of the way the trees meet overhead to form an archway of rippling green through which shards of sunlight sparkle a mosaic of fractured brilliance, but every so often there's the surprise of a gate or the rooftop of an isolated – and possibly luxurious – dwelling where some lucky person lives in perfect peace.

At the end of the lane a broad gravelled parking area opened up on the right. I swung into it, looking around as I did so for Dad's car. It wasn't there, and for once I was actually not sorry. Much as I love Dad, glad as I usually am to see him, at that precise moment all I really wanted was a few hours alone with only myself for company, and the wind and the salt spray blowing away the cobwebs.

I pulled up on the seaward side of the clearing, where a tree-studded lawn slopes away towards a tumble of trees, grabbed my baseball cap from where it was lying on the front passenger seat and put it on, pulling the ponytail of hair that I'd caught up in a scrunchy through the gap above the buckle at the back. Then I headed across the parking area towards an impressive grey stone building that nestles against a high, shrub-covered bank on a plateau cut deep into the steep hillside. It's the home of the Jeavons family, who own the strip of land that runs from here all the way down to the river, and it also accommodates the clubhouse for the sailing folk who keep their boats there.

The door was ajar; I pushed it open and went inside, taking off my sunglasses to allow me to see in the gloomy hallway.

A solidly built middle-aged woman in jeans and a bright

checked shirt emerged from a doorway. Pam Jeavons. Like the rest of this place, there is something unchanging about her. I suppose she must have aged in the years I've known her, but it seems to me she has always looked exactly the same, her hair – iron grey – curly and windswept, her face weather-beaten and leathery.

'Emma!' She looked pleased to see me, but that's Pam all over. She greets all the folk who use her river mooring as long-lost friends; it's another of the charms of the place.

'Hi, Pam. Dad not here today?'

'Not so far. Last time he was here he did say he was pretty busy. One of his sales team is on maternity leave, isn't she?' Pam tucked an irrepressible curl behind her ear; it promptly sprang back again. 'It's time he retired, if you ask me.'

'Dad retire? And let someone else take over his precious business? Never!' I laughed. 'It would be good if he took things a bit more easily though. Is it all right if I launch my boat from here?'

Pam snorted. 'How long have you been coming here? Thirty years?'

'Probably,' I said ruefully. 'I don't want to take advantage, though.'

'You know darned well it's all right. Just as long as you don't bung up the turning circle with that trailer of yours. Saturdays we get quite busy.'

'I won't.' But I was thinking guiltily of the haphazard way I'd parked outside the clubhouse. I didn't want some crusty paying member storming in to complain about a car and trailer causing an obstruction.

'If Dad does come in, will you tell him I'm here?' I said.

'Will do. How long are you likely to be out?'

I checked my watch, a chunky black sports model.

'I should be back around lunchtime, maybe a bit later. Low tide's not until four-ish, is it?'

'Half-four. I'll see you later, then. You will look back in, won't you?'

'Will do.'

It's always sensible to tell someone when you are out on the water alone, and courteous to let them know when you are safely back.

There are those, of course, who don't bother. They are often the ones who cause problems for the coastguard and the rescue services, the ones with little experience and no sense of responsibility. Whilst you need a licence to drive on a road or take a plane into the skies, there is no such restriction on taking a boat out to sea. How can there be, when England is an island with endless miles of shoreline, accessible beaches and hidden coves? It would be unworkable. And yet the sea is the most dangerous and unforgiving of places. It isn't only the reckless or the unwary who come to grief. Understandably, my father drilled that into me from an early age.

My mother was an experienced sailor. Boats and sailing had been her life. Yet she was lost at sea. She'd gone out on what should have been a routine day's sailing off the Cornish coast – more or less the same waters as I was heading for today. The weather had been good, and in any case she was used to much more challenging conditions. But something had gone wrong – just what no one ever knew for sure. That's the way it is with the sea. Make a mistake or simply cross swords with luck and, like my mother, you may never make it home.

I don't remember my mother. Not really. Sometimes a perfume – such as the scent of Imperial Leather soap – or a snippet of music will arouse a hazy memory in me, something that feels almost like a haunting regret; sometimes I look at a picture of her and believe for a moment or two that I really can recall sitting on her lap, playing with her long blond hair. But in reality I think that's just fancy. I was, after all, only two years old when she was lost. The only mother I have ever really known is Maggie and the rest is just wishful thinking. Much as I love Maggie, there's still a little lost part of me that yearns for my real mother, though mostly I acknowledge that I'm just being sentimental and romantic. My mother – Felicity, or Fliss, as she liked to be known – is just a sort of fairy-tale princess from the storybooks I read when I was a little girl, and though I left those books behind long ago, the princess is still there, buried deep in my psyche.

The lesson is that Fliss was a brilliant sailor, and it didn't save her. If she'd told someone that day where she was headed and for how long, maybe the alarm would have been raised earlier and she would have been found before the tides took her. So I abide by the rules. I sign out and I sign in. Usually, anyway.

I said goodbye to Pam and went back outside. I turned my car and trailer and drove out of the parking area, taking it slowly – from this point on the lane is no more than a rough track bordered by woodland on either side. At the bottom of the incline the river opens up, a broad expanse of sparkling blue water dotted with craft of all kinds. Beyond it, Falmouth rises high above the marina and the dockyard; to the left, the Penryn River flows out to meet the sea.

A couple were launching a Topper from the slipway. I waited for them to clear it, then backed up, unloaded the dinghy into the water, tied it up and drove my car and trailer to a spot at the far end of the turning area, where it was unlikely to be in anyone's way. I passed the time of day with a man working on a boat jacked up on timbers, repairing and painting the hull, as I slipped into my waterproof jacket and buoyancy aid and pulled on my fingerless sailing gloves. Then I went back to the dinghy and paddled my way through the craft bobbing between the buoys.

Once I was clear of them, with open water ahead of me, I set sail and headed out towards the open sea.

As I'd hoped, the minute I was out on the water my head was miraculously clear. Trickles of moisture ran in rivers from the corners of my eyes, drying into salty streaks on my cheeks, burning tight and rosy from the wind, and the taste of the salt on my lips along with the salve I plaster on to keep them from drying out was like an elixir. Freedom! A few hours of total, blissful freedom! But I couldn't stay out for ever, much as I would have liked to. If for no other reason, I had to get back in while the tide was high enough to reach the slipway. I tacked back across the Carrick Roads and into the sheltered waters of the river, reloaded my boat on to the trailer and drove back up the narrow lane to the clubhouse.

Still completely unaware that my life was about to change for ever.

There's still no sign of Dad's car outside the clubhouse; clearly he's been too busy with the business to come down to Penryn today. Or maybe he and Maggie have gone out somewhere. I'll give them a quick ring before I make the detour to Porthtowan. There's no point going all the way over there if they aren't at home.

I stop to go in and let Pam Jeavons know I'm safely back. There are two men talking beside a car parked just a few feet from the main entrance to the clubhouse. One I recognise as a regular – he works in a Truro bank, I think – and the woman in the driver's seat, with her window open so that she can join in the conversation, is his wife. The other man is a stranger to me, though – dark hair cropped fashionably short and receding a little at the temples, tall, strong-featured, rather good-looking, with a nose that looks as if it might have been broken at some time. He's wearing chinos and a dark blue polo shirt – not dressed for sailing. None of the three so much as glance at me. They're far too engrossed in their conversation.

Pam is in the outer hall, talking on the telephone. She smiles at me and waves a greeting. I go to the whiteboard to sign myself back in, and by the time I've done it, Pam has finished her phone call.

'You're back, then.'

''Fraid so. Dad never did turn up, I suppose?'

'No.' Pam hesitates. 'Something a bit strange, though. I've had a man here asking about your mother.'

'You mean Maggie,' I correct her.

Pam shakes her head; a strand of iron-grey hair comes loose and springs on to her cheek, which has turned a little pink.

'No. Your real mother. Felicity.'

'What?' I can feel my eyes widening in surprise. 'Someone was here asking about Felicity?'

'Yes. And the sailing crowd from the old days. At first I thought it was someone who used to know her, then I suddenly realised he was too young for that. Stupid, really. I find myself forgetting that time's gone on; I'm no longer the girl I used to be, and the people who were young with me are all middle-aged now. Anyway, when I came to my senses I asked him what his interest was, and he said something about researching for a book.'

'A book,' I repeat, trying to get a handle on this.

'That's what he said.' Pam flicks again at the offending lock of hair. 'The thing is, I told him you were out sailing and you'd be coming back later, but I've been wondering ever since whether I did the right thing. I'm not convinced he was being strictly truthful. Some of the questions he asked were . . . well, a bit odd, and after he left I saw him talking to some of the regulars outside. Ed Brinkworth, for one, and his wife. He'd been out sailing, and she'd come to pick him up . . .'

Ed Brinkworth, that's the name of the Truro banker. Who was in conversation with a man I didn't know at all and was presumably the person who had been asking about my mother.

'I think he's still here,' I say. 'At least, he was when I came in. OK, thanks, Pam, I'll have a word with him, find out what it's all about.' I pick up my car keys from the table beneath the whiteboard and head back out to the parking area.

The stranger is still there, talking now to Ed Brinkworth's wife through the open window of the car. Ed has gone round to the passenger side and is half in and half out of the door. I walk towards them, wait, watching them pointedly. I'm not near enough to hear what's being said, but Mrs Brinkworth appears to be enjoying herself. Eventually, with a smile and a wave, she closes the window and moves off. I walk purposefully towards the stranger.

'I'm Emma Dunning. I understand you're interested in my mother, Felicity Penrose.'

For just a moment he looks slightly disconcerted, then he recovers himself.

'Emma. I'm very pleased to meet you.' He holds out his hand; I ignore it. He looks OK, in fact he looks rather nice, but I'm suspicious of him all the same. It's a bit peculiar to say the least that he is asking questions about my mother.

'I'm Mike Bond. I'm a writer.' He gets a business card out of his wallet and offers it to me.

I glance at the card and push it into my pocket.

'Yes, Pam Jeavons told me. I'm rather puzzled, though, as to what your interest is in my mother. It's almost thirty years now since she died.'

'Right.' There's a strange, wary note in his voice, though, almost as if there is some question about that, and an almost rueful expression in his rather nice dark-brown eyes.

'You're writing a book about women sailors, is that it?'

'Not exactly . . .' Again the wariness.

'What, then?' My curiosity is beginning to be tinged with something that feels strangely like alarm, though for the life of me I don't know why.

He's silent for a moment, those brown eyes narrowed and looking not at me, but past me. Then he seems to make up his mind.

'I think it might be better if we went somewhere a bit more private. If there's a pub near here, maybe I could buy you a drink . . .?'

Is he trying to pick me up? Somehow I don't think so. But I have no intention of going somewhere 'more private' with a man I don't know from Adam, and certainly not until I know what all this is about.

'No thank you,' I say crisply. 'All I want to know is why you're asking questions about my mother and her friends.'

He hesitates. 'This isn't really the right place. It would be better if we could—'

'Surely you can just tell me what your interest is.'

Still he hesitates. 'I'm afraid you might find it upsetting . . .'

16

I'm becoming irritated. 'I've had thirty years to come to terms with the fact that my mother died in a sailing accident,' I say shortly.

He removes his sunglasses so that he is looking at me very directly. 'You're sure about that, are you?'

'Of course I'm sure!' I snap. 'I'm quite capable of talking about my mother without getting upset.'

'No. What I meant was . . . are you sure that she died?'

His words startle me so much that I almost laugh.

'What on earth do you mean?'

'Your mother. Are you quite certain she isn't still alive?'

'This is ridiculous,' I say impatiently. 'You've got hold of the wrong end of the stick somewhere. My mother was lost in an accident at sea. In 1959. She was drowned.'

'*Presumed* drowned.' The way he emphasises the word, and the fact that he is watching me expectantly, suddenly makes me want to hit him.

'Her body was never found, if that's what you mean. Well of course it wasn't! She was well out to sea when the accident happened. But . . .'

And then he drops the bombshell.

'Look, I realise this may be one hell of a shock for you . . .' He hesitates, and his eyes, narrowed, are on my face. 'The thing is, there's some suggestion that your mother didn't drown at all. That she is actually still alive.'

Words fail me. This is beyond crazy. And yet uncertainty is jolting in my stomach and I have the dreadful feeling of standing on the edge of a precipice, a yawning chasm at my feet.

'This is preposterous!' I flare. 'I never heard such nonsense in my life!'

And then he says the thing that really tilts my world on its axis.

'I'm sorry, Emma, but the fact is that your mother was seen alive, in America, some time after she supposedly died.'

TWO

MIKE

The girl – Emma Dunning – couldn't look more shocked if I'd hit her in the face with a hammer drill, and I feel like a complete and utter heel.

There are times when I hate what I do, and this is one of them.

Investigative reporter. Not the sort of job to earn you many brownie points with Joe Public – unless the person you're exposing happens to be a banker, a member of parliament or an estate agent, about the only professions that rank lower in the popularity stakes than a journalist of any persuasion.

More often than not, of course, that's exactly what my marks are. A fraudster of some kind, destroying the lives of others for his own greedy ends; a captain of industry who has cheated his employees out of their pensions; a local politician on the make. There's a huge satisfaction in laying their exploits bare and showing them up for the despicable characters they are. But this . . . this is something else entirely, and I really don't like it.

From my information it would seem that Felicity Penrose faked her own death thirty years ago. At the moment I haven't a clue why she did it – and I'm not even one hundred per cent sure whether she did it at all. But whether she did or didn't it's not the fault of her daughter, who was only two years old when she was presumed lost, and she's the one in the firing line now. The repercussions are going to hit her hard – the publicity, the emotional fallout, the whole damn kaboosh – and that's what makes me feel such a swine.

She looks like a nice ordinary girl, even if she does bear an almost uncanny resemblance to the Felicity whose profile I've checked out. Same dark blond hair, same clear-cut features, similar build – slimly athletic, yet at the same time rounded. Not even the clothes have changed that much – shorts, deck shoes, loosely buttoned shirt over a vest top. But she's the one whose world is going to go arse over tip, and I wish I could spare her that.

Trouble is, I can't. I need this story and the money it's going to bring me – if it turns out there *is* a story. If I don't make a decent killing soon, I'm going to be in big trouble financially – and we're talking serious stuff here, like the mortgage company repossessing the house that I call mine, but which is technically theirs. I could take that, I guess, if it was just me who'd be out on the street. I've managed in tight situations before and I'd manage again. But it's not just me. It's Daisy, my seven-year-old daughter, and I can't play games with her security.

Sorry as I might feel for this Emma Dunning, it's no way enough to make me back off. When her comfort and well-being is in conflict with Daisy's, it's no contest. Daisy comes first every time. A strange girl is nowhere in it.

Which is why I stand my ground, look her in the eye and harden my tone.

'Suppose I was to tell you that my information is that your mother was seen in Florida some time after she was supposed to have died by someone who knew her? That the suggestion is that in fact she is still very much alive? Does that surprise you, Emma? Or have you known all along?'

Whatever you may think, however it looks now, I haven't always been a heartless shit. Once upon a time, in what now seems like another lifetime, I was an honest-to-goodness journalist with a skin no thicker than most – chief reporter with a regional daily in the Midlands.

Life was good, unbelievably good. Besides the job, which I enjoyed, I was a happily married man with a lovely wife and a beautiful little daughter.

And then it all fell apart.

Sometimes, when I'm looking at life through the bottom of a whisky tumbler, it seems to me that things started to go wrong with the Stamford case. Though of course that had nothing whatever to do with the decimation of my private life, it somehow marks the boundary between 'then' and 'now'.

Frazer Stamford was a prominent local councillor, chair of God knows how many committees, trustee of this and that, on the board of governors of several schools. He'd been invited to garden parties at Buckingham Palace, and awarded an OBE. His beneficent face and portly stomach regularly graced the pages of the *Advertiser*. A man most admired. A pillar of the community. And then I was told, very quietly, about the wads of money in brown envelopes that were changing hands, wads of money that were finding their way into various bank accounts belonging to Frazer Stamford in exchange for certain firms gaining lucrative council contracts.

Naturally, I went after the story. And the deeper I dug, the more muck I uncovered. Far from being the upright citizen he pretended to be, Frazer Stamford was little more than a crook, and the losers, ultimately, were the taxpayers, who believed him to be something between a saviour and a saint.

Trouble was, Stamford had friends in high places, some of them, no doubt, as corrupt as he was. When I tried to run the story I was told in no uncertain terms to bury it. I refused. The people Stamford represented deserved the truth. I got my way, the story aired, and a police investigation ended up with Stamford being sent to prison. But my position on the paper was no longer tenable. I wasn't sacked, exactly, but you could say I'd have had a case for constructive dismissal if I'd chosen to take it to tribunal.

I went freelance. The Stamford case had attracted the attention of the nationals and I was able to make a good living stringing for them, writing articles, features and comment, and, when the chance arose, getting my teeth into other exposés too.

Bev, my wife, wasn't keen on the exposés, though I must admit I got a buzz out of them. She didn't like the subterfuge and she was nervous that one day I'd be attacked and have my own hidden camera or tape recorder broken over my skull.

'What would I do if anything happened to you?' she used to say.

'You'd run off with one of your rich ex-boyfriends and live a life of luxury,' I'd joke – Bev had the sort of looks that always made me wonder why she'd given me a second glance, much less married me, when she could have had her pick from practically every red-blooded male who entered her orbit.

'I don't want a life of luxury,' she'd say. 'At least not with any of them. I want you. So don't you dare get yourself killed. If you do, I'll never forgive you.'

And I'd kiss her and tell her I had no intention of allowing myself to be killed, and neither of us had the faintest premonition that Bev was the one who would die and I was the one who'd be left. Why would we? Who thinks, in this day and age, that having a child is going to kill a fit, healthy young woman?

That's what happened, though. And all the more ironic since we were both so delighted when Bev fell pregnant again. Daisy – four years old at the time – was delighted too at the prospect of a baby brother or sister, though she was determined it would be a sister, who, she announced, should be called Cinderella. (Cinderella was actually second choice – for some unfathomable reason her first choice was Calibrese.)

Truth to tell, I've never quite been able to forgive myself for not spotting something was wrong, though how I could be expected to know when the health professionals missed it I don't know. I'd never even heard of pre-eclampsia. But it's not a word I'm ever likely to forget now. It's what killed Bev and the little unborn Cinderella/Calibrese too. Suddenly I was a widower, half crazy with grief and shock, with the sole care of a four-year-old who couldn't understand where her mummy had gone, and why, when she cried for her, she didn't come back.

I don't know how we'd have got through if it hadn't been for Tom and Judy, Bev's parents. Though they were in a hell of a state too over Bev's death, they rallied round in a way I'll never be able to repay, arriving on the doorstep and promising to stay as long as they were needed.

It couldn't be a permanent arrangement, of course, and since I was freelance and not tied to an office desk it made sense to move to Somerset where they live so they could help me care for Daisy. I put the house on the market, glad to be going somewhere where the memories of happier times weren't constantly smothering me, and found a semi on a newish estate half a mile or so from Tom and Judy's home. It would be ideal for Daisy and me – or so I thought. I didn't expect to be happy – happiness was a concept that had died with Bev – but at least we'd be OK, and I could build a secure life for my daughter.

Trouble is, nothing has really worked out as I hoped. Three years on and Daisy certainly seems bright and well adjusted, so that, I suppose, is something to be grateful for, but I'm struggling, and I'm worried that if I don't make a breakthrough soon her world is going to fall apart all over again.

In the beginning I worked like a maniac, not only to pay the bills but because when I was concentrating on a story I wasn't thinking about Bev. But after a while things started getting difficult.

At first I blamed the pressures that were distracting me and eating into my working day. Wonderful as Judy and Tom were, in the last resort Daisy was my responsibility. She had to be taken to school each morning and collected each afternoon – at ten past three, for goodness' sake. That meant me packing up work at quarter to at the latest, and getting back to it when she was at home wasn't that easy. But as time went on I began to realise it was more than that.

Somewhere along the line I'd lost the will to work. Grief was destroying me in insidious ways. I couldn't seem to concentrate on anything. Inspiration deserted me. The more desperate I became, the more the fog of doubt around me thickened. What the hell was I going to write that would sell? And if I couldn't sell, how were Daisy and I going to get by?

And then the Felicity Penrose story dropped out of a clear blue sky and struck me on the shoulder, courtesy of my old drinking pal and former colleague, Gerald North.

Gerald called me last Sunday morning, which took me a bit by surprise. I hadn't heard from him lately.

'How are you doing, mate?' he asked. 'Busy at the moment?'

I groaned. 'Suffering at the moment.'

It was no less than the truth. The previous night, in a fit of melancholy, I'd polished off the best part of a bottle of whisky, and I had a monumental hangover. To make things worse, I'd promised Daisy we'd go for a bike ride this morning, and the thought of jolting along the cycle track on my ancient tourer was not an enticing one, given my throbbing head. I'd asked Daisy to cut me a bit of slack for an hour, and she'd disappeared to the walk-in cupboard in her bedroom that I'd turned into a little den for her, with a desk-height shelf and a stool, and which could be anything she wanted it to be. Sometimes it was a shop, sometimes a house. More often it was the HQ of a spy ring or a Tardis. But whatever it was today, it would not distract Daisy from the bike ride for ever.

'You do sound a bit groggy,' Gerald agreed. 'Perhaps I can cheer you up. A piece of info came my way the other day, and it crossed my mind it might be of some use to you – if you're still into the investigative stuff. I don't know whether there's anything in it or not, of course. But if there is, it could be quite a story.'

The kettle was boiling; I reached for it, poured water on to coffee granules and stirred.

'Go on.'

'Have you ever heard of a yachtswoman called Felicity Penrose?'

'Can't say I have.'

'No, me neither. But back in the late fifties she was pretty well known. She and her sailing partner, Jo Best, were into ocean-going racing amongst other things, and making their mark by all accounts. Besides which she was intrepid, good looking, a bit of a pioneer. Sailing was still very much a man's world back then. Women had to fight to be accepted.'

'Right.' So far I wasn't exactly fired up. 'This is going to be a latter-day women's lib story, is it?'

'Patience, young man! Would I be ringing you on a Sunday morning with a women's lib story? Believe me, this has got everything. Or the potential for everything.'

'OK. Go on.'

'Fliss was hitting the headlines pretty regularly back in those days. High-profile sponsors coming out of the woodwork, records broken, even a near-disaster when she and Jo got caught in a catastrophic storm. Then, less than a year later, she went missing off the Cornish coast. In relatively calm water. Her boat was recovered, but there was no sign of Felicity. The boom was flapping loose and it was assumed she'd had some kind of accident and gone overboard. These things happen apparently. Anyway, she was given up for dead.'

I took a sip of still-scalding black coffee.

'And . . .?'

'Well, you can guess what I'm going to tell you next.' He sounded smug.

'You're going to tell me she's turned up somewhere, alive and kicking.' It didn't take a genius to work it out, even if I was pretty thick-headed this morning.

'On the button. My information is that she was seen in America some time after she was supposed to have drowned.'

'Some time. We're talking . . . what?'

'A long time ago, I grant you. But if she didn't die in that accident, if she just did a disappearing trick and fooled everybody, what does it matter when it was? The story still holds good. It certainly made the news at the time, and there was an insurance payout involved, I shouldn't wonder. Anyway, I just thought I'd pass it on in case you might be interested.'

'That's very good of you, mate.' I reached across the breakfast table, pushing aside Daisy's Peter Rabbit egg cup and a glass containing the remains of her orange juice, and reached for a discarded envelope and a pencil. 'So, who's your informant?'

Gerald chortled.

'The wife.'

'Your wife? Molly?'

'Well, around and about. She's just come back from a golfing holiday in Florida with her sister. She got talking to this chap who hails from Cornwall, though he's been in the States for more than thirty years. It was his wife, now dead, it seems, who spotted Felicity – she'd known her back in England.'

'And they've waited all this time to say anything about it?'

'Apparently so. But you know the old saying – there's nowt as queer as folk. Anyway, let me give you the chap's name and contact number and you can get in touch with him yourself. If Molly wrote it down right, of course. But I expect she did. I often say she should have been the newspaper reporter, not me.'

I took down the details, thanked Gerald again and we chatted for a few minutes. For all my early scepticism, I was beginning to feel optimistic. Years of being a journalist has given me a good nose for a story, and it was twitching now. All of a sudden the old enthusiasm was stirring in my veins, my headache was miraculously easing and I actually wanted to get started on looking into this. It was a feeling I hadn't experienced in a long while.

But, keen as I was, my investigation would have to wait. I'd promised Daisy we'd go for a cycle ride and I couldn't let her down.

I went upstairs. As I'd expected, the DO NOT DISTURB sign was hanging on Daisy's door. I tapped, and opened it a crack, causing Daisy to shriek at me indignantly.

'No, Daddy! You can't come in! I'm busy with top-secret stuff! Don't you *dare* come in!'

'Oh, right. So you don't want to go for a bike ride any more? Well, that's OK by me.'

The cupboard door scraped open hastily, and the bedroom door was flung wide.

'Daddy! Did you say . . .?'

'A bike ride, yes. But if your spy stuff is more important . . .'

'No! Well . . .' Daisy made a determined grab at her dignity. 'I expect it can wait.'

Like my research into what might, or might not, be a story to save our bacon, I thought wryly.

That was last Sunday. Since then I've been busy.

It took me several attempts before I got hold of the man in Florida whose name and contact details Gerald had given me, and in the meantime I researched everything I could lay my hands on regarding Felicity Penrose.

As Gerald had said, it seemed she had been pretty well known in the sailing world and beyond in the late fifties, and there was a good deal of coverage of her exploits in the tabloids. Hardly surprising, really: she and her sailing partner, Jo Best, were two very attractive girls, Felicity – or Fliss, as she apparently liked to be known – a petite blonde, Jo a statuesque brunette. The icing on the cake was that their boat was named after their sponsor – *Pretty's Pickles* – a gift to the caption writers and subeditors. I could well imagine their delight at being handed an opportunity to dream up the headlines. 'Pretty Pair in a Pickle' was pretty typical. The rest I'll leave to your imagination.

The girls didn't look to be in a pickle, though. Posed beside a winch, brief shorts exposing long suntanned legs, they looked happy and confident. What really shook me was learning that Felicity was married with a daughter. How the hell could a mother go off sailing and leave a small child behind? Bev hated spending so much as a night away from Daisy – actually it used to annoy me that the few times we snatched some time away together she'd been totally unable to relax and enjoy the break. Instead she'd worried constantly, and rang home several times a day to make sure Daisy was all right. Not what I'd had in mind when I'd booked a weekend in a hotel on the Rialto in Venice. But there you go, that was Bev, and the way she was was one of the reasons I loved her.

Clearly this Felicity Penrose (she still went by her maiden name in the sailing world – for ease of identification, I presumed) had no such qualms.

And if there was any truth in the suggestion that she had faked her own death, then it was even worse than that. She'd abandoned her daughter not just for a few weeks, but for good.

That made me pretty damned angry. I don't usually allow myself to get emotionally involved with the stories I'm working on, but I know from bitter personal experience just how desolate a little girl can be when she's crying for a mother who doesn't come. It could be, of course, that this particular little girl was so used to being left in the care of others that it didn't affect her that much. But I could still feel my jaw tightening as I looked at that pretty face, the smile of a girl without a care in the world, who must have been selfish at best and callous and cruel at worst.

That's probably the reason why I had no qualms approaching the daughter just now. She's the living image of the girl in those old photographs. When I saw her I somehow projected my disgust for Felicity on to her. Only to realise that she is very likely the injured party in all this. She's the one whose world is going to fall apart. If there's any truth in the story. And always provided she doesn't already know – it hasn't escaped me that the family might have been in on the whole thing for some reason or other, an insurance scam, perhaps. But I have to admit that seems fairly unlikely, given what Maurice Gooding told me when I finally got hold of him – Maurice Gooding is the man in the States Gerald put me on to.

Getting hold of him was a feat in itself. Apparently, since he has been widowed, Maurice spends most of his time at the golf club – which was where he got talking to Molly, presumably.

And could the man talk! Bad – very bad – for my phone bill, but good for getting every last detail of the story.

It was Maurice's late wife, Barbara, who had seen the woman she was convinced was Felicity. She too had been born and brought up in Truro and for a time had moved on the periphery of the same circles. When Felicity was lost, Barbara's mother had told her about it in one of her letters and sent her cuttings from the local paper.

It had given her 'quite a turn', Maurice said, when she'd seen Felicity 'alive and kicking' in Naples.

'Naples?' I repeated, thinking for a moment I'd somehow got my wires crossed and ended up in the wrong country.

'Naples, yes. Over on the west coast. Barb had gone over for a day out with some of her ladies' club, and they were walking round the marina when she saw her. She was with some guy. Twined all round one another, according to Barb. She didn't know who he was, but she thought he was one of the sailing crowd. Brown as a nut, in shorts and those boots they all wear.'

'But she was sure it was Felicity?'

'Sure as dammit. She never got the chance to speak to her, though. The marina was pretty busy, and in any case Felicity was otherwise engaged, but she was adamant it was her.'

'And she never saw her again?'

'No. Never. I told her she had to have been mistaken, but she still stuck to it, right up until the day she died. "I'd love to know the truth of it," that's what she used to say.'

It really wasn't a great deal to go on. A sighting of a girl who might or might not have been Felicity in a Florida marina almost thirty years ago by a woman who could no longer verify her impressions.

It's all too easy to make a mistake in any case. I know that from bitter experience. How many times have I thought I've caught sight of Bev on a crowded street? Same slim build, same burgundy hair, same oversized shirt and black leggings. My heart would start pounding, and although I knew it couldn't be, I'd hurry to catch that ghost of my dead wife. Only to discover when she turned around that not only was she not Bev, she didn't even come close. Besides which, Barbara Gooding, by her own admission, hadn't known Felicity all that well, and the chances were that the girl she'd seen had been wearing sunglasses and maybe a baseball cap as well, a blonde in the sort of clothes they all wore for sailing. But I didn't want to let this go. Whether my antennae were waving because there really was a story here, or just because I was hoping there was, I still intended to follow it as far as I could.

Which, to begin with, was not very far at all. For all my efforts, I couldn't find any trace of Jo Best; she seemed to have disappeared as completely as Fliss. And when I drove down to Falmouth this morning I didn't make much progress there either. The sailors messing about on boats on slipways and in the marina were too young to be any help, and gave me blank looks when I mentioned Felicity's name, and access to the Royal Yacht Club, where I guessed I'd find most of the older, richer, more committed sailors, was denied me. After a couple of fruitless hours I had nothing to show for my efforts but a sunburned nose and a raging thirst. I treated myself to a pint of lemonade and lime and a pasty in one of the harbourside pubs, and there I struck lucky. The barman knew the Penrose family, and told me that Martin Dunning, Felicity's husband, kept a boat on the Penryn River. So, without a great deal of hope, I followed his directions and found the clubhouse at the bottom of the well-concealed lane.

The woman in the clubhouse was friendly enough, but fairly unhelpful, and I was on the point of deciding this was a wild-goose chase when my luck changed.

First, there was the lady in the car park who'd come to pick up her husband in her 4x4. To begin with, I wasn't hopeful. She didn't look the outdoor type, with her expensive hairdo, glossy make-up and military-style jacket with power shoulder pads, but she was about the right age, and sure enough, when I mentioned Felicity's name, she couldn't wait to have a good bitch.

According to her, Felicity had been – not to put too fine a point on it – rather popular with the men, and the fact that she was married with a child hadn't been much of a deterrent. 'If she hadn't been alone on that boat of hers, I'd suspect that one of the wives or girlfriends of one of her admirers pushed her in,' she said archly.

My antennae were twitching again now, rejuvenated all over again as I remembered that Barbara Gooding had said Felicity had been with a man when she had supposedly seen her.

'She had affairs, then?'

'Flings, certainly.' Her lip curled. 'She was certainly the type. Simon Beacham, for one, was besotted with her. Whether they had an affair I couldn't say, but I certainly remember them whispering in corners.'

'Simon Beacham?' I prompted.

'Yes. He had a sail repair shop in Falmouth, and taught part time in one of the sailing schools as I remember it. He was in a terrible way when she drowned; went off to sail the world soon afterwards, to get over her, I always thought.'

'Did he ever come back?' I asked, striving to sound casual.

'Not to my knowledge. He was somewhere in America the last I heard.'

America again. This was beginning to look good. Before I could ask any more, however, the woman's husband emerged from the clubhouse. He was less inclined to be chatty; in fact, I got the distinct impression he was anxious to change the subject. Had he been one of the men who'd been under Felicity's spell? I wondered. That would explain why his wife was so ready to dish the dirt on Felicity.

And then I hit the jackpot. The pair of them suddenly clammed up, looking embarrassed. And when they drove off, I discovered the reason for it.

A girl was crossing the car park, approaching me. A girl who looked uncommonly like the photographs I'd seen of Felicity Penrose. And who, a moment later, was introducing herself as Emma Dunning, and asking me what my interest was in her mother.

Which brings me to where I am now. Feeling like a complete and utter heel. All the colour has drained from the girl's face; her suntan looks as if it has been painted on to a blank canvas.

'I'm sorry,' I say. 'I really didn't want to have this conversation in a car park. But . . .'

'Where on earth did you get this ridiculous idea from?' she flares. But there's something that might almost be uncertainty in her face. 'What sort of a writer are you anyway?'

'A journalist,' I say. 'Look, why don't you let me buy you that drink. I can explain, and you—'

'You must be joking!' she snaps. 'A journalist! I have nothing whatever to say to you.'

She turns her back on me, begins to walk away across the parking area, pace fast, shoulders rigid.

'Emma . . .'

She ignores me.

I think of going after her; change my mind. There's really no point just at this moment. It may be that when she's had time to think she'll get in touch with me – she still has my card. But I'm fairly certain she was totally shocked by what I'd said. If Felicity is still alive, Emma doesn't know anything about it.

Besides which, I'm still feeling bad about what I've done to her. And little does she know, there's worse to come. If there's anything in all this – and I'm beginning to think there is – then it would seem likely Felicity faked her death in order to run off with a man. This Simon Beacham, if I'm not much mistaken. That is going to hit Emma pretty hard. I can't imagine what it would be like to discover your mother could abandon you so lightly.

I can't stop now, though, just because I feel sorry for her. It's too important to me. And at least I now have a few facts to work on. A name for Felicity's lover, and an occupation. A 'last heard of' location that seems to tie in with Naples, where Felicity was allegedly spotted. Looking for a sailing school in Florida might be like looking for a needle in a haystack, but I'll give it my best shot. I hope Emma Dunning doesn't get hurt in the process, but if she does, there's not a lot I can do about it.

THREE

THE LINK

The fat A3 envelope is propped up on the ledge in the minute hallway that is the communal entrance to the block of flats, too big to fit into a basket in the wire mail tray. Melanie Thomas sees it the moment she comes in the front door, and her heart gives a little skip. She's pretty sure, even before she picks it up, that it's the brochure she's been waiting for ever since Anna, her mother, suggested she send for it. The logo inscribed along with the franking confirms it. The Jubilee Sailing Trust. Mel tucks it safely under her arm while she swivels the keys on her key ring to select the one that opens her own door, then puts it down on the kitchen table, intending to change out of her work clothes and pour herself a glass of wine before opening it. But she can't wait. She gets a knife from the wooden block on the counter and slices the envelope open neatly – is it working in a bank that makes her so pernickety? she wonders – and extracts the glossy brochure.

There's a picture of a tall ship in full sail on the cover, billowing white canvas against a clear blue sky. The sea is blue too, a deeper greeny blue, smudged with a light shadow that seems to be the reflection of the sails. The imp of excitement skips in Mel once again, and for the first time in months she's looking forward rather than back.

The sea has always drawn her, though she'd never in a million

33

years have thought of taking up sailing. Unsurprising, really. Living in London, it isn't as though the sea is on her doorstep. And it's good that she's planning to do something completely different. Stretching herself, moving out of the comfort zone that has become a prison. Distancing herself from the person she's become – a victim. She hates that image of herself, although it's not far from the truth. Victim of a freak accident that would never have happened if she hadn't been running away that awful night from a husband she didn't love and was actually beginning to actively dislike. Victim of her own stupidity in rushing into a marriage she'd known was wrong for her even before the ring was on her finger.

She should have called a halt then, before it was too late, but she hadn't. She was too desperate to fill the gaping hole that Mark had left in her life and in her heart.

Oh Mark! Just the whisper of his name is an aching echo deep inside. Mark, whom she had adored, and whom she had been so sure loved her back, even when to believe it seemed a dream too far. Mark, whom she had thought was her soulmate. Mark, whom she can't forget, even now, three years after he unceremoniously dumped her, still tugging at her heartstrings, still a yearning in her soul.

How could she ever have been so stupid as to think that marrying Brian could be the answer? But in the beginning the attention he'd paid her had been balm for her wounded pride and her aching heart. He'd made her feel good again, spoiling her with presents and compliments, taking her on special surprise outings. He was handsome and generous and popular – everyone liked him. And so she'd allowed herself to be led along a path she should have known was the wrong one, sleepwalking to disaster.

The problems hadn't been long in coming.

Mel had known from quite early on that Brian was possessive, forever imagining that every other man had designs on her, but after they were married, things became much, much worse. He didn't like her going out alone, to meet her girlfriends, even tried to come between her and her mother. He criticised the clothes she bought as 'too revealing'. In a club one night he practically got into a fight with a young man who approached her and tried to chat her up while Brian was at the bar buying drinks. He opened her mail and listened in to her phone calls. He put her down both in private and in public, as if he wanted her to feel small, and thus dependent on him. It was absolutely getting to her but she couldn't help blaming herself. He probably knew that deep down she was still in love with Mark; she should never have married him feeling the way she did. And the fact that he was so good to her in many ways – buying her flowers and extravagant gifts, taking her out for candlelit meals in expensive restaurants, bringing her breakfast in bed on Sundays – only made her feel more guilty, more to blame.

She had to have some freedom, though, otherwise she'd have gone mad, even though she sometimes wondered if it was worth the Spanish Inquisition she had to face every time when she came home. She tried very hard not to rise to the bait, but that was getting to her too.

The night that changed everything came just before Christmas. All seventeen of the girls at the bank where Mel worked had gone out for a celebratory seasonal meal. It had been a good night: they'd had a private room at a pub, they'd sprayed each other with party poppers and pulled crackers, donned the paper hats and hooted with laughter at how weak the jokes and mottos were. They'd eaten melon, and turkey with all the trimmings, Christmas pudding and mince pies, and drunk a good deal of sparkling wine. By half past ten they were all rather merry and not yet in the mood to go home.

Brian had said he'd come and fetch Mel about eleven, but two or three of the others said they had a taxi booked, so why didn't she share it with them, since it would be going practically past her front door. It seemed silly to get Brian out on a cold, foggy night. Mel rang him and told him not to bother coming for her, which he seemed to accept as sound good sense. But when she eventually got in, at half past eleven, it was a different story entirely.

She'd thought Brian would be in bed, but he wasn't. He was watching for her from the window – she saw the curtains twitch as the taxi pulled up outside. The minute she got inside the house, he went for her.

'Where have you been?'

'You know where I've been! The office party.'

'Until this time of night?'

'Brian – it's not that late.'

'And who was that man in the car with you?'

'Man?' Mel was totally bemused.

'There was a man. He came round and opened the door for you.'

'That was the taxi driver,' Mel said, exasperated.

'It didn't look like a taxi to me.'

For once Mel didn't feel like appeasing him. Perhaps it was all the wine she'd drunk, but she really couldn't be bothered with this. She turned away impatiently.

'Oh for heaven's sake! I'm going to bed.'

'Don't you walk away from me!' He grabbed her by the arm, and something snapped in Mel's head. She wrenched herself free and swung round to face him.

'And don't you tell me what to do! I've had enough of it, Brian. You don't own me.'

'You're my wife. You'll do as I say. And I won't have you cavorting around town making a show of yourself and coming home at all hours with strange men. Understood?'

'Is that so! Well, I might just go out again, see if I can find another *strange man*.'

She headed for the door. She had no real intention of going anywhere, she just wanted to make her point, but with Brian still yelling at her, she didn't want to back down. Tears had sprung to her eyes; she couldn't bear this any more. She'd had such a lovely evening, and now . . .

Mel rushed out, on to the narrow pavement that curved around the corner into a minor road. Afterwards she could never understand why she didn't hear the motorcycle or see its lights; she could only suppose she was blinded by tears, deafened by the roar of angry despair in her ears. The first thing she was aware of was a strange sensation of flying, followed by a dull thud as her body hit the ground and the screech of tearing metal as the motorbike veered into the railings of the pedestrian crossing she should have used. She felt no pain, only profound shock. Brian was there, turning her over, cradling her in his arms, and the light of a street lamp was a fuzzy orange corona floating in space. And then the darkness was closing in and she could no longer see it.

One little act of defiance, and what had it cost her! As well as a broken leg and a dislocated shoulder, Mel's spleen was ruptured and had to be removed. She could, perhaps, have lived with that – or rather, without it – even though she had to be careful of the infections she was prone to without its protection, but much harder to bear, almost impossible at first, was that she had also lost an eye. A total freak, they said, meaning the accident – there'd been a jagged piece of brick in the road, thrown, no doubt, by hooligans earlier in the evening, and she had managed to land face down on it. But Mel thought the choice of expression was pretty tactless, since it could well refer to her now, too.

She was devastated, by both the disability – though she did adjust to that sooner than she'd anticipated – and the disfigurement. They could do wonderful things with prostheses these days, they said; hers would look so good no one would ever know. Mel doubted that was true. And in any case, *she* would know. She couldn't imagine her face ever returning to normal, either; the egg-like swelling on her cheekbone showed no sign of subsiding, even when the bruising had faded.

When she came out of hospital she had gone home to Bromley, staying with Anna, her mother, while she convalesced. There was no way she could be left alone all day while Brian was at work, and in any case, she didn't want to go home. Whilst she was in hospital she'd had plenty of time to think, and she knew she couldn't face going back to her horrible marriage. What was more, she didn't think Brian actually wanted her any more; he could barely bring himself to look at her, and she knew he was disgusted by her disfigurement. The pretty girl he'd married and was so jealous of had become a monster in his eyes; he hadn't liked to think of other men desiring her, but now that, in his opinion, they wouldn't, she had lost her attraction for him. When she told him she wanted a divorce, he raised no objection; they'd filed for a 'quickie' and it had gone through with practically no trouble at all, since they'd been in rented accommodation and had no possessions to speak of to argue over.

Throughout it all, Anna was a tower of strength, but that was only to be expected. She had always been Mel's refuge – strong, wise, totally supportive – and Mel thanked her lucky stars that Anna had not still been on her year's round-the-world sabbatical when the accident had happened – a sabbatical she'd taken following the death of Goff, Mel's father.

'There was no such thing as a gap year when I was young,' she'd said. 'I missed out on that, so I'm going to do it now – see all the places I've always wanted to see.' And so she had. She'd taken off with little more than a backpack, trekked in the Himalayas, ridden an elephant in Thailand, spent three months in New Zealand with old friends she hadn't seen in years. Pretty amazing really, Mel thought, but she was glad her mother had found a way to cope with the loss of the man she'd been married to for more than a quarter of a century.

Mel had missed her dreadfully, though, and really didn't know what she'd have done if Anna had still been on the other side of the world when she was facing her own personal trauma. Anna was there for her, just as she always had been, nursing her, counselling her, encouraging her. But although she was now alone, she didn't try to get Mel to move back in with her permanently, as many mothers might have done, though it was perfectly possible for Mel to get to work each day by commuting. Instead she helped her find a little garden flat just a bus ride away from the bank.

Slowly Mel was getting her life back on track. Her confidence was still rocky, though, and it was Anna who had come up with the suggestion that was now exciting her.

'Have you heard of the Jubilee Sailing Trust?' she asked one day when Mel was visiting.

Mel shook her head. 'I don't think so, no.'

'I heard a programme about it on the radio the other day. They have a tall ship – the *Lord Nelson* – which is specially equipped for people with disabilities . . .'

'Well thanks for reminding me, Mum,' Mel said drily.

'No, just listen. The idea behind it is to give everyone the chance to sail, as a valued member of the crew, not just a passenger. It's geared for people much worse off than you – the totally blind, the wheelchair-bound, those with Asperger's, anyone really. You can book for a week or two-week voyage, and you get the whole package. Taking your turn on watch, helping to raise and lower the sails, taking the helm, climbing the rigging if you fancy it.'

'How do people in wheelchairs climb the rigging?' Mel asked.

'Well, they can't climb exactly, of course. But there's a special hoist, apparently, that takes the wheelchair up.'

'Amazing!'

'I thought so. I think you'd enjoy it, Mel. You've always liked the great outdoors, and you can't get more outdoors than a sailing ship in the middle of the ocean.'

'Oh Mum, I don't know. I don't know the first thing about it . . .'

'I don't suppose many of the others do either. But there are professional crew to show you the ropes – you'd soon learn. It would be a fantastic experience, and it would do you the world of good to try something totally different. Meet new people.'

'Maybe . . .'

'Why don't I find out about it for you? If I can get an address and phone number for this Jubilee Trust, I'm sure they'd send you some literature about it.'

Mel smiled wryly. When her mother had the bit between her teeth, it was pointless to argue.

'OK, do that. I'll have a look and see what I think. But I'm not making any promises.'

Strangely, though, she was beginning to feel a spark of interest. There was something very seductive about the sea, she thought. She'd always loved the sound of waves breaking on a beach, sucking at the shingle, pounding the base of the cliffs. She loved the vastness of it too, and the feeling of immense power. She pictured being somewhere in the middle of the ocean under full sail, the silence and the freedom and the peace, and the more she thought about it, the more it appealed to her. So much so that before she knew it she was watching eagerly for the post and the arrival of the brochure.

Well – now it's here! Exercising serious self-control, Mel lays it on top of the envelope on the kitchen table and goes to change out of the navy skirt and patterned blouse that is her bank uniform. She tugs on black cotton leggings and a jade tunic and lets her hair down from the French pleat she fastens it into for work. She's avoiding looking in the mirror, as she always does nowadays, but in her haste she catches a quick glimpse, and instantly the cloud of depression is hanging over her again, shutting out the light. She hates what has happened to her looks. Her prosthetic eye appears huge to her, totally unmissable, and the deep indentation runs in an ugly diagonal across her cheek. Everyone says it hardly shows now, but to Mel it's horribly obvious, with the reflected light in the mirror highlighting the place where the flesh has melted away. She swallows hard, desperately trying not to be drawn back into self-pity.

Don't think about the way you used to look. Don't think about Brian. Most of all, don't think about Mark. You can't change the past, not a single thing. But the future is a fresh start. The future is up to you . . .

She makes herself look in the mirror again, lifting her chin, staring defiantly at her own face, even forcing an ironic smile. Then she turns away, goes back to the kitchen, pours herself the glass of wine she promised herself, and sits down with the brochure.

The Jubilee Sailing Trust. The tall ship – the Lord Nelson.

The picture on the front cover is drawing her in. Even before she reads a single sentence of the information inside, Mel feels sure she's made up her mind. She's going to do this. And it could well be the fresh start she so desperately needs.

FOUR

EMMA

I'm driving, too fast, back up the narrow winding lane − quite some feat, given that I'm towing a boat and climbing a hill. But I'm not giving a thought to what might be coming the other way. I just want to get away from the journalist. As I round a bend, I come face to face with a Range Rover taking up most of the road. I slam on my brakes and pull in as close to the hedge as I can, and the other driver does the same. We skid to a halt, bumper to bumper. The driver of the Range Rover glares at me and throws his arms theatrically into the air, but at least he has the sense to realise it will have to be him who gives way. He reverses rapidly up the lane until he reaches a passing place, and I'm able to squeeze past him.

I'm shaking from head to toe, and the shock of the near miss, coming on top of the horrible, unexpected encounter with that man, has brought me perilously close to tears. I try to get a grip on myself, but I can still hear Mike Bond's voice clamouring in my head: *The fact is that your mother was seen alive, in America, some time after she supposedly died.*

It's nonsense, of course − nothing but muck-raking by a low-life newspaper hack desperate for a sensational story. Total, utter nonsense. And yet . . . much as I'm trying to deny it, there's just a sliver of doubt in my mind. Seen alive . . . by whom? Who could it have been? They must have been pretty convincing if he'd come to Cornwall to follow it up.

I drive on, more slowly now, all too aware that I shall have an accident if I'm not careful, and when I come to a lay-by I pull in and switch off the engine. Then I sit staring unseeingly down the sunlit ribbon of road while the wild thoughts chase around in my head.

Can it possibly be true? Certainly Felicity's body was never found. Yes, her boat was well out to sea when it was spotted, with the boom swinging free, so the natural assumption was that she'd been hit by it and gone overboard. But almost certainly she would have been wearing her life jacket, and that would have made her pretty buoyant. She wasn't floating in the vicinity, and her body had never been washed up anywhere – or if it had, no one had ever discovered it. Theoretically, it is possible. There's no proof whatever that Felicity died that day. Just as there's no proof that she didn't.

A sharp prickle that feels almost like hope stirs deep inside me suddenly, and that shocks me all over again. It has never occurred to me for a moment that Felicity might still be alive; I've grown up without her, and Maggie took her place so completely that I have not really missed her. Yet in this moment I want my mother. There's a need that's aching fiercely in an unidentifiable place that I suppose is what you might call my heart. A tug of longing deep inside at roughly the place where I was joined to her by the umbilical cord.

It doesn't last long, though. Almost simultaneously the full import of what I'm wishing for becomes clear to me. If she is alive, it can mean only one thing – that for some reason she faked her own death. The thought that she could callously and calculatedly walk away from us, leaving us to grieve for her, and then start a new life somewhere as we'd never existed at all – that's pretty devastating. How could she do something like that to Dad . . . to me? It doesn't fit at all with the image I have of her. To me she's always been the pretty woman smiling out of the old photographs, whose sailing trophies are still kept polished, though the silver plating has worn thin with age. Now, the thought that she may have deceived us all is tarnishing that image like the thirty-year-old trophies, making her feel phoney like them, not precious at all, but worthless dross, valuable only for what they represent. And that is hurting me, far more than the loss of my mother. Niggling under my skin like a sliver of wood when I've cleaned the rail too vigorously and picked up a splinter. Making me uncomfortable as well as shaken. If fate robbed me of my mother, that's one thing. If she went of her own accord, because she didn't want to be with us any more, that's quite another.

I'm going to have to tell Dad and Maggie about this, I realise. It's something I'd prefer not to do — if it's upsetting me, how much more is it going to upset them? But I really think they should be warned. I have a sneaky feeling that journalist is not going to let it go, and it would be better coming from me than having him turn up unannounced on their doorstep. And I'd intended to go over to Porthtowan today anyway.

I start the car and pull back on to the road. I had meant to phone from the club and make sure someone was home, but I'd forgotten all about it. I'll just have to hope they haven't gone out somewhere for the day.

Generally speaking, it takes about half an hour to cross the peninsula to Porthtowan. Today, though, there are quite a few caravans and camper vans on the road, which slows things up, and for a good mile or more I get stuck behind a farm tractor and trailer. I fume with frustration until he pulls into a gateway and I'm able to put my foot down again.

It's getting on for four o'clock by the time I come over the crest of the hill and the Porthtowan bay opens up beneath me, an expanse of blue trapped between the outcrop of cliffs on both sides. The blue is crinkled with white streaks like the frills on a petticoat — the surf is good here, and the beach will be peppered with enthusiasts, their boards tucked beneath their arms, making their way to and from the car park and Blue, the bar just beyond the breakwater where the surfers congregate. From here they are just dark dots like a swarm of ants, but the scene is so familiar to me I don't need to be able to see it to picture it clearly.

The road dips down, forking away to the beach. I pass the turning and drive on up the rise on the other side, then swing off the main road into a lane that climbs steeply up to the clifftop. Up, up, another turn to the right, and I'm turning into the drive of my old home. It's square, solid-looking, built of Cornish stone and surrounded by lawns and flower beds where the roses are in the first flush of full bloom. There's a gnarled old apple tree where Dad put up a swing for me when I was little, and a plum that always attracts the wasps. I was stung more than once. But the memories are mostly happy ones, of a secure childhood when the sun always seemed to be shining, as it is today.

The doors of the double garage are open; I can see Maggie's Fiat, but there's a space where Dad's car should be. He's not here, then, but Maggie almost certainly is. If they were both out, the garage would be locked up. I park, walk round the side of the house. I'm actually quite glad Dad isn't here. I think it might be easier talking to Maggie first about what's happened. I open the kitchen door.

'Hello! Anyone home?'

No answer, but the kitchen is full of the smell of baking. I go in, cross to the door that connects with the hall and call again.

'Maggie? Hello?'

'Emma? Is that you?' Maggie emerges from the sitting room, carrying a vase of lilies. 'What a lovely surprise!'

She goes to put her arm round me to hug me, then draws back.

'Hang on, let me get rid of these. They're dropping everywhere, and you know how the pollen stains . . .'

She passes me, heading for the outside door and leaving a trail of petals and orangey-brown stamens in her wake. I get the dustpan and brush from the cupboard under the sink and sweep them up. Through the window I can see Maggie tipping the dying flowers into the composting bin and think how good she looks – still trim, still fit, though I know she's not far off sixty now. Her dark blond hair has been touched up to cover the places around her face that have turned grey, and it's square-cut and crimped up into a mass of tiny curls. She dresses well, too – though she's only messing about at home today, she is wearing beige linen trousers, a crisp white blouse and a paisley print waistcoat. And her face is smooth, almost unlined – I've sometimes thought that if my mother were still alive, it's quite possible she'd look as if she were the elder sister rather than the younger. The sun and the wind and the salt spray are notoriously bad for the complexion. Now it occurs to me that I might just get the chance to find out, and the thought makes my stomach fall away and a glitch of nervousness pulse in my throat.

'Well, how are things going then, Emma?' Maggie asks, coming back in and putting the vase in the sink. 'You've been sailing, I take it?'

'Yes. Where's Dad?'

'He's gone in to the showroom. You know Marilyn is on maternity leave, and Deana called in sick this morning with summer flu.'

She glances at the wall clock, which is of a strange back-to-front design, anticlockwise rather than clockwise. I've never got totally used to it; I still have to work out the time laboriously. 'He'll be home soon, I should think.'

So – I may not have very long.

'Maggie,' I say. 'I really need to talk to you.'

She throws me an anxious look.

'That sounds ominous.' When I don't answer, she says: 'Look, I boiled the kettle just before you came. Why don't I make us a cup of tea? There are some rock cakes, too. Still warm I should think. Would you like one?'

Earlier, before my encounter with Mike Bond, I'd been thinking how much I'd like to tuck into one of Maggie's rock cakes. or scones. Now I'm not at all sure I'll be able to eat a thing. But . . .

'Go on then,' I say.

She makes the tea, sets the mugs down on the kitchen table and unloads some rock cakes from a wire cooling tray on to a plate, which she places between us. I don't say a thing until she's sitting down. Then: 'You're not going to like this, Maggie,' I start. 'I don't like it. But I really think you should know . . .'

'What? What on earth are you talking about, Emma?'

I take a deep breath and tell her.

'Oh my God,' Maggie says. But very quietly, and it's muffled because it's coming from behind her fingers, which are pressed to her mouth. She closes her eyes momentarily, and she's gone so pale I'm afraid she might be about to faint.

'I'm sorry, but I really thought you ought to know,' I say, apologetic as if this was all my fault.

And then, seeing just how shaken up she is, I'm angry again. How dare this man appear in our lives like the demon king in a pantomime bursting out of the trapdoor of the stage in a cloud of smoke? How dare he suggest my mother faked her own death? How dare he go round asking questions about us and poking about in our lives as if we had no rights, and no feelings, at all?

'We can't let him get away with it,' I say decisively. 'He was at Penryn, talking to anybody who'd talk to him about Felicity. Heaven knows what he'll do next. We've got to put a stop to it!'

Maggie spreads her hands helplessly.

'And just how are you going to do that?'

'I don't know. I'll find out who he works for, tell them in no uncertain terms it's got to stop. He gave me his card . . .' I fish it out of my pocket, look at it, and feel the wind go out of my sails. 'Oh – it doesn't look as if he works for anybody. He's a freelance. Well, I'll ring him then. Tell him if he continues with this we'll sue.'

'Emma, no – no.' Maggie is shaking her head vigorously. 'Just stop – think. If you rush in with all guns blazing, he'll think we've got something to hide.'

47

I'm puzzled. There's something slightly odd about Maggie's response. She's terribly shaken, and yet . . . I don't know. I can't put my finger on it.

'Maggie, this man is suggesting my mother faked her own death,' I say. 'It's serious stuff. If we don't nip it in the bud, we could end up all over the papers. He's got to be stopped.'

'But there's no way you *can* stop him.' Maggie is regaining some of her self-control. She reaches across the table and covers my hand with hers. It's shaking a bit, but her grip is firm over my knuckles, much more like the old Maggie, who is so good at managing life's traumas and crises. 'If he thinks he's got hold of a story then he's going to go on digging, whatever you might say. But if you leave well alone it'll probably die a death. We're talking about something that happened thirty years ago. The trail is going to be very cold. Thirty years, Emma. Honestly, I don't think there's anything to worry about.'

Again I'm puzzled; again I feel the edge of disquiet. My first reaction had been that Mike Bond's suggestion was absolutely ludicrous. But Maggie hasn't once said anything resembling that. Rather, it's as if she's accepting there might be some truth in it. Where I'm ready to go in fighting for my mother's reputation, Maggie's response is almost defensive . . .

'Maggie?' I say, giving her a hard stare. 'You don't believe he's really on to something, do you?'

'No, of course not.' But somehow it's unconvincing.

I give my head a shake to clear it.

'For goodness' sake, you don't really think she could do something like that, do you?'

Maggie gets up, goes to switch the kettle on again – gaining time, I think, since neither of us has drunk our first cup of tea.

'Maggie?' I say sharply.

She half turns.

'Your mother was a very determined person, Emma. If she wanted something, she'd go after it, no matter what.'

'You *do* think!' I say, shocked.

'I'm saying it's possible, that's all. And if she did do something like that, the last thing we want now is for it all to come out. We're not just talking about a newspaper story, are we? There could be a criminal investigation, and the insurance company would certainly want their pound of flesh if they could prove they'd been defrauded. Just think what that alone would mean . . .'

She breaks off, cocking her head. She's heard a car on the drive; I can hear it too.

'Your father's home,' she says. 'Don't say anything about this to him, please.'

'But he's got to know! Apart from anything else, Pam is going to mention it when he goes to Penryn . . .'

'I'll tell him. But I'll pick my moment. And this isn't it.'

'OK.'

I don't know how I'm going to keep this from him, but I don't fancy broaching it with him either. Best leave it to Maggie, which was, after all, what I'd intended.

Dad comes in, looks pleased to see me.

'Emma! You haven't completely forgotten us then.'

'As if!' I give Dad a hug.

I adore my dad. Always have. To me it seems as if he hasn't changed one jot since I was a little girl, but of course that's not true. His hair is iron grey now and receding at the temples, and he's put on a bit of weight, but he has a healthy tan from the hours spent out on his boat and the extra weight suits him.

'So – how are you doing, my love?'

'Oh – you know . . .' Actually I'm struggling with the weight of the secret between us. 'Dad . . .'

Maggie throws me a warning glance, but Dad doesn't notice a thing. He's too busy snaffling one of Maggie's rock cakes, devouring it in two healthy bites.

'How's Philip?' he asks, brushing crumbs from the corner of his mouth.

Philip. I haven't spared Philip, and our problems, a thought since I came ashore and walked into all this.

'I don't know, Dad. I don't think it's going to last much longer if I'm honest. We seem to be coming from totally different directions.'

'Hmm. Pity. He seems a decent bloke.'

'He is . . . I'm just not sure he's right for me.'

We talk some more, but it's awkward and I hate not being able to mention the thing that's occupying every corner of my mind. How Maggie can act so normally I can't imagine. To me, everything feels false and unreal. After a while, I can't stand it any longer.

I tell Dad and Maggie I have to get back. Maggie puts some rock cakes in a polythene bag for me to take home with me. Dad gives me another hug. Maggie comes out with me to the car.

'Just don't do anything hasty,' she says.

'OK.'

At this moment, I honestly don't know what, if anything, I am going to do.

There's a message from Philip on my answering machine: he's back from Exeter, he decided against buying the motorbike, do I want to go out for a drink and something to eat this evening?

The short answer is no, I do not. I call Philip, pleading a headache. Then I make myself a salad and a cheese omelette. I have very little appetite, though I've not really had much to eat all day. My stomach is tying itself in knots when I try to swallow. I force down the omelette, but the salad is a step too far. I scrape it into the bin, pour myself another glass of wine and try to make sense of all that's happened.

I absolutely cannot. I'm just going round in circles. One moment I think the whole thing is absolutely crazy, the next I think that if there wasn't something in it, Mike Bond wouldn't be chasing the story. I can't get what Maggie said out of my head either. That she could actually believe that Felicity was capable of faking her own death, leaving Dad, abandoning me, is pretty devastating.

But to just leave it, as Maggie had suggested . . . I really don't think I can do that.

Of course I should have asked Mike Bond where his information came from, what exactly he had been told, while I had the chance. I was so totally in shock I just ran away, but now I'm getting a strong urge to find out more. It may be, of course, that he really is on a wild goose chase. But supposing he's not . . . supposing my mother is still alive . . . supposing he finds her . . .

If there's anything to know, I want to know it. As soon as Mike Bond does.

I get out the card he gave me. There's an address in Somerset and a telephone number, plus a mobile number. A mobile – he is up with the times! But then, I suppose a newspaper reporter would be – he wants to be in touch to call in his latest nasty scoop.

I don't suppose he'll be at home yet; for all I know he's still poking around in Falmouth, and even if he has headed back to Somerset it's unlikely he'll have arrived yet.

With another glug of wine to fortify myself, I dial the number of the mobile. After what seems an age it starts to ring. Then the answering service clicks in, saying the number is unable to take my call at the moment, but asking me to leave a number after the bleep.

I take a deep breath.

'This is Emma Dunning. Let me give you my telephone number. I'm sorry if I was a bit short this afternoon. But I really think we should talk again.'

FIVE

MAGGIE

This is a total nightmare. I can't believe it's happening. After all these years. And yet I suppose I've always known that it might.

In the beginning, when Fliss first disappeared, I lived on a knife edge, my nerves stretched tight so that they seemed to sing like the telegraph wires used to in the days before they took them all down and buried them underground. Do they still sing, those wires, down there with no one to hear them? My nerves certainly did, though they too were buried deep, hidden beneath what everyone thought was grief for my sister.

And of course I *was* grieving for her. I missed her dreadfully. Knowing she'd gone for ever, that there would be no more giggles at wicked jokes that only we understood, no more reminiscences and shared memories, no more late-night confidences, was an ache in the pit of my stomach, the sharp pain felt in a limb that is no longer there. She was my little sister, my naughty little sister, impossible, infuriating, yet totally adorable. Whom I was supposed to look after but who constantly got me into dreadful trouble with our parents because she refused to do as I told her and did her own thing anyway, be it climbing trees or paddling in the river or clambering under barbed-wire fences, and when she fell out of the tree and winded herself, or got a bootful of water in the river, or tore her clothes on the barbed wire, I was the one in hot water when we got home. My cute and cheeky little sister, who grew into a beauty, and was brave and funny and spirited. Of course I grieved for her!

But it was more than that. Much more, though no one knew it. At first it was the wondering, and the worrying about her, and the terrible regret that I hadn't been there for her when she needed me, hadn't been able to stop her from doing whatever it was she had done. And later, when I learned the truth, there was the guilt that came from both the secret I was keeping and the inescapable feeling that I was failing her all over again, not to mention the fear that everything was going to come unravelled. My whole life was built on a lie; if the deception was revealed, I would lose everything I cared about. Martin. Emma. Everything. And so I did what I had to do.

I concentrated on being a good wife to Martin and mother to Emma and gradually managed to tuck all the negative things away in the recesses of my mind, where they became shadowy and insubstantial and only very occasionally crept out to haunt me. I've been happy and blessed, and I almost forgot that the whole of my life is built on quicksand.

That's changed now, in the blinking of an eye.

When Emma told me about the journalist who had spoken to her at Penryn, the kitchen went dark around me, as if someone had turned out the lights, and everything seemed to be spinning and whirling and becoming fainter, more distant. I think in that moment I was closer to fainting than I've ever been in my life. But some instinct for self-preservation pulled me back from the brink. I went into defence mode.

How much good that has done, I don't know. The first, most important thing as I saw it was to prevent Emma from doing anything hasty. Not that I can blame her for that – she's obviously shocked to the core and in denial. But heaven only knows what sort of a hornets' nest she'll stir up if she goes in fighting. I had to try to stop her. It may be too little too late, though. As I said, I would think the trail to the truth is very, very cold after all these years, but there's always the danger this journalist might dig up something. If he does, people are going to be hurt – badly. And I have to admit I include myself amongst them.

I am the one who stands to lose the most, and it frightens the life out of me. I'm shaking all over once more just thinking about it.

Emma is like a daughter to me; I couldn't bear to lose her.

And Martin . . . Martin is my life. I've loved him so much, for so long. Everything I've done I've done for him. And it's been worth it.

We've had a good marriage – we have! Three years ago we celebrated our twentieth wedding anniversary with a big family party at the Greenbank Hotel in Falmouth, and we're planning on doing a Caribbean cruise in September as a sort of belated second honeymoon. But lovely as those special occasions are, it's the fabric of our daily life that really matters, and that shows how close we are. We never have rows – little arguments, maybe, but not rows. If I see a discussion heading that way I nip it in the bud, capitulate, make the peace. And that's fine by me – my happiness comes from making Martin happy. Since we've been married we've never spent a night apart – quite a novelty for him in the beginning, since it was so different to the way he and Fliss lived – but now I think it would feel as wrong to him as it does to me. Making his life run like clockwork, ensuring all his needs are met, smoothing his feathers when they are ruffled, bolstering his confidence if it takes a knock – all these things have been my mission in life. We're a team. A partnership. So why am I so afraid that it would all collapse in ruins if Fliss came back from the dead?

The obvious answer to that of course is that legally I would no longer be his wife. That our marriage would be null and void. At least I presume it would, though I don't actually know for sure, since she was declared dead all those years ago. But it's not really the legal aspect that worries me so much as the wondering if Martin would still be as besotted with her as he was back then. If even now she would have the power to come between us.

It's one of the reasons I haven't yet told him about the journalist. I have to tell him, of course. Better that it comes from me than from someone else, and he will hear it from someone else if the wretched man is asking questions of anyone who might have known Fliss. But I'm dreading it all the same, and not just because it's bound to shock and upset him. No, the thing that really makes me shrink is that in that first unguarded moment I might see a flash of hope in his eyes.

Like the guilt and the fear, the knowing that I am second best is something I've learned to live with. Something I rarely think about any more. And Martin denies that it is true. He says that he was over Fliss a long time ago. If I press him, he'll even say it's me he loves. But though my head tells me the reason he won't say it spontaneously is because he is the least romantic man imaginable, my heart has never quite been able to believe it. However good our marriage, however close we have become, I am very afraid that deep down there is a part of Martin that will always belong to Fliss. And I don't want to see it lighting up his face when I tell him that a journalist believes that she isn't dead at all, but still alive.

Well, for the moment my chance to talk to him has come and gone. Martin has gone out again – he got a phone call from an old pal of his, Tony Baggott, who is apparently trying to get his trailer tent sorted for a holiday in the Lake District and has run up against some problem that requires the attendance of Martin and his tool kit. So I have a brief respite. Unless Tony has heard the news from someone . . . The journalist hasn't been to Porthtowan, as far as I know, but if he's sniffing around at Penryn it's only a matter of time before he does.

I'm shaking again, with anxiety and dread. And yet at the same time I'm experiencing a peculiar sense of longing. *Oh Fliss . . . where are you now? What happened to you, after . . . ? Did you find happiness with the man you loved so much? I do hope so! Knowing that you have had the life you wanted with him is really the only thing that could assuage my guilt . . .*

My throat closes; tears are gathering in my eyes. Tears not only for a lost past, for a closeness we once shared, but also frightened tears for an uncertain future. And without really knowing why, I find myself going upstairs, to the spare bedroom, opening the rather stiff door of the wall cupboard and getting out the battered cardboard box that's stored at the back. It's years now since I looked inside that box, and part of me resists the urge to do so now. But the compulsion to see the photographs and mementos is stronger. For some reason I can't explain, the past seems to be reaching out to me and I need to connect with it.

Not everything inside the box is unexploded dynamite, of course. There are all kinds of bits and pieces – theatre programmes, yellowed with age, newspaper cuttings of family weddings and funerals, a photograph of me and Fliss with a sailor from the nuclear submarine *Nautilus*. I well remember that photograph being taken – we were on holiday in Weymouth when the submarine docked after having made news by going under the polar ice cap. The crew had come ashore and Fliss persuaded this sailor to pose for a photograph with us. He was a lantern-jawed American, in the uniform of the American navy, looking a bit awkward; Fliss was smiling her usual sunbeam smile. Though he had an arm round each of us, the sailor appeared to be leaning towards Fliss. Well – typical. I probably didn't exist, as far as he was concerned. Story of my life.

I put the photograph to one side and go on rootling through the box. I'm very aware of what it is I am looking for. It's a letter that, if the worst happens, may make it a bit easier on Emma. It'll be no help at all to me, of course, quite the opposite. In fact, I'm not yet sure whether I'll have the courage to give it to her. It will be like opening a Pandora's box. But I want to read it again, see exactly what it says and does not say, think about the consequences of giving it to Emma after all these years. Because it was intended for her, if ever this eventuality should occur. And maybe even if it didn't. And the fact that she has never seen it is down to me; something else I have to feel guilty about.

Why did I keep it from her? *Why?* But that's a rhetorical question. I know very well why I did it, and can still, even now, make excuses for myself.

The letter is at the very bottom of the box, as if, though I hadn't been able to bring myself to throw it away, I wanted to bury it as deep as I could, out of sight of prying eyes, and where even I couldn't see it unless I really wanted to. A blue airmail envelope, and inside matching blue paper. Feather-light, thin, brittle. Covered with Fliss's none-too-tidy scrawl.

I sit on the floor, smooth out the creases, and begin to read.

My dearest Emma,

I don't know how to begin this letter. I don't know how to make you understand. You're only a little girl now, but when you read this you will be grown up. And you will have grown up without me. But I want you to know that I have never stopped loving you and I never will. That this isn't the way it was meant to be. I can only try to explain and hope that you won't blame me too much . . .

The words are blurring because my eyes are filling with tears. *Oh Fliss . . . Fliss . . . I am so sorry! This whole mess came about because we loved too much, both of us. And both of us were to blame. It wasn't all my fault — was it? But whatever, now it's time to face the consequences. And we are not the only ones who are going to pay the price . . .*

Fliss should never have married Martin, of course. In fact, as she herself was the first to admit, she shouldn't have married anyone, at least not then, when her freedom was still the most important thing to her, and her thirst for adventure unquenched. It was always going to be a recipe for disaster. She wouldn't have married, I'm sure, if the moral climate had been as it is today. But this was the 1950s and we lived in a small Cornish town. There was very little choice. Well — there was a choice, but Fliss took what seemed to her to be the least bad option.

It's just one of the things she tried to explain in her letter to Emma. The letter that, for my own selfish reasons, I have never passed on. Now, through the blur of tears, I look at it again.

Where do I begin, Emma? I honestly don't know. So perhaps the best place is at the very beginning . . .

Across the miles and the years it is as if I can hear my sister's voice. And because I was there, and party to most of what happened, I can fill in the bits that she's left out to spare Emma's feelings. She'd never tell her just how desperate she was when she found she was pregnant – that would be far too hurtful. And unfair, really, given how much she loved and wanted Emma once she held her in her arms. But I remember, oh yes, I remember, the tears and the regrets and the sleepless nights. I remember it well. Because the decision she reached broke my heart.

Part Two
1956–1959

SIX

Felicity Penrose sat on a smooth boulder on the clifftop, knees drawn up to her chin, arms wrapped around them, staring at the panoramic vista of sea and sky that spread out before and beneath her and wondering how in the world she had come to be in this terrible mess. Well, she knew how it had happened, she was hardly that naïve. She just couldn't believe she could have been so stupid.

Pregnant. By a man she didn't love, who wasn't even really her boyfriend, but who had once been her sister Maggie's. Pregnant, because of too much to drink at a party – Babycham, for goodness' sake – how had she got drunk on *Babycham*? Or had someone spiked the silly wide-topped, slender-stemmed glass with something a good deal stronger? Possibly. It was the kind of prank some of the young crowd at the party might well think was funny. The one thing she was sure of was that it wouldn't have been Martin Dunning, though he was the one she'd gone for a walk with along the beach, the one with whom things had got out of hand. Martin was too decent to do something like that, even if he hadn't been quite such a gentleman when they were alone in the dark and Fliss was leading him on.

And she had led him on, she knew it. She was a flirt, and she knew that too. She just hadn't meant things to go so far. But she'd been drunk, and she'd been enjoying herself, and one thing had led to another, and then it had reached the point where it seemed morally wrong to call a halt, and now . . .

Felicity swallowed the lump of shame and sheer terror that was knotting her throat. She felt horribly sick – had done for weeks now. At first she'd tried to convince herself it was just nerves because she was so worried, the sickness of apprehension. But the trembling heart of her knew it was more than that. At last, when she couldn't bear a second longer the suspense of waiting for a period that didn't come, she went to see Dr Myers. He examined her and confirmed what, deep down, she already knew.

'There's no doubt, I'm afraid, Felicity. You are going to have a baby. In about six months' time, I'd say.'

He was regarding her solemnly over the top of his wire-rimmed spectacles; no joyous celebration this, he knew. Just another young woman who'd got herself into trouble and had to cope with the consequences.

Fliss said nothing. She stared down at her hands, tightly clasped in her lap, and fought back the tears of shame and despair that were aching in her throat.

'Does the father know about this?' Dr Myers asked. 'Will he be willing to marry you?'

'No!' Fliss looked up sharply. 'No – he doesn't know, and I don't want him to. I don't want *anyone* to know! You won't tell him, will you?'

Dr Myers shook his head sadly. 'Of course I won't tell him – or anyone else. What happens between these four walls is absolutely confidential. But you are going to have to tell him. He has a responsibility here.'

'I don't want anything from him. I just want . . .'

'For it all to go away? Well I'm afraid it's not going to. You're going to have a baby, my dear, whether you like it or not. And that means making plans.'

'Couldn't you . . . Couldn't you arrange . . .' Fliss was stumbling over the words she was afraid to speak, but which were the hope she was clinging on to. 'Couldn't you . . . *do* something?'

Dr Myers sucked in his breath sharply.

'I'm afraid not.' His tone was stern now. 'If you are talking about a termination, you must know it's illegal. And I would strongly advise you against pursuing such a course either by yourself or with the help of anyone else. It's not only illegal, it's very dangerous. I've seen the results of botched abortions, and I can assure you, you do not want to risk that. At best it could mean you'd never be able to have another child; at worst it could cost you your life. Please, put any such thoughts right out of your head.'

Fliss lowered her eyes, chastened.

'Look, my dear, if you are set against marrying the father – which I honestly feel would be for the best – there are other options. You're not considering keeping the baby and bringing it up alone, I presume?'

'No!' Fliss said, horrified. In all her deliberations, the thought had never crossed her mind. This was, after all, 1956 – only the brave and the brazen raised an illegitimate child alone. Especially in a small Cornish town where everyone knew everyone else.

'In that case, then, I would suggest adoption would be the best answer. There are plenty of couples who are unable to have children of their own and are desperate to adopt.' Dr Myers leaned back in his chair, sliding open a desk drawer and rifling about inside it. He drew out a couple of sheets of foolscape paper, covered with typescript and stapled together. 'I'll give you the contact details for someone who will be able to help you. A social worker. They will talk you through what will happen, help you find somewhere to stay until the baby is born, and put you in touch with the adoption agencies.'

There was a coldness now in Fliss's stomach; it reached out and gripped her heart with fingers of pure ice. 'I don't know . . .'

'It need not be someone here in Truro. You could go further afield, where you're not known, if you'd prefer it. But I assure you, whoever you see will treat anything that passes between you in complete confidence.' Dr Myers settled his spectacles back on his nose and ran his finger down the list of names and telephone numbers, then jotted some details on a pad, tore off the sheet and passed it to Fliss.

She stared at it dully, the doctor's scrawl blurring before her eyes.

'Talk it over with your parents,' he advised. 'You are still living at home, aren't you?'

Fliss nodded. Though she was past the magic age of twenty-one and legally an adult, it was still quite the usual thing for young people to stay in the family home until they married. Maggie, her older sister, was twenty-four, but she too still lived with their parents. Very few, except those who went away to university, or to take a job, left home. Maggie was a junior with a firm of accountants in Truro; Fliss worked on the production line in a pickle and chutney factory in Camborne – not a very demanding job, and one that was well beneath her capabilities, but it allowed her to take time off for her sailing. The factory owners – Ralph and Norman Pretty – actively encouraged it, in fact. Pretty's Pickles had actually sponsored Fliss and her sailing partner, Jo Best, helping to finance some of their adventures. They were proud to be associated with her, and glad of the publicity her achievements brought to their business.

The knot in Fliss's throat tightened again as she thought of it. She'd let them down, all of them. There would be no more high-profile voyages or races for the next six months at least. She couldn't be seen with a spreading waistline and a baby-shaped bump even if she was still physically capable of the rigours of sailing two-handed, which she actually doubted she would be. Everything would have to go on hold, all their ambitious plans would have to be shelved, and there was no guarantee the opportunities would ever come again.

Fliss felt horribly claustrophobic suddenly. She had to get out of here, out of this small, stuffy room that smelled of antiseptic and carbolic soap, away from Dr Myers, who was saying all the things she didn't want to hear.

'Felicity?' His voice penetrated the fog that seemed to be suffocating her. 'You must talk it over with them. They'll be far more understanding than you think, I'm sure. You're not the first girl this has happened to, and you won't be the last.'

Fliss gave a small, strangled laugh. That others had been in the same position was of no comfort whatsoever.

'No,' she said, 'but they weren't me.'

'Quite. But believe me, it's not the end of the world, however it may look to you at the moment. Now, I'd like you to come and see me in a month's time, just so that I can check that everything is as it should be. Which I'm sure it will. You're young and strong, in good health, and there's no reason why you shouldn't sail through this pregnancy.'

He stood up, crossed to the door and opened it. There were several people in the waiting room through which she had to pass, amongst them a woman with a small boy, whom Fliss recognised as Molly Treadworth, the butcher's wife. Fliss's face flamed. It seemed to her that the waiting patients would know exactly why she was here, and might even have overheard something of what had been said. But thankfully Molly Treadworth at least seemed hardly to notice her. Her attention was focused on her little boy, who was flushed and coughing.

Fliss scurried between the two rows of chairs feeling horribly conspicuous and escaped through the door. Her Vespa scooter was parked outside; she started it up and headed for Porthtowan. She wasn't going home yet, though. Instead she headed for the lane that led steeply up to the clifftop. When Fliss was upset or worried about something she always came here, where the stiff salt breeze seemed to blow the cobwebs away and the feeling of space and peace and wild nature at her feet and all around her calmed her spirit. The lane became a path; the path petered out into a carpet of gorse and heather. Fliss stopped beside a smooth boulder and parked the Vespa.

More than anything she wished that Jo, her sailing partner and friend, was here. She was the one person Fliss would have willingly confided in. But Jo was away, crewing on a tall ship, gaining experience for what the two girls had been hoping would be their next adventure, and Fliss didn't know when she would be back. Under sail, you were completely at the mercy of the winds and the tides.

Fliss sat down on the boulder, the sun warm on her face, but unable to touch the cold place deep inside her, staring out to sea and trying to decide what she was going to do.

Dr Myers was right, of course, when he said she must tell her parents – there was absolutely no way she could keep it from them. But oh, was she dreading it!

They were going to be so disappointed in her. So ashamed. This was a small place; everyone knew everyone else, and everyone was censorious. People sniffed at a girl sleeping with someone before she was married – she was considered to have let herself down – and to actually fall pregnant was total disgrace. Fliss's mother, Greta, a pillar of the community, was going to be mortified. But it was the thought of how her father would react that Fliss really dreaded.

When Fliss was little, her father had been her hero, and the years had changed nothing. She still adored him, this strongly built man who looked exactly like the sailor he had once been, with his weathered, sun-browned face and eyes as blue as a summer sea – though he had long since left the merchant navy and worked now at Nancekook, the mysterious Ministry of Defence establishment on the cliffs above Porthtowan, he still loved to sail. Bill Penrose was a man of few words, but they were always wise ones, and Fliss had never heard him speak ill of anybody. He was also calm in a crisis and pragmatic to a fault. But Fliss thought that was because he didn't allow people or circumstances to impinge too deeply into the fabric of his life.

This, she knew instinctively, was something quite different. Bill idolised both his daughters. Nothing was too good for them; nobody who hurt them was allowed to get away with it. This was going to upset him dreadfully, and imagining the look she would see in those very blue eyes made Fliss cringe inwardly.

Perhaps it would be best if she were to break the news to her mother first, she thought, and this evening would be as good a time as any. Bill would almost certainly be out – when the weather was fine, as it was today, he spent pretty much every spare minute working on his boat, if not actually sailing – and she thought that Maggie was going to be as well – at breakfast she'd said something about going to the pictures. Fliss was dreading telling Maggie almost as much as she dreaded telling her father. Maggie could be very strait-laced, and just to make matters worse, Fliss thought she still carried a torch for Martin.

It was going to be horrible; she could imagine the most dreadful atmosphere was going to ensue. But the bottom line was she had no one to blame but herself. She'd got herself into this mess, she'd have to get herself out of it. But for all her resolve, Fliss felt frightened and alone and utterly helpless.

That evening, when Bill and Maggie had both gone out, Fliss told Greta. To her surprise, her mother was not as shocked as she had expected.

'I thought as much,' she said, her face as tight as her voice.

'You knew?' Fliss said.

'I had my suspicions.'

They were in the kitchen, putting away the last of the tea things. Greta untied the strings of the frilly apron she wore in the afternoons – in the mornings she was always completely covered up in a voluminous pinafore – folded it, and put it in the kitchen drawer. Then she turned and gave Fliss a straight look.

'Do you think I don't know the signs, my lady? And you've been too quiet as well. Not at all like yourself.'

'Oh Mum . . . I'm so sorry.'

'It's a bit late to be sorry. Who's the father?'

'Martin Dunning.'

That did take Greta aback.

'Martin *Dunning*? The one our Maggie used to go out with? Dunnings the garage people? Over at Redruth?'

'Yes.'

'Well!' There was a certain respect in Greta's tone. A garage, even if it was quite small – a couple of petrol pumps on a narrow forecourt, a small shop that sold cigarettes and sweets as well as motor oil and batteries, and a vehicle repair shop – made the Dunnings business people, and business was well placed on the social ladder in Greta's book. Not as elevated as a doctor or solicitor or optician, but more or less on a par with a schoolteacher or clergyman, and certainly a step up from a Nancekook labourer, a housewife, an office junior and a girl who worked on a pickle production line.

Greta came from Redruth; she knew the garage and its history, could even remember the days when old Jack Dunning, Martin's grandfather, had owned the grandest car for miles around, a big black Humber that transported the bride at weddings, the chief mourners at funerals, and was hired by anyone requiring a taxi – something that was quite an occasion in itself. 'We'll have Jack Dunning,' people would say. And Jack, chauffeur-smart in a black cap with a shiny peak, would turn up, always five minutes early, load any luggage into the boot and help his passengers into the spacious interior, which smelled of leather polish and cigarette smoke. Greta had loved riding in the taxi when she was a little girl, sitting on one of the 'dickey seats' and feeling terribly grown-up and important. In those days there was a little café, which later became the shop, and Jack's wife, whose name she could not remember, and had possibly never heard – everyone would have called her 'Mrs Dunning' in those days – served coffee in the mornings and tea in the afternoons and home-cooked meals – liver and bacon, minced beef and onion, rabbit stew – between twelve and two.

Over the years, the business had grown. Ted, Jack's son, had taken it on when Jack retired, and started selling used cars from a plot of land across the road. Martin, Jack's grandson, had trained as a mechanic and was fully expected to inherit the family business when the time came. Greta had been secretly pleased when Maggie had started going out with Martin, and disappointed when their relationship had come to an end. He was, in Greta's eyes, quite a catch.

'Don't even think it, Mum,' Fliss said, reading her mind.

Greta, on the point of saying that Martin must be made to shoulder his responsibilities, thought again.

'It would be a song and dance, I suppose. It would be better, really, if we could keep the whole thing quiet. You could go away to have the baby, and if it's adopted, nobody need be any the wiser. We'll have to find out . . .'

'Dr Myers gave me the name of someone who can help. He thought adoption was the best thing.'

'Well of course it is! You don't want anybody knowing what a silly girl you've been, do you? And this woman can sort it all out for you, can she? You'd better give her a ring, Fliss, see what she's got to say. Or do you want me to do it for you?'

'No! No!' Fliss said, horrified at being treated like a child.

'Well make sure you do, and soon. We must get something sorted out before you begin to show. Then if you disappear until it's all over you can come back here and carry on as if nothing has happened. I'm even wondering if we could fix it so your father and Maggie needn't know . . .'

Fliss was feeling totally overwhelmed. When Greta got the bit between her teeth, there was no stopping her. If she'd already suspected Fliss was pregnant, she must have been turning options over in her mind, Fliss supposed.

'You mean . . . we wouldn't tell Daddy?' she asked.

'We'll have to see. But I'd rather we didn't have to. This is going to break his heart . . .'

Fliss bowed her head. It was exactly what she'd thought. And for the moment, the possibility that she could keep this from her beloved father outweighed any doubts that were niggling deep inside when she thought of having her baby adopted.

It really would be for the best. In fact she couldn't see any other way out of the mess she was in.

Fliss phoned the contact number Dr Myers had given her and met the social worker. Mrs Adams was middle-aged, pleasant, straight-talking, and not a bit judgemental. She was also very efficient. She would arrange accommodation for Fliss for the last three months of her pregnancy – she had a list of landladies who were prepared to let a room to a single girl 'in trouble'. She would register her with a doctor in the same town and book a hospital bed for her confinement. She thought this would be more suitable than a mother-and-baby home, since Fliss was considerably older than most of the girls who took this route, who were likely to still be in their teens. Another advantage was that Fliss could give up her baby as soon as she left hospital, whereas in a home, mothers were expected to care for their babies for a minimum of six weeks, and sometimes longer. According to Mrs Adams, this made it much harder to give up the baby. Many girls just couldn't do it. But ten days – the length of Fliss's stay in hospital if all went well – ten days would be manageable.

Mrs Adams would arrange the adoption too – or at least she would put Fliss in touch with a suitable agency. Did Fliss have a particular religious denomination? Fliss, who rarely if ever attended church services, since she was forced to go to Sunday school each week when she was a little girl, said she supposed she was C of E, and Mrs Adams made a note of that.

It was always possible, she said, that suitable adoptive parents would be found before the baby was born, in which case he – Mrs Adams always referred to the baby as 'he' – could go directly to them. (*Go directly to jail, do not pass Go*, Fliss, who had once upon a time played a lot of Monopoly, thought dully.) Failing this, he would be placed with a foster mother until permanent arrangements were made.

It seemed to Fliss to be a done deed. She wasn't happy about it – how could she be? – but it appeared to be the best possible outcome to a horrible mess.

And then two things happened to sow the seeds of doubt in her mind.

The first was that she bumped into Martin Dunning – almost literally.

Since that night on the beach, Fliss had assiduously avoided Martin, and she thought he might be avoiding her. But one day, a week or so after she had first met Mrs Adams to set the wheels in motion, she saw his Zephyr Zodiac parked up in the lay-by opposite the factory gates when she left work riding her Vespa. She could think of no earthly reason why he should be there unless he was waiting for her, and as she pulled out on to the road he tooted and waved, indicating that he wanted to speak to her. It was the last thing Fliss wanted. So far nobody but her mother, Dr Myers and Mrs Adams knew her secret, and she wanted it to stay that way. Though sweet reason told her Martin could easily catch and overtake her, Fliss took off as fast as the Vespa would go, which, in reality, was not very fast. Its top speed was about fifty miles an hour, and the small wheels made it unstable round bends, of which there were plenty on her route home. She hadn't gone very far before she heard a car engine behind her. Unable to overtake her around the blind bends, he just sat there, and his presence so close behind her was unsettling. When the gradient of a steep hill slowed the Vespa to a crawl, she panicked. She changed down from second to first gear, at the same time accelerating hard and also looking back over her shoulder. The snatch of the gear change and the lack of concentration were her undoing. The front wheel of the Vespa bucked, and before she knew it, Fliss was sliding off the back of the scooter and being dumped unceremoniously in the road.

It wasn't a serious accident given the low speed at which she was travelling, and Martin had left enough distance between them so she was not at risk of being run over. It was the ignominy

71

that was the worst thing; that and being forced, now, to face Martin.

'Are you all right?' He was out of the car and running up the hill towards her long before she had the chance to pick herself up, leaving his car door swinging wide open.

'It's your fault!' Fliss shot at him, dusting herself down with hands that stung from having impacted the gravel on the road. 'Why are you following me? You've been right on my tail since—'

'I could hardly overtake you on those bends,' Martin said.

'But you were waiting for me outside work.'

'Maybe I was. Look, let's get your bike out of the road, shall we?'

'I can do it.' Fliss bent over and gasped as a sharp pain knifed through her stomach. She straightened up, pressing her hand to the spot beneath which the pain had shot and experiencing a moment's completely unexpected alarm.

Martin seemed not to have noticed. He righted the Vespa with ease – really, there was no weight to it at all – and pushed it to the side of the road.

'I'm sorry if I scared you, Fliss. I just wanted to talk to you, and you haven't been in any of the usual places since—'

'Well no – perhaps there's a reason for that,' she snapped. 'Perhaps I don't want to talk to you.'

He winced. 'Right. I see.'

'No, you don't see.' The shock of falling off her scooter coming on top of the stress she'd felt on being waylaid and followed by Martin was making her shake, and also loosening her tongue. 'You've done enough damage. Just stay away from me, OK?'

She saw the uncertainty in his eyes then.

'Fliss . . .?'

'Just leave me alone!' She turned away, getting on to her scooter, riding off. He didn't follow her. In fact, when she reached the top of the hill, she looked around and the Zodiac was still in the middle of the road, though the door was no longer swinging open. She took the turning for Porthtowan, and though she listened out for the throaty engine, she didn't hear it, or see Martin again.

He did telephone her, though, that evening. The Penrose family were one of the few homes in the village that boasted a telephone – most people made any necessary calls from the public kiosk in the village. But Greta did dressmaking to bring in some extra income, making clothes for local people and doing alterations for a couple of the big stores in Truro, and a telephone was pretty well a necessity.

It rang that evening just as *The Archers* was finishing. Maggie answered it and came into the living room looking as if someone had forced her to eat a crab apple.

'It's for you, Fliss. Martin Dunning.'

Fliss's first inclination was to refuse to speak to him. But she could hardly do that; Maggie would think it very odd. She could feel her mother's gaze boring holes in her back as she went out to the hall and picked up the black Bakelite receiver.

'What do you want?' she hissed.

'Fliss – what you said this afternoon . . . Did you mean . . .'

He sounded hesitant, uncertain, quite unlike himself, really. At twenty-five, Martin always seemed totally confident and sure of himself.

'I meant I want you to leave me alone,' Fliss said.

'No – not that. You said I'd "done enough" . . .'

'You have.'

'Are you saying I've got you into trouble? Is that it?'

For a moment she couldn't speak. The words simply would not come. She cast a nervous glance over her shoulder, checking whether she'd closed the living room door behind her properly – the last thing she wanted was for Maggie to overhear the conversation.

'Yes,' she said at last.

'Bloomin' heck, Fliss.'

'Exactly. But if you tell a soul . . .'

'What are you going to do? We really ought to talk.'

73

'I don't want to talk. And what I'm going to do is none of your business.'

'Surely you don't think I'm going to walk away and leave you in a mess? What sort of a bloke do you take me for? If you're in trouble because of me, then of course I'll do the decent thing.'

'Didn't you hear me? I just want you to leave me alone, Martin. I'm sorting it out. I can't let this ruin my life. And before you put on the sackcloth and ashes . . . it was my fault as much as yours. So I don't see why your life should be ruined either.'

'That's not the way I see it, Fliss.'

'I don't care how you see it just as long as you don't tell anybody about this. If you do, I'll kill you.'

'OK, OK, if that's the way you want it . . .'

'It is.'

'I don't like this . . .'

'Neither do I!'

'. . . and if you change your mind, just . . . get in touch, Fliss. I want to do the right thing.'

'The right thing is to keep this between ourselves. The right thing is to find a good home for the baby, have it adopted and try to forget it ever happened. As far as I'm concerned, Martin, that is the right thing,' Fliss said.

And she put the phone down.

The second thing that happened was that Jo Best came home.

Cornwall was not, strictly speaking, Jo's home. If asked, she would have been hard put to it to name any particular place as the one where she belonged.

Her father had been an army officer; as a young child she had lived in Burma and Hong Kong as well as Bridgnorth and Corsham. When she was eight years old, she had been sent to her first boarding school – there had been three in all, as Jo had a habit of getting expelled. The war put an end to her mother's camp-following; she took a house in Cheltenham and for a while Jo went to live with her, but it wasn't a success. Marie, who had

74

become accustomed to a full social life, was lonely and began drinking too much, and when Jo's father was killed at El Alamein she went on a downward spiral. Unable to cope with her own alcoholism, let alone a rebellious daughter, she sent Jo to live with an aunt in Falmouth. It was here that Jo discovered her love for sailing and forged her friendship with Fliss, a friendship that was to change the course of both their lives.

The two girls made a formidable team, skilful, adventurous and dedicated. Incensed by the way women were treated as second-class citizens in the sailing world, they set out to prove they were as good as any man. They were barred from being full members of most sailing clubs, so they made their own independent arrangements, and when Jo's mother died – drink as the root cause, combined with an overdose of sleeping pills – and Jo came into a not inconsiderable inheritance, she used it to buy a boat of her own, newer and faster than Fliss's beloved, but ageing, *Mesmaid's Song*. The two girls began racing and their fame spread with the success they achieved; as Jo's money dwindled, Fliss managed to persuade her employers, Pretty's Pickles, to sponsor them.

But the girls' ambition knew no bounds. It was their dream to sail the Atlantic together, just the two of them, not as crew for a male skipper. They were a way off achieving that yet, but in the meantime there was a project that had excited their interest.

A replica of the *Mayflower*, the ship on which the Pilgrim Fathers had sailed to the New World in 1620, was being built in a Brixham shipyard, and the plan was to recreate the historic voyage. It would be a celebration of the special alliance that had been forged between Great Britain and America as they fought together in the war. When they heard about it, Jo and Fliss made up their minds – they were going to apply to be part of the thirty-three-strong crew. Their chances, they knew, were slim – they suspected that the captain, Alan Villiers, who had been sailing square-rigged ships for forty-odd years, would not be impressed by the idea of having women in his crew – but they hoped the high profile they now enjoyed would work in their favour.

A ship like the *Mayflower* II was a far cry from what they were used to, of course, so when the opportunity arose for Jo to crew on a voyage on a tall ship she grabbed it with both hands. Experience could, after all, make all the difference when it came to trying to get taken on for the *Mayflower* voyage.

Jo had been gone for seven of the most traumatic weeks of Fliss's life, but now she was back. Fliss was dreading having to tell her friend that their plans had been thrown into disarray, but glad she would at last have someone with whom she could discuss her plight, someone who wouldn't judge her. Jo was very much a free spirit, in many ways more unconventional than Fliss herself, and Fliss expected her to take a laid-back approach to the situation, even if she was disappointed and even annoyed that she would have to try for the *Mayflower* without Fliss.

In the event, however, she was totally taken by surprise by Jo's reaction.

'There's something I've got to tell you,' Fliss said.

She and Jo were in a coffee bar in Falmouth, one they often frequented. As usual it was crowded, leather-jacketed youths and girls in full dirndl skirts layered over paper nylon petticoats gathered around the tables drinking frothy espresso coffee whilst the jukebox blared the hits of the day – Frankie Lymon and the Teenagers, 'Why Do Fools Fall in Love'; Kay Starr, 'The Rock and Roll Waltz'; Bill Haley, 'Rock Around the Clock'. Fliss and Jo sat on high stools at a corner counter, divorced from the rest of the social scene.

'I'm pregnant.'

'Oh Fliss, no!'

''Fraid so. It's a nightmare, isn't it?'

'But who . . .? When . . .?'

'Do you remember that party at the beach bar? When you were with Simon Beacham?'

'I wasn't with Simon Beacham. I was dancing with him because you'd given him the cold shoulder and gone off with Martin Dunning . . . Ah. I see. It's Martin Dunning, is it?'

Fliss nodded miserably. 'I can't believe I could have been so stupid. I mean – Martin Dunning's a nice chap, but . . . I was so drunk, Jo. I think somebody must have spiked my drink.'

'Hmm. Simon Beacham, I wouldn't be surprised. He's so besotted with you, he might have thought he stood a chance if you were tiddly. And he was on shorts – vodka, I think. You probably wouldn't have tasted that if he'd tipped one in your Babycham.'

'The creep!' Fliss shook her head in disgust. 'Anyway, that hardly matters now. I'm in a real mess.'

'What are you going to do?' Jo asked. Her face had gone pinched; she looked very shaken.

'What can I do? I'm going to have it adopted, of course. I've been in touch with a social worker and she's arranging everything—'

'No!' Jo said sharply.

'What?' Fliss looked narrowly at her friend, puzzled by the vehement response, and saw just how emotional she had become.

'Don't do it, Fliss. Don't have your baby adopted. You'll regret it for ever if you do.'

'But there's no way I can keep it. How could I? And Mum and Dad . . . Dad doesn't even know about it.'

'You can't give up your baby, Fliss,' Jo said passionately. 'Believe me, it's a very bad idea.'

This was not just about her, Fliss realised suddenly. This Jo, so emotional she appeared to be on the verge of tears, wasn't one Fliss knew at all. Jo was intrepid and funny and strong, a little bit wild; it always seemed to Fliss she cared for nothing and no one. 'Jo?' she said. 'I don't understand. Why . . .?'

'Let's get out of here.' Jo pushed the clear Pyrex cup and saucer that had contained her espresso to the back of the counter and stood up abruptly, threading her way between the crowded tables and heading for the door. A gaggle of motorcycles and scooters was parked on the forecourt outside; Jo caught her hip on the handlebars of one, but strode on as if she hadn't even noticed. Fliss had to half run to keep up with her.

'What is the matter?' she demanded, catching at her friend's bare arm.

Jo stopped walking; swung round.

'There's a lot you don't know about me, Fliss.'

'But what has it got to do with me being pregnant?'

'Everything.' Jo's face was set, her jaw tight, yet trembling, and there was despair in her voice. 'When I was sixteen, Fliss, I was where you are now. I had a baby. A little boy – Peter, I called him. He was adopted. I really didn't have a choice. I mean – *sixteen?* No real home of my own. No parents. I absolutely could not keep him. But I can tell you, there's not a single day of my life I don't think about him. Well – perhaps not every single day, not now. But at Christmas . . . his birthday . . . all sorts of other odd times when it just . . . suddenly . . . Well, it's all there, and I want him so much, and I wonder where he is, what he's doing, what he looks like, and I'll never know . . . It's hell, Fliss. Absolute hell.'

'Oh Jo . . .' Fliss put her arms around her friend, hugging her. 'Why have you never told me?'

'What would be the point?'

'I could have . . . You should have told me . . .'

'And what could *you* do? You couldn't get my son back, could you?' Jo took a long, shuddering breath, regaining control. 'No, it's too late for me. But you, Fliss . . . I didn't have a choice. But you do. And I'm telling you. Don't go there. If you value your sanity, don't go there.'

'Oh Jo! I don't know . . .'

'Think again, Fliss. Please, please, think again.'

Fliss did think again. She turned it over and over in her mind, shocked at the deep-rooted agony that Jo secretly lived with, frightened by the thought that it might well be the same for her, wondering if she was making the wrong decision, whether there was a way she could keep this baby. But in the end it didn't really change anything. Not only was the prospect of bringing up a baby alone as frightening as the idea of parting with it, the deciding factor was the shame it would bring on her parents. She couldn't do it to them, she absolutely couldn't.

And so, in spite of serious misgivings, she went ahead with her plans.

SEVEN

It was every bit as bad as Jo had said it would be. The birth was long and complicated, and it was some hours before a nurse brought Emma into the ward Fliss was sharing with three other new mothers, but the moment she held her in her arms, to her utter amazement Fliss felt the most overwhelming rush of love. She was so small and so perfect, though her head was a bit pointed because she had taken so long to be born; she stared up at Fliss with amazingly blue eyes, an unwinking, trusting stare. She was tightly swaddled, but through the blanket her body felt firm and warm, and the baby smell of her was warm too and quite unlike anything Fliss had ever smelled before.

Fliss was going to bottle-feed her, obviously – since she would be giving her up in ten days' time, starting her on breast milk would have been pointless – but she was horribly envious of the other new mothers who were nursing their babies. Never mind that they complained that the frenzied sucking was giving them sore nipples; she'd have changed places with them in an instant. In any case, bottle-feeding wasn't exactly pain-free – the tablets they'd given her to stop the milk from coming in didn't seem to be working, and her breasts were swollen and throbbing. She cradled Emma as close as she could whilst holding the bottle as the nurse had shown her, and when they took her away, back to the nursery, where all the babies were lined up in their cots in rows, she buried her face in the pillow and fought back the tears.

'When is your husband coming to see you then?' the woman in the next bed asked. She was called Mrs Donovan, she had a sharp face and sharp eyes, and Fliss was horribly certain she suspected that Fliss had no husband. The nurses were addressing her as 'Mrs Redfern' – she was going by her mother's maiden name, since 'Felicity Penrose' might be recognised – and she had a ring on the third finger of her left hand, a wide, cheap ring she'd bought at Woolworths, but there were giveaways. The bottle-feeding; the suitcase under the bed full of her clothes and those she had bought for the baby, because she wouldn't be going back to her lodgings when she left hospital, but straight home to Porthtowan; the fact that her only visitors had been Jo and her mother.

'He won't be coming,' Fliss said. 'He's away working.'

'Oh. I see,' Mrs Donovan said, and Fliss saw her exchange a glance with Mrs Fenton in the bed opposite.

To be honest, though, Fliss was past caring what they thought. When she left hospital she'd probably never see them again, and she'd got used to feeling like a fallen woman in the weeks she'd been lodging with Mrs Blacker in her little terraced house on the outskirts of town. Mrs Blacker seemed to feel that doing her Christian duty by taking in an unmarried girl in Fliss's condition gave her the right to show her disapproval in a hundred little ways; though she never actually said so in as many words, she made it apparent all the same. She'd even set a curfew so that if Fliss went out in the evening, to the pictures, or just for a walk, she had to be back by ten or the door would be bolted. No, the only thing Fliss really cared about now was Emma, and the awful prospect of having to part with her.

Whereas before Emma was born it really hadn't bothered her at all – she'd just wanted this whole thing to be over – now she could think of nothing else. At night she tossed and turned; when she was allowed up to have her first bath she lay in the warm salty water staring at the flabby tummy that had so recently held her beloved baby and wondered if even now it was not too late to change the plan and keep her. She had a respite – an adoptive couple had been lined up had the baby been a boy, but as she had turned out to be a girl, there were no prospective parents in the frame and for the time being Emma was going to a foster mother. At least it meant she wasn't doing anything final just yet, Fliss thought. She could still change her mind. If she could come up with a workable alternative.

The registrar came to the hospital on the fifth day – Fliss was allowed to walk down the corridor to a small office where she would have some privacy as she reported her details for Emma's birth certificate. Mother – Felicity Penrose. Father . . . She had intended to have 'Unknown' recorded in the appropriate space. But in the event she heard herself saying: 'Martin Dunning.' It gave her quite a jolt, and she wondered just how far she had come towards deciding Emma's future.

And yet, for all that her thoughts and emotions never stopped whirling, it was as if she was somehow paralysed, locked in to the programme of events. Fliss, who usually made her own decisions, felt strangely institutionalised, numbed and helpless, capable only of doing what was expected of her. Mrs Adams came to collect her and Emma on the day she was discharged; she carried Fliss's case down to her car, held Emma while Fliss got into the rear seat and then settled her on Fliss's lap, a sweet-smelling bundle in a pink pram suit Greta had bought for her and brought to the hospital, and a lacy white shawl Fliss had fallen in love with when she saw it in a shop window.

Fliss held Emma tightly; her eyes were full of tears.

'You are doing the right thing, Felicity,' Mrs Adams said, getting into the driver's seat and starting the engine. 'Emma is going to be a much-loved baby, and whoever adopts her is going to be so grateful to you for giving them the child they want so badly. That's what you have to cling on to.'

Fliss couldn't answer. Perhaps Emma would have the sort of

life she would never be able to give her, but at that moment she was overwhelmed by wretchedness and a sense of impending loss that was exactly like grief.

The drive to the foster mother's home took about half an hour; Fliss tried to make each minute of it stretch to eternity. And then they were drawing up in the drive of a country cottage, getting out of the car, walking towards a front door that was already open and a plump, comfortable-looking woman who had come to welcome them.

'This must be Emma,' she said, pulling the shawl aside so she could look at her. 'She's beautiful.'

Fliss nodded. If she said a single word she was going to burst into tears, she knew. The woman – Mrs Price – showed her into a small, cosy parlour where a crib stood in front of the window.

'Here we are. Would you like to put her in her cot?'

No! No! Fliss's heart was screaming. But she bent over the crib and laid Emma down on the flannelette sheet and took off the little pink bonnet and loosened the pink jacket at the throat.

Mrs Adams touched her arm.

'She'll be fine now with Mrs Price,' she said, gently but firmly. 'Best not to prolong this, Felicity. It'll only make it harder for you.'

Fliss pressed her hands to her mouth, staring down at Emma's face, memorising every detail of it for the empty months and years ahead. She kissed her fingers and touched them to Emma's peachy cheek.

'Goodbye, my darling. Be happy.'

Then she turned and walked away, out of the house, away from her beloved child. Only then did the tears come, and when they did, it seemed they would never stop.

'Jo, you were right, I can't do this,' Fliss said. 'I can't bear it. I think of her every moment of every day.'

'I know. I did warn you.'

'But I didn't realise . . . I feel . . . I feel as if my heart's been torn out. I keep telling myself it's for the best, that I'm just being selfish wanting her when she will be so much better off with a proper family, but it really doesn't help. I'm just a wreck.'

It was true, she was. Night after night she sobbed uncontrollably, her arms wrapped around her empty stomach, bent double with a pain that was physical in its intensity. Day after day she went through the motions of life like an automaton, trying to keep up a pretence and all the while bleeding from every pore, every nerve ending.

'It's not too late,' Jo said.

'It soon will be.'

A couple had been found who wanted to adopt Emma; who they were Fliss didn't – and never would – know, but according to the adoption agency they were a professional couple with their own attractive home. They desperately wanted a family; in a year or two's time they would probably adopt another baby, so Emma would have a brother or sister. It sounded idyllic; Emma would have two loving parents and a wonderful life, Fliss was sure. But still she couldn't bring herself to sign the papers. They lay on her dressing table still in their envelope, and the lady from the adoption agency had begun to press her. Emma couldn't stay with Mrs Price, the foster mother, for ever. Fliss was not being fair to the couple who wanted to adopt Emma, or indeed to Emma herself. She really had to make a decision and act upon it. Once or twice she got out the papers and read through them, pen in hand, but still she couldn't do it.

'I don't know what to do, Jo,' she groaned.

'Well, you know what I think.'

'Yes, but . . . I just don't think I can bring up a baby on my own. I'd have to give up my job, and what would I do for money?'

'Perhaps your mum would look after her while you went to work.'

'I don't know that I can ask her. She's so anxious nobody should find out I've "let myself down", as she calls it. Even Dad doesn't know. He thought I was staying with a sailing friend. I don't know how on earth I could tell him now . . .'

'You'll find a way.'

'What sort of a life could I give Emma?'

'You're her mother.'

'I know, but . . .'

'I think,' Jo said, 'that you ought to talk to Martin Dunning. He has a responsibility here to help with the expense if nothing else. They're not short of a penny or two. And he did offer, didn't he?'

'Yes, he did. And I told him to get lost.'

'Well I think it's time for you to go back and eat humble pie,' Jo said bluntly. 'Pride is a luxury you can't afford. Come on, let's go over to the garage and see him.'

'Now?'

'There's no time like the present. There's room for me on the back of your scooter, isn't there, now you haven't got that bump in front.'

'You're coming with me?'

'Too true. I want to make sure you don't chicken out. If I can stop you from making the same mistake I did, Fliss, then I'm going to do it!'

Martin Dunning was on the garage forecourt putting petrol into a customer's Austin. Fliss pulled up under the wall beside the machine that checked tyre pressures and took off her crash helmet. She didn't like her crash helmet – she thought the peak made her look like a duck. Dark blond hair cascaded over her shoulders. It wasn't her intention to seduce Martin Dunning all over again – nothing could have been further from her mind – but if it had been, she was going the right way about it, Jo thought. Sometimes, it seemed to her, Fliss was totally unaware of the effect she had on men. She could tell from Martin's body language when he looked across and saw her that he was definitely smitten by Fliss. There was something just a bit too studied about the way he nodded and then pretended to ignore her whilst all the time it was perfectly obvious that he was very aware of her.

When Martin finished filling the Austin with petrol, he and the driver went into the little office and Fliss followed them in. She was shaking inwardly with nervousness, but very determined. Something had to be done; she couldn't let Emma go. The customer paid and left; Fliss approached the counter.

'Fliss,' Martin said. There was a stiff formality in his voice. 'This is a surprise. How are you?'

Fliss dug her hands into the pockets of her jacket, clenching them into fists.

'I need to talk to you, Martin.'

'I thought you never wanted to see me again.'

Fliss bit back the retort she would have liked to make. She really couldn't afford to antagonise him.

'What I want is neither here nor there. We have a daughter, Martin, and—'

'A daughter.' He looked a little stunned, as if until this moment none of what had happened was quite real.

'Yes. A little girl. I called her Emma. I went away to have her, as I expect you realised when I disappeared off the scene. She's with a foster mother now, and she's supposed to be going to be adopted, but I don't think I can go through with it. In fact, I'm sure I can't. I want to keep her, bring her up myself.' She broke off, almost unable to believe what she was saying.

Martin's eyes narrowed; he was still wary.

'That's not what you said before.'

'I know. But, like you say, that was *before*. Now she's here, I've held her, fed her . . . it's not a bit how I thought it would be. I don't feel at all the way I thought I'd feel. To be honest, nothing really matters any more except getting her back . . .' Her chin trembled, the tears that were never far away these last weeks aching in her throat. 'I want to keep her. But I don't think I can do that without your help.'

Martin blew breath out over his top lip.

'What sort of help?'

'Well, financial, obviously. I'll have to buy a pram, a cot, a baby bath. She's got to be fed and clothed. I don't earn much, and if I'm going to carry on working I'll have to pay for child care on top of everything else. I just can't do it on my own.'

A black Morris Minor was pulling up beside the petrol pumps – another customer.

'I'll have to serve.' Martin flipped up the trapdoor in the counter, came through, letting it drop back into place behind him. Fliss watched impatiently through the window as he crossed to the car, speaking to the driver and then unscrewing the Morris's petrol cap. What a moment to be interrupted! she thought in agitation. Just to make things worse, the man also wanted his oil and water checked, and both needed topping up. The customer gave Martin some notes from his wallet, and when he came into the office for change he did not even glance at Fliss; it was almost as if she wasn't there.

Annoyance flared, all the more potent because of her emotional state.

'You can't just ignore me, Martin,' she said sharply when he returned. 'And you can't ignore the fact that you've got a baby either. You have a responsibility here. You're going to have to support her one way or another.'

'Who said I was going to ignore her?' Martin snapped back. 'Of course I'll support her – and you – if that's what you want. But have you really thought what it's going to be like for you – and for her?'

'I think so, yes. It's going to be pretty awful to start with – people are going to have a field day tearing me to shreds. But it'll be a nine-day wonder. They'll have something else to talk about before long.'

'And what about . . . she's called Emma, you say? How is it going to be for her, tarred as illegitimate? When she goes to school and she's the only one in the class without a father? Children can be very cruel.'

Fliss swallowed hard.

'I know – I know. But my mind's made up. At least she'll be

with her real mother, who loves her. So I'm afraid you're not going to get off scot-free by painting a black picture. If you won't help me willingly, then I'll just have to—'

'Oh, for goodness sake, Fliss!' he interrupted her. 'How many times do I have to say it? I am not trying to escape my responsibilities. It's just that I'm thinking there's a better way, a way that you can keep Emma without causing quite such a scandal. There will still be talk, of course, but like you say, it'll soon be forgotten. And at least Emma won't have the stigma of being illegitimate like a millstone round her neck.'

Fliss frowned. 'What are you talking about, Martin?'

'Pretty obvious, really, I'd have thought. What we should have done in the first place.'

'*What?*' She was beginning to understand what he was going to say, but she still couldn't quite believe it.

'Well,' Martin said, giving her a straight look, 'the obvious solution is for us to get married.'

'He said *what?*' asked Jo, astounded.

'That we should get married.'

'And what did you say?'

'I said I'd think about it.'

'But Fliss – *marry* him? It's a bit extreme, isn't it?'

'Actually, it probably is the best solution.'

'But . . . it was just a one-night stand. It's not as though you're in love or anything.'

'No. But he is a really nice guy. I think we'd be all right. As he said, it would be awfully hard on Emma without a proper family. And it wouldn't be quite such a matter for shame for Mum and Dad . . .'

'But *marrying* him!'

'You're the one who's tried to talk me out of having her adopted, Jo,' Fliss snapped. 'What else do you suggest I do?'

'I don't know,' Jo admitted. 'I just think . . . well, I'm afraid it's a recipe for disaster.'

'The disaster's already happened,' Fliss said flatly. 'All we can do now is make the best of it.'

'So you are going to do it.'

'To be honest,' Fliss said, 'I don't think I have much choice.'

The path to the altar was far from plain sailing, but Fliss was so elated by the thought of having Emma back that everything else paled into insignificance. Nothing really mattered, not the talk in the town, not her own misgivings, not the terrible fuss at home.

And there was a fuss at home!

To begin with, Greta tried to talk her out of such a huge step, but perhaps not as wholeheartedly as she might have done – she too had been surprised by the strength of the attachment she felt to the baby, who was, after all, her first grandchild.

But Bill was in a terrible way, desperately disappointed in Fliss and terribly hurt that what had been going on had been kept from him. The very fact that he normally took everything in his stride meant that when something did upset him it was all the worse for it. He simply was not used to handling emotion, and when he cried, as he cried in private over this, the tears seemed to him to be a sign of weakness, and as much of a shock as discovering what had happened without his knowledge.

When Fliss told him, he simply sat in stunned silence.

'I'm sorry, Daddy,' she said. 'I shouldn't have kept it from you. But I didn't want to upset you.'

He looked up at her for a moment, the pain raw in his eyes before he lowered them again.

'I'm your father, Fliss.'

'I know. But I was so ashamed.'

'And you, Greta!' He turned to his wife. 'How could you? I can't believe all this has been going on and you never said anything.'

'We thought it best,' Greta said tightly.

'Well, I don't know . . .' He shook his head, then got up and headed for the door.

'Where do you think you're going?' Greta demanded.

'Does it matter? I'm not needed here, am I?'

'Oh Daddy, that's not true! Please don't walk away!'

'I want to be on my own for a bit.'

'But we've got to talk about the wedding,' Greta objected.

'You can talk about it. I don't want to. I don't want to know anything about it.'

Fliss was distraught. 'But . . . you will give me away, won't you?'

'I suppose I shall have to. But it's a bit late for that, isn't it?'

He went out; the back door slammed after him.

'He'll come round when he's had a chance to think about it,' Greta said.

But in the event it was a very long time before Bill could bring himself to even look at Fliss. When she married Martin three weeks later, by special licence, he did walk her down the aisle but he held himself stiffly, keeping his distance between him and his beloved daughter, and when Fliss brought Emma home he couldn't bear to look at her either.

Time would alter that, of course. But for the present he was too badly hurt to be able to forgive.

Bill was not the only one to be upset by the news. For Maggie it was the bitterest of blows.

The fact that Fliss had gone away to have an illegitimate child did not come as a shock to her. She'd guessed what was going on. Fliss's expanding waistline had not gone unnoticed by her, nor had the whispered conversations between her sister and Greta, nor the peculiar atmosphere in the house. Maggie had said nothing, waiting for Fliss to make the first move, and when she did not, Maggie too was dreadfully hurt.

But the fact that her sister had not seen fit to confide in her was as nothing compared to the awful discovery that the father of Fliss's baby was none other than Martin Dunning. And the news that she was going to marry him was an end to all Maggie's hopes and dreams.

Maggie had been in love with Martin for as long as she could remember. She'd been over the moon when he asked her out, but it had only lasted a few brief months before he'd 'finished' with her, as they called it, saying he wanted his freedom. She pleaded, said she'd never tie him down, that he could do exactly as he liked as long as he still saw her sometimes, and Martin had said OK, as long as they both understood the situation, they'd stay friends. And so they'd gone to the pictures every so often, and he took her home from the youth club on the back of his motor-bike, and she'd pretended to herself that everything was all right. But it wasn't, of course. He was seeing other girls, which, under the terms of their agreement, should have been permissible, but in the end Maggie couldn't stand it any more. She gave him an ultimatum; he told her he was absolutely not her property. And that was that.

She tried to put him out of her head. But still the torch burned, bright as ever. Just as she thought she was getting over him, their paths would cross, her heart would do the same old somersaults and the magic would begin all over again. Crazy magic. Black magic. Magic that meant she could think of nothing but him. He got inside her head and pulsed through her veins. Maggie, normally so sensible, so level-headed, was totally obsessed by Martin and nobody else would do. There were other boys, and then men, who took her out, treated her well, but they just didn't measure up to Martin, and she continued to hope that when he'd sown his wild oats he'd come back to her and they would be together.

Now the chance of that happening had been utterly destroyed, and by her own sister. Maggie was devastated – and angry. When she'd been going out with Martin there had been times when he'd tried it on, and always she had stopped him, worried he would think her fast. And where had it got her? Precisely nowhere! Fliss had allowed Martin all the liberties he wanted and as a result she was going to marry him. It simply was not fair!

All her life she'd played second fiddle to Fliss. Mostly she hadn't minded too much. She was proud of her pretty, talented, feisty little sister. But there had been times when it was hard to take. She recalled how, when they were little, adults would act as if she was invisible, making much of Fliss, saying what pretty hair she had, what a pretty face, trying to get her to say something – Fliss had learned that refusing to talk, just looking at the grown-ups with big innocent eyes and a tightly buttoned mouth, was a sure-fire way of getting attention. As they grew up, it was the same with the boys – they flocked around Fliss as the gulls followed the fishing boats. Then when she began to make a name for herself in the world of sailing it was yet another attraction – everyone wanted to know Felicity Penrose. Once again Maggie had been pushed into the background, but on the whole it suited her. She wasn't one to seek out the limelight. Let Fliss have the glory; Maggie couldn't think of anything she'd like less than having her photograph in the papers and people asking for her autograph. She enjoyed her job, training to be a chartered accountant, and, like Fliss, she had a scooter, though hers was a Lambretta. If only she'd had Martin, life would have been perfect just as it was.

And now . . . this.

Maggie felt as if the sky had fallen in on her world. It would have been bad enough if Martin had been marrying someone else, but Fliss! He'd be around all the time. She'd have to watch them together, and try to pretend she really didn't care when all the time she was bleeding inside. Maggie didn't know how she was going to bear it.

EIGHT

It might just have worked. It could have worked. Fliss and Martin were both determined it would. They'd caused enough talk locally with their shotgun wedding; they didn't want the next scandal to be divorce. Besides which, they both wanted to make a stable home for Emma. It could have worked in the way arranged marriages work – love growing from a shared life. They were two attractive young people – Martin had fancied Fliss for a very long time and, drunk as she had been on the night Emma was conceived, it would never have happened unless she had fancied him too.

But it wasn't long before Fliss discovered that married life could be a great deal harder than she'd ever imagined. She and Martin found a cottage to rent on the outskirts of Redruth, one of a row that had been built originally for tin-miners. Their neighbours were all elderly folk with whom she had nothing in common, and though Hattie Firks, the widow who lived next door, was friendly enough, Fliss was very lonely. Martin left for work early each morning and it was often late in the evening before he came home, and she was left isolated from her family and friends – with Emma to consider, she couldn't use her scooter any more to get about. Delighted as she was to have Emma back, the endless round of washing nappies, cleaning the house and preparing meals soon became horribly tedious when her only company was a baby who seemed to do nothing but sleep, feed and cry.

The bright spots were the times Jo came to visit her; she hung on to them as a lifeline, but throughout that first summer Jo was frequently away, crewing on one boat or another. And the most enormous blow fell when Jo became involved with a man and moved to Plymouth to be near him.

'Oh Jo, you can't go!' Fliss wailed when her friend broke the news to her. It was what she'd been dreading; there'd been a glow about Jo ever since she'd met Yves Delors, a handsome French sailor.

'Fliss – I'm sorry, I really am. But I've got my life to live too.'

'I know. I'm just being selfish.'

'No, you're not. I can understand how you feel. But you'll be fine, you'll see. Emma won't be a baby for ever – you'll be able to sail again, and take her with you. She'll probably be the youngest girl ever to get a skipper's ticket.'

'Probably.' Fliss forced a laugh. She was glad for her friend; Jo deserved some happiness. Knowing how she herself had felt giving Emma up for those brief weeks, her heart went out to Jo, who had lost her baby son for ever, and she'd seen the wistful expression on Jo's face when she looked at Emma. Perhaps Yves was the one for her; perhaps they'd go on to have children together and Jo would be able to fill a corner of that empty place inside her. She mustn't begrudge her that – she didn't! And yet . . .

And yet there was no way she could stop the feeling of desolation at the thought that Jo's regular visits would be no more, and no way she could stop the creeping edge of envy either. She wondered how it would feel to be as head-over-heels in love as Jo clearly was. It wasn't something she'd ever experienced, and she didn't expect she ever would now.

It was towards the end of the summer when a local used-car business came up for sale, and Martin immediately took an interest in it.

'It doesn't do that much trade at the moment,' he said, 'but the potential is there all right. Finding the money to pay for it will be a stretch, but now that I've got you and Emma to provide for I'd like to build up a business of my own.'

'Sounds good,' Fliss said.

'You don't mind taking the chance? Or tightening our belts for a bit?'

Fliss shook her head. Money wasn't important to her. She'd never had much to spare; every penny she earned had gone on her boat, *Mermaid's Song*, and she'd never wanted to spend on the fripperies that gave other girls such pleasure – clothes, make-up, gramophone records. But she'd never been really hard up either. Her parents had always made sure there was food on the table and coal on the fire; now she managed quite happily on the housekeeping allowance Martin gave her and let him take care of everything else.

'Go for it,' she said.

'I'll certainly look into it,' Martin said.

He did. Fliss wasn't party to the negotiations, or to his meetings with the bank manager to arrange the finance, but by Christmas, the new venture was under way. She wasn't party either to any of Martin's business plans. Presumably he talked it over with his father; he certainly didn't discuss it with her, and in the beginning the only thing that really affected her was that he was later home from work than ever and she became used to spending her evenings as well as her days alone.

Winter seemed to last for ever and tragedy followed tragedy. In December a horrific train crash in Lewisham killed eighty-eight people; the following February Fliss was stunned by the deaths of so many of the Busby Babes when the plane that was bringing them home from an important football match in Switzerland crashed on take-off in icy conditions. She listened to every news bulletin to see which of the young sportsmen had survived and to get news of the condition of those whose lives were hanging on a thread; she pored over newspaper pictures of the familiar faces of the nation's heroes and read every printed word. But it wasn't long before something far closer to home put it right out of her head.

Bill had not been well since he had contracted Asian flu back in the autumn, and at the end of February he suffered a massive heart attack and died. Fliss was devastated. She'd done her best to put things right with her father, especially when he was so unwell, but their relationship had never really recovered. Now it was too late. In a way she blamed herself for his death; if he hadn't been so upset by what had happened, perhaps his reserves wouldn't have been so low and he would never have caught the flu in the first place. Martin told her not to be silly, that she shouldn't torture herself that way, but it didn't help.

The dark depression that winter could always bring hovered over her now like a lowering storm cloud. Fliss felt horribly trapped and knew there was nothing she could do about it. This was the life she'd opted for; it was too late now to change her mind. And she didn't want to. Really she didn't. The thought that she had so nearly lost Emma was enough to make her count her blessings, but still the low feelings and the restlessness persisted. She yearned for the warmth of spring, for the long sunny days, for the chance to take her boat out to sea, taste the salt on her lips and feel the wind in her hair. Without it she wasn't living, she was existing.

But at least Emma was more fun now, and Fliss was beginning to enjoy her company rather than simply doting on her. She took her for long walks in her pushchair, pointing out the lambs' tails in the hedgerows and the snowdrops nestling in the banks. One day Martin brought a little car home for her – an Austin Seven that someone had traded in for a newer model – and he arranged for her to have a driving lesson once a week from a local school of motoring. Fliss passed her test first time, and was delighted with her new-found freedom.

She could drive over now to visit her mother; it was there that Emma took her first faltering step, much to Greta's delight. And one day, when the weather was improving, she had a suggestion to make.

'Why don't I have Emma for the day and you could go sailing?'

Fliss's face lit up. 'Oh, that would be marvellous! But are you sure?'

'I'd love to have her. And it would take my mind off . . .' Greta broke off, her eyes filling with tears. She was missing Bill badly, though she tried to hide her grief from Fliss. 'She's a little sweetheart, aren't you, my love?' She straightened Emma's dress over her chubby knees. 'If she can't cheer me up, nothing can.'

'Mum, you're a life-saver!' Fliss said.

Things were definitely beginning to change for the better.

After having been laid up for so long, of course, Mermaid's Song was going to need some tender loving care and attention. Fliss still kept her at Falmouth; though Martin had tried to talk her into moving to Penryn, where the cost of mooring was much cheaper, she'd so far managed to avoid it.

One day in April she packed her car with all the things Emma would need and took her over to Porthtowan. It would be the first time she'd left her daughter since she had been out of her foster care. Fliss was knotted up with anxiety, and was soon driving Greta mad with an endless list of instructions.

'This is how you use the Baby Mouli to purée her vegetables . . .'

'Be sure to put her changing mat on the floor, not the table, when you're putting on a clean nappy – if she fidgets she might roll off . . .'

'She'll need a good long nap in the middle of the day . . .'

'For goodness' sake, Fliss, I managed to bring up you and Maggie!' Greta said, exasperated. 'I'm sure I can look after Emma for a few hours.'

But the moment she'd kissed Emma goodbye and set off for Falmouth, the worries melted away as if by magic and Fliss was floating on a cloud of elation.

She was free for the first time in almost a year! It was wonderful!

As she'd expected, Mermaid's Song was looking a little the worse for wear. The visible grime on the decks and in the cockpit and cabin was nothing that couldn't be cleaned with a bucket of hot soapy water and a scrubbing brush, and she could soon have the teak and stainless steel polished and buffed to a high shine. But the spinnaker needed patching, and Fliss thought she really should make arrangements to investigate what was going on out of sight below the waterline. Since the boat had been kept in the marina, her hull should still be tight, but she was probably going to need repainting and anti-fouling. Fliss paid a visit to Sam Green, under whose eagle eye the marina ran smoothly as clockwork, and asked him to make the necessary arrangements for Mermaid's Song to go on to the hard, where she could be inspected and painted.

'I'll do that myself,' Fliss said, looking to save money. It didn't take much expertise to splash a few pots of paint about, and she'd enjoy doing it, always provided Greta was willing to look after Emma again, which Fliss was pretty sure she would be.

The spinnaker repair, however, was a different matter. She couldn't possibly manage that without professional help and for that she'd have to pay a visit to the sail company. For the first time since she'd arrived in Falmouth, her heart sank. Visiting the sail company meant having to deal with Simon Beacham, something Fliss avoided wherever possible.

She'd never liked Simon and still wondered if he had spiked her drink on the night she had become pregnant with Emma – she wouldn't put it past him. She didn't like his over-effusive manner or his habit of telling porkie pies in order to impress, and she didn't like that he seemed to be besotted with her, though she thought she might only have herself to blame for that. No one else liked him either, he was very much an outsider, and Fliss, feeling sorry for him, couldn't bring herself to cut him or belittle him as the others did, with the result that he latched on to her like an eager puppy. He was forever finding some excuse to walk by when she was working on her boat, or popping up in the bars and cafés she visited, and it made her uncomfortable. But such devotion had its uses, and getting a good deal on the spinnaker patches she needed was one of them, particularly now, when she had no money of her own and was going to be going cap in hand to Martin to foot the bill for the repairs.

Fliss walked along the harbour, looking at the moored craft as she went. Many of them she knew of old – they'd been here as long as she had, the bobbing yachts and motorboats, the little fishing smacks, the bigger cabin cruisers, their names as familiar to her as her own. Amongst the flags and bunting she spied the jokey skull and crossbones of the *Pirate Queen*, owned by Viv Tallow, one of the old crowd, and smiled. Many a fun time they'd had on the *Pirate Queen*, much to the disgust of the rather pompous old-timers of the yacht club, who throughly disapproved of such junketing.

A smart new Ohlson she didn't recognise caught her eye, and she broke stride, gazing at it enviously. The name inscribed on the hull was *Jersey Gal*, and she wondered who it belonged to. Someone with money to spend, obviously. Oh, what she wouldn't give for a craft like that!

The sailmaker's workshop was situated in what had once been an old warehouse. Peeling double doors stood ajar; Fliss pushed one wider and the familiar smell of grease and canvas wafted out to meet her.

'Simon?' she called. 'Are you there?'

He emerged from the gloom at the back of the workshop, a stockily built young man with slicked-down hair and a sly grin that revealed a snaggle tooth.

'Fliss! What a surprise!' he greeted her. 'Nice to see you! How's tricks?'

'I'm OK. And you?'

'All the better for seeing you. You've been much missed. So, what can I do for you? I suppose it's too much to hope you came just to see me?'

''Fraid so. My spinnaker is in sore need of your expert attention. It's beginning to get awfully thin, but I'm sure you can work your magic on it.'

'I'd like to work my magic on *you*, sweetheart.'

'I'm a married woman now, Simon.'

'So I heard,' he said regretfully. 'Well, if that's not on the agenda, I suppose your spinnaker is the next best thing.' He was standing too close, invading her space, but Fliss gritted her teeth and put up with it.

They talked business for a few minutes, then Fliss raised the subject that was intriguing her.

'There's a very nice boat not far from mine that I haven't seen before. The *Jersey Gal*. Have you seen her?'

Simon's irritating grin turned to a scowl.

'You couldn't miss her, could you?'

'Who does she belong to then?' Fliss asked.

'Hmm!' Simon snorted. 'That would be Hank the Yank, big-headed sod. He did a transatlantic crossing in reverse and thinks it makes him something special. Well, that and his poncey boat.'

'She's beautiful!'

'If you like that sort of thing. You know what they used to say about the Yanks in the war? Oversexed and over here? Could apply to him. The girls seem to think he's Rock Hudson – he's been out with half of Falmouth since he's been here. Plus he's stealing business from the locals.'

'In what way?'

'Touting his services for valeting and general maintenance. Says he needs to earn enough money for his next jaunt, but he doesn't seem short to me. That boat of his must have cost a pretty penny.'

'Right.' Perhaps it would be politic to end this conversation, Fliss thought.

They chatted a while longer, then she escaped and walked back along the quay. When she reached the Ohlson she stopped, gazing at it longingly. Simon might scoff, out of jealousy, she rather thought, but she certainly wouldn't say no to it. The only way she'd ever get her hands on something like that was if she found a millionaire to sponsor her. Some hope! She sighed enviously, and headed back to the weather-beaten but much loved *Mermaid's Song*. At least she was hers, all hers, and as long as she could get her seaworthy and sail her sometimes, Fliss really wanted nothing more.

Except her little daughter. A sudden longing for Emma surged through Fliss, and with it an edge of anxiety that everything was all right at Porthtowan. She'd been gone for hours now. She really must be getting back. Fliss did what she had to do with Mermaid's Song and set out for home.

Emma had, of course, been absolutely fine and Greta had enjoyed having her.

'We've had a lovely time, haven't we, my pet?' she said. 'Bring her over again, Fliss. Whenever you like.'

'I'm going to take you up on that,' Fliss said.

A few days later Sam Green called to tell her Mermaid's Song was now on the hard and ready for repainting.

'We've given her a good wash-down, and she looks pretty fair to me,' he said amiably.

'Oh Sam, you shouldn't have!'

'Why not? I had a half-hour to spare.'

'I'm sure it took you longer than that.'

'Give over! Anyway, she's all yours now. If you're still set on doing the job yourself. But there's a young fellow, an American . . .'

'So I heard. But I've got to do it myself. I don't want to shock Martin with a big bill.'

'If you're looking to save money, there's a paint sale on at—'

'Definitely. Brilliant.'

'You want me to get some for you before it all goes?'

'Would you? You're an angel, Sam!'

'Not just yet, I hope,' he said drily. 'When will you be over?'

'As soon as Mum can have Emma.'

'Can't imagine you with a baby, Fliss.'

'No,' she said with a wry smile. 'Neither can I.'

Good as his word, Sam had obtained two gallon cans of ablative paint, and while the Mermaid's Song was still in the water he had marked off with painter's tape a good six inches above the water-line so that Fliss would know the depth she needed to cover. She'd come prepared with brushes, rags, a paint tray and roller and a stick for stirring the paint – boat paint, with its metal components, which settled on the bottom of the tin, took an awful lot of stirring – and she was dressed for the job in overalls and an old shirt of Martin's, a kerchief tied bandanna-style over her hair.

She worked for a couple of hours, totally engrossed. She didn't notice the man until he spoke, and when he did she jumped out of her skin.

'You're doing a good job there, but . . .' He broke off. 'Oh, oh my!'

Turning abruptly, Fliss had managed to step into her paint tray.

She swore, an unladylike expletive.

'Looks like I spoke too soon.' There was amusement in his tone.

'It's not funny!' Fliss was shifting her foot gingerly, looking in horror at the thick black paint that coated her deck shoe and had thrown splatters up her bare ankle.

'From where you're standing, I guess not.' The drawling accent was certainly not Cornish; it sounded distinctly American. Fliss looked up sharply, curiosity making her forget her ruined shoe. The man, who had been leaning against an old boat hull watching her, was tall and athletically built, wearing faded denims and an open-necked shirt, the sleeves of which had been rolled up to reveal deeply tanned forearms. His fair hair was bleached blond by the sun, his face as bronzed as his arms.

Fliss, about to make a sarcastic retort, was suddenly struck dumb. Something in the way he was looking at her, his narrowed eyes, his half-smile, paralysed her momentarily, and for a moment she could do nothing but look back at him, stunned by the bolt of electricity that had jolted through her. Then embarrassment kicked in, for both her totally unexpected reaction and her undignified situation.

'It was your fault!' she snapped. 'You made me jump.'

'Sorry about that.'

'You don't look very sorry.' Fliss jiggled her foot, wincing with distaste. 'Oh – what a mess!'

'Stay where you are.' The man, clearly the American Simon had called Hank the Yank, put on the sunglasses he had been swinging between thumb and forefinger and crossed to the box of cleaning materials Fliss had brought with her. 'You've got rags here, I presume?'

'In there somewhere . . .' Now that those disconcertingly blue eyes were hidden behind sunglasses Fliss felt more in control of herself, if still a complete fool, and she was even more mortified when the rag he pulled out of her box turned out to be a piece of striped winceyette that had once been the leg of a pair of Bill's pyjamas.

'They're not mine!' Fliss flared defensively.

He cocked a grin at her.

'I didn't think for a minute they were.'

'They belonged to my father.'

'Reckon you'll need the whole suit to clean that lot up,' he said easily. 'What else have you got in your box of tricks?'

He was about to delve in again when a bolt of horror shot through Fliss. This could get worse; among the rags were old vests and a pair of her mother's voluminous knickers. The last thing she wanted was for him to wave those like a flag!

'Oh – just give me the rag!' she snapped hastily. 'For all the good it will do!'

She was trying to kick off her shoe and wobbling precariously.

'Hey, careful!' he warned. 'We don't want you falling over again.'

'I did not fall over!' She found a bit of unpainted hull to lean against while she got out of her shoe, hobbled to the box of cleaning materials and fished out an innocuous old tea towel and a bottle of turpentine, slopping it liberally on to her paint-stained foot. As she scrubbed at it he took the turps, soaked Bill's pyjama leg and attacked her shoe.

'Guess we're never going to get this off,' he said ruefully. 'They've had it, I'd say.'

'They were my best ones, too!' Fliss groaned, worried about having to ask Martin for the money to buy a new pair. 'How could I have been so stupid!'

'And there was I thinking it was my fault.'

'Well – it was! If you hadn't made me jump out of my skin . . . What were you doing there anyway? Creeping up on me like that!'

'I don't creep, ma'am. I was just admiring the very pretty scenery. Here you are . . . that's about the best I can do.'

Fliss took her proffered shoe.

'Thanks for trying, anyway.'

'At your service, ma'am.'

'Oh, will you please stop calling me ma'am! I'm not the Queen.'

'So what do I call you?'

It was there again, that disconcerting twist of her stomach.

'Really,' Fliss said coolly, 'there's no need for you to call me anything.'

'Now that is a darned shame,' he returned, unfazed. 'I was hoping we might get to know one another and I could buy you a drink maybe to make up for landing you in this mess. Hey, I'll go first, if you like. My name's Jeff Hewson, and I—'

'Oh, I know who you are,' Fliss interrupted. 'You're the owner of the Ohlson, and you're running a valeting outfit and putting the locals out of business.'

He laughed. 'So you had the advantage of me all along.'

'I usually do,' Fliss said sweetly. 'And I should warn you your valeting business isn't the only thing I've heard about you. You've got quite a reputation with the girls, I understand. So I'll put you straight right away.' She waved her left hand, displaying her wedding ring. 'I'm Felicity Dunning, Mrs Felicity Dunning, and much as I appreciate the offer of a drink, I really have to get on and finish painting my boat.'

For a moment he looked a little taken aback, then recovered himself.

'Ah well, there's always tomorrow.'

'Not for me,' Fliss said crisply. 'Not only am I married, I

also have a baby. My mother is looking after her today, but it could be ages before I have another chance to get my boat finished.'

'Looks like you could do with some help then. And I'm your man. Never mind the valeting, I'm pretty handy with a paintbrush too.'

Was there no end to the cheek of him?

'I don't have the money to pay a professional,' Fliss said curtly. 'I wouldn't be doing the job myself if I could.'

He smiled disarmingly. 'No charge. Reckon it's the least I can do. Come on now, give me a brush – you won't regret it.'

Fliss shook her head, conceding defeat. Jeff Hewson might be everything Simon said he was – brash, overconfident, an impossible charmer who fancied his chances. But painting the *Mermaid's Song* all alone was a daunting task, and she'd be a fool to turn down an offer of help. Besides, where was the harm? She could handle him.

'OK, you've talked yourself into it,' she said breezily. 'There's a spare brush in that bag. And now I really have got to get on.'

She turned away, pouring more paint into the seriously depleted paint tray.

'Right, ma'am. Where do I start?'

'Anywhere you like,' Fliss said. 'You're the expert.'

Apart from a couple of brief breaks for refreshment – Fliss had brought a bottle of lemon barley water and a flask of coffee with her – they worked solidly, Fliss moving anticlockwise around the boat, Jeff in the opposite direction, so there was no danger of him making more suggestive remarks and she had begun to relax her guard. It was four in the afternoon before they met on the far side of the boat. Jeff had taken off his shirt so as to avoid ruining it with paint splashes; the bright spring sunshine turned the feathering of fair hairs on his arms and chest to molten gold, and long muscles rippled across his back as he stretched to reach the last unfinished patch.

'There we go, ma'am – all done I reckon.'

'Don't call me that!'

'OK – Felicity, was it?'

'My friends call me Fliss.'

'Hey – this is progress!'

'I wouldn't count on it.'

'You're still not on for that drink, then?'

'Absolutely not. I have to get home.'

'So when am I going to see you again?'

Fliss shook her head despairingly.

'What are you like? I told you – I'm a married woman with a little daughter.'

'I'm only asking when I'm going to see you, not trying to get my wicked way. What do you take me for? And after I've helped you out here, too!' He was pulling his shirt back on, buttoning it loosely. 'I'd have thought you'd take pity on a poor guy far from home and lonely.'

'From what I hear, you're certainly not lonely!' Fliss retorted, 'And in any case, I haven't a clue when I'll be back. It all depends on my mother and when she can look after Emma.'

'Emma – that's a pretty name.'

'She's a very pretty girl,' Fliss said proudly. 'Now – I've got to go and see Sam Green, tell him Mermaid's Song can go back to her berth when the paint's had a chance to dry.'

'You want me to tell him for you? I'm going back that way.'

'That would be great – if it's no trouble. And thanks for all your help,' she added, relenting. 'I am grateful, really.'

'My pleasure, ma'am . . . Fliss,' he corrected himself with a grin. 'I'll see you when I see you then.'

'Yes. See you.'

As she watched him walk away along the marina Fliss felt a pang of regret. If she wasn't a married woman . . . if he wasn't a terrible flirt . . . if things were different . . .

But they weren't. She had a husband and a child. Her days of freedom were over.

106

With a sigh Fliss packed her things together and headed for home.

'So – how did you get on?' Greta asked Fliss when she collected Emma.

'I've finished the painting,' Fliss said over Emma's head – though she had been perfectly happy all day, the minute she had seen Fliss she had demanded to be picked up, and Fliss was cuddling her close, her chin nestled in the soft baby hair that was now growing in loose curls.

'You did well, then,' Greta said.

'A friend gave me a hand.' Fliss didn't want to admit that the friend was a man she'd never met before. 'I had a bit of a disaster, though . . .' She held out her foot, displaying her ruined shoe.

'Oh dear! However . . .?'

'Don't ask!' Fliss said grimly. 'At least the painting is finished now, and Simon Beacham should have the spinnaker mended soon. All I have left to do is a bit of polishing and cleaning and I'll be up and running.'

Greta was collecting Emma's things together and packing them in the pram bag that Fliss still used for the purpose though the Silver Cross coach-built perambulator had long since been consigned to the attic.

'I could always have Emma again,' she suggested. 'Then you could go over and finish up. What about . . oh, say, Tuesday?'

'Are you sure? That soon? I don't want to impose on you . . .'

'Emma and me are just fine, aren't we, my ducks?' Greta said. 'I love having her. It takes me out of myself.'

'Mum, you are a star!' Fliss said, delighted.

NINE

Fliss went to Falmouth several times in quick succession to make Mermaid's Song ready for the summer season. She felt a little guilty that she might be taking advantage of her mother, but Greta was insistent that she was more than happy to look after Emma, and the little girl was always eager to see her grandmother. Fliss worried too that Martin might think she was spending too much time on her boat and not enough on her daughter, but he was all too aware of the depression Fliss had been sinking into through the winter months and was pleased to see her happy and purposeful. In any case he was so busy with the new garage that he was working ridiculously long hours, and since Fliss was always home with a meal waiting for him by the time he eventually finished for the day, he raised no objection.

In the time it took Fliss to finish cleaning and polishing Mermaid's Song she didn't once see Jeff, and she had almost forgotten about him, engrossed as she was in her preparations and bubbling with eager excitement to be out on the water. If she thought about him at all, it was to assume that he was busy with his valeting business; Falmouth was beginning to buzz as the fair-weather sailors arrived for the summer season.

When at last she was satisfied that Mermaid's Song was ready, Fliss took her out for a short trip and then celebrated by visiting the cafeteria where many of the sailing crowd congregated for soft drinks, snacks and a chat.

The place was busy. A class from the school of sailing that had its HQ in the boathouses beneath were talking earnestly over their glasses of orange squash, and a group of lads and girls she knew well were seated untidily around a couple of pushed-together tables by the windows that overlooked the harbour. When Fliss had got herself a long cool drink she went over to join them.

'Haven't seen much of you lately, Fliss,' Tilly Grantham, one of the girls, said, and another cracked: 'She's a married woman now! Her water wings have been well and truly clipped!'

'I've been working on *Mermaid's Song*,' Fliss said. 'She's ready now. I took her out this morning.'

'Yes, I saw you! Thought it was you,' another of the group put in. 'She's going very well for an old boat.'

Although for some reason Fliss felt something of an outsider, she was enjoying the company when an unwelcome figure sauntered across the cafeteria, obviously intent on joining them.

Simon Beacham. Fliss's heart sank. She'd managed to avoid him when she'd dropped off the cheque to pay for the repair of her spinnaker, but there was no avoiding him now. He pulled up a chair beside her, so close that his knees were practically touching hers. Fliss shifted back, he shifted forward; her chair was now right up against the table and she could go no further.

'So, Fliss, how's the world treating you?'

'Fine, thanks. And you did a great job on my spinnaker. You found my cheque, I hope?'

'I did. But I was sorry to miss you.' He was grinning his ingratiating grin, gazing at her with those puppy-dog eyes. 'You're a very elusive little mermaid, Fliss.'

'That's me.'

But he was making her uncomfortable, and it didn't help that Tilly Grantham, sitting more or less opposite, caught her eye, raised an eyebrow with a knowing look and turned to whisper to the girl sitting next to her, who giggled.

'Help!' Fliss mouthed silently, but Tilly only smiled, clearly amused, and ignored her plea.

No way! that look said. He's your problem, lady!

Out of politeness and a feeling of indebtedness, since he had mended the sail for her so cheaply, and also feeling sorry for him since the others were, as usual, pointedly ignoring him, Fliss endured another ten minutes or so of Simon's annoying attempts to chat her up. But she was growing more uncomfortable by the minute, and it pained her, too, that the other girls were secretly enjoying her predicament. They thought her a flirt, she knew; worse, not just a flirt but too easy with her favours – 'fast' as they called it – and they were jealous of the way all the boys flocked around her. Now she'd got her comeuppance – a shotgun marriage and a baby. And if she had ingratiated herself with Simon Beacham to get her repairs done on the cheap, then she'd have to put up with the consequences.

Suddenly Fliss wanted to get away from them – all of them. They were a clique she was no longer a part of. She'd never been one to form close friendships – Jo, her soul sister, excepted – and now the gulf yawned deeper than ever. But in particular she wanted to get away from Simon Beacham, who was making her skin crawl. She checked her watch pointedly.

'I've got to go.'

She tried to rise, couldn't, because Simon's chair was so close to hers. He had to stand up to let her out, then he was at her shoulder, invading her space, muttering something about going her way.

'Bye, all.' She moved away; he followed, across the cafeteria, down the flight of wooden stairs. Fliss's irritation was beginning to turn to desperation. Would she never shake him off? But even now she couldn't bring herself to make the sort of cutting remark the other girls would have made in her position.

Someone was waiting at the foot of the stairs for them to come down before going up himself. A tall, tanned figure with sun-bleached blond hair, eyes narrowed as he squinted up at her.

Jeff Hewson.

'Well hi there!'

'Hi!' Her heart had skipped a beat.

'You made it back, then?'

'A few times. My boat's ready now. I sailed her this morning.'

'Well good on you!' Simon was hovering; Jeff glanced at him. 'Hey, sorry, are you two . . .?'

'No!' Fliss said hastily. 'We just both happened to be leaving at the same time.' Seeing her opportunity, she turned to Simon. 'Nice to have seen you, Simon. Catch you again sometime.'

'Oh – right . . .' He had no option but to withdraw, though he didn't go far, pretending interest in something down on the pebbled shore.

'Keep talking to me, please!' Fliss said. 'I just can't shake him off.'

Jeff cocked an eyebrow.

'At least he had good taste.'

'He drives me mad!'

'So maybe this is a good time for me to ask you again if I can buy you a drink.'

'Thanks, but I've had enough orange squash to sink a battleship.'

'A proper drink then. A nice cold cider. Come on now, I'm going to get a complex if you refuse me again.'

Fliss glanced at Simon, still lurking just yards away.

'Oh, all right then,' she said, smiling. 'You win.'

'Well hey, that's great, ma'am.' He shot a grin at her. 'Fliss. Looks like this is my lucky day!'

'So,' said Fliss as they settled at a corner table in the Quayside Bar and waited for the half-pints of cider they'd ordered. 'Just exactly who is it I've agreed to have a drink with?'

'A persistent Yank, you could say.'

'Well, yes, but apart from that.'

'Pretty well sums me up. What about you? That's a much more interesting subject.'

'You know all about me,' Fliss said. 'I told you – I'm married with a little girl.'

'Emma.'

'You remembered!'

'Uh-huh. How old is she?'

'Just over a year.'

'And your husband?'

'You want to know how old my husband is?'

'Course not. Just wondering about him. What he does. Is he a sailor too?'

'When he gets the chance. But that's not often these days. He has a garage business over on the north coast, where we live, and it keeps him pretty busy.'

'In any case, you like to sail alone.'

'I do, actually. Unless it's with Jo. She's my sailing partner. We've done a lot of stuff together . . .'

'*Pretty's Pickles*,' he said slyly.

'How do you know that?'

'You're famous round here. Didn't take a lot to find out about you and your exploits.'

Fliss blushed, but she couldn't help but feel rather pleased he'd taken the trouble to ask around about her.

'A lady after my own heart,' he said. 'I like to sail alone too. Did the transatlantic crossing last summer single-handed. That's how I came to end up in Falmouth.'

'You did a single-handed transatlantic?' Fliss said, impressed.

'Sure did. And I'll have to do it all again the other way round if I'm ever to get home again. But right now I'm happy where I am. Just as long as I can earn enough to keep my head above water, so to speak.'

Their drinks had arrived. Fliss took a long pull; the cider could have been colder, but it tasted good.

'So where do you call home?' she asked, setting the glass back on the little cardboard beer mat.

'Maine, New England. You heard of it?'

'Heard of it, yes . . .'

'Up on the east coast, not far short of Canada. But I was down in Florida before I came here. Little place called Naples, in easy reach of the Ten Thousand Islands and the Keys.'

'It sounds idyllic,' Fliss said. 'Why in the world would you want to be in England when you could be in Florida?'

'Guess I wanted a challenge. There's only so much bumming around in the sunshine a guy can take. Especially with the threat of the draft hanging over him.'

'The draft?'

'Compulsory military service. You had it here, didn't you, until recently?'

'You mean National Service.'

'Yeah, that's it. Our system is a lot more hit-and-miss than yours was, though – bit of a lottery, really. I dare say they'll catch up with me sooner or later, but I figured I'd rather it was later. I've had enough of being institutionalised – dropped out of college because I didn't like being pushed around, and I reckon the military will be more of the same, only worse. I like my freedom, Fliss.'

'Me too,' Fliss said, the longing for what she had lost evident in her voice.

'I'm guessing marriage and a baby put an end to that, though.'

'Yep. And I do miss it. Oh, don't get me wrong – I absolutely adore Emma, but . . .'

'But you still wish you could be free.' He hadn't missed the fact that she hadn't also said that she adored her husband.

'I do really,' she said honestly.

'So why did you get married?'

Fliss pulled a face. 'I didn't have much choice.'

'Ah.'

'I couldn't bear to give Emma up, and being a single mother wasn't an option. Not in a little place like Porthtowan. I've been lucky really. Martin – my husband – is very good. He lets me do more or less as I like. I mean – he could object to me leaving

Emma with Mum so I can come down here to my boat, but he doesn't. But . . . well, I've got responsibilities now. Ties. I'm not used to that. I wasn't really ready to settle down . . .'

She broke off. She couldn't believe she was opening up in this way to a virtual stranger. But there was an ease between them that she rarely experienced with anyone, man or woman. It had been there, really, from the first moment she'd met him. Even when she'd been sparring with him, furious over the damage to her shoe, there had been a sort of familiarity on a level far deeper than mere words – she'd never have agreed to his offer to help her paint the boat otherwise. It was as if she'd known him all her life. Now she was sharing with him feelings she hadn't shared with anyone except Jo, and she knew instinctively that he wouldn't judge her, that he understood. Because in some indefinable way they came from the same place, two sides of a coin fitting neatly together.

'There were so many things I still wanted to do,' she said. 'Jo and I had such plans. Sailing the Atlantic, for one. You've done that; I haven't, and I don't suppose I ever will now. Even if I didn't have Emma to think about, I could never afford a good enough boat.' She pulled a wistful face. 'What I wouldn't give to have a boat like yours! She's a beauty!'

'I've got to admit I'm pretty proud of her.'

'So you should be! Ah well, I've got *Mermaid's Song*. I can still sail her sometimes. And when Emma's a bit older I can bring her with me – teach her to sail. Perhaps she'll do all the things I'll never be able to now.'

'Hey!' he said, reaching across the table and covering her hand with his. 'You'll still be young enough to do them yourself.'

'Will I?' She left her hand where it was. There was nothing of the seducer about him now; the gesture was one of solidarity, of comfort. 'I don't know. I honestly don't know. I think I had my chance and I've blown it.'

A bell clanged loudly, followed by the landlord calling: 'Time, gentlemen, please!'

Fliss glanced at her watch. 'Closing time? Already?'

'Seems so. Better drink up.'

He drained his glass; with regret, Fliss did the same.

'I suppose I'd better head for home.'

'What time do you have to be back?'

'Oh – four, five . . . but there won't be time to take the boat out again, and I've got her pretty shipshape now.'

The landlord was moving between the tables, collecting empty glasses and crisp packets, asking lingerers to drink up, casting baleful glances at those who did not. Jeff guided Fliss across the bar with a light touch of his hand on her waist, opened the door for her.

'Well,' he said as they stepped out on to the sunlit quay. 'Would you like to have a look at my boat?'

'Oh . . . yes!'

'Come on then.'

He touched her waist again; she glanced at him and he winked at her, a slow, wicked wink accompanied by a half-smile, and it hit her again, that bolt of quivering excitement she'd experienced the first time they met. She caught her breath, awareness suddenly taking the place of the ease that had been there between them, and almost changed her mind about going with him. But the temptation was too great; she kept on walking, his hand dropped to his side and the moment passed, though it left her inwardly reeling.

'I don't suppose she's as tidy as your *Mermaid's Song*,' Jeff said apologetically as they neared *Jersey Gal*. 'I'm not the neatest guy. But then, show me one who is, left to his own devices.'

'Martin's pretty good,' Fliss said, feeling perhaps it was time to remind Jeff – and herself – that she had a husband.

'I'll bet he is,' Jeff returned amiably. 'Wouldn't surprise me if he needs to be, married to you.'

'Why, you cheeky . . .!' She aimed a playful blow at him.

He laughed. 'Steady on now!'

For just a moment as he warded off her blow she thought he

115

was going to put his arm round her again, but he did not. And then they had reached *Jersey Gal* and Fliss was thinking of nothing but this beautiful boat and how much she would love to sail her.

In spite of Jeff's assertion that he was an untidy soul, everything on deck was, Fliss noted, in perfect order, sails neatly stowed, ropes coiled, gadgetry clearly well maintained. The cabin, however, was a different matter. Cushions, pillows and a rug lay haphazardly over one bunk; assorted clothes were strewn on the other, lying where he had dropped them.

'You live on board?' Fliss said.

'Where else? No sense paying for lodgings when I've got all I need here.' He shifted some of the clutter. 'Have a seat. Can I get you a coffee? Tea?'

'Oh, go on then. Coffee. No sugar.'

He disappeared into the tiny galley. Fliss looked around, curious about this man, who fascinated her on every level. A pile of books was stacked untidily on a locker; she checked the titles. Mostly travel books, a couple of Perry Mason paperbacks, a dog-eared copy of *The Great Gatsby*. There were also some sailing magazines and a couple of out-of-date newspapers, a *Telegraph* and *The Cornishman*. Fliss heard the rattle of cups in the galley and hastily replaced them. She didn't want to be caught snooping. She shifted the pile of clothes further along the bunk, making room for him to sit down, and caught a whiff of perfume. Peculiar – Jeff was hardly the type to wear Californian Poppy. The sweater that had come to the top of the heap didn't look like Jeff's either – pink and fluffy.

Fliss was shocked by the twinge of something that might almost have been jealousy. Stupid – stupid! She'd always known he was a womaniser; worse, she had absolutely no right to be put out by the fact that she wasn't the first woman he'd brought back to his boat. But she was – she was! – and the realisation disconcerted her.

He was coming back, a mug in either hand.

'So,' Fliss said, pointing to the jumper. 'Who's your friend?'

'What?' He followed her glance. 'Oh – God knows!'

'You have that many girls back here you can't keep count of them?'

He laughed. 'You really do have a very low opinion of me.'

'You're the one who started it!'

He put the mugs of coffee down on the low table.

'Unlike you, I'm a free agent.'

'Very true,' she retorted, nettled. 'And don't forget it. I don't want you getting any ideas about adding me to the notches on your bedpost.'

He held up his hands in surrender and sat down on the opposite bunk, jean-clad legs splayed comfortably.

'Don't worry, you're quite safe. I'm not about to leap on you. I wouldn't dare. You're way different to any of the other girls I've met here in Falmouth – or back home, come to that. They're just looking for a good time. But you . . .'

There was something in his tone that set Fliss's skin prickling.

'I expect I'm looking for a good time too – but in my own way.'

'Your way – exactly. We're kindred spirits, you and I. Which is why I enjoy your company.'

Fliss picked up her coffee, cradling the mug between her hands as if to create a barrier between her and this man she found so easy to be with and yet so unsettling, both at the same time.

'Just as long as you know I'm not one of your conquests.'

'I wouldn't insult you by thinking for a minute you might be. So, now we've got that out of the way, if you like my boat so much, do you want to sail her?'

Fliss's heart leaped. But . . .

'I can't. I told you – I've got to go home.'

'I didn't mean today. Next time you can get away.'

'Could I? Really?'

'I just offered, didn't I? Come down when you can, and if I'm free we'll take her out.'

'That would be great!'

'That's settled then. And by the way, I do know who the owner of the sweater is. She's called Maureen Wicks, she works in the post office, and I'll be seeing her again tonight. OK?'

Again, that small imp of jealousy.

'You didn't have to tell me that,' Fliss said.

'Don't want you thinking I'm a complete heel.'

'Actually,' Fliss said, 'I don't think that at all. You're just a typical man.'

'And will be until I meet the right girl.' For just a moment she had the feeling he was being perfectly serious. For just a moment there was something in his voice, in the way he was looking at her, that made her tummy tip again. For just a moment she might almost have imagined that he was telling her he *had* met the right girl, except that she was already spoken for. For just a moment there was something there between them, an unspoken under-standing, as if their souls had reached out and touched.

Then he was tasting his coffee and making a face.

'Ugh! No sugar!'

Fliss tasted hers, mirrored his expression.

'Ugh! Sweet! This must be yours.'

They exchanged cups and it never occured to either of them to get fresh ones, or even to drink from the other side.

When Fliss left, Jeff stood leaning on the rail and watching her walk away along the quay. In all his life he'd never before felt like this about anyone. As he'd admitted, there had been girls, and plenty of them, but always they'd been fleeting fancies. The minute one tried to tie him down, he moved on.

More than one had tried. At home, in Maine, and when he'd been at college, he'd thought that part of the attraction was down to his background, who he was. But after he'd dropped out, headed for Florida, it was still the same story, though he kept very quiet about his family connections, and not just to keep the gold-diggers at bay.

Oddly enough, Jeff was as ashamed of his privileged background as any boy from the wrong side of the tracks might be of a squalid one. To him it represented everything he found abhorrent – a snobbery he'd witnessed over and over again when he was growing up, and an assumption that it was the God-given right of the Hewsons to be top of the heap. That he would go to Harvard had never been in doubt. That he would take over the helm of the shipbuilding company that had made the family fortune was also preordained, unless he decided to follow another family tradition – politics – in which case he would be one of the youngest and most dynamic senators in the House, and might even run for president one day, like Jack Kennedy, carrying on the golden image of a golden family.

But Jeff didn't want to go into politics and he didn't want to be tied down to Hewson Enterprises either, or at least not for a very long time, and he detested Harvard. After almost two years of studying hard and being bullied by his father to run for student president – which he had not the slightest intention of doing – he dropped out and headed for Florida. Whatever the expectations of his family, all Jeff wanted to do was sail.

He'd learned as a youngster – his family owned a holiday home on an island off the coast of Maine. They'd spent the long summer months there each year, and the freedom to sail his boat off the secluded sandy beaches was the reason Jeff continued to go to the island long after the friends he'd played with as a child and partied with when they grew older had given up the retreat for more exciting holidays in Europe or the Caribbean.

In Florida he spent time in Naples and the Keys, 'bumming around' as his father disgustedly described it. He was happy simply being one of the crowd, who neither knew nor cared about his illustrious family background. It was only when he decided to sail the Atlantic that he realised he couldn't escape his heritage as easily as he'd thought he could. He needed a decent boat; there was a tidy sum left to him by his grandfather sitting in a trust fund. Not to draw on it seemed stupid, but at the same time it reminded him of the conflict between his personal circumstances and his ideals. Eventually he used the trust fund to buy the *Jersey Gal*, but he saw it open up a gulf between him and his sailing friends; some were openly jealous, some became ingratiating as they tried to muscle in and take advantage. Jeff made up his mind that from there on in he would forget about Hewson money, pay his way as they did, live only on what he was able to scrape together one way or another. And since he had arrived in England, that was exactly what he had done.

Yet still the girls flocked around him. For all they knew he was a penniless sailor, yet he found it ridiculously easy to pick up a date. Puzzled, Jeff shrugged his shoulders and made the most of it. But he was also careful to move on the moment any girl tried to tie him down. He had no desire to get seriously involved with any of them.

Felicity Penrose – Dunning – was different. Special. He felt a connection to her, as well as the physical attraction. But she was married to another man. No point hankering after her. He'd just enjoy her company and leave it at that.

When she disappeared from view, Jeff stood for a moment, staring along the harbour, at the boats bobbing at their moorings and the gulls swooping over the sea wall. Then, with a sigh, he pushed himself away from the rail and went below.

TEN

The summer of 1958 was a happy time for Fliss. Once and occasionally twice a week she took Emma to Porthtowan and headed for Falmouth. Sometimes she sailed alone, taking *Mermaid's Song* out for a whole glorious day; sometimes she sailed with Jeff on *Jersey Gal*, which was every bit as exhilarating as she'd expected it to be. The boat was both fast and easy to handle, equipped as it was for single-handed sailing, and she loved working in unison with Jeff, who liked nothing better than to push his boat to the limits.

But it wasn't just the excitement of sailing close to the wind; she loved simply being with him too. In his company she was her old self, exuberant and light of heart, intrepid and sharp-witted. She could talk to him easily, about anything, in a way she couldn't with anyone but Jo. And always there was the added frisson of the electricity between them, sometimes at the most unexpected moments. A touch of hands as they hauled together on a stubborn rope could send a shiver through her; a shared glance made her stomach twist deliciously. They scared her a little, these bolts of unfamiliar desire; she had no right to be feeling them. She was Martin's wife; he was the one who should arouse her. But she had never felt this way with Martin, nor indeed with anyone before, and she allowed herself to savour her feelings in secret, whilst promising herself that that was exactly what they would remain – a secret pleasure.

Even when she was at home, engaged in housewifely duties, they could catch her unawares, those delicious little thrills, when she thought of him. And she was thinking of him a good deal too often, she admitted. But that, too, was her secret, and she hugged it to herself, singing as she washed the dishes, ironed Martin's shirts or prepared a meal for Emma, and counting the days until she could be in Falmouth again. Where was the harm? Nothing untoward had happened between them, nothing ever would. She was a wife and mother, he was a water gypsy who would soon move on to another marina, or even go home to America. The shadow that thought cast over her sun should have warned her that she was becoming far more involved emotionally than she cared to admit, as should the deep disappointment that engulfed her when she went to Falmouth and didn't see him, but if she did feel the occasional qualm, she quickly dismissed it. If she was happy, Martin and Emma were happy. All Fliss wanted was for this wonderful summer, this blissful hiatus, to go on for ever.

By the end of July, however, two small clouds had appeared on the horizon of the endless blue of Fliss's sky.

The first was more of a niggling concern than a real worry. Greta, normally incredibly energetic for a woman of her age, wasn't quite her usual self.

It was Maggie who first drew Fliss's attention to it. 'Mum seems to get awfully tired very quickly these days,' she said. 'I can't help wondering if having Emma so often is getting too much for her.'

'Oh, I'm sure if she couldn't cope she'd say so,' Fliss replied, but the next time she collected Emma she noticed – Greta did look rather weary.

'Are you all right, Mum?' she asked.

'Oh, I've got a bit of a headache, that's all,' Greta said dismissively. 'We went for a longer walk than usual – I find it's the best way to get Emma to sleep for her afternoon nap, pushing her out in her pushchair, but this afternoon she took for ever to drop off, and I just kept going.'

'So you missed your own snooze.' Fliss was only too eager to accept this explanation.

'Exactly. I do like a little nap after my dinner.'

Fliss nodded, relieved. If Greta was no longer willing or able to look after Emma, it would be the most enormous blow. But the possibility that her mother might be overdoing things did worry her a bit all the same. She wasn't getting any younger, and Fliss didn't like to feel she was taking advantage of her.

The other cloud, however, appeared much more threatening.

Martin was quieter than usual, with a worried look, and one night when he had still not come to bed at well past one o'clock she went downstairs to look for him. He was sitting at the kitchen table with the garage ledgers and a pile of what looked suspiciously like bills in front of him.

'For goodness' sake – what are you doing?' she asked.

Martin massaged his forehead and tired eyes.

'Trying to do the impossible. We're struggling, love. The money just isn't coming in but the bank loan still has to be paid, and the electricity bill, and the oil company.'

'It'll be fine, I'm sure,' Fliss said. Money, or lack of it, never figured very highly on her list of priorities.

Martin sighed wearily. 'I've got to find a way of cutting expenditure. I've been looking at every possibility but I'm running a tight ship at the garage as it is. We're going to have to cut our personal expenses, I'm afraid. It's the only way.'

'Whatever,' Fliss said. 'Just come to bed now and we'll talk about it in the morning.'

Martin didn't make a move, just rasped his hand across his jaw, where the stubble had begun to cast a dark shadow.

'You do realise, don't you, that your boat is one of the first things that's going to have to go?'

That drew Fliss up sharp. '*What?*'

'Oh, love, don't get upset. I'm not talking about selling her – at the moment, anyway. I don't suppose she's worth a lot anyway. But the mooring at Falmouth is an expense we really can't afford.

123

What I was thinking is that it would be a whole lot cheaper on the Penryn River.'

'True.' Fliss knew the Penryn River well. Her father had kept his boat there and she liked the friendly atmosphere – the people who used it were less competitive than those at Falmouth. But it was not without its drawbacks. Since it was a tidal river, the boats were grounded when the sea was out; launching meant wading in knee-deep water and mooring involved pulling the boat into a position where she wouldn't be capsized by the rush of the incoming tide.

'What I'm going to suggest is that I store the *Mermaid* at the garage over the winter and then we make a decision when we see how we're placed next spring,' Martin said.

'You mean we might be better off by then?' Fliss said, brightening.

'Let's hope so. And you're right, it's no good losing sleep over it. Let's go to bed.'

Next morning the subject wasn't mentioned and Fliss hoped it wouldn't be again. The threat of having to leave Falmouth, and maybe even lose *Mermaid's Song* altogether, was something she didn't want to contemplate. But although it lurked behind her shoulder like a spectre, Fliss was determined not to allow it to spoil her wonderful, joyous summer.

And then something else happened to put both the niggling worries right out of her head.

Though Jo was still based in Plymouth, seemingly settled happily with her Frenchman, she and Fliss had stayed in touch. When they weren't able to meet, they wrote regularly – long, newsy letters. And in one, towards the end of August, Jo had an exciting suggestion to make. The Fastnet Race, crowning glory in Cowes Week Regatta, was held biannually, and she and Yves had planned to enter next year. Now, however, Yves had been asked to skipper a big boat with a crew of fifteen and he was keen to take on the challenge. Left in the lurch, the first person Jo had thought of was her old sailing partner. Was there any chance that Fliss would like to take his place? And if so, would she be prepared to do a trial run in a few weeks' time?

Would she! Fliss was giddy with excitement at the prospect. Without a great deal of hope, she put it to Martin, and to her surprise and delight he didn't immediately squash the idea.

'You really want to do this, don't you?' he said.

'Oh I do! I do!'

'Well, if your mother is willing to help out with Emma, I suppose we could manage . . .'

Greta was willing; everything was arranged, and on a Friday evening at the beginning of September, Fliss took Emma to Porthtowan and set out to drive to Plymouth.

Jo and Yves lived in a tiny rented cottage close to the harbour. Jo had made up a bed for Fliss on a put-me-up in the minuscule living room and the three of them spent a memorable evening over a fish-and-chip supper and a shared bottle of Blue Nun.

For Fliss and Jo it was old times revisited, and Fliss quickly warmed to Yves. He was exactly the sort of man she'd imagined, easy-going and unfettered, yet meticulous in his planning, and Fliss envied Jo her uncomplicated relationship. Martin treated her well, very well, but she wasn't in love with him and never would be. Though she adored Emma and couldn't for one moment regret having kept her, at times like this she certainly regretted trapping herself in a relationship that would never be more than a marriage of convenience. Seeing Jo and Yves so wrapped up in one another, sharing a life they both loved, started a restlessness in her and made her sad for what might have been.

Next morning they were up with the dawn, heading down to the marina, and Fliss promised herself that nothing would spoil these few precious days when she could forget everything but the wind and the tides and the salt spray on her face and pretend she was still the girl she used to be.

The Fastnet Race begins at Cowes and heads westward across the Irish Sea, round the Fastnet Rock off the coast of Eire and back to Plymouth, but for the trial run Jo had decided to cut the first leg and start from Plymouth; it seemed unnecessary to go all the way to Cowes simply to retrace the route. Yves came with them to the marina to wave them off, two girls who had achieved so much together and were about to relive their glory days.

The boat was riding to wind and tide; with other craft moored close to her on either hand. They hoisted the mainsail, let go the mooring and as soon as there was sufficient room, raised the jib and sheeted it in. Though it was more than a year now since they had last sailed together, all the old telepathy was still there and they were soon in clear water. The sun was high and warm, the breeze fair, and by using the genoa they were able to make a good pace windward. Fliss was hungry already; they tucked into sardine sandwiches and drank hot sweet tea as the coastline slipped by.

The sunset – spectacular scarlet – was fading and dusk was falling as they approached the Lizard. Flashes of light from its beam cut regular swathes through the mist that almost always seemed to shroud it, but once past and heading for Land's End, the visibility cleared and Fliss leaned contentedly against the cockpit and watched the rise and fall of the waves against the dark sky.

It was in the wee small hours of the morning that a feeling of foreboding began to creep insidiously in her veins. She was on watch again – she and Jo were taking it in turns to get a few hours' sleep – when she realised the night had become very dark. She checked the barometer – it had fallen sharply, and the wind was rising. In Fliss's experience they were all the signs that a storm was on the way. There had been no mention of any serious problems when she'd listened to the weather forecast earlier, but nevertheless she was fairly sure something rather nasty was brewing.

Fliss put on her oilskins and checked that everything was well stowed and securely fastened down, then reefed the mainsail. The barometer was still falling, and in the first pale light of dawn, angry clouds scudded across a yellowish sky. Not bad enough yet to wake Jo, not bad enough to reef down to bare poles, but definitely one to watch. The winds were so strong now that the boat was skimming along at a speed that it was difficult to achieve even when under full sail.

And then, quite suddenly, it happened. A sudden gust, gale force, rolled the boat. The mainsail swung, the spinnaker pole dipped, the world turned topsy-turvy. Fliss, on her safety harness and line, was catapulted from one side of the boat to the other, catching her shoulder a painful blow. She squealed, but the sound was lost in the roar of the wind and the waves.

'What the hell . . .?' Jo emerged from the cabin wrapped in her sleeping bag, then ducked back hastily as water broke over the deck in a surging rush and spray flew like rain.

'I'm going to set the trysail and jib,' Fliss called over the deafening noise of the storm. She was hoping desperately that the spinnaker pole had not damaged the mainsail when the boat had rolled, but in any case it was time to lower it now. The other option would be to heave to – take off all sail and ride out the storm – but her gut feeling was that they'd probably be better off running before it. Heaving to was all very well, but with the sea becoming ever more mountainous, she thought they might well take on a great deal of water if they followed that course.

'Be right with you,' Jo called back.

A few minutes later she re-emerged clad in her oilskins and wearing her safety harness. They were riding the waves now, and there was something exhilarating, if terrifying, about the way the boat climbed high, then plunged into emptiness on the far side of the wall of water. This was what Fliss loved most of all – this feeling of living close to the edge. She didn't like being cold, she didn't like being wet – and in spite of her oilskins, she was very wet, her clothes beneath them clinging soddenly to her skin – she didn't like having to pump filthy seawater out of the bilge every quarter of an hour; she was thinking with longing of a warm bed and a good hot meal. But there was nothing quite like the adrenalin rush that came from pitting her skills against a storm, and she knew that when it was all over, the satisfaction of knowing that she had taken on the elements and won would sustain her spirits long after she was back ashore and living the mundane life of a housewife and mother.

Time had taken on a strange dimension now – hours became minutes and minutes hours. Fliss and Jo made no attempt to run for harbour – though they were at the mercy of the wind and waves, it was much safer, they knew, to be well out in the Irish Sea than to attempt to find a place to land. Around the coast there would be rocks and sandbanks, unknown, unseen, and with the gale buffeting them helplessly there was always the danger that they might be driven on to them.

It was midday before the storm began to spend itself, but the light was still as grey as if it were pre-dawn. They were sailing now on storm jib and triple main, which helped the central balance of the boat, and thankfully she didn't seem to have suffered too much damage. But the radio wasn't working and they could see that the aerial had gone from the top of the mast, a victim of the force of the gale.

Decision time.

'Do we go on or turn back?' Jo asked, though there was hardly need. Neither of the girls was a quitter, and the Fastnet Rock was now not that far off.

'Let's go for it,' said Fliss. 'I think the storm's spent now.'

'OK. But oh my God – do you need to wash your hair!'

'You too.'

They looked at one another and burst out laughing. Their hair was standing up in stiff spikes so that it looked as if they'd suffered a severe electric shock. It wasn't the first time, and both hoped it wouldn't be the last.

Soaked and chilled to the bone, their lips and cheeks caked with salt, Fliss and Jo headed for the rock that was the turning point of their expedition.

Maggie had thoroughly enjoyed her weekend. Since Martin was fully occupied all day on a Saturday at the garage, Greta had suggested Emma should stay with her until Fliss got back. There was no problem with Emma's sleeping arrangements, as Greta had bought a second-hand cot, which she'd put up in the spare room, and it would be better than moving the little girl from pillar to post, as she described it.

Maggie was delighted about this. She adored her niece, and never seemed to get to spend enough time with her. On Saturday she took Emma shopping in her pushchair, then played with her in the garden until it was time for lunch and her nap. When she woke again, bright-eyed and full of energy, Maggie took her down to the beach, carrying her over the pebbles, then taking off her socks and sandals and letting her paddle in the lacy rivulets that were the tail-end of the surf waves. It was a lovely afternoon stolen out of time; Maggie got talking to a family whose children were also playing at the water's edge, and it was clear from the things they said that they thought Emma was her daughter. Maggie did not enlighten them. The misconception actually pleased her; she could almost pretend for a little while that Emma did belong to her.

When they returned home it was to find that Greta wasn't well. What she termed 'a sick headache' had developed, and certainly she looked very white.

'Go and lie down, Mum,' Maggie said. 'I can give Emma her tea.'

'Are you sure?'

'Of course I'm sure. Have a couple of aspirin and a good sleep.'

She prepared Emma's meal: fingers of bread and butter and a boiled egg. When she looked in on Greta later, taking her a cup of tea, her mother was fast asleep, so Maggie didn't disturb her. She bathed Emma, read her a story, and put her to bed with a bottle of warm milk. Emma was asleep in no time, but still Maggie sat beside her cot, gazing at her chubby cheeks and rosebud mouth, still pursed from sucking at her bottle, and feeling the love well inside her in a warm flood. And with it a prickle of envy. If only Emma was hers . . . if only *Martin* was hers . . .

Emma stirred, jamming her thumb into her mouth, and with a sigh Maggie smoothed the soft hair away from the little girl's forehead, straightened the covers over her firm little body, and dragged herself away.

Next morning quite early she was awakened by Emma calling out. The door to Greta's room was still closed, so Maggie warmed a bottle of milk and took Emma into bed with her, where the little girl feel asleep again nestled into the crook of Maggie's arm. Maggie was dozing too when a sudden crash followed by a metallic drum roll catapulted her back to full wakefulness. What the hell was that? She eased away from Emma, got out of bed, went to the window and pulled back the curtains. Outside, the sky had darkened so much that it might almost have been night again, rain was beating against the window in torrents and the trees at the end of the garden were thrashing about in the wind, shedding twigs and clusters of leaves on to the lawn. The dustbin, which normally stood outside the back door, was halfway down the path, its contents strewn in an untidy trail behind it – it had been the bin blowing over that had caused the crash that had wakened her, obviously.

'Good grief!' Maggie muttered, shocked. She hadn't heard that any violent weather was on the way, and this seemed to have erupted from nowhere.

A split second later she thought of Fliss. Just how localised this storm was she had no idea, but the thought that Fliss was at sea and possibly at the mercy of a gale as strong as this was an alarming one.

Leaving Emma still sleeping, she padded into the kitchen and put the kettle on. As she was spooning tea from the caddy into the pot, Greta appeared in the doorway. She was wearing her dressing gown and her face, bereft of powder and lipstick, looked pouchy and heavy as uncooked dough.

'Mum! What are you doing up?'

'What a wind! Nobody could sleep with all that going on.'

'How's your head this morning?'

Greta pressed her fingers to her temples, closing her eyes and giving her head a small shake.

'I thought it was a bit better when I woke up, but now I'm on the move . . .'

'Why don't you go back to bed?' Maggie suggested. 'I'll bring you a cup of tea, and some more aspirin.'

The phone was ringing; she headed to the hall to answer it. Martin. As always, her tummy tipped at the sound of his voice.

'Just ringing to make sure Emma's OK.'

'She's fine. She's still asleep.'

'Good. Look, I know I said I'd be over first thing this morning, but I've got an awful lot of paperwork piling up at the garage. Would it be all right if I got that done first? I should be with you by midday.'

'No problem.' She was disappointed, though. She'd been looking forward to seeing him without Fliss there to spoil things, she realised. The plan had been that Martin would come over early, spend the day with Emma and then leave her at Porthtowan for another night. And of course he'd share Sunday lunch with them – the meal that, with Greta so poorly, it was looking increasingly likely that Maggie was going to have to cook.

She didn't mind that, though. In fact she'd enjoy doing it – spoiling Martin a bit. Maggie doubted Fliss had ever cooked a decent Sunday roast in the whole of her life.

'I'm a bit worried about Fliss,' she said now. 'It's blowing an awful gale.'

'She and Jo are more than capable of handling a bit of heavy weather,' Martin said, rather nonchalantly, she thought. 'They're probably enjoying it.'

A sound from upstairs attracted Maggie's attention; she looked up to see Emma at the top of the stairs, about to attempt to clamber down.

'Stay there, Emma!' Maggie warned sharply. 'Don't try to come down by yourself!'

'She's fine on stairs. She bumps down on her bottom.'

'Not my stairs, she doesn't,' Maggie said sharply. 'I don't want her falling down and breaking an arm or leg when she's in my care.'

'You're a star, Maggie. I'll see you later.'

A warm glow suffused her. She ran up the stairs and scooped Emma into her arms. *You're a star*, Martin had said. It meant nothing whatsoever, of course, but it felt good just to have him say it.

'That was your daddy on the phone,' she said to Emma. 'He'll be here presently.'

Emma thrust her bottle into Maggie's hand.

'M-ulk,' she demanded.

'All right, darling, we'll get it,' Maggie said.

And felt the warm glow spread and grow into a bubble of contentment.

It was another lovely cosy day. Maggie cooked lunch − roast pork with crisp crackling, apple sauce and stuffing balls, followed by stewed plums and custard. Martin cleaned his plate, and complimented her on her cooking. Later, when Emma woke from her nap, they took her out in the car to a playground where there were swings, a solid metal roundabout and a see-saw, because although Greta's headache had lifted a bit she was still feeling groggy, and they thought it would be better if Emma wasn't running about disturbing her now that the rain seemed to have stopped.

At six thirty, Maggie and Martin were bathing Emma when the phone rang. Greta, up and about now, answered it, and called up the stairs.

'Martin − it's for you.'

Maggie squinted at him, puzzled.

'For you − here?'

'It'll be Yves, I expect.' Martin stood up, drying his hands on the towel that was warmed and waiting for Emma. 'I told him I'd be here today if he wanted me.'

He left the bathroom door open behind him and Maggie cocked an ear, listening out. But there wasn't much to overhear.

'Right . . . right. You'll let me know if you hear anything? OK . . . Thanks . . .' He came back and resumed soaping Emma as if the interruption had never happened.

'Was it Yves?' Maggie couldn't stop herself from asking. Martin nodded. 'Has he heard anything?'

'No.' Just the one word.

'What do you mean – he hasn't heard anything from Fliss and Jo?' she pressed him, anxiety flooding in once more.

'That's right.'

'But hasn't anybody tried to contact them?'

'They've tried. They can't make contact.'

'Oh my God! You don't think . . .?'

'Maggie!' He made a warning face at her over Emma's glistening wet head. 'I'm sure they're fine. There could be any number of reasons why . . .'

'Oh, I suppose . . .'

'There could be. You know that as well as I do.'

'Has the coastguard been alerted? Shouldn't somebody . . .?'

'Yves doesn't want to get a full-scale search under way yet, and I agree with him. Like me, he thinks the chances are that it's just radio contact they've lost. They'd be furious if there were helicopters scrambled, the whole palaver of it, when they're perfectly fine. He trusts them, and so do I.'

She was shaking. How could he be so calm? It was unnatural for him to react like this. She thought again of the ferocity of the storm even here, on land. Tearing branches from healthy living trees. Tossing fully laden dustbins about like toys. Her heart was in her mouth, yet Martin seemed hardly concerned at all, and he was Fliss's husband, for goodness' sake.

Perhaps he really doesn't care what happens to her, she thought. He only married her, after all, because of Emma. Maybe it would be a relief not to be tied any more to a wife he doesn't love . . .

'Isn't it time you were out of that bath, Emma?' Martin said.

Maggie wrapped the towel around the warm, squirming little body, hoisting Emma on to her lap; Martin, sitting on the edge of the bath, tickled her toes as Maggie patted her dry, playing 'This little piggy' to make her laugh. She was glad of the distraction, yet the terrible, suffocating anxiety remained, and Maggie knew that the night ahead would be a long and sleepless one.

Her family were not the only ones who were desperately worried about Fliss. As he listened to the howling of the wind, saw the fury of the waves, heard radio reports of the gale that had the whole of the southern part of England and Ireland in its grip, anxiety knotted in Jeff's stomach like an undigested meal.

He wasn't, by nature, a worrier; it wasn't like him to imagine the worst. By and large he tended to take things as they came, deal with them as necessary, but not anticipate trouble and waste time and energy fretting about what might never happen. So it came as something of a shock to him to realise that he was unable to get it out of his head that Fliss was out there on this raging sea.

She'd be fine, he told himself. She and Jo were experienced sailors and they'd deal with whatever the storm threw at them. But the nagging anxiety refused to go away. He wouldn't be happy until he knew she was safely back. It was a new experience for Jeff, and one that he didn't care for. With a sense of shock he realised just how deeply he had come to care for Fliss. Just how far she'd got under his skin, into his head and his heart.

Jeff wasn't quite sure how he felt about that. Or what he would do about it.

Maggie didn't go in to work the next day. She couldn't have faced it, and in any case, the worrying had made Greta's migraine return with a vengeance. She couldn't even get up from bed, but lay with the curtains closed and a cold flannel on her throbbing temples.

Martin did go to the garage – he couldn't afford not to open up, he told Maggie. He was deeply in debt and struggling – it would help nobody if he went bankrupt. But Maggie knew from the dark shadows beneath his eyes and the gaunt lines of his face that he hadn't slept much – she'd maligned him in thinking he didn't care.

The hours dragged by, endless, anxious hours, but it was night-fall before the news came.

When the telephone rang, Maggie snatched it up.

'Yes?'

'They're OK,' Martin said. 'I told you they would be.'

'Where . . .? What happened? How do you know?'

'I've had a call from Yves. They did get caught in the storm, and lost their radio, amongst other things. But they weren't far from Fastnet and they decided to carry on anyway.'

'And they're all right? Really all right?'

'They're fine. You can stop worrying.'

Maggie's knees gave way beneath her; she sank on to the bottom stair, sitting there cradling the receiver long after Martin had rung off.

'Fliss is OK,' she called out to Greta.

The relief was enormous, swamping her just as the anxiety had done before. And then, quite suddenly, she was angry too, so angry she was shaking with it.

How could Fliss put them through this? How could she be so selfish? And how come everything fell at her feet, whether she wanted it or not? She didn't deserve Emma and she certainly didn't deserve Martin. It would serve her right if she lost them both.

But she wouldn't, of course. Not untouchable golden girl Fliss.

Life was absolutely not fair.

ELEVEN

It was several weeks before Fliss went back to Falmouth. After leaving Emma with Greta for so long while she did the Fastnet trip, she didn't like to call on her again too soon, and in any case she was becoming concerned that Maggie might well have been right when she said looking after the little girl was becoming too much for her. She really didn't look well, and Maggie had told her how poorly their mother had been all over that long weekend.

Fliss would have put it down to the stress of worrying about whether she was safe – Greta had always had a tendency to head-aches when she was stressed – but Maggie had told her the headache had started on the Saturday, before the storm had struck, and that left Fliss wondering if it was having Emma that was the trigger.

Greta, however, denied it hotly.

'I haven't got to the stage yet where I want you fussing over me,' she said tartly. 'It's come to something if you think I'm past looking after my granddaughter.'

'I'm only concerned . . . She is a bit of a handful now she's walking . . .'

'She's no trouble at all. It does my heart good to have her,' Greta insisted.

And so, one day at the beginning of September, Fliss went to Falmouth.

There might not be many more chances, she thought. The end

of the season was coming and Martin was still saying that *Mermaid's Song* would have to be stored at the garage for the winter – something Fliss was dreading. And it wasn't just the thought of not being able to sail her boat that depressed her. It was also the prospect of not seeing Jeff. Though there would almost certainly be people she could crew for, her principal excuse for going to Falmouth would have gone, and Fliss admitted to herself how much she had come to depend on their easy-going relationship.

The shadow of the long and lonely winter months lay heavily on her as she drove across the peninsula, and she stepped on the accelerator, anxious to reach Falmouth and talk to Jeff.

But when she reached the marina, the *Jersey Gal* was missing from her berth. Fliss's heart sank. Jeff must have gone out early, she thought, and hoped he'd be back before it was time for her to go home.

She prepared *Mermaid's Song* and took her out for a couple of hours, but when she got back there was still no sign of the *Jersey Gal*. Fliss stowed her sails, made her boat safe and headed for the cafeteria.

It was less busy today – but the first person she saw as she went in was Simon Beacham.

'Hear you had a bit of a blow on the Fastnet trip,' he greeted her.

'All good fun,' Fliss said, edging away.

As usual, he followed her.

'I take it you know about Hank the Yank.' Fliss froze; Simon puffed up with importance and sly pleasure at the look on her face – a combination of shock and anxiety. 'I take it you don't. Well, I expect you'll be sorry to hear he's gone.'

'Gone? Gone where?' Fliss hated having to admit her ignorance, to Simon of all people, but she absolutely had to know.

'He's got a job refitting a boat. Hayling Island, I think. Sorry to be the bearer of bad news.'

'Did he say when he'd be back?' The words were out before she could stop them. Simon shook his head, but his expression was smug.

'I don't think he will be. From what I can make out, he was

ready to move on.' He smiled, the snaggle tooth grazing his lip. 'You're just going to have to make do with me, I'm afraid.'

'I'll have to take a rain check on that one.' She sounded for all the world exactly like the old, breezy Fliss, but inwardly she was in turmoil.

'Oh well, you know where I am if you get lonely.'

This time she could find no answer. She turned away, hurrying out of the cafeteria and down the wooden stairs to the quayside.

Jeff – gone. Without so much as a goodbye. She couldn't believe it. But why would Simon make up something like that? He'd know she'd find out soon enough if it wasn't true.

Hurt and loss welled inside her; the stiff breeze off the sea whipped at her hair and stung her cheeks, but it wasn't responsible for the tears in her eyes. They came from the awful chasm that had opened up inside her, and she felt as if they were choking her. How could he do it? How? Oh, she'd always known he was a flirt, a gypsy, a free spirit. But she'd thought that what they shared was worth more than this.

Fliss caught at the wooden handrail, holding it tight as she tried to stop those tears from flowing and feeling as if her world had come to an end.

There was a quotation, Fliss knew, about troubles coming not as single spies but whole battalions. She couldn't remember it exactly, but her mother had a saying that meant the same – 'It never rains but it pours.' And that, it seemed, was what was happening now. Bad enough that Jeff had gone and *Mermaid's Song* was in dry dock; to make things a thousand times worse, she and Maggie were dreadfully worried about Greta. Her headaches were coming more and more frequently and were more and more debilitating. But Greta was stubbornly refusing to seek help for them.

'She won't listen to me,' Maggie said. 'You know what she's like when it comes to doctors and hospitals. Will you talk to her, Fliss? She might take more notice of you.'

But Fliss had no more success than Maggie.

'He won't be able to do anything for me except give me pain-killers, and I've got my aspirin,' Greta said, stoic as ever. 'It's something I've got to live with, that's all.'

Then, one day, Martin got a phone call at the garage from a panicked Maggie. Greta had collapsed – Maggie had found her unconscious on the bathroom floor. An ambulance had been summoned and Greta had been taken to hospital in Truro – Maggie was there now, waiting for news.

Martin shut the garage and rushed home to inform Fliss, then took both her and Emma back with him. He sorted out a Mini from his used car stock, filled it with petrol and handed Fliss the keys. He'd look after Emma until Fliss got back, no matter when that might be.

It was a nightmare journey – Fliss, unused to the car and shaking with anxiety for her mother, managed to stall the engine every time she had to stop at a road junction or traffic lights, attracting a good deal of ill-tempered honking from other motor-ists. But she made it in the end, and found Maggie in the relatives' room of the hospital.

Greta had regained consciousness, Maggie told her, but she was behaving very strangely, talking a lot of nonsense and apparently unaware of where she was or what was happening to her.

'What is it – a stroke?' Fliss asked.

'They don't seem to think so. I told them about the headaches she's been having and they're doing tests now.'

'You think it's connected?' Fliss asked, more worried than ever.

Maggie pulled a grim face.

'Don't you? It's more than coincidence if you ask me. I don't like the sound of it at all. Oh, why wouldn't the silly woman go to the doctor?'

It was hours later before a white-coated registrar came to see them and broke the news they'd been dreading.

A tumour had been growing in Greta's brain. They could operate, though the chances of a good outcome were, frankly, slim. But the alternative was, perhaps, even worse. It could only be a matter of months, or even weeks, before the tumour killed her, depending mostly on whether it was benign or malignant, something they wouldn't know until a sample had been analysed under the microscope.

'But if it's benign . . . surely that wouldn't be so bad?' Fliss said, grasping at a shred of hope.

'Not as bad as malignant, certainly, but it doesn't mean it won't continue to grow, I'm afraid,' the registrar explained. 'Your mother is going to be in a lot of pain, and she's going to gradually lose more and more of her faculties, depending on which direction the tumour spreads. My feeling is that the best option is to remove as much of the growth as possible. But that, of course, is something only she can decide – if she's capable of making a decision.'

'And if she isn't?'

'We'll cross that bridge when we come to it.'

In the event, after Fliss, Maggie and the doctors had talked to her, Greta was deemed to understand the situation well enough to sign the consent forms herself.

Two days later she underwent surgery. Maggie took time off work and Fliss went over to Porthtowan, both for moral support, and because the fact that they were on the telephone there meant that they could keep in touch with the hospital easily.

The hours dragged by; when the telephone rang, their hearts sank. They had been told to ring for news at about five o'clock; it was now just after three. If it was the hospital calling it didn't look good.

It was the hospital; it wasn't good. They were very sorry, they had done everything they could, but Greta had died on the operating table.

Fliss and Maggie looked at one another, at each other's stunned and crumpling faces. Then they dissolved into tears and into one another's arms.

Greta's sudden and unexpected death brought the sisters closer together than they had been for years. They supported one another through all the grim formalities and the planning of the funeral, taking it in turns to be the one who was strong and the one who was falling apart. Fliss moved into her mother's house in Porthtowan so that she could field the phone calls while Maggie was at work, and one evening they got drunk together on the remains of a bottle of sherry, reminiscing about old times, remembering incidents that seemed hilariously funny and which made them almost hysterical with laughter until suddenly they were in floods of tears again. Together they prepared food for the wake – canned salmon sand-wiches and sausage rolls and cheese and pineapple chunks on cocktail sticks – and they walked side by side behind Greta's coffin, unable to see one another – or any of the other mourners – because of the tears that were swimming in their eyes, but taking comfort in the feeling of sisterly unity. There was another opportunity for nostalgic reminiscing when they went through Greta's things, neatly packing clothes that were still good to go to charity, stuffing the rest into bin bags, and trying to sort drawers full of old photographs, letters, even bills on which 'Paid in Full' had been written in good old-fashioned ink. Greta seemed to have thrown nothing away – there was even a small card stamped with the name of the cycle shop in St Agnes, and beneath it, column after column of payments marked off – 5/- per week. The date confirmed that the payments were for her first bicycle, Fliss realised, a very special present the year after she had passed the scholarship to go to grammer school.

The house had been left to the two girls jointly, but though she was strapped for cash, Fliss couldn't have brought herself to insist it should be sold so that she could have her share. Instead, Maggie gave her most of her share of the money that Greta had stashed away in a post office saving account – seventy-five pounds – with the promise of more later.

Fliss's first thought was, of course, for her boat, but it didn't seem right not to offer it to Martin when he was in such dire financial straits.

Martin, however, wouldn't hear of it.

'Your mother meant it for you, Fliss,' he said. 'It will mean you can keep Mermaid in Penryn, if not Falmouth, when the sailing season starts, and pay for any running repairs she may need.'

'Oh Martin . . .' Fliss was not only grateful, but humbled, and wished with all her heart that she could have the same feelings for him that she had for Jeff. He was such a good man and he deserved a wife who loved him as much as he loved her. But she didn't have those feelings, she couldn't see she ever would, and knowing it was a weight of despair around her heart.

The depression crept up on Fliss gradually, an echo of the way she'd felt last winter, but much, much worse. While she and Maggie had been sorting out all the things that needed to be done following Greta's death, she hadn't had much time for thinking or even grieving, but when everything had been tied up and Fliss was at home once more, she felt as if she were sinking into a bottomless pit of wretchedness. She wept for her mother; she wept for the hopelessness of her situation, trapped in a marriage to a man she didn't love; she wept for Jeff, who had come to mean everything to her, with whom she though she had shared a special bond, but who had abandoned her without a word. Sometimes she thought the tears would never stop.

Christmas came and went, a surreal parody of the festive season. For Emma's sake, Fliss made a huge effort to hide her despair, making paper chains with her to deck the house and finding an old pillowcase for her to hang up at the end of her bed for Father Christmas to fill with new toys and the obligatory apple, mandarin orange and Brazil nuts.

Maggie joined them for Christmas Day and took over the cooking of the capon, roast potatoes and Brussels sprouts when Fliss got herself into a state trying to juggle saucepans and roasting tins and a complicated timetable. But although they did their best to create a festive atmosphere, with crackers and paper hats, sherry and carols, the empty place where Greta should have been sitting loomed large, and Jeff continued to occupy Fliss's thoughts and heart. She wondered what he was doing for Christmas, whether he was spending it with some new girlfriend, and felt the tears welling again. Stupid, stupid! She'd always known what he was like, always known that nothing could come of the way she felt about him. But castigating herself did no good. It didn't lessen the hurt and it didn't lessen the longing. Without him she felt incomplete, as if she had lost a part of herself, and she didn't think she would ever be whole again.

Fliss felt the most enormous relief when the whole charade was over, but it was a brief respite only. As she cleared away the wrapping paper and coloured twine, discarded when the presents had been opened, it occurred to her that it was a metaphor for what her life had become, shiny and full of promise, yet no longer containing anything of value. Except, of course, for Emma. But much as she adored her daughter, Fliss couldn't escape the dreadful feeling that it wasn't enough.

On a cold, blustery Saturday towards the end of January, Martin telephoned Maggie.

'Have you got any plans for today?'

Maggie's heart gave the same lurch it always did when she heard Martin's voice.

'Not specially, no. Why?'

'I was just wondering if you'd go over and look in on Fliss. I'm really concerned about her. She's been acting very strangely, and this morning she was worse than ever. I didn't want to leave her – wouldn't have if Saturday wasn't one of my busiest days at the garage – and I really don't think she should be on her own all day.'

'Of course I'll go over,' Maggie said, worried.

She finished clearing away her breakfast things, tidied up, and made a list of essential shopping she could do in Redruth whilst she was there. Then she bundled herself into her duffel coat, two scarves and the peaked crash helmet that made her look like a duck, and set out on her Lambretta.

The front door of the cottage would be locked, she knew, so she went around to the back. But to her surprise, when she knocked on the back door and tried to open it, that was locked too. Had Fliss gone out somewhere? She hammered again, hard, and when there was still no response, went to the kitchen window, peering in. All she could see was a clutter of used crockery on the worktop beside the sink; what sunlight there was was reflecting off the glass and making it impossible to look further into the kitchen, but she rather thought it was empty. She walked around to the front of the house, ringing the doorbell, then looking in at the living room window. The light was on, making it easy to see in. Emma was sitting in the middle of the floor, but of Fliss there was no sign. She hadn't gone out then, but where was she? In the bathroom? Upstairs, making the beds? Why wasn't she answering the door? Maggie gave the bell another long twist and heard it shrilling loudly, but still there was no sound of Fliss coming to answer it.

Growing increasingly alarmed, Maggie was just wondering if she should try to find a way of breaking in when she heard the key being turned in the lock and the door opened. Fliss was standing there, barefoot, and still wearing her dressing gown. She was very pale, and it didn't look as if she'd brushed her hair this morning – it was still tousled from what might well have been a restless night.

'Oh,' she said. 'It's you.' Her voice was dull and flat and she made no attempt to open the door fully.

'Aren't you going to let me in?' Maggie asked.

'Oh – yes. Sorry.' She moved slowly, as if it was all a dreadful effort.

The front door opened directly into the living room. As Maggie had seen through the window, Emma was sitting on the floor, still in her sleepsuit, surrounded by what looked like the entire contents of the bottom drawer of the chiffonier, including a Stanley knife. Horrified, Maggie swooped on it.

'Emma! You mustn't play with this!'

'Mag-gie!' Emma was up in a moment, stumbling a little because her feet were still encased in the towelling fabric of her sleepsuit, and holding out her arms to her aunt. Maggie scooped her up and gave her a hug, noticing that her bottom felt damp, there was still sleep in the corners of her eyes, and a crust of egg yolk on her chin.

'Why didn't you answer the door?' she asked Fliss over the little girl's head. 'I was getting really worried.'

Fliss's eyes were dull and empty.

'I didn't want to see anyone.'

'And why aren't you and Emma dressed?'

'I couldn't be bothered.'

'Well you have to be bothered!' Maggie exploded. 'You've got a child to look after! What on earth is wrong with you, Fliss?'

Fliss's lip wobbled, her face crumpled, tears welled in her eyes. She sank down on to the sofa, covering her face with her hands.

'I don't know, Maggie. I honestly don't know,' she groaned. And began crying in earnest.

It was at least partly true. Fliss simply didn't recognise the dark place she found herself in, where nothing had any real meaning, the simplest task required an effort and energy she no longer possessed, and the tears were never far away. Though there had been times before when she had been dreadfully miserable, nothing had come close to the way she felt now, and she knew it was far more than the understandable grief at the loss of her mother.

There was a darkness inside her head as well as all around her, a thick, suffocating cloud that dulled her thought processes and made her limbs heavy. There seemed to be a black aura around everything. She didn't want to talk to anyone, but she didn't want to be alone either. She cried too easily, but the tears were not healing, they merely left her feeling even worse, as if crying had congested what little space there was inside her head. And it wasn't just mental, it was physical too. The slightest confrontation made her shake all over, as did the thought of leaving the house. She felt sick and had no appetite. She couldn't sleep – well, she could fall asleep, exhausted, but a few hours later she would be wide awake again, her nerves twanging, her thoughts racing. It was horrible, utterly horrible, and she had nothing to draw on to lift herself back to normality.

'For goodness' sake, Fliss, pull yourself together!' Martin said.

But she couldn't. Fliss was sinking in a morass that she couldn't fathom, let alone pull herself out of. She was useless. A total failure. They'd be better off without her. But what would happen to Emma if she wasn't here? She couldn't leave Emma motherless. The vicious circle was complete. And began all over again.

'Oh Maggie, I'm no use to anyone,' she moaned now.

'That is stupid talk, Fliss.'

'It is not! Just look at me! Look! I'm a terrible wife to Martin. And Emma – I can't even care for Emma properly. I'm a total disaster.'

'You're a lovely mother.'

'I'm not. I'm useless.'

'Stop it, Fliss. Go and make yourself look halfway respectable. I'll get Emma dressed and make a cup of tea. Or better still, we'll go into town, find a café and have a coffee and a slice of saffron cake.'

'I don't want—'

'Yes you do. You love saffron cake. Anyway, that's what we're doing, so don't argue. Off you go now.'

Fliss went, obedient as a child. She was gone a very long time, but when she came back she was bathed and dressed in a pair of black ski pants that skimmed her long legs and an oversized man's sweater. She looked a great deal more like her usual self, though she was still ghostly pale.

'You need some make-up,' Maggie decreed. 'You look as if you've dipped your face in the flour bag.'

'I've only got lipstick and mascara.' Fliss was never one for much make-up.

Maggie dived into her bag for her cosmetics purse and pulled out a panstick.

'Here you are. Put on some of this.'

Fliss took it, smearing thick lines of panstick down her cheeks and rubbing it in. Then she spat into her mascara, scrubbed some on to the little brush and applied it.

'That's better. Now, let's find your coat, and Emma's, and we'll go.'

Fliss sighed.

'I'm pathetic, aren't I?'

'Don't start that again, or I'll take you to the doctor's instead of the café.'

Unexpectedly Fliss laughed, though it was as brittle as a bare branch on a frosty morning.

'Nothing's changed. You're still the big sister, Maggie. Still bossing me about.'

'I should think so too! You need me to keep you in order.'

'Yes,' Fliss said ruefully. 'I think I do.'

After the saffron cake and a frothy espresso coffee Fliss was a lot more like her old self, though still visibly shaking, and Maggie wondered whether the effort of going out, whilst it was doing her good in the short term, might actually be taking its toll on her fragile nerves. She stayed at Redruth until late afternoon, when Martin got home, because she really didn't think Fliss should be left alone.

Martin looked tired and worried – he'd had a busy but not very profitable day; a sale he'd been banking on had fallen through and there hadn't been any other new business to make up for it. Besides which, Fliss had been constantly on his mind.

'She was in a dreadful state when I got here,' Maggie told him when Fliss disappeared to go to the bathroom. 'She's a bit better now, but I don't know how long it will last. I think she's having a nervous breakdown. She really needs to see the doctor.'

Martin huffed breath over his top lip, more worried than ever. A friend of his mother's had had a nervous breakdown when he was a boy; she'd been taken off to 'the asylum' and he remembered his mother muttering darkly about awful electrical treatments and drugs that kept her 'out of it' for days on end.

'Do you really think that's necessary? She'll get over it again, won't she?'

'I certainly hope so! But . . .'

'If I took her on holiday, wouldn't that help?' He sighed again, shaking his head. 'The trouble is, I haven't any cash to spare for holidays, and I can't afford to close the garage either. Truth to tell, I'm struggling.'

'She's in no fit state to be left here alone with Emma,' Maggie said. 'The way she was talking this morning . . . saying you'd both be better off without her . . . well, there's no knowing what she might do.'

'Oh my God!' Martin said, shocked. 'You don't think . . .?'

'I honestly don't know.'

She fell silent for a moment, an idea beginning to take shape in her mind.

'I wonder if she could go and stay with her friend Jo for a bit? It might do her good to get away from all her responsibilities here, and she and Jo are really close. She'd make sure Fliss didn't do anything stupid.'

'It's a thought. But what about Emma?'

Maggie took a quick decision.

'I'm due some holiday. I could look after Emma for a couple of weeks. After that . . . well, we'll just have to play it by ear.' A door slammed. 'She's coming back. Do you want me to get in touch with Jo, see what she says?'

Martin nodded. 'Would you?'

'Of course. So, Emma has been a really good girl today, haven't you, darling?' she said, quickly changing the subject.

The moment Maggie got home she telephoned Jo, who was horrified to hear that Fliss was in such a state, and agreed unhesitatingly that of course she'd be glad to have her to stay. Yves was away, crewing on a long-distance voyage; it would be just the two of them. Jo was working for a sailing school, teaching theory at the moment, though she would soon be out on the water too when the weather improved, and she couldn't see that there would be any objection to Fliss helping her. Fliss could give her a hand with getting her boat ready for the new season too, and they could do some trips together in preparation for the Fastnet Race later in the year.

'You're a life-saver, Jo,' Maggie said. 'Fliss is going to be so bucked, I know.'

And, she admitted to herself, so was she. The thought of having Martin and Emma all to herself, even if it was only for a couple of weeks, was rather a delicious one.

Away from the claustrophobic cottage, away from her responsibilities, away from Martin, the improvement in Fliss was dramatic. She missed Emma dreadfully, of course, but she spoke to her regularly on the telephone and sent her postcards with pictures she thought Emma would like, and bought little presents for her – a sun hat, a handmade rag doll, a stick of rock.

She and Jo went sailing, and had long heart-to-hearts when she confessed her feelings for Jeff and Jo told her bluntly she had to forget him. She couldn't of course, but the sadness she still felt at what might have been took on more normal proportions. Jo was right, she had to accept he'd gone, and try to move on, hard as that might be. Her appetite returned, encouraged by the light meals Jo prepared – Martin never felt he'd had a proper meal if it didn't consist of meat and two veg. She was sleeping better – the depression was always worse when she was tired from a bad night – and she didn't feel like crying helplessly all the time. Her nerves were still fragile, an unexpected problem could set her trembling, and decisions were still beyond her. But on the whole she was on a much more even keel.

At the end of two weeks Martin came over to see her, bringing Emma, and they spent a pleasant enough day together, but it set Fliss back, and it was decided that she would stay with Jo for another couple of weeks.

She had to go home soon, though; she couldn't opt out of normal life for ever. Martin promised to arrange for *Mermaid* to be transported to Penryn and to ask around about child care so that Fliss could go sailing, and that, at least, gave her something to cling to, something to look forward to.

She had to go home for Emma's sake. She was missing her more and more, the same ache, the same empty place in her arms and her heart that she had felt in those bleak days when she had left her little daughter with the foster mother.

She had to go home. Back to her old life, back to being a wife and mother. This time, she was determined to make a much better job of it.

After a winter spent under a sheet of polythene in a corner of Martin's used car lot, the *Mermaid's Song* was in need of a coat of paint but otherwise in good condition. Fliss took Emma with her to the garage while she readied the boat, which slowed down progress considerably, since she couldn't take her eye off her daughter for more than a minute, and Emma's attention span with her toys was short – they were not nearly as interesting to her as all the things Fliss didn't want her meddling with. But at last the job was finished, and Martin arranged for *Mermaid* to be transported to Penryn. He'd also found a lady in the village willing to have Emma once a week. In view of their financial situation Fliss was worried that they couldn't really afford to pay for child care, but Martin was insistent.

'Things aren't so bad that we can't afford a pound a week,' he said. 'In any case, your health comes first. I don't want you getting depressed again.'

On a bright day in March Fliss set out for Penryn. There was a brisk breeze blowing and she headed out to the Mallen Roads and began to tack towards the open sea. Several other boats were doing the same; Fliss waved a hand in greeting and called out cheerily to one that passed close by.

There was a bigger boat away to her right, sail billowing,

white-painted hull shimmering in the bright sunlight. Fliss stared at it, her heart beginning to beat a tattoo. It looked for all the world like the *Jersey Gal*!

It can't be, she told herself. You're imagining things.

Her first instinct was to flee, to put as much distance as she could between her and the man she was trying so hard to forget, and who had left her without so much as a goodbye. But even now he was drawing her in like a magnet – if indeed it was him. She changed tack, closing the distance between them, catching every bit of wind to take her skimming in pursuit. Then, when she was close enough to be sure she was not mistaken, she took fright again. Too late. He'd seen her. He raised an arm in salute and she waved back, heart thudding.

How could he *do* this to her? How could just a glimpse of him rob her of all her good intentions – all reason? In total panic Fliss took off again, skimming towards the open sea.

But try as she might, there was no way she could outrun *Jersey Gal*. Jeff was following her, playing games, racing her. As he passed her he whooped, raised his hand again, shouted something. She couldn't catch the words, but they set her heart pounding once more. For over an hour they danced around one another, and her trepidation turned to exhilaration. This was wonderful! This was living!

At last Fliss checked her watch; time to go in if she wasn't to miss the tide. She turned for home; Jeff followed her. She expected him to head for Falmouth Marina, but he didn't. As she passed through the Mallen Roads he was still on her tail, showing no sign of changing direction, and when she took down sail he was right behind her.

'Hey!' he called. 'Are you trying to avoid me?'

'What do you think?'

'You'd better not be! I'm buying you a drink!'

'Here?'

'No, in Falmouth. Come on, dump *Mermaid* and get on board a *real* boat.'

She shouldn't, she knew. She should be strong enough to tell him no. But . . . 'You'll have to wait!' she called back.

'I'm in no hurry.'

She laughed with sheer exuberance.

'You will be if you miss the tide.'

'Get a move on, then.'

She did, though she told herself he'd have no one but himself to blame if he got marooned here at Penryn. She beached *Mermaid's Song*, and by the time she'd made her safe he was waiting for her with his dinghy, leaving *Jersey Gal* anchored in the deeper water beyond the receding tide line.

'Hey, gal, how ya doing?' he asked as she scrambled aboard.

'I'm OK.'

'You look pretty damn good to me!' He winked at her, a wicked, heart-stopping wink.

'You don't look so bad yourself,' she countered.

It was the understatement of the century. He looked wonderful, she thought, blond hair curling beneath a white cap, face still tanned by the wind and last summer's sun, shirt open at the neck to reveal a gold medallion on a slender chain.

'I'm not sure I've forgiven you yet, though,' she said.

'How so?'

'Going off like that without so much as a word. I can't believe you'd do that!'

He gave her a sideways glance.

'I had my reasons.'

'Which were?'

'I'll tell you over that drink,' he said.

They didn't go to their usual bar; instead he drove her out of town in his beat-up old Ford Consul – sailors inevitably drove rackety old cars that were held together with nothing more than willpower and string; all their spare cash went on their boats.

They found a village pub, all old oak beams and horse brasses, with a ship's figurehead over the chimneypiece, and ordered beers and rounds of roasted beef sandwiches and potato crisps.

The old ease was there between them as they talked. Fliss told Jeff about the loss of her mother, and as she fought back tears his hand covered hers and her pain was reflected in his face. Then he told her about the job he'd had in Hayling Island, working on the refit of a luxury yacht.

'How the other half live!' Fliss said, shaking her head.

'You're joking!' Jeff took a long pull of his beer. 'Something like that isn't much fun. Jeez, the guy who owns it doesn't even sail it himself. He has someone to do it for him.'

'It would be nice to be able to afford it, though.'

'If you say so.' Jeff didn't say that he had grown up in the sort of circles that took luxury for granted; his origins were still strictly off limits.

'So,' Fliss said, 'what are you doing back in Falmouth?'

He raised an eyebrow, sneaking her a sideways grin.

'Well, looking for you, of course.'

'Liar!'

'Sure am.'

'After you went off without so much as a word? Oh, you'll have to do better than that.'

Her tone was light, flirtatious, a camouflage for the tumultuous emotions that were seething inside her.

'I told you – I had my reasons.'

'And you told me you'd explain over a drink. Which I don't think you have the slightest intention of doing.'

'That depends.'

'On what? Come on, you're just making excuses because there isn't a single good reason.'

'Wrong.' His very blue eyes narrowed and levelled with hers, holding them. 'You really want to know?'

'Yes.'

'Suppose I was to tell you I realised I was getting a sight too involved with a lady I had no business to be getting involved with. A lady . . .' his fingers curled round his glass, twisting it restlessly on the beer mat, 'a lady not a million miles away from me right now.'

Fliss's heart seemed to have stopped beating. And not only her heart; the world around her had stopped too, ceased to exist at all, reduced to nothing but her and the man sitting across the table from her.

'Fact is,' he went on, 'I've always known we were good together, you and I. But I thought that was OK, we were just sharing some good times. I fancied more – of course I did – but you were off limits, being a married woman and all that, and I had plenty of girls to keep me satisfied. And then you got caught in that gale and I realised just how damn much I care for you. Couldn't have that, could I? Not me, the footloose and fancy-free Jeff Hewson. Couldn't see any future in it either. So I reckoned the best thing I could do was hightail it and forget all about you. And I tried, God knows I tried, but it didn't work like that. You were still there, dammit, all the time, and it was driving me nuts. I figured the way things were between us had to be something pretty special, so I came back. Just to see whether I might be in with a chance. Pretty damn-fool thing to do, I know, but then I've never been the wisest of guys.' He grinned crookedly. 'Just tell me to get the hell out of here, and I'll go, with my tail between my legs. But I reckoned I just had to know.'

Fliss could scarcely breathe. An aura of unreality was surrounding her now, but within it joy leapt. She hadn't been alone in thinking that what they shared was special. She hadn't imagined the meeting of hearts and minds, the electric animal attraction. Jeff felt the same way too, and for all that she knew that nothing could come of it, her heart soared.

'Yes,' she whispered.

'Yes, you want me to get the hell out of here?'

She shook her head, her hand snaking across the table so that her fingers met his, the lightest, most tentative of touches.

'No. I mean . . . yes . . . it's just the same for me. You knew that, didn't you?'

'I sure as hell hoped.'

'I couldn't stop thinking about you either. Every minute of every day.' The words were pouring out now in a torrent. 'All I wanted was to be with you. I tried not to, but I couldn't help it. Nothing means anything without you. Really, nothing. I think . . .' She stopped short. *I love you*, she had been going to say, but it was too soon for that, too deep a commitment, though it was what she felt with all her heart.

His fingers closed over hers.

'So – what are we going to do?'

'I don't know.' She didn't want to confront reality yet, just to savour this marvellous moment.

'Ah well,' he said. 'I guess we'll think of something.'

'Oh Jeff . . .'

He drained his glass.

'Come on. Let's get out of here.'

He got up and so did she. But she still clung to his hand as they left the pub. The beef sandwiches remained, uneaten, on the table.

Outside, he pulled her into the shadow of the old stone walls and kissed her, holding her so close that it seemed they had become one. The aura of unreality was still surrounding her, the joy of discovering that Jeff felt as she did and the urgency of their unleashed passion banishing any trace of guilt. All her commitments and responsibilities belonged in another world; here there was only Jeff. They kissed until she was dizzy, until the world spun around her, until the need in them, aching and pulsing in every inch of their bodies, became unbearable. Like a pair of drunks they staggered to his Ford, kissed again. He started the engine and drove with his arm around her and her head resting against his shoulder, changing gear right-handed, unwilling to let her go for a single second. And she felt the same way. There was

155

a cramp in her back and her right hand felt like a pin cushion, but she stayed exactly where she was, afraid that if she moved she would wake up and find this was all just a dream.

She knew where they were headed, and she was right. The *Jersey Gal* was bobbing at her mooring; they went aboard and straight down into the snug little cabin, where they clung together again before tearing one another's clothes off in a frenzy of desire.

And then, on the little bunk with its rough blanket and hard mattress, they made wonderful, passionate love.

Of course, as they emerged from the languorous aftermath, the question had to be asked again. 'What are we going to do?' And again, there was, as yet, no answer. But for the moment it really didn't matter. Though she knew they would have to be faced eventually, those hard, life-changing decisions so momentous she couldn't bear to think about them, they could be put off for another day. For now, she and Jeff were together, and could be whenever she could escape to Falmouth.

In the blissful euphoria that suffused her, it was more than enough.

TWELVE

'It's really good to see you so much happier, Fliss,' Martin said.

Fliss was ironing a pile of laundry, singing as she worked. She *was* happy, euphoric almost, floating on a cloud of bliss, and had been ever since she had begun her affair with Jeff. And it seemed to her almost to excuse her deception. She didn't snap at Martin any more, she felt a kindly warmth towards him, and strove to make life good for him in a hundred little ways. She had far more patience with Emma, who was at a very trying age, following Fliss everywhere, even to the bathroom, emptying dressing table drawers whilst Fliss was making the bed, pulling out the sheets again when she was repacking the drawers, never giving her a moment's peace. Whereas before Fliss would have scooped her up crossly and dumped her in her playpen, now she merely shook her head and laughed.

'Oh Emma, what am I going to do with you?'

Her good humour towards her family went a long way to assuaging her feelings of guilt. If she was happy, Martin and Emma were happy. As long as they didn't know the reason behind it, where was the harm? And they didn't know, she made sure of that.

So far they had made no long-term plans, looking no further than the next time they could be together. Fliss didn't want to face decisions she wasn't ready to contemplate. And Jeff, footloose, easy-going Jeff, didn't press her.

Those weeks of early summer were the most wonderful time of Fliss's entire life; she wanted them to last for ever. But of course they couldn't.

'I'm going to have to go home, Fliss,' Jeff said.

They were in the cabin of *Jersey Gal*, where they had just made the most ecstatic, wonderful love.

A chilly hand grasped Fliss's heart. '*Home?* To America?'

''Fraid so. My mother is ill. I've booked a flight, and I leave tomorrow.'

'You never said!'

'I don't tell you everything.' He said it teasingly, but it touched a nerve anyway. There was still so much she didn't know about Jeff. Strangely, since they were so close, he never talked about his family. She'd gained the impression he'd disassociated himself from them, but he'd never said why, and she hadn't pressed him, though she longed to know every detail of his past life. It could be he was ashamed of his origins – that possibility only added to the aura of romance that surrounded him, and made her feel fiercely protective. It could be there'd been some terrible falling-out. But whatever it was, he'd tell her when he was ready.

Now, however, Fliss could contain herself no longer.

'I didn't even know you were in touch with your family,' she said.

'It's not something I'm very good at,' he admitted. 'I got a letter from my father telling me he's worried about Mom.'

'What's wrong with her?' Fliss asked.

'He wasn't specific. "Women's troubles" was as far as he went. Guess it's something Mom finds embarrassing. But he did say he thinks I should go visit, which has got me real worried. I must go and see her. I'd never forgive myself if . . .'

'You must go, of course.' Fliss, still raw from her own mother's death, agreed. And then, as the sneaky fingers of foreboding closed around her heart: 'You will come back, though, won't you?'

For a long moment Jeff was silent. Then he said: 'Honey, I'm honestly not sure. I'll have to come back for my boat, of course, unless I decide to sell her, and I don't want to do that. But whether or not I stay . . . Truth to tell, I think it's time I went home. I can't bum around here for ever. I reckon it's time to think about the future – and that includes us. This has all been very nice, but . . . it's not exactly ideal, is it?'

'What are you saying?' Fliss sat up. This wasn't the sort of conversation she could have in a state of undress, with her face against his bare shoulder. She reached for her shirt, slipping it on and holding it around herself protectively.

'That we can't carry on like this for ever. Well, I can't. I don't want to go on sharing you any more. How do you think I feel when you go home to your husband? It damn near drives me crazy. So what I'm proposing is that if I do decide to go home for good, you come with me.'

Fliss's heart seemed to miss a beat.

'Tomorrow?'

'No, of course not. As I said, I have to come back for *Jersey Gal*. My return flight is booked for a week's time. I'll get in touch then and you can let me know what you've decided.'

'You're really asking me to leave Martin and go to America with you?'

'That's about the size of it.'

'But it's not that simple . . . What about Emma?'

He reached into the pocket of his jeans, cast off on the floor beside the bunk, pulled out his cigarettes and jammed one between his lips.

'I'm guessing you'll want to bring her with you. Well, that's fine by me.'

Fliss had begun to shake.

'Oh Jeff, I don't know! This is crazy!'

'I love you, dammit!' His eyes narrowed behind the curl of

cigarette smoke. 'I want a proper life with you, not a few snatched hours. Don't you want the same?'

'Well of course I do! But . . . oh, I just don't know what to say!'

Jeff's eyes levelled with hers. 'As I see it, in the end it comes down to whether you want us to be together enough to make the break.'

Fliss was panicking. 'I can't decide just like that! You can't ask me to!'

Jeff swung his legs over the edge of the bunk, and stood up, stooping slightly to pull on his jeans.

'Here's the deal. I'll be back for the *Jersey Gal*, and you as well, I hope, in a week or so. Come with me, and we'll have a great life together, you, me and Emma. But if you decide you can't do it – heck, if you can't work up the courage – then it's got to be over. What we're doing isn't fair on anybody, and I can't carry on.'

He sounded so matter-of-fact it was chilling. Obviously he had given this a lot of thought. And of course he was right, deep down she knew that. What they were doing wasn't fair to him and it wasn't fair to Martin. Besides which, happy as this brief interlude had made her, she knew she wouldn't be satisfied to go on as they were for ever. Jeff was her soulmate and she wanted to share her life with him. But was she brave enough to do what he was suggesting? Could she turn her back on her family, her friends, and run away with him? Could she hurt Martin this way? Take Emma into the unknown?

The questions raced in a confused melee around her brain; for the moment she simply did not know.

'Maggie – I've got to talk to you,' Fliss said. She looked, Maggie thought, as though she had a high fever – cheeks flushed, perspiration glistening at the neck of her shirt, hands shaking.

'What on earth is it, Fliss?'

Fliss glanced over her shoulder at Emma, who was playing happily in the sandpit Maggie had made for her in the garden.

'It's really serious.'

'I can see that.'

'I need a drink.'

'You'll be lucky. Unless you want a tipple of medicinal brandy.'

'Yes. Yes, I do!'

'OK. It's your funeral.' Maggie disappeared into the house, and while she was gone Fliss stared at Emma, thinking how happy and settled she was here, and wondering how she would adapt to a new life in America.

When Maggie re-emerged with the brandy in a small tumbler, she took it and tossed back a mouthful so fast it made her splutter, but as the warmth hit her stomach it almost instantly steadied her a little. Maggie touched her arm, indicated the rustic garden seat that her father had made many years ago.

'Come and sit down. Then you can tell me what in the world is going on.'

Obediently, Fliss crossed the lawn and sat. Maggie settled beside her.

'Come on then. Spill the beans.'

And Fliss did.

'What are you going to do?' Maggie asked.

The heat had gone out of the sun as they talked; they'd had a short break while Fliss made Emma's tea, and then resumed again, sitting in the deepening shadow while Emma scooted around with her dog-on-wheels.

'Well I want to go, of course! I love him, Maggie!'

Totally shocked as Maggie was, a small voice inside her was saying she should have seen this coming. Fliss had never been in love with Martin, would never have married him unless she'd been forced into it by circumstances. Really, it was almost inevitable that she would meet someone else, someone who would be to her all the things that Martin could never be.

But Martin adored her so! Painful as it was for Maggie to acknowledge it, she knew it to be true. He was going to be devastated.

And Emma – he doted on Emma. This would break his heart . . . Her own love for him surged; somehow she had to protect him from this.

'Martin will never let you have Emma,' she said matter-of-factly.

'He'll have to! I'm her mother!'

'He won't, Fliss, I'm sure of it. He'll go to court to keep her if necessary.'

'They'll find for me!'

'I wouldn't bank on it. He'll tell them how you leave Emma with me every chance you get to go off sailing with your boyfriend. That she comes way down your list of priorities. I know – it sounds horrible – but that's the way it's going to be presented. And he'll drag up your mental history too – how you weren't fit to look after her properly, and had to go away for a month to recover. By the time he's finished with you, no court is going to award you custody.'

Fliss was reeling.

'I'll just take her, then!'

Maggie shook her head. 'You wouldn't get away with it. By the time you got to America the authorities would be waiting for you, and any chance that you might be given the benefit of the doubt would be well and truly scuppered.'

'Oh my God.' Fliss groaned. 'You're right. I can't do it, can I?'

'I don't think you can. Or at least, you can't take Emma with you. You're going to have to make a choice, Fliss.'

'I couldn't leave Emma!'

'There you are then. Decision made.'

Fliss buried her head in her hands. Maggie was right, she knew. Martin wouldn't let her take Emma, and no court would take her side if she applied for custody. Her only hope would be to smuggle Emma out, but she couldn't see how she could get a passport for her without Martin's knowledge. Without a passport she couldn't fly, and she couldn't possibly subject a two year old to an Atlantic crossing in a small boat. But she couldn't go without her either. It was utterly unthinkable. Fliss remembered that dreadful time they had been separated when Emma was just a few weeks old. If it had been unbearable then, how much more so would it be now? She couldn't do it, she absolutely couldn't do it. Even if it meant losing the only man she had ever loved. Fate had dealt her an impossible hand; there could be no winners here, however she played it.

The week that followed was one of the longest of Fliss's life. She counted off the days, feeling like a prisoner on death row with the prospect of the noose coming ever closer. At the end of the week she pictured Jeff catching his flight back to England, driving down to Cornwall from Heathrow. They'd arranged that he would call her the next day at the phone box down the lane; she was shaking all over again as she put Emma in her pushchair and set out. Emma had sensed her mother's tension; she was grizzling and restless. When Fliss parked the pushchair beside the telephone box to wait, she kept trying to climb out.

'Sit still, Emma, for goodness' sake!' Fliss thrust a rag book with pictures of dogs into her hands – Emma tossed it down on the grass verge. 'Please, please, will you behave!'

She kept checking her watch as she waited for the phone to ring – eleven o'clock, the appointed time, a minute past, three minutes, five . . . Why didn't he phone! Had something happened to him? Had he come back to England at all? Had he changed his mind about wanting her to run away with him? Was he dead? She went into the kiosk, jiggled the receiver, went out again. Emma started to scream – one of her rare but extremely powerful tantrums.

'Oh, stop it, Emma . . .!' Her voice tailed away. A car was coming up the hill, a bright yellow car with a very distinctive shape to the bonnet. It couldn't be . . . could it? Oh my God, it was – she was sure it was – Jeff's Ford Consul! It was slowing, pulling into the side of the road. Jeff was getting out . . .

'What are you doing here?' she demanded.

'Well I figured it would be better than a phone call. I wanted to see you, honey, not just hear your voice.'

'Oh Jeff!' The love was welling up in her, and fierce longing. And with it, the terrible, choking despair. Hard enough to tell him on the telephone that she couldn't go with him, but to have to do it in person, looking at the face whose every line she knew and adored, was the most terrible prospect imaginable. How could she do it? But she had to. She had no choice.

'This is Emma, I presume,' he said, smiling at the little girl, who had forgotten her tantrum to gaze at him, wide-eyed.

'Yes. But you shouldn't have come.' She glanced up and down the road anxiously. 'Suppose someone should see us?'

He raised a quizzical eyebrow. 'Does that matter now?'

Sudden tears thickened her throat.

'Well . . . yes. It does. Jeff . . . I'm really sorry, but . . .'

His jaw tightened, but all the life seemed to have left his face. 'Right. You're not coming with me.'

'I can't. Jeff, I can't. I want to. I really, really want to, but . . .'

'Not enough.'

Her heart felt as if it was breaking. 'There's nothing in the world I want more. But . . . I can't leave Emma. Just look at her, Jeff. She needs me!'

'So bring her with you.'

'Martin would never let me have her. I know that now. Oh, don't look like that, please, I can't bear it. You must understand. I can't abandon my child!'

'No. I guess I can see that.' But he looked hurt, all the same, so terribly hurt. 'Well, if that's what you've decided, there's nothing more to say.'

She caught at his hand, her tear-filled eyes gazing into his.

'I love you!'

A bleak smile twisted the corner of his mouth. 'And I love you. But I guess it's not enough. Right, well, in that case there's no point prolonging the agony.' He had reverted to his old, blasé self.

The tears were hot in her eyes, spasming in her throat. 'You will keep in touch?'

'I shouldn't think so.'

Panic filled her at the thought of losing contact so completely, so finally.

'Don't you have an address you could give me? Just so I'd know where I could find you if . . .'

'I didn't think that was going to happen.' But he fished in the glove compartment of his car, found a scrap of paper and a pen, and wrote down an address in Maine, New England. 'That's my home address. I don't suppose I'll be there, but I expect it would find me eventually.'

As he passed it to her, his fingers squeezed hers briefly.

'That's it, then, hon.'

Her throat spasmed again. *Don't go! Please don't go!* she wanted to cry, but no words came. They would do no good. And she couldn't even hug him, here on a public road, just a few hundred yards from her home.

He got into the car, raised a hand briefly to her, his mouth twisted into a tight grimace. The car's engine revved hard and the tyres screamed as he executed a manic three-point turn, and then he was gone. Fliss watched through a mist of tears as the yellow Consul raced away down the hill, disappeared round the bend at its foot.

There was nothing left for her to do but go home.

The darkness was enveloping her again. She could feel it closing in, the same suffocating fog she had experienced before, and it terrified her. She fought it, but it was stronger than she was. She tried to hide it, but she couldn't. She trembled constantly, was forever on the verge of tears, couldn't take the slightest interest in her appearance, couldn't face leaving the house. Martin noticed it, and shook his head wearily. 'Oh Fliss, not again, please!' She wanted to say she couldn't help it, but that sounded so pathetic; she wanted him to understand, though she knew she had no right to expect it. She wanted him to treat her gently, give her some ray of hope that she would get through this, find life worth living again. But Martin had worries of his own; the year the bank had given him to turn the business around was almost up and he was nowhere near out of the woods. The debt was dragging him down; he thought the chances were that he was not only going to lose the garage, but be declared bankrupt.

And then one night as she lay sleepless, the idea came to her like a bolt of lightning. A wild, crazy idea that emerged from the shadows and would, no doubt, retreat with first light.

But it didn't. As Fliss thought about it, she was filled with euphoria, surging in her veins, lifting her out of the depths of despair into which she had sunk. Would it work? Could it work? Oh, it must – it must! She couldn't live without Jeff and she couldn't live without Emma. This way . . .

Like a crazed woman Fliss set about working out the details that would turn fantasy into reality and change the course of all their lives.

Part Three
1989

THIRTEEN

MIKE

It's Sunday morning. Sunday is the day I usually devote to Daisy, and I feel guilty as hell that instead of being at home with her, taking her out perhaps, to Weston-super-Mare or Bristol Zoo, I'm sitting over a pot of coffee and the remains of a full English breakfast in a Falmouth B&B. But needs must where the devil drives, as they say. If I don't make some serious money soon we're going to be in deep schmuck and there won't be any cash to spare for an ice cream or a donkey ride on the beach, never mind the entrance fee to the zoo. If only I can make this story work, I can turn things around.

Yesterday afternoon that was beginning to seem increasingly unlikely. To my relief, though, I've had a couple of breaks. Small ones, it's true, but hey, a small break could lead to a big one.

The first came after I left Emma Dunning – or rather, she left me, with depressing haste. I went back into Falmouth to have another crack at talking to people in the sailing community and gathering all the background information I could, since it had occurred to me that if the biggie – the Felicity Penrose story – hits the buffers, I might at least be able to salvage a story, or even a series, about women sailors from the wreckage. Of course I also asked questions about Simon Beacham, the name that came up as a possibility for a man she might have run off with. But apart from one weathered old boatman, no one had ever heard of him, and the old fella wasn't much help.

'Simon Beacham! Now there's a name from the past!' he said, looping a bowline round a bollard to make his little boat fast.

Hope sprang. 'You knew him?'

'Oh ah, I knew 'im all right. Funny bugger. 'E used t' 'ave one o' them lock-ups.' He jerked his head in the direction of the road that runs between the marina and the town. 'Did repairs, mended sails, that kind of thing. 'E's been gone years now, though. Went to Americky, I 'eard.'

America again. It seemed to keep cropping up.

'And Felicity Penrose . . . did you know her?'

'Oh, I knowed Fliss all right. We all knowed Fliss. She was a cracker and no mistake. Terrible thing that were. She drownded.'

'Were they friendly, Simon and Felicity?' I asked.

'Couldn't say. 'E did work on 'er boat, that I do know. Al'us boasting about it, 'e was. 'E fancied 'er, I reckon. Well, we all did.' The old man's face cracked a smile, deepening the creases in his weather-beaten cheeks. 'A cracker. That's what she were. A proper little cracker. And always a friendly word. Never got above 'erself, that one.'

'Was he a local, Simon Beacham?' I asked. The woman I'd spoken to at Penryn had said not, but she could have been mistaken.

The old boatman's eyes narrowed.

'What's your interest in 'im?' he asked suspiciously.

He's the only name I've got for a link to Felicity Penrose. But I couldn't say that.

'My father used to sail — I'm trying to trace old pals for him,' I lied.

'Sorry — can't 'elp you. And no, 'e weren't local. Something in me water tells me 'e came from Bristol, but I might have that wrong. It's a long time ago, and I never knew 'im that well.' He straightened up, wiping his hands on the seat of his trousers and extracting a tobacco pouch from a pocket.

'I got to get going. If I'm late for me tea my missus'll 'ave my guts for garters.'

'Thanks anyway.'

He nodded sagely. 'Good luck to you. You'll need it, I reckon.'

He was right there! But at least I had one smidgeon of information. If Simon Beacham *had* hailed from Bristol, there was a chance that he had family still living in the area, and Bristol is only half an hour or so's drive up the road from where I live in Somerset. Added to which, Beacham isn't exactly a common name. If he'd been called Smith or Jones I might have had a problem, but Beacham . . . I could check local phone directories and voters' registers when I got home and I might just strike lucky.

My second break came when I got back to my car and retrieved my mobile phone from the glove compartment. I don't tend to carry it around with me unless I'm expecting a call or think I'm likely to want to make one – it's too damn heavy, like lugging a brick around. I should have made the effort, though – I'd missed two calls.

The first was Daisy.

'Where are you, Daddy? Just wanted to tell you Gran's bought me a Sindy horse. How super is that? It's not even my birthday! Oh, and a new pair of sandals – *bor-ing*! Night, night, Daddy!'

I grinned, shaking my head. How long would it be before it was sandals, or clothes of some kind, rather than toys that Daisy got excited about? Not nearly long enough, I suspected. If I so much as blinked, my little girl would be a young woman before I knew it.

Then, as the second call clicked on, I forgot all about Daisy growing up, doing a double-take in shock. It was Emma Dunning, apologising for being short with me earlier, and saying we needed to talk again.

Now that really was a turn-up for the books! I listened to the message twice, and felt like punching the air in triumph, though to be honest, I don't really think she knows anything about her mother's disappearance. I'm pretty sure she was totally shocked by what I had to say. But if I can get her onside it will give me a foot in the camp, and hey – you never know what that might lead to.

I phoned her back right away, sitting there in my car, looking out over the sea, turned scarlet on the horizon by the setting sun.

It took a while for her to answer; I was just beginning to think she couldn't be home when she picked up.

'Emma Dunning.'

'Emma, it's Mike Bond. You called me.'

In just the smallest of telltale silences I could picture all over again the look of shock on her face when I'd approached her. But when she spoke her voice was steely, determined.

'Are you still in Falmouth?'

'I am, yes.'

'I really need to talk to you again. Do you think we could meet?'

'Sure thing.'

'Tomorrow?'

'I don't see why not. Where do you suggest?'

'I live in Launceston. I know a nice pub that would be about halfway for both of us.'

'OK, give me the details.'

Searching for something to write on, I spotted an envelope that was lying in the well between the seats. A red reminder for the electricity bill. Shit – I still hadn't done anything about that!

My notepad was there too; I flipped it open and scribbled down her directions.

'What time?'

'Say midday?'

'I'll be there.'

After the call ended I sat a while longer, thinking. Then, before I forgot all about it again, I made out a cheque for the electricity bill, put it in the envelope, and walked till I found a post box. The last thing I wanted was to have our electricity cut off – though I hoped there was enough cash in my current account to cover the cheque. I didn't want to have to pay overdraft charges either. But who knew? Better times might be just around the corner.

I'm still feeling quite cheerful as I sit over the remains of my breakfast. I have a couple of hours to kill before I head up the A30 to meet Emma. If I get my ass into gear I can go down to the marina and do a bit more asking around. Something about this story is going to break soon, I'm sure of it. And where my instincts are concerned, I'm not often wrong.

I get to the pub early – I allowed myself plenty of time in case I had problems finding the place – but Emma is already there, perched on a bar stool with a glass of something long and cold at her elbow. This morning she's wearing grey drawstring trousers and a tight-fitting little cardigan over a vest top in acidic green, and her hair, which was tied back in a ponytail yesterday, is falling loose across her shoulders. When she catches sight of me she doesn't smile a greeting, but then I wouldn't expect her to. She just gives me a direct look, those greeny-blue eyes challenging.

'You found it then.'

'No trouble. Sorry if I've kept you waiting.'

'No, I was early.' She nods in the direction of double doors on one side of the room. 'There's a beer garden outside. It might be a bit more private.'

No preliminaries, no beating about the bush. Emma Dunning is clearly a woman who goes straight to the point, and I rather like her for it.

'Can I get you another drink?' I offer.

'No, I'm OK thanks.'

The bartender, who has been talking to a couple of men at the far end of the bar, slopes up and I order a pint of lemonade and lime. While I'm paying for it Emma slides off her stool, drink in hand, and stands waiting for me by the open double doors. Outside, we find a seat at the far side of the beer garden, well away from a family gathered around a wooden picnic-style table and incorporated bench and the blue plastic slide on which their children are playing noisily.

'I was quite surprised to get your call,' I say, when we're sitting down. 'I got the impression yesterday that you really didn't want to talk to me.'

'I was pretty shocked yesterday,' Emma says. 'Now I want to know what this is all about.'

'OK.' I take a long pull of my lemonade and lime. 'To be honest, though, I already told you pretty much all I know. That your mother was seen in Florida some time after she supposedly drowned.'

'By whom?'

'A Mrs Barbara Gooding.'

'Who the hell is she?'

'Someone who lived in Cornwall before she and her husband moved to the States.'

'And that's it? You're trying to rake muck on the basis of the say-so of someone who probably hadn't seen my mother for years?'

'According to her husband, she was pretty sure.'

'According to her husband?'

'Barbara died some years ago. But her husband says she was convinced it was Felicity she had seen.'

'So why didn't she say something at the time? Why has this only come up now?'

'I don't know.' I don't want to admit that in the beginning Barbara's husband had talked her into believing she must have been mistaken. It weakens my case, already pretty thin on hard evidence, to the point of collapse.

'Do you know a Simon Beacham?' I ask bluntly.

'Never heard of him.'

Damn. Perhaps I should have saved that question for Martin and Maggie Dunning if – when – I get to see them. Now they'll be forewarned, unless I can get to them first.

I'm toying with whether or not to tell Emma that Barbara

Gooding had said Felicity had been with a man when she saw her, but before I've decided Emma pushes her drink to one side and leans forward on her elbows.

'Is he the man my mother is supposed to have run away with?'

I set my own drink down sharply on the table.

'What makes you say that?'

She shrugs. 'You don't have to be a genius to work it out. If there is any truth in this story – and I say if – then she must have had a reason for faking her death. She didn't benefit financially; it was my father who got the insurance payout on her life.'

Ah – so there was an insurance payout. Interesting.

'It couldn't have had anything to do with her wanting to be free to continue sailing,' Emma continues. 'My father never stood in her way, and in any case she could hardly do something spectacular like a solo round-the-world trip without being recognised, and no one has ever claimed that a Felicity Penrose lookalike has popped up in any of the big races. That leaves love – or lust. Though to be honest, if it was that, I can't see why she didn't just bolt.'

I nod. The same thing had occurred to me. But given her extreme reaction yesterday, I'm a little surprised that Emma should have reached the same conclusion, and even more surprised that she should couch it in those terms, and the hard, matter-of-fact tone of her voice. It's a protective shell, I guess – beneath it, I'm pretty sure, she must be devastated by the thought that her mother could abandon her so heartlessly.

'Unless, of course, she wanted to give us a leaving present – the insurance money,' Emma goes on in the same brittle tone. 'I have to be honest with you here – I think my father's business was in pretty dire straits financially around the time she disappeared, and it was the payout on her life that got him out of a mess, paid for the franchise, and set him on the road to success. Having said that, I don't think it helps your case much. The insurance company wouldn't have paid out if there'd been the slightest suspicion that Fliss wasn't actually dead.'

Again, I'm a bit taken aback by her directness, but hey, I'm not about to look a gift horse in the mouth.

'Have you talked to your family about it?' I ask.

'Well of course I have!' she says shortly.

'And?'

'Maggie was as shocked as I was.'

But there's just the tiniest hesitation before she says it, which makes me wonder if in this, at least, she isn't keeping something back.

'Look,' she goes on, as if reading my thoughts, 'I'm sorry if I gave you the impression I was going to tell you something relevant to my mother's disappearance. If so, I'm afraid I've wasted your time. I've got absolutely no reason to doubt that she died when I was two years old. Nothing!' She emphasises the word with a fierce nod of her head, and the dark blond hair comes loose from behind her ear, framing her heart-shaped face.

'All right,' I say, 'I believe you. To be truthful, I wasn't hopeful that you could tell me anything new. But . . .'

'The reasons I wanted to see you are entirely selfish, I'm afraid. If there's a chance that my mother is still alive – which I'm not for one moment admitting – I want to know about it. And not by reading about it in some newspaper exposé.' She finishes her drink and sets the empty glass down on the table, looking at me very directly. 'Will you keep me in the loop, please? If you do find out anything, will you let me know? I don't want any nasty surprises. OK?'

'OK.' I indicate her empty glass. 'Can I get you another drink?'

She hesitates. 'I'm driving, but I'll risk a spritzer.' She smiles bleakly. 'I could do with something a good deal stronger, but . . .'

I go back into the pub, leaving her sitting in the beer garden. When I come back with the drinks, she cuts a lonely figure, sitting with her chin cupped in her hands, staring into space, and once again I feel sorry for her. This might be just a story to me – albeit one that could improve my fortunes no end – but it's her life. I can't imagine how she must be feeling, and I don't want to. I have to remain detached.

When I put the drink in front of her she takes a long pull, then looks at me over the rim of the glass.

'This man you mentioned, Simon . . .?'

'Beacham.'

'Yes. Him. What makes you think he might have been involved with my mother?'

I wonder how I can put this delicately. 'Someone I was talking to suggested it. She thought they might have been having an affair. And apparently he disappeared off the scene shortly after your mother went missing. The general consensus of opinion is that he went to America. And has not been heard of since.'

'Right.' I can see her thinking about this, and not liking it. 'That does seem a bit strange, I must admit. Unless he was in love with her, and so upset by her death that he wanted to get as far away as possible from anything that reminded him of her.'

'You seem quite prepared to accept that Felicity might have had an affair,' I say, probing gently.

'From things Maggie has said, I'd gathered that my mother was no angel.' She pulls a wry face. 'But it's actually running away with him, leaving me, that I find so hard to stomach,' she adds.

'I'm sure it is, and I'm sorry . . .'

She gives me a look that says she rather doubts that, then straightens her shoulders.

'Anyway, I want to get to the bottom of it now as much as you do. I'll see if I can find out anything about this man. Trouble is, apart from the locals, the sailing community is quite transient. A lot of them tend to go where the wind takes them. And if you're right, and he did help my mother pull off a stunt and then went off to meet up with her somewhere, I don't imagine he would have kept in touch with anyone who knew her. He'd cut all ties, wouldn't he? Maybe even change his name.' She pauses. 'And so, I suppose, would my mother. Change her name, I mean.'

'Almost certainly she would have had to,' I agree. 'If she left the country soon after she was supposed to have drowned – before the story, and her photograph, hit the news – I dare say she could have used her own passport. But to start a new life . . . that would be a different matter entirely. Even if she managed to keep below the radar, I can't see that she could go on being Felicity Penrose. Much too risky.

'Simon, though . . . He wasn't a missing person, or a wanted one, and getting a new identity isn't that easy. I imagine it's pretty expensive, not to mention illegal. I have to hope he didn't think it was necessary, since he's really the only link we have.'

Emma is silent, pushing her hair behind her ear again and resting her chin on her hand. Then she says:

'Even if that is what happened, there's no guarantee they're still together.'

'True. But it would be a good starting point.'

'The one sure thing is that my mother would never have given up sailing,' she says decisively. 'Maybe she could never have gone high-profile again, but she would have to be around boats. And actually, now that I come to think of it, that is the strongest argument that says you are wrong. Sailing the big races was my mother's life. She'd know that if she faked her death, all that would be over. A new identity would be worthless unless she got a face transplant too. The first time her picture appeared in a newspaper or on TV she'd be recognised. In fact, now that I come to think about it, there would have been a good chance of her being recognised anywhere in the sailing community.'

'America is a big place, and not very interested in anything, or anyone, not American,' I say. 'And in any case, she *was* seen, and recognised, remember.'

'By a woman who hadn't seen her for years. By sheer chance. Sailing isn't a parochial sport. All nationalities are in it together.'

'At the top level, yes. But recreationally . . . there must be thousands of little marinas where you could go unnoticed. All the races your mother did were UK-based, weren't they? I'd lay bets none of them got more than a paragraph's coverage in the

US press, if that. And though her death might have been big news here in Cornwall, I can't imagine it would have been in America.'

But who am I trying to convince? If she had faked her own death and started a new life under an assumed identity she was taking a hell of a risk, especially if she wanted to go on sailing, which apparently had been something of an obsession with her. Could it be that I'm wrong about the whole thing? That I'm so desperate for a big story that I've let my enthusiasm run away with me? So far I've got nothing whatever to go on but a supposed sighting by a woman who might very well have been mistaken, and my own instincts.

Instincts I've learned to trust. There is something here, deep down I'm sure of it.

I remember the tiny hesitation when I asked Emma about her family's reaction to the news that I was investigating Felicity's death.

'You mentioned Maggie,' I say. 'She was your mother's sister, wasn't she?'

Emma's eyes narrow slightly.

'Yes.'

'So how long after Felicity disappeared did she and your father get married?'

'Well, after my mother was declared dead . . . Oh!' She breaks off, covering her mouth with her hand. 'Of course! That means . . . if my mother isn't dead . . . Oh, what a mess this all is!'

I try to distance myself from her obvious distress.

'And were they together before they were able to get married?' I ask.

'Oh yes . . . Maggie stepped in to look after me, and . . .' Again she stops short, a look of outrage sharpening her features. 'Hey, hang on, you're not suggesting . . .?'

'I'm not suggesting anything, just trying to get the facts straight,' I try to pacify her, though actually she's read my thoughts pretty accurately. Felicity might not have been the only wayward one in that marriage. And if her husband had been carrying on with her sister, it added a whole new dimension to the scenario.

'I won't have you casting aspersions on Dad and Maggie,' Emma said furiously. 'They are two of the most morally-minded people I know. Maggie can be quite strait-laced, actually, and Dad . . . well, I know he adored my mother. He would never have cheated on her, it just wouldn't be in his nature. Especially with her own sister. That's one thing I am absolutely sure of.' She breaks off as another thought strikes her. 'Look, I don't know whether he knows yet that you're here, muck-raking. Maggie asked me not to say anything to him yesterday – she wanted to tell him in her own time. She knew how much it's going to distress him. So I'd very much appreciate it if you promise me you won't go over there doorstepping them. Anything you want to know, please ask me, and I'll help you all I can. But I don't want you upsetting them. Do I have your word?'

Damn. I had planned to call on them before going home to Somerset. But on balance I think it is probably more use to me to have Emma on board at this stage. They would almost certainly be hostile; Emma, at least, seems to want to get at the truth, whatever that might be.

I look at her, this feisty young woman who looks so much like her mother, and wonder what outcome she is hoping for. Does she want Felicity to be alive so much that she's prepared to pay the price of knowing she has been abandoned and deceived? Or would she prefer to keep her illusions and what few memories she has intact? I don't know, and I'm not going to ask her, but I find myself hoping that whichever it turns out to be, she isn't going to be too badly hurt. I like her, a lot. I like her directness, and I like the edge of vulnerability beneath the bravado. She's just a nice, and very attractive, girl who's been landed with a situation in which she can't win. She doesn't deserve all this. And I'm sorry I'm the one who's opened the can of worms. But I can't allow myself to be sidetracked, or get emotionally involved. It's too important for me and for Daisy, and besides, it's now much too late to back off. The damage has been done.

Emma finishes her drink.

'That's about it, then, isn't it? I'll ask around, see if I can find out anything about this Simon Beacham, and if I do, I'll let you know.'

'That would be good.'

'And you'll keep me posted on anything you might find out?'

'I will.'

'Thank you.' She sighs. 'I wish none of this had ever happened, but it has, and I can't just ignore it and hope it will go away. If my mother is alive I want to find her.'

'You and me both.'

'I know. Which is why I'm prepared to help you.'

We walk out to the pub car park.

'Bye then,' she says.

I watch as she drives away and am surprised by a sudden feeling of regret. No time to ponder it now, though. I have far too much to do and time is running out. I get into my own car and head back to Falmouth for one last crack at learning something new.

FOURTEEN

EMMA

I'm driving on a familiar road, but I know I'm not concentrating as I should. I feel as though a feather pillow has exploded inside my head; though my thoughts are spinning, I can't seem to catch any of them.

Is it possible Fliss did the unthinkable and faked her own death? If so, why? Who is this Simon Beacham, and was he involved with her? Where is he now? Has my mother actually been alive the whole of my life and I never knew it? Does Maggie know something – is that the reason she was so against me pursuing this, because she is afraid of what I might find out? And Dad – did Maggie not want me to tell him in case he blurted out something that might give the game away? There was something very odd about her reaction when I told her about Mike Bond and his allegations. She was shocked and upset, yes, but not in the way I'd have expected her to be. And it was that, more than anything, that made me think there *was* more to Mike Bond's story than just sensational fiction dressed up as fact.

I have to talk to Maggie again. I have to talk to Dad. I'm already halfway to Porthtowan – I might as well head on down there now.

Philip won't be best pleased – though we haven't made any firm arrangements, he'll be half expecting to see me today. Could be he's been around to my place already, knocking on the door and wondering why I'm not home. But I'm afraid Philip is way down my list of priorities just now. In fact, he's barely on the radar. Only yesterday morning I was all chewed up because I'm not at all sure our relationship is working any more, wondering whether perhaps the best thing would be to end it so that we can both be free to find someone we're better suited to; now yesterday seems like a lifetime ago. Sometime soon I am going to have to make a decision – do I want to be with him or not? But one thing at a time. I'm already in emotional overload; I can't handle anything else just now.

Trying to concentrate on the road, I head for Porthtowan.

Of course I should have thought this through. Sunday lunch is a ritual for Dad and Maggie. A roast with all the trimmings, a bottle of wine, a lazy hour afterwards when they pretend to read the Sunday papers but actually have a sneaky nap. They haven't quite reached that point when I arrive; they're still eating pudding – one of Maggie's legendary apple pies with home-made custard and a plop of clotted cream.

'Emma!' Maggie exclaims as I appear in the doorway, having rung the bell and let myself in. 'What are you doing here? Why didn't you let me know you were coming? We'd have waited for you.'

The delicious aroma of roasted beef is lingering, but for once I'm not at all tempted.

'It's OK. I'm not hungry.'

'You don't eat properly, my girl! Sit down and I'll make up a plate for you. There's plenty over.'

There would be. Maggie cooks for an army.

'No – really . . .'

'Don't argue.' She's abandoned her apple pie and is putting slices of beef on a plate. 'I'll pop the vegetables and gravy in the microwave. They'll be hot again in sixty seconds flat.'

It's pointless to argue, I know that from bitter experience. But I'm puzzled and a bit perturbed. After our conversation yesterday

Maggie must know why I'm here, yet she's behaving as if nothing has happened.

Dad, though . . . Dad's a different animal. I've been wondering if Maggie has told him about Mike Bond; now I know instantly that she has. Dad hasn't said a word since I arrived, apart from 'Hello, Emma,' and his discomfort is palpable. That's Dad all over; when he's upset about something he goes into his cave. I decide to let him finish his apple pie before I drag him out by saying my piece, and Maggie makes that easy by keeping up a constant stream of chatter, fussing over the dinner she's determined to make me eat, then sitting down at the table with us.

I can't help noticing, though, that her own apple pie is more or less untouched, and she is refilling her wine glass rather frequently. When I've struggled through roast beef, Yorkshire pudding, cauliflower cheese and carrots, and Maggie is making coffee, I feel the time has come when I must say something.

'Maggie's told you what happened yesterday, I suppose,' I say to Dad.

'She has, yes.' But he's avoiding looking at me.

'And?'

He shrugs, shaking his head and sighing, but saying nothing. This is like pulling teeth.

'Dad? You don't think there's any truth in it, do you?'

I don't quite know why I put it like that when I have the most horrible gut feeling that there is something in it. Probably I'm just looking for reassurance. I'm not a little girl any more, but he's still my dad, and a part of me still looks to him to make bad things better.

It's Maggie who answers, though, banging the cafetière down on the table for emphasis.

'Of course there's nothing in it!'

'What do you think, Dad?' I persist.

He looks up then, and I'm shocked and saddened by the way his face seems to have aged suddenly, the contours less defined, the creases more pronounced.

'I don't know, Emma,' he says.

'Of course you know!' Maggie says forcefully. 'Fliss would never have done something like that. It's ridiculous. Why anyone should come up with such an outrageous suggestion is beyond me. And I can't believe that you could give credence to it for a single moment!'

'She was behaving very strangely for some time before it happened,' Dad says. He's talking to Maggie, not to me, and I get the feeling they've had this conversation before, when she told him about Mike Bond and his assertions, presumably. 'You know how depressed she was. You were as worried about her as I was. And you know what we thought at the time.'

Maggie huffs loudly.

'Well, yes. And that would have been halfway feasible, given her state of mind . . .'

'What did you think at the time?' I ask.

Dad looks back at me.

'We thought she might have done something stupid.'

I'm horrified. 'You mean . . .?'

'That she'd taken her own life, yes. She had bouts of depression – really bad bouts. When they hit her she just . . . changed. It was awful. She was in this dark place and there was no getting through to her.'

I shake my head, trying to take in this image of my mother that is so unlike the one I've always cherished.

'You never said.'

'There wouldn't have been any point, would there? And it wasn't the real Fliss. The real Fliss was full of life, full of fun . . . she's the one I want to remember. The one I wanted you to know.'

His eyes tear up; he looks away abruptly, regaining control of himself. Maggie squeezes his shoulder; he brushes her away. He's impatient of shows of emotion, my dad, in himself or anyone else.

'Anyway,' he goes on after a moment, 'she said more than once that we'd be better off without her, and we did wonder if she'd

185

been in such a state that she really believed that, and did away with herself. Now . . .' He breaks off.

'Now you wonder if she couldn't bring herself to do that, and ran away instead,' I say.

Actually, it's quite a comforting thought. Still pretty awful, especially if I stop to imagine for one moment just how wretched she must have been to even contemplate doing something so drastic, but from my point of view, less hurtful than thinking she'd cared so little for me that she simply abandoned me for selfish reasons. A mother who runs because she think you'll be better off without her, and loves you too much, is, however misguided, infinitely preferable to one who doesn't care about you, doesn't love you at all.

But it still leaves too many unanswered questions. Where did she go? Why has she never come back? How did she manage to disappear so completely? Someone must have helped her – she couldn't have swum to shore from way out to sea where her boat had been found. Someone else must have been involved, and who could that be but a friend – or a lover? Which bring us right back to the man Mike Bond is looking for. The man who seems to have disappeared as completely as my mother.

'Do either of you know a Simon Beacham?' I ask.

Dad hardly seems to hear me; he's gone back into his own private world. But Maggie hears all right. In the act of depressing the plunger in the cafetière, she freezes, and shock and alarm are written all over her face.

'You do know him,' I say.

Maggie is struggling to recover herself.

'*Used* to know him, yes. A very long time ago.'

'We're talking about a long time ago. More than thirty years.'

'Surely you're not suggesting . . .' Maggie looks outraged.

'His name has come up,' I say. 'He disappeared, it seems, not long after Felicity was reported drowned. And no one knows what happened to him. A bit of a coincidence, don't you think?'

'I don't see why,' Maggie snaps. 'The sailing crowd come and go all the time – you know that. Where did you get this from, anyway?'

'I've met Mike Bond again. I—'

Maggie reacts violently. 'Emma – I warned you! I told you not to . . .'

'Well I'm afraid I don't necessarily do as I'm told any more. I want to get to the bottom of this. Mike Bond is doing a lot of digging, and if he comes up with anything, I'd like to know about it. You know the old saying – better to have him inside the tent than outside. At least that way we get to know what he's up to – what he's found out. And I want to know the truth, even if you don't.'

'She's right, Maggie,' Dad says decisively. 'Who is he, Emma, this reporter? Do you have a number for him? I'd like to talk to him myself.'

'Oh for goodness' sake!' Maggie explodes. 'What is the matter with the pair of you? Fliss is dead! Why can't you accept it?'

'We don't *know* that she's dead, Maggie,' Dad says. 'She's been *declared* dead. But what if she isn't? What if the silly girl faked her own death because she couldn't go on any more, because she was deluded into thinking we'd be better off without her? What if she regretted it afterwards, but couldn't come back and admit what she'd done?'

'This is nonsense!'

'You may be right. But she wouldn't have been able to, would she? Think of the implications! It's a really serious thing to have done. She'd have been ashamed, afraid of the repercussions . . . However desperate she was, she'd feel there was no way back. What if she's still out there somewhere, lonely, unhappy . . .'

'You want her to still be alive, don't you?' Maggie shoots at him, her voice trembling. 'Doesn't it mean anything to you that we've been together for thirty years?'

'Well of course it does!'

'It doesn't look that way from where I'm standing. You've never got over her, have you? You've never stopped loving her!'

'Maggie!' I protest, horribly embarrassed.

She rounds on me, more out of control than I've ever seen her.

'And *you* want her back too, Emma. That's what this is all about. I've brought you up, always been there for you, but it's Fliss you want. You're determined to find her, never mind how much you hurt *me* in the process!'

'Stop this, Maggie!' Dad's tone is dangerously low, the tone that used to put the fear of God into me when I was a little girl. He never laid a finger on me, never needed to. That tone was enough.

She stops. Her eyes go wide, then squeeze shut; she covers her mouth with her hand. There's a flood of tears still locked inside, I know, that will erupt through the fragile barrier at any moment.

'Maggie . . .' I go to her, put my arm around her. 'Maggie, we love you – we both love you. This isn't a popularity contest – we're not choosing her over you. It's just that we have to know the truth. I'd have thought you'd want that too. She was your sister, after all.'

Maggie mumbles something unintelligible.

'Come on,' I say, 'sit down. Have another drink.'

She laughs hollowly.

'You think I'm an alcoholic or something?'

'Don't be silly. I just think a drink would do you good. You're upset.'

Dad is doing nothing to comfort Maggie. He's looking at her very hard.

'Do you know something we don't, Maggie? Is that what this is all about?'

She doesn't answer; I flash him a warning glance. *Don't make things worse.*

I find a bottle of Tia Maria in the chiffonier, pour some into a little shot glass, put it down on the table in front of her. In spite of her protestations she drinks it in one swallow.

'You don't understand, either of you,' she mutters. And then, louder: 'Don't either of you realise the implications of all this?'

'Of course we do. We're not stupid. But we can't just pretend this hasn't happened. We have to get to the bottom of it, love,' Dad says reasonably.

But Maggie shakes her head. 'Fliss is dead. That's all there is to it. Why can't we just leave it at that?'

I'm uncomfortably sure that there is a reason for her being so upset, something she's not saying. She knows far more than she'll admit about what happened to my mother.

I shiver as a goose walks over my grave. But I'm more determined than ever. I have to find out the truth. How I'm going to do it, I'm not sure. And if Maggie is going to be hurt by it – and Dad too – I'm sorry. But I simply cannot rest until I know what happened to my mother. And in this at least I have an ally, if a very unlikely one.

Mike Bond promised to keep me in the loop. I only hope he keeps that promise.

It's six o'clock by the time I get home, and as I let myself in I hear the telephone ringing. Damn! I really don't feel like answering it, and I hold off a moment or two, hoping it will stop. It doesn't, and the insistent shrilling gets to me. I find it difficult to ignore a telephone at the best of times, and right now it's impossible. It could be Dad. It could be Mike Bond. If I don't catch it, I'll never know.

I pick up, half expecting to hear the dialling tone that will tell me my unknown caller has rung off. But no. And it's not Dad or Mike Bond, it's Philip.

'Emma! Where have you been? I've been trying to get hold of you all day.' He sounds peeved.

'Not all day,' I object. 'I was here until about half past eleven this morning.'

'Well where have you been since then?'

I'm becoming irritated. Hardly surprising, really, after the day I've had.

'Out.'

'So I gather. But where?'

Typical Philip, but absolutely the wrong thing to say to me, especially at the moment, as (a) I don't want to go into it all just now, and (b) I don't like him assuming I have to answer to him. I feel like snapping back that it's none of his business, but I stop short of that. It would, after all, be unkind and uncalled for.

'I've been to Porthtowan,' I say reluctantly.

'You went to Porthtowan yesterday,' he objects.

'There's no law that says I can't go again. They are my family, after all.'

'Well, now that you are there . . .'

'Philip, if you're going to suggest going out, please don't,' I say. 'I'm dreadfully tired. I'm sorry. And I've got an awful lot going on at the moment.'

'There's a long silence, then Philip says:

'Are you trying to give me the brush-off?'

'Oh Philip . . .'

Perhaps I am doing just that; if I find his persistence annoying rather than endearing, if I can't be bothered to talk to him, then perhaps I've made up my mind without realising it. But I really don't need this just now. And if I am going to end things, it shouldn't be over the telephone. Philip deserves better.

'Look, can we talk about this some other time? It really isn't a good moment.'

'When is?' The emphasis is sarcastic rather than a legitimate question.

I sigh, feeling horribly guilty now on top of everything else.

'Oh, all right, come over if you want to,' I say, with not very good grace. 'But don't expect me to be good company. Something pretty devastating has happened, and I can't really think about anything else.'

'What?'

'I'll tell you when you get here.'

While I'm waiting for him to arrive, I change into a Dash tracksuit because unaccountably I suddenly feel cold, chilled through and through, and huddle myself into a ball on the sofa with a tartan travel rug wrapped round me and a large glass of Lambrusco within easy reach.

Philip comes in, a tall, dark, good-looking bloke with longish hair that's not quite a mullet and a Tom Selleck moustache.

'God, Emma, you look awful!' he says by way of greeting.

'Well thanks a lot! That makes me feel much better! There's some Lambrusco there if you want a glass.'

'I'd rather have a beer.'

'There's some in the fridge. Help yourself.'

He disappears into the kitchen, comes back with a Becks, which he proceeds to drink straight from the bottle.

'What's all this about then?'

'Oh Philip, it's such a mess. I don't know where to start . . .'

But I think that perhaps it would be good to talk it all over with someone not emotionally involved.

As I talk, Philip sits down beside me and tries to put his arm around me. I shrink away. 'Don't, please.'

He looks hurt, but withdraws.

'Well,' he says when I've finished. 'This is bloody unbelievable.'

'I know. I just don't know what to think, Philip. I don't even really know what I want the outcome to be. Part of me would like her to be alive, and part of me . . . Well, the implications are huge, aren't they? Not only for me, but for Dad and Maggie too . . . It's an absolute nightmare.'

'I can see that.' The phone is ringing. 'Do you want me to get that?' Philip asks.

'No, it's all right, I will.' It's well past ten o'clock now and I can't think who would be calling at this time of night unless it's Dad or Maggie. I shake off the rug and stand up. I'm feeling warmer now, and also calmer. Though I hadn't wanted to talk about this whole thing, actually it has helped. I go through to the hall and lift the receiver.

'Hello?'

'Mike Bond here.'

My stomach twists.

Philip is in the doorway. 'You want another drink, Emma?' he asks, quite quietly, but augmenting the words with mime. I shush him, shaking my head.

'I'm sorry to ring so late,' Mike says, 'but I imagine you'll be out at work tomorrow, and I thought you'd like to know straight away—'

The breath is tight in my chest suddenly.

'Know what?' I interrupt him.

'I've been making some calls since I arrived home this evening and I've got a lead for Simon Beacham.'

'You've found him!'

'Not yet. But I have tracked down a cousin in Bristol, who says the last he heard of Simon he was definitely in Florida. Running a canoe-for-hire business on a river. The cousin doesn't have an address, but at least it gives me something to go on. I've got contacts in the States who should be able to find him – if he's still there, that is. I'll keep you posted when I know more. But I thought in the meantime I'd just let you know that things are moving in the right direction.'

'Thank you.' I've started to shake again, and my thoughts and emotions, which had steadied, are frothing once more. 'That's really good of you.'

'No problem. I'll be in touch.'

'Who was that?' Philip has been to the kitchen to fetch another beer while I was on the phone; now he is standing in the doorway, leaning against the jamb and watching me curiously.

'Mike Bond. The reporter. It seems as though . . . well, this isn't just a crazy nightmare. Things are really happening . . .'

'Come here.' He draws me into his arms, and this time I don't pull away – the familiar is oddly comforting. But when he asks: 'You want me to stay tonight? I will if you like,' I'm immediately on the defensive again.

'No, no. I'll be fine.'

'You're sure?'

'Of course. I don't need a nursemaid.'

'Nursemaiding wasn't what I had in mind.'

'I know.'

And that, of course, is the crux of the matter. I might have been glad of a friendly chat, but I'm recoiling from the thought of making love. And not just a lack of interest – I actively don't want to, and I know that it really is over between us.

I don't think I can face telling him that right now, though, coward that I am. I can't face the inevitable discussion, and possibly the pleading, that will follow. I'll have to find the courage to do it sometime soon – it's not fair on either of us. But for now I just can't do it.

'I'd really rather be alone,' I say, hating myself for my weakness. But knowing that it is no more than the truth.

FIFTEEN

THE LINK

Melanie Thomas is on the Tube with her mother, Anna, when she catches sight of him. The train is pulling out of Oxford Circus as he emerges on to the platform from one of the entrances. A glimpse, nothing more, but it's enough to make her gasp. She jerks round, heart racing, to peer out of the window, but all she can see is the back view of a man in a tan leather jacket amongst the other passengers who have just disembarked from the train and those who, like him, who have just missed it.

'Oh my God!' she whispers.

'What?' Anna, settling into the seat beside her daughter, is puzzled and a little alarmed.

'Mark! I saw Mark!'

'Oh Mel, no. Surely not? It was just someone who looks like him, I expect.'

'No! It was Mark!'

Mel can hardly believe it, yet she's absolutely sure. It was him.

When they first split up it hadn't been unusual for her to think she'd seen him, on a crowded pavement, in a cinema queue, walking along the Embankment. Her heart had leaped then too, but common sense had told her it couldn't possibly be him, even before the man she'd homed in on turned around and she saw that really he looked nothing like Mark at all. She'd known it couldn't be Mark, because Mark had gone to Singapore, accepting the posting that he'd turned down once before because she'd said she didn't want to leave England and he'd said no way was he going without her. In some ways she was glad he'd gone; if he'd still been in London and she'd had to see him – really see him, not just imagine seeing him – she didn't think she could have borne it. In others, the distance between them, the fact that he was no longer around, made the split harder to accept. For a long while it hadn't seemed quite real, though the terrible ache in her heart, the hollow place inside, had told her it was.

'I'm going to take the job in Singapore,' he'd said, and his hard, matter-of-fact tone of voice, the whole of his demeanour, stiff, distant, had made her go cold inside.

'Oh,' she said in a small voice. 'They're putting on the pressure, are they?'

'It's a good career move,' he said. 'I really can't turn it down.'

'Oh,' she said again. She was waiting for him to ask her to go with him, and when he didn't, the cold place inside her grew and spread. 'You will be back, though, won't you?' she asked. 'It won't be too long before I see you again?'

'I don't think that's a good idea, Mel,' he said. 'Long-distance relationships really don't work. I think it would be best if we called it a day.'

And nothing she could say could change his mind. She'd tried, she'd swallowed her pride and argued and pleaded, though she could see it was a lost cause. Though he was still there, in the same room, close enough to reach out and touch, he'd gone away from her already.

She *did* try to touch him, and he shrank away as if she was a leper. Mark, who had been the sweetest, most tender of lovers; Mark, who had held her and caressed her and told her she was special, that he'd never felt this way about anyone before. Mark, who was the air she breathed, the beat of her heart.

She was confused as well as devastated; she couldn't understand what had happened, how she could have got it so wrong. Her confidence, her faith in her own judgement, her faith in everything and everyone, had been shattered, along with her dreams.

Small wonder she'd allowed Brian to console her wounded pride and ease her broken heart. And small wonder it had all gone horribly wrong. For the unvarnished truth was that she'd never forgotten Mark, never stopped loving him. Though he was no longer in her life, he was still locked away in her heart, and so many small things could turn the key. The Last Night of the Proms. The haunting sweetness of Karen Carpenter's voice, especially when she sang 'Goodbye to Love'. The merest whiff of the after-shave Mark used to wear. The flicker of firelight. The soft kiss of snowflakes. The sun setting over London, spreading scarlet ribbons on the dark water of the Thames. Any or all of them could catapult her back to the time they had spent together, the days when she had been truly happy, except that now the only emotion they stirred was an ache of sadness so poignant it was hard to bear.

That she never sailed with Mark, never so much as set foot in a boat, let alone a tall ship, is one of the reasons she is so looking forward to her planned trip on the *Lord Nelson*. She absolutely needs to experience new adventures, create new memories that have nothing whatever to do with Mark – or Brian. Life has to begin again, a completely fresh start.

She's already booked her trip – well, she's put a cheque to the Jubilee Sailing Trust in the post, at least. At Anna's suggestion, she chose one of the shorter voyages, just six days, and sailing out of Portsmouth; it seemed sensible to see how she likes it before committing to several weeks away, and she can always book another week or more later if she enjoys it as much as she thinks she will. She's checked that her passport is up to date – she'll need it in case they go to France, though nothing is guaranteed, apparently – it depends on the winds. The uncertainty of not knowing where she'll end up is an added attraction, and makes the whole thing seem like a real adventure. Today she and Anna have been shopping for some of the things she'll need – sailing gloves, a warm woollen hat, a small torch. She's bought sun cream, too, and a pair of thick-soled training shoes with ridged soles. The carrier bags containing her purchases are piled on her lap, and by now she would have been unable to resist peeking inside them if she hadn't seen Mark. Now, though, they are completely forgotten.

'It was him, Mum, I know it was,' she says. 'He's back in London! He must be!'

'Oh Mel.' Anna looks worried. This is the last thing Melanie needs, just as she's making a start towards building a new life. She has to look forward, not back. 'Darling, even if it was him . . .'

'It was! If he'd got to the platform just a minute earlier he'd have got on to our train! Maybe even into our carriage . . .'

She presses her hand over her mouth. If that had happened, if they'd come face to face, what would she have said? What would he have said? Would he have been pleased to see her, or would it have been horribly awkward?

Awkward, most likely. After all, she's never heard a word from him since he left.

'What if I bump into him again?' she says fearfully.

'Pretty unlikely, surely? London's a big place, and his company offices aren't anywhere near your bank, are they?'

'He loved West Ken, though. If he's living there again . . .'

Anna sighs. 'Well, if you do bump into him, you're just going to have to deal with it, darling. But don't, please, get your hopes up. I don't want to see you hurt all over again.'

Easy for her mother to say; Mel's never really stopped hurting. She wishes with all her heart that she could be more like Anna, who is always so prosaic, who seems to take everything in her stride, rather than her emotional, highly strung self. She's turned into a jelly inside, all jangling nerves and churning thoughts.

The Tube rattles through the tunnel, emerges into Victoria station, where they need to change trains. As she climbs down on to the platform Mel is tempted to simply stand there, waiting for the next train, hoping to see Mark again, to find out if he is, like her, heading back to West Kensington. But she knows Anna won't have it, and in any case, it could just force the awkward encounter she's afraid of.

'You want me to take one of those bags?' Anna asks. She's going back with Mel and they plan to have a meal in the Italian restaurant just down the road from Mel's flat before she heads home.

'It's OK, I'm balanced nicely,' Mel says, and then laughs hollowly, silently, at the irony of it. Balanced, her! That's the last way to describe her emotional state.

Mark, oh Mark!

One glimpse, one fleeting glimpse, and she's right back where she was five years ago. Hopelessly obsessed with a man who is never again going to be hers.

They complete their journey, emerge into the street, which is dappled with late afternoon sun. Mel juggles the bags containing all the accoutrements for what is supposed to be her great new adventure, and feels she has left the only person she has ever truly wanted in the darkness of the London Underground.

SIXTEEN

MIKE

I don't like flying. Not great for my street cred, I grant you, but a fact. When it comes to taking a plane I'm a wuss. Well, there you are. I've admitted it. I don't like the feeling of being cooped up like a sardine in a can thousands of feet above the land, or worse, the ocean. I don't like being at the mercy of computers and instruments that would spell disaster if they had a glitch – and goodness knows, my own experience of computers doesn't exactly inspire confidence – not to mention bird strikes and thunderstorms and ash clouds from erupting volcanos. I once heard that a jumbo-jet pilot, when asked why he flew four-engined planes, replied that it was because they didn't make them with five, and I wholly agree with that sentiment. Except that I'm not sure I entirely trust the pilot anyway – I fear he may fall asleep from boredom on a long flight, and if he's awake will be engrossed in a crossword or an argument with his first officer, or chatting up the pretty stewardess who takes him his plastic meal on a plastic tray and umpteen cups of coffee. When he emerges from the cockpit to use the loo, the snaking queue melts away as if by magic, and I'm one of the first to give up my place even if I'm busting a gut.

Best not to drink alcohol before or during a flight, they say, but if I didn't have a good strong whisky in the departure lounge I doubt you'd get me on board at all.

Besides the perceived danger, there's the discomfort. I'm six foot two, and sitting for hours with my knees squashed up to my chin and the seat of the person in front of me angled back so it's inches from my nose is my idea of hell.

So, to recap, I don't like flying. But in this modern world there is sometimes no way of avoiding it. Especially if you're researching a story that takes in two continents, as this one does. If I want to find out the truth of what happened to Felicity Penrose, I'm going to have to bite the bullet and fly to Florida.

So I'm at Heathrow, nursing a large whisky on the rocks, with my travel bag parked close by me so that it doesn't get mistaken for a suspect package, and no would-be terrorist can slip a bomb inside when I'm not looking, waiting for the call to board, and getting more jittery by the minute. Not my idea of fun, but hey, it had to be done. And while I wait I try to distract myself by running over all I've learned so far, and what my plans are when – if! – I land safely in Orlando.

At least I have the consolation that things are moving at last. It's ten days now since I located a cousin of Simon Beacham in Bristol, most of which I've had to spend kicking my heels, which has been pretty frustrating after the adrenalin rush I got when I struck lucky.

The first thing I did when I got home from Cornwall – well, the first thing after I'd picked Daisy up from her grandparents' and seen her safely to bed – was to get out the phone book – luckily we just about come in the Bristol area, which spreads from Falfield (Gloucestershire) in the north, to Weston-super-Mare in the south.

I was quite surprised to find there was a good half-column of Beachams, and also a Beachham, with a handful of Beauchamps for good measure – nobody had told me how Simon spelled his name, and I hadn't thought to ask. But at least it was a manageable list, unlike the three pages plus that I knew would be dedicated to the various Smith clans.

I made a start right away, ringing a few numbers without

success. None of them admitted to any knowledge of a relative named Simon; two were not answered – I made a note as to which they were so I could try again later – and one irate lady told me that if I didn't get off the line immediately, she would be reporting me to the police. By that time it was too late to make any more calls – possibly I'd already overstepped the mark, and the last Miss Beacham would have been less crusty if it had been earlier in the day, so I decided the rest would have to wait for tomorrow. Trouble was, tomorrow was Monday. A lot of people would be at work.

Then my phone rang and unbelievably it was one of the first people I'd spoken to, who had told me her husband was out but she'd never heard of him having a relative called Simon. Apparently when her husband got home she'd told him about my call, and luckily I'd left her my number, as I had all the others – apart from the irate lady who threatened me with the police.

'Dennis tells me he does have a cousin named Simon,' she said. 'He hasn't had any contact with him since the late fifties, which is why I didn't know anything about him. He went to America, it seems.'

'Does your husband know where in America he went?' I asked, revitalised.

'I'm not sure. Do you want to speak to him? He's here now . . . I'll put him on.'

The man who came on the line had a faint but unmistakable Bristol accent.

'This is Dennis Beacham. You're asking about my cousin Simon, I understand.'

'I'm trying to find him, yes.'

'Can I ask why?'

'I'm writing about sailing in the nineteen fifties. Simon was involved, I understand. In Falmouth . . .'

'He was, yes, but in a very small way. I wouldn't have thought he'd be of much interest to you.'

'You'd be surprised at the details that make a story interesting,'

I said easily. 'He went to America, I believe. Would you happen to know whereabouts?'

'Florida — at least that was where he was when I last heard of him. He was running a canoe business on a river somewhere north of Orlando. But I haven't a clue as to whether he's still there.' From his tone of voice I could tell Dennis Beacham was still puzzled as to my interest in his long-lost cousin.

'OK — well, thanks anyway,' I said. 'You've been a great help.'

'I don't know about that. We were never especially close, Simon and I. He was a bit of a loner.'

'You didn't know any of his friends, then?'

I felt reasonably safe in asking. If he hadn't heard from Simon for years, didn't know where he was, he wasn't likely to warn him I was asking question. Unless, of course, he knew more than he was letting on, pretending ignorance in order to protect Simon. If Simon had helped Felicity fake her own death, the family might be rallying round to keep his whereabouts secret, and the last thing I wanted was for him to take fright and go into hiding. But if that was the case, why had Dennis rung me back? And, though clearly puzzled, he didn't seem to be being evasive.

'No, sorry, I never met any of them,' he said in answer to my question. And then: 'If you do find him, will you let me know? I'd be interested to know where he landed up and how he is.'

'Will do. And thanks.'

When I put the phone down I poured myself a whisky — the last of the bottle — and wondered whether it was too late to ring Emma. She'd like an update, I imagined. Not that I had much to tell her, but all the same . . .

I picked up the phone again, and called her, realising to my surprise, as I waited for her to answer, that this was as much about wanting to speak to her as to impart my meagre information.

What the hell was that all about? She's a pretty girl, yes, and I like her. But I haven't so much as looked at another woman since Bev died. I've been in a sort of limbo as far as my personal life is concerned, and that's the way I've wanted it. Anything else seems to me to be a betrayal of her memory, and it was something of a shock for me to realise I was feeling a little too interested in Emma Dunning, and not just because of who her mother was.

Then she picked up, and almost immediately I heard a man's voice in the background, which successfully squashed any foolish ideas I might have been getting.

And a good thing too! I thought. *The last thing you want is to get emotionally involved with Felicity Penrose's daughter!* But there was no mistaking the twinge of regret that she has a man in her life. A man she's undoubtedly going to need before this is over.

Annoyingly, the regret was still there when we'd finished our conversation and it was just me and the remains of my glass of whisky again. I couldn't get Emma Dunning out of my head – kept seeing her face, hearing her voice, wishing that I'd met her under different circumstances and I hadn't been the one to turn her world upside down. But at least it seems she has come to terms with the situation, and now wants to know the truth. The best way I can help her is to give her some kind of closure.

With that in mind, I made my next phone call. Walt Flanaghan is a long-term friend. He's a private investigator by trade, one of the best, and our paths have crossed a few times over the years. If anyone could track down Simon Beacham it was Walt, and I could probably get him to agree to put the work on the slate – a nice fat fee if he comes up with information leading to a saleable story.

I checked my watch – mid-afternoon in the States. Whether he'd be answering his phone on a Sunday was another matter. But he was. I suppose if a private eye wants work he has to be available pretty much 24/7.

I told him what I wanted, and as much as I know.

'Can you have a crack at finding him, Walt?' I asked.

'Sure thing.' He sounded reassuringly confident. 'If the guy's still in Florida, I'll find him.'

'I'll wait to hear from you then?'

'I'll be in touch as soon as.'

'Great stuff.'

And then, of course, there was nothing I could do but wait.

It was Friday before Walt got in touch.

'Got him!'

'You have?'

'Didn't I say I would? There's a canoe outfit on the Wekiva River . . .'

'Which is where?'

'An hour's drive north-west of Kissimmee. Pretty isolated country. It goes by the name of Simon's Landing. Not that inventive, as names go, but pretty useful to the likes of you and me.'

'He doesn't know you were asking about him?'

Walt huffed. 'What d'you take me for? How long d'you think I'd last in my line of business if—'

'Just checking. I want to take him by surprise. Has he got a significant other?'

'There's a Mrs Beacham, if that's what you mean. You want me to find out more?'

However good Walt might be, I didn't want to risk alerting Simon Beacham.

'No, I'll come over myself, as soon as I can fix it. Thanks, Walt.'

'My pleasure. Just as long as it all works out and . . .'

'You get your share of the spoils. I know. I'll see to that.'

So I made arrangements for Tom and Judy to look after Daisy and booked a ticket to Orlando, which appeared to be the nearest major airport to the area Walt said Simon is living.

I called Emma to tell her the latest developments.

'I can't believe you've found him,' she said.

'Neither can I. I thought it would be like looking for a needle in a haystack. Anyway, I'm going over to try to see him. And it just occurred to me to wonder if you'd like to come with me.'

I left the unspoken implication hanging in the air. If Simon Beacham had helped Felicity to fake her own death so that they could run away together, I might not only find Simon in Florida, but Felicity too.

Emma didn't give me an outright no.

'When are you going?' she asked.

'On Wednesday, from Heathrow.'

'In that case I can't.' She sounded regretful. 'I'm still teaching until the middle of July. Would it wait till then?'

So she's a teacher. That surprises me a bit. I can't imagine her in a classroom; she seems too much the outdoor type.

'Pity,' I said. 'But there's nothing I can do about it now. My ticket's booked.'

'Right. I understand. You will keep me posted, though, won't you?'

'Of course.'

So here I am, looking at the Heathrow departures monitor, which shows that my flight is more or less on time, and waiting for the tin-can voice over the tannoy that will summon me to the breach. When suddenly I see someone I recognise.

Emma Dunning! She's wearing denim jeans, a black blazer and white shirt, and carrying a patchwork tote bag. She's looking around anxiously as she makes her way between the knots of waiting passengers and plastic bucket seats. I hastily down the last of my whisky, deposit the cup on a handy table, and thread my way towards her.

'Emma!'

'Mike! God, I thought I was going to miss the flight! The traffic on the M4 was awful!'

'What are you doing here?' I ask, rather unnecessarily.

'Well, coming with you, I hope!'

'I thought you said you couldn't get away.'

'I've wangled it.' She runs a distracted hand through her hair, which is falling loose to her shoulders. 'Don't ask! I've managed it. That's good enough, isn't it?'

'I'm glad.'

And I am, on all sorts of levels. If I do find Felicity Penrose,

Emma, more than anyone, has a right to be there. And I'm glad for myself, too, though I'm unwilling to admit it.

The tannoy screeches into life.

'Passengers on Flight . . . make your way now to Gate . . .'

'That's us.'

'Don't suppose we'll be sitting together, but . . .'

'You never know, someone might be prepared to change places.'

'You never know.'

We join the queue for the departure gate.

At least now I have a good reason to hide my discomfort about the flight ahead. Heck, who knows, I might just enjoy it!

SEVENTEEN

MAGGIE

It's four in the morning, but I'm wide awake. That's how it's been with me ever since Emma dropped the bombshell that a newspaper reporter is investigating Fliss's 'death' back in 1959. I manage to fall asleep when I first go to bed, but a couple of hours later I'm wide awake again. My nerves are jangling like tightly stretched wires, and they send little shocks of electricity to tingle in my hands and feet, a never-ending shower of pinpricks. My stomach feels as if a cloud of moths are fluttering there, trying to escape. And my thoughts churn endlessly until my head feels as if it's about to burst.

There's absolutely no chance of me going back to sleep, I know – at least not a proper refreshing sleep, though I do sometimes doze restlessly at about the time when I should be getting up to make Martin's breakfast, and I hate that. I do like to make sure it's on the table for him when he's finished his shower and shave. The women's lib brigade would probably label me a doormat, but that doesn't bother me one iota. All I care about is making life good and comfortable for him; all I want is for him to be happy.

Oh Martin, Martin! I love him so much that it's a pain inside me still, even after all these years, and especially now, when I'm so afraid I may lose him. How will he ever forgive me for the secret I've kept from him all this time? Goodness knows, I can hardly forgive myself for deceiving both him and Emma, for living a lie. There's so much I've kept from them, and if the truth comes out they're going to hate me for it, as I hate myself. Because however I may try to convince myself I did it for them, I know that I was being far from selfless. I also did it for me, in the hope that things would work out in just the way they did.

Fliss will hate me too, I expect – probably already does. She'll think I stole her life, and that's not far from the truth. But she doesn't know that I betrayed her too; that's something she won't know until Emma finds her.

Besides worrying about the consequences of all this for myself, I'm being torn apart by seeing Martin so hurt. Since I told him – as I had to – that a journalist was claiming that Fliss didn't die at all, but faked her death so as to run away to a new life, he's been a shadow of himself. He's become very silent and withdrawn, he picks at his food – Martin, who normally wolfs it down with enormous gusto, enjoying every mouthful. He's sick at heart, I know, at the suggestion that Fliss might have been so desperate to get away from him that she could do something like that, sick, and hurt, and uncomprehending. But in that first moment when I told him, I saw something that looked like a flicker of hope in his eyes, and it left me in no doubt that even after all these years he still loves her.

Something else that's worrying me, as I'm sure it must be worrying him, is the legal implications. Not only will our marriage be null and void if Fliss is found alive, there's the financial aspect too. The insurance company paid out a lot of money on Fliss's life – it's how Martin was able to afford the franchise for the garage that set a business that was failing on the road to success. They'll want it repaid, of course they will. Our nest egg, meant for our retirement, will be gone in one fell swoop, and it could be even worse than that. He might have to sell the garage in a hurry, which would also mean cheaply, or go on working well past the date he intended to retire, or both. Who knows? In my nightmares I fear the house might have to go as well. It's all overwhelmingly awful.

And it's just got a whole lot worse. I'd pinned all my hopes on

Simon Beacham being untraceable after all these years, but it seems I was being overoptimistic. Apparently this reporter, Mike Bond, has found him, and is planning to go to America to talk to him. All I can hope for now is that Simon won't know where Fliss is, and will deny any involvement. I'm trying to think that he won't want to incriminate himself, but I'm not altogether convinced. Simon was always an oddball, and he might well take the opportunity to make himself important. Besides which, if he is offered a goodly sum for his story by way of inducement, I can't see him turning it down.

It's all a total nightmare, and the worry of it is driving me crazy. For the first time in my life I glimpse the abyss Fliss fell into all those years ago, the darkness closing in as she described it. I am in danger of losing everything I hold most dear, and I know that if that happens life will not be worth living.

In the soft half-light of dawn that's filtering in through a gap in the curtains, I raise myself on one elbow and look at Martin. His back is towards me, so I can't see his face, just the angle of his jaw, the plane of his forehead, and I fill up with love and with despair. Martin doesn't seem to be having trouble sleeping, but then he hasn't got this sword of Damocles hanging over him. He might be sad, he might be anxious, but he doesn't face the demolition of his integrity. There's no risk to him of the layers of deception being stripped away to reveal a secret that will irreparably change the way his loved ones see him.

Shame and despair knife through me; I cringe inwardly so that it feels as if every bit of my stomach is tying itself up into a tight knot. I curl myself around Martin's back, burying my face in his shoulder; he stirs a little and moves away. It's unconscious, I know, but it feels to me like an omen; already he has begun to go away from me.

I get up, pad downstairs, and make myself a cup of tea.

At seven thirty the phone rings. When I answer it, it's Emma. The minute I hear her voice, I get a bad feeling.

'What's wrong?' I ask, desperately anxious.

'Oh no, nothing's wrong, Maggie. I just wanted to let you know. I'm leaving for Heathrow in a minute.'

'Heathrow?' I can't quite believe I've heard this right.

'Yes. I've managed to wangle some time off and I'm going to Florida with Mike Bond.'

'What!'

'I know you don't approve, but I really need to be there, know what's going on at first hand.'

'Emma, no, you can't . . .'

'Don't try to talk me out of it, Maggie. My mind's made up. Look, I've got to go now – you never know what the traffic will be like. I'll be in touch.'

And she's gone.

I can feel the red-hot panic rushing through my body; I'm stunned with horror. Emma is going to be there if Simon Beacham talks. Maybe she'll meet Fliss and learn the truth. And I haven't had the chance to put my side! It's total disaster, and there's not a thing I can do about it. I bury my face in my hands and burst into tears.

EIGHTEEN

EMMA

It's quite beyond me how politicians and celebrities can cope with criss-crossing the world and still emerge bright-eyed and bushy-tailed to hold vital meetings or make glittering appearances on red carpets. I suppose it might have something to do with travelling first class rather than economy, but even so . . . A comfortable seat, a glass of champagne and a meal served on proper plates instead of in a horrid plastic tray can't make that much difference, surely? It's the thrum of the engines that gets to me, and the jet lag, the enforced inactivity and the boredom.

This time, of course, I had a lot on my mind, and too long to think about it. Though I'd met up with Mike at the airport and we'd boarded together, our seats were miles apart, me on the left-hand bank, right over those horrible thrumming engines, his in the very middle of the centre block, towards the rear of the plane. I'd have liked the opportunity to talk things through with him, and even get to know him a bit, this man who appeared out of the blue and turned my world upside down, but it wasn't to be. Hardly surprising, really, since we'd booked separately – me at the very last minute, after I'd wangled some leave on compassionate grounds. The only chance we got to exchange a few words was standing in the area outside the galley, and then we had to keep moving because we were getting in the way of the queue for the loo.

Mike seemed a bit edgy, I thought, and I wondered if he was annoyed that I'd managed to fix it to come along. He probably never imagined for a moment that I'd be able to get time off work at such short notice, and was now regretting asking me. But when he asked where I was staying and I admitted I hadn't had time to book anything and was going to have to make arrangements when we arrived, he told me he was using a low-budget place within easy reach of the airport and suggested I do the same.

'Not the last word in luxury, but convenient, and it won't break the bank,' he said.

'Sounds fine to me. As long as they've got rooms free.'

'I'm sure they will have. Another couple of weeks, when we get into the school holidays, I'm not so sure. We are talking Orlando, after all. Disney World. My daughter is furious with me for not bringing her along.'

'You have a daughter?' I said, surprised.

'Daisy. She's seven.'

The queue for the loo was pushing us ever closer to the galley; a stewardess answering a passenger's call for a bottle of water asked us to move, and at precisely the same moment the plane lurched and I cannoned into Mike.

'Oh – sorry . . .'

'No problem.' But he wasted no time in disengaging himself, and when the tannoy cranked into life and the captain's voice instructed us all to return to our seats and fasten our seat belts as we were encountering some turbulence, he seemed rather too eager to get away.

I was embarrassed, suddenly, that I'd managed to fall into him. Surely he didn't think that I'd done it on purpose? That I'd taken it he was propositioning me, by suggesting I should accompany him to Florida, and then that we should stay at the same hotel? That I was making some kind of move on him? As if! Any kind of romantic liaison is the last thing on my mind. Especially with a man who's ruthless enough to pursue his story without giving a shit as to who gets hurt in the process. Especially with a man

212

who has a seven-year-old daughter and, I've now noticed, wears a wedding ring.

The journey seemed to take for ever, made worse by having to change planes in Detroit, and by the time we arrived in Orlando I was dropping with tiredness. I'd hardly slept the night before, and it was now past what would have been my usual bedtime at home. On top of this, my ears had blocked up and I couldn't hear properly, which added to the feeling that my head was full of cotton wool. Luckily neither of us had hold luggage – we'd both opted to manage with what we could stuff into carry-on bags – so we didn't have the endless wait at the carousel, but there was a long queue at the car hire desk and the formalities seemed endless.

'All I need now is to get to the hotel and be told they haven't any vacancies,' I said.

'Well, in that case you'll just have to have my room,' Mike said – at least, through the layers of cotton wool, I thought that was what he said. 'But don't look so worried. It's not going to happen.'

Mercifully he was right. We checked in, I dumped my bag in the room I was allocated, and grabbed a quick shower. When I'd made myself look respectable I went back down to the bar to meet Mike as arranged. He was already there, sitting at a corner table with a beer. As soon as he saw me he signalled to a waiter and I ordered a glass of dry white wine.

'So, what's the plan?' I asked.

'We'll head straight up to Simon's Landing first thing tomorrow,' Mike said, taking a pull of his beer. 'No sense wasting time.'

A nerve jumped in my throat. It was what we were here for, but suddenly I wasn't sure I was ready.

'You look all in,' he said, eyeing me critically. 'Do you want something to eat, or would you rather just go to bed?'

'Bed, definitely. Well . . . maybe a sandwich or something. There's no way I could cope with a full-scale meal.'

'My sentiments exactly. It's been a long day, and we need to be fit for tomorrow.'

We ordered sub rolls, piled high with tuna and salad, which

we ate in near silence. I was far too tired to have a conversation, and for all I knew Mike felt the same, though he looked surprisingly fresh.

When I'd finished my roll and my drink I left Mike still sitting in the bar and headed back to my room, where I fell out of my clothes and into bed. For just a minute I pondered how surreal this was – being in America with a man I barely knew, looking for a mother I'd always thought had died when I was two years old. Then, without any warning, I was asleep. A deep, dreamless sleep. A sleep that lasted until I was woken by the shrilling of the telephone beside my bed.

I didn't have a travel clock, and couldn't see the time by my watch – it was dim in the room, the thick window blinds filtering out light – but instinct told me it was morning. I reached for the phone, and heard Mike's voice.

'I thought you were meeting me for breakfast.'

'I am – what time is it?'

'Half seven.'

I could hardly believe it – I'd virtually slept the clock round.

'Oh shit! I'm sorry! Give me ten minutes and I'll be there . . .'

I leapt out of bed, splashed cold water on my face, threw on the same travel-weary clothes as yesterday. The long sleep hadn't refreshed me at all; if anything I felt thicker and woollier than ever, and my ears were still bunged up.

Which is why I say I honestly don't know how the influential, the rich and the famous manage to do it, and appear totally unscathed. Because at this moment, sitting across the breakfast table from Mike, trying to eat a bagel that sticks in my throat, I feel like a total zombie. If today is the day when I find my mother, how the hell am I going to cope? And, almost more to the point, what in the world is she going to think of a sorry, jet-lagged specimen like me?

When we've finished breakfast I go back to my room for my sunglasses, baseball cap and sunscreen. Then I go down to the lobby, where I meet Mike, and we set out in his hire car.

Although it's still early, the sun is already bright and hot and the road ahead of us shimmers silver and crystal. My stomach is tying itself in knots.

Mike gives me a narrow look. 'This isn't much fun for you, is it?' he says.

'Not a lot.' I try to sound nonchalant, but who am I fooling? Not Mike, it seems.

'I am sorry, landing it on you the way I did,' he says. 'If I'd known . . .'

'You'd have backed off?' I laugh bitterly. 'I don't think so.'

'No, you're probably right. It's pretty important to me, this story.'

Suddenly I'm angry, an anger that explodes from my tight-strung nerves.

'*This story!* That's all it is to you, a story! May I remind you it's my mother's life we're talking about. My life. My father's and Maggie's. We're real people, not just characters in a book or a film. This is devastating for us. But you don't give a shit about that, as long as you get *your story!*'

There's an awkward silence, then:

'I guess I asked for that,' Mike says ruefully. 'It's rough on you, I know. And actually I think it shows a lot of guts, confronting it head on.'

'I don't know about that,' I say, still snappily. 'All I hope is we can get some answers that will settle it once and for all.'

Mike glances at me. His eyes are hidden behind his Aviator sunglasses, but his tone is surprisingly gentle.

'Don't bank on it, Emma. We don't know for sure that Simon Beacham had anything to do with this. And even if he did . . . he's not going to want to incriminate himself. We might very well run into a brick wall.'

He's right, of course.

'But there's always the chance, isn't there, that . . .'

I break off. I can't quite bring myself to say what I'm thinking. That I might actually find my mother at Simon's Landing. Mike seems to read my thoughts, though. He reaches over, squeezing my hand briefly.

'It's possible. But even if they were together once, it's a very long time ago, and I can't see, somehow, that this is the sort of place where Felicity would have settled.'

There's a sort of desperation seething in me, all knotted up with the nervousness, and I realise just how much I want to meet my mother. If she is alive, that is. How much, actually, I want her to be. Though it hurts like hell that she might have chosen to abandon me, I still long for her, need to ask her why she did what she did, and, perhaps, come to build some kind of relationship with her. It's a primal instinct that has been gnawing at me ever since Mike raised the possibility that she was not dead at all, and it owes nothing to the sweet voice of reason.

But I know it's a mistake to get my hopes up. The country we're travelling through seems to be sparsely populated – an ideal place for someone who doesn't want to be found to hide away – but it's an awfully long way from the sea, and from all I know of my mother, I can't somehow imagine that she could be happy for long if she wasn't able to sail. It seems much more likely that she'd choose somewhere more like Naples, where she was supposed to have been seen, than an inland backwater. But then again, if she'd known she'd been spotted, it's just the sort of place she might have run to. From the map, spread out on my knee, I can see that Simon's Landing seems to be the last outpost of civilisation in a vast expanse of open country and National Park, the least likely place where anyone would look for her.

We travel for a while in silence, then Mike spots a sign for Simon's Landing. The road we turn into is narrow and wooded on either side. Every so often we pass a chalet-style building in a clearing with cars parked outside, and I wonder if it's possible my mother lives in one of them.

Again, Mike seems to read my mind.

'They look like holiday lets to me,' he says, and I have to agree he's probably right. A couple of children are chasing one another around a big old Chevvy outside one of them, and there's a washing line strung up between the trees that's festooned with swimwear, towels and smalls, typical of a family on holiday. We keep going, following the white arrows that are tacked to trees at intervals along the way, and eventually we reach a place that looks like a parking area. It's deserted. We pull up beneath the canopy of trees and walk towards a cluster of timber huts that appear to be an office, a small café and a shop, though they are all locked up and there are no signs of life. My heart sinks, but there's a notice stuck to the door of the office giving an opening time of 10 a.m., and when Mike checks his watch, it's not yet half past nine.

'We're too early.'

'Looks like it.' I'm peering in at the windows of the office and shop, but I can see nothing. Mike is setting off down a narrow track to the riverbank. I follow him. The river is broad and calm; barely a ripple breaks the surface. A couple of dozen canoes are pulled up neatly on the bank on either side of a landing stage. A nerve jumps in my stomach. Did my mother beach any of these canoes? The thought that she might have is the weirdest feeling. Half a world away from the only place that connects us, I might be standing on the very spot where she stood – yesterday?

'We might as well go back to that town we passed through a while back while we're waiting,' Mike says. 'I could kill for an iced Coke.'

I'm not that bothered about the Coke, but it seems a better idea than sitting in the clearing waiting for someone to turn up and open the office.

We return to the car and drive slowly back along the forest track in the direction that we came. The small town we'd passed through on the main road is only a mile or so further on, no more than a straggle of stores, a church and a garage. They are all festooned with patriotic bunting, apart from the church, which has a huge poster proclaiming that 'Jesus Loves You'. Mike pulls on to the forecourt of the garage, parking well away from the pumps; he doesn't need petrol yet – 'gas' as they call it over here – but it looks as if they sell snacks and newspapers in the kiosk. I'm unbuckling my seat belt, but Mike stops me.

'Let me do this.'

He disappears into the garage, I wait, puzzled. He re-emerges a few minutes later carrying two paper mugs of iced cola and a couple of bottles of water.

'Why did you make me wait in the car?' I ask as he hands me one of the paper cups and settles the other in the drinks holder between the seats.

'I didn't want you seen. You look too much like your mother. Suppose Simon called in here for gas on his way to the Landing and they told him someone looking exactly like Felicity had been in? I don't want him forewarned.'

'But surely . . . my mother is . . . well, she's well into her fifties now,' I object.

Mike raises a laconic eyebrow. 'We're in the land where people don't age. Wrinkles get airbrushed away by the plastic surgeon and nobody goes grey.'

I shake my head. 'I can't believe my mother would have a facelift.'

Strange how confident of it I feel. I'm so much like her in so many ways, not just my looks, and I can't imagine ever going under the plastic surgeon's knife, ergo, neither would she.

'Well, let's hope you're right. Just to be on the safe side, though, I'd like you to wait in the car at Simon's Landing too, until I've sussed out the lie of the land. Simon would certainly recognise you as Felicity's daughter, even if she doesn't look that much like you any more. I want to pretend to be a day tripper, thinking about hiring a canoe. If he gets suspicious, he'll clam up and we'll get nowhere.'

I open my mouth to object, but actually I can see where he's coming from. There's a good chance Simon would recognise me, even if it is more than thirty years since he saw my mother. Actually, if that's the case, it would be even more likely he'd spot the likeness, because I look pretty much as he would remember her. If Fliss isn't here – and to be honest, I'm beginning to doubt she is – then Mike will have to ask some pertinent questions without arousing Simon's suspicions, and I mustn't mess things up.

We drive back through the forest. It's now just before ten, and there's a Suzuki jeep and a people carrier parked under the trees, and a motorbike outside the office.

They're here then! My heart starts hammering.

A young guy in shorts and sneakers emerges from the office and heads down to the landing stage and the canoes. The owner of the motorbike, no doubt. That leaves the drivers of the jeep and the people carrier.

Mike takes a last pull of his Coke and replaces the carton in the cup holder. But before he can get out of the car, two more people appear in the office doorway – a man in baggy jeans and a T-shirt and a woman. They appear to be having an argument; raised voices carry across the open space to where we're parked under the trees.

'That's got to be him,' Mike says.

'But that's not my mother,' I say with certainty, looking at the woman. She's about the right age, as far as I can judge from this distance, but she's olive-skinned, with glossy black hair, and the brightly patterned blouse and black leggings she's wearing do nothing to hide the fact that she is, to put it kindly, well-upholstered. They're still arguing, the woman gesticulating theatrically, the man backing away from her, arms raised in an attitude of surrender. Then he turns abruptly, and starts walking towards where we are parked.

'Get down!' Mike hisses, and I duck my head, more or less burying it in the map I still have on my lap.

He's not coming over to us, of course, he's headed for the jeep. As I hear the engine roar into life I dare to look, just in time to see it skidding on to the road, leaving a trail of dust in its wake. Mike swears. He opens the door of the car.

'I'll see if I can find out in a roundabout way when he'll be back. We can't sit here all day on the off chance.'

'Now we know he's not there, can I come with you?'

'Better not. Stay out of sight in case he comes back.'

Frustrated and disappointed, I wait. It's really hot in the car now that the engine is switched off and the air conditioning out of action, and my skin feels damp with perspiration. Eventually Mike re-emerges. He's carrying what looks like glossy leaflets, promoting the canoe trips, I imagine. He gets into the car.

'Whew, it's like an oven in here!'

I don't want to talk about the heat. I want to know what has happened.

'How did you get on?'

'Well, the woman is definitely not your mother.'

'I could have told you that. But the man . . . was that Simon Beacham?'

'It was, yes. But I don't think he'll be back today. Judging by the smell of bourbon in that office, and a half-empty bottle the woman was trying to hide, I'd say he's got a drink problem, and he's probably gone home to sleep it off. Or demolish another bottle. His wife is pretty mad at him, I could tell.'

'His wife . . .?'

'Well, that's surmise. She's wearing rings on every finger, including a huge emerald, an eternity ring and a wedding ring on the third finger of her left hand. And if she was just an employee, I don't think she'd have been yelling at him in quite the way she was, do you?'

'No.' I have to concede the point, and don't know whether I'm glad or sorry. If this woman is Simon Beacham's wife, it's unlikely I'm going to find my mother here. But I'm rather glad she isn't with him – he looked like a red-faced old soak to me, a man who'd let himself run completely to seed, and thinking of my lovely, still-trim father, I can't believe that Fliss could have chosen this unsavoury-looking character over him.

'So, what next?' I ask.

'I've booked a canoe trip for tomorrow. It seemed the best excuse to come back again without it looking fishy. It's just for me, though. I said my wife didn't fancy it – thought she'd be food for the mozzies. You're going to have to stay behind tomorrow, I'm afraid. We know now that Fliss isn't here, and I can't risk Simon seeing you.'

'No, I suppose not.' But I'm feeling frustrated, fed up and disappointed.

Mike starts the engine. 'There's nothing more we can do here today. We might as well go sightseeing, if you'd like to.'

I shrug despondently. 'Might as well.'

Anything to keep me from thinking too much about the fact that this lead seems to be ending in a blind alley. Anything to keep me from going over and over the same old questions. Is my mother still alive? If so, where is she? And am I ever going to find her?

NINETEEN

MIKE

It's a funny thing. When I started investigating this story, I felt like a shit for turning Emma's world upside down by telling her that her mother might still be alive. Now I get the feeling that it's very much what she wants, and I feel bad about shutting her out. She wants to be on the spot if I find Felicity; she wants to be the first to know. But I can't include her in everything. She has to take a back seat if I'm to find out the truth. I can't let her foul things up, either by being recognised, or by losing her cool and letting the cat out of the bag. She can be a bit fiery, doesn't always stop to think before she speaks.

It's one of the things I like about her, though – what you see is what you get. Just one of the things, actually, of which there are rather too many. Sometimes when I'm with her it's a struggle to keep my mind on the job. Which is why I enjoyed yesterday – apart from the abortive visit to Simon's Landing.

When I found out Simon Beacham wasn't likely to be back all day, I suggested a spot of sightseeing. We settled on Cape Canaveral, which I was actually quite keen to visit since we were so close, but I didn't expect Emma to be up for it. Perhaps I was being sexist, but I could just imagine what Bev's response would have been, and thought it was probably more of a man's thing. To my surprise, though, Emma was enthusiastic, which just goes to show how wrong you can be when you generalise.

We drove over and spent a fascinating day touring the compound. We saw the shuttle, and an astronaut or two, and we even had a discussion over lunch about the moon landings. I'm a bit of a sceptic, I'm afraid. A subscriber to the conspiracy theories. Emma, though, takes a much more romantic view.

'I'll never forget that first time!' she said, and it was nice to see her face alight instead of anxious and stressed. 'We were on holiday in Bournemouth. Dad let me stay up late specially and I remember standing in the garden outside our hotel, staring up at the moon and thinking: "Men from earth are walking there!" It was incredible!'

'Exactly.'

'Why would they fake something like that?'

And why did Felicity fake her own death? The parallel here strikes me forcibly. But I don't want to bring the conversation back to Felicity right now.

'To win the space race?'

'No! They did it! I know they did! You've seen the pictures . . .'

A discussion ensued with all the usual arguments – the flag blowing in the wind on the one side, the piece of moon rock we'd just seen on the other. In this, I thought, Bev and Emma *were* alike. Bev had believed it all too.

'Have it your way,' I said, feeling generous towards her, though not in the least convinced. But I'd enjoyed the sparring, was enjoying her company.

The connection between us, and Emma's lightened mood, lasted until we got back to Orlando. We went out to a Chinese restaurant – nothing too posh, since neither of us had brought suitable clothes – and over the crispy Peking duck, king prawns and lemony chicken she became serious again.

'We're not going to find her, are we?' she said, pushing egg-fried rice round her bowl with one chopstick.

'I don't know.'

'I just can't see it. That man . . . oh, I might be wrong, but I can't imagine Fliss with him at all. He was . . . well . . . gross!'

'He might not always have been.'

'Hmm.' She didn't look convinced. 'Well, anyway, it doesn't seem as though she's with him now. If she ever was. He won't know where she is. Why would he? And America is such a vast country. Talk about needles and haystacks . . .'

She suddenly looked very small and very lost. I thought of the dreadful state Daisy was in when Bev died, the little girl crying inconsolably for a mother who didn't come, and remembered that was where Emma had been. She might be a grown woman now, but that little girl is still there, locked away inside. I wanted to put my arms round her, but that would have gone down like a lead balloon. Words were the only comfort I could offer.

'If she's still alive, we'll find her,' I said, striving to sound more confident than I felt.

She looked up at me from beneath a thick fringe of lashes.

'Oh yes? How?'

'We will. We've been lucky so far, haven't we? And once I've talked to Simon Beacham, we'll start searching in earnest, anywhere and everywhere sailors congregate. If she's alive, she'll still be around boats – you said that yourself. Someone, somewhere will remember her. And she may well have got careless. She'd have hidden away in the beginning, but after thirty years . . . she won't think she has any reason to do that any more. She won't think for a moment that anyone would be looking for her after all this time.'

'Do you really think so?' Hope was flickering across her face, and I was suddenly more determined than ever to find Felicity Penrose, and not just so that I would have a scoop of a story.

'Definitely.' Again I saw that little girl lost who's hiding inside the very attractive woman that Emma grew into, and experienced a flash of anger. 'And when I do, I'm going to tell her exactly what I think of her.'

'Oh no!' Emma shook her head. 'You mustn't judge her. Not yet, until we know why she did it. She must have had a good reason. She must have!'

Oh yes, I'm sure she did, I thought scathingly. A good enough reason to abandon your own daughter, and let her believe you were dead, just doesn't exist in my book. But I didn't want to upset Emma by saying so.

'Have some chicken,' I said instead, pushing the carousel round so the lemony chicken was in front of her.

'I'm not really hungry.' But she spooned some into her bowl, and watching her I thought that I was getting to like Emma Dunning a whole lot more than was good for me.

I kept thinking about her after we got back to the hotel and parted company – couldn't seem to get her off my mind. I haven't seen her this morning, though. I decided to make an early start, do a bit of the scouting around that I would have done yesterday if Emma hadn't been with me, and ask a few pertinent questions of Simon's nearest neighbours. I grabbed a breakfast of ham and eggs, sunny side up – nobody does them quite like the Americans – with one eye on the entrance to the restaurant, but she didn't appear. Perhaps she had a sleepless night; perhaps she got stuck into the miniatures in the fridge in her room and is sleeping it off. I don't know – only that I'm glad she's not around to distract me.

Now I'm heading for Simon's Landing. I've booked a canoe trip for ten fifteen, though hopefully I won't have to actually take it. The thought of paddling for hours, with the mozzies taking me for a Michelin-starred meal, is not appealing. But what has to be done in the line of duty . . . I'll just have to do it. That's the name of the game. And if I'm to get myself out of the doldrums of debt and unemployment, it's one I'd better win.

I pull into the parking space under the trees a little after ten. I stopped off at the same garage where we bought the Cokes yesterday and asked the girl in the kiosk if she knew Simon. She rolled her eyes, chewed her gum, and muttered something unintelligible.

'I'm going out there for a canoe trip,' I said.

I didn't much care for her evil chuckle.

'Good luck to you!'

'That doesn't sound promising,' I said, but she wouldn't be drawn further.

'The guy's a loser,' was as far as she would go.

I risked showing her a photograph of Felicity that I'd filched from the archives and asked if she knew her, but she shook her head and went back to chewing her gum and fiddling with her nails.

I had no more luck with any of the other residents I talked to. So as things stand everything rests on Simon himself. I hope he's here, and I hope he's alone. The motorcycle, which presumably belongs to the young man who works here, is parked outside the office, but there's only the Suzuki jeep in the clearing under the trees. No people carrier.

Simon was driving the jeep yesterday, but presumably his wife does too, so I have no way of knowing which of them I'll find in the office. When I walk in my heart sinks. It's the woman – no sign of Simon.

'Ah, Mr Bond. You are early,' she says briskly. Her accent is a strange mixture of American and something that might well be Italian.

'A bad habit of mine, I'm afraid.'

'Well, never mind. I had you down for the ten thirty shuttle, but . . .'

'The shuttle?'

'Didn't I explain yesterday? We drive you upriver to the point from which you will set off. The people carrier we use is not yet here. But luckily for you, since we have no more bookings this morning, I can take you by jeep.'

'I don't mind waiting,' I venture, hoping for Simon and the people carrier to appear.

'The trip will take you about five hours, so no sense wasting time,' she says briskly. 'I will get Dean to mind the office while I drive you.'

Really there's nothing I can do but go along with it. The woman takes me down to the landing stage and makes me look at the geography of the river from this point.

'There are many stages on this stretch,' she says sternly. 'You need to be able to recognise which is ours. And be sure not to go beyond that bridge. If you do you have gone too far, and you will have to paddle against the current to return. Not good.'

'I'll try not to do that,' I say lightly. 'I don't want to end up in the sea.'

'No, you do not. We do not want to lose one of our canoes.'

I have the unpleasant feeling she's not joking. It's the canoe she's concerned about, not me. It doesn't inspire confidence.

She instructs the boy, Dean, to load a canoe into the jeep and mind the office while she's gone. Then we set out, back through the forest that I am beginning to develop a heartly dislike for.

'So – do you own this place?' I ask, trying to elicit as much information as I can whilst I have the chance.

'We do. Yes.'

'We being you and . . .?'

'My husband. Simon. You will meet him when you return.'

That's good news. And I was right. She is his wife.

'Have you been here long?' I ask conversationally.

She snorts.

'Too damned long! But it's a living.'

And also a good place for someone who has something to hide. Remote, thin on population, a veritable backwater. And not a sailing boat in sight.

Eventually we turn off the road into a lay-by where a landing stage has been erected on a curve in the river. We unload the canoe and I carry it down to the water's edge, the woman following with the paddle.

'This we call the Little River,' she says. 'A few miles downstream it joins with the Big River, on which is Simon's Landing. It shouldn't take you more than five hours or so, but I should warn you we have had some trees down in recent storms. We do our best to keep the course clear, but sometimes it is not possible. Simon and Dean should have worked on it yesterday. But . . .'

But Simon was, no doubt, too hung-over to lug fallen branches out of the river. Great.

'I am sure you will find a way' she says breezily.

Hmm! I wish I was! I haven't paddled a canoe since I was a boy scout, and this looks as if it's going to be a lot more challenging than anything I did then.

The woman − I still don't know her name − holds the canoe steady while I climb in, waits for me to pick up the paddle, and pushes me off. Then, without another word, she turns away. The engine of the jeep is already gunning as I take my first few tentative strokes, and I'm on my own.

Five hours! Five bloody hours of this ahead of me, and no promise of anything more than I've got already at the end of it!

It's not long before I come across the first of the fallen branches. It's been quite pleasant until now, paddling along beneath a green tracery of foliage that creates canopies and tunnels, and open stretches where the sun is hot on my bare arms and legs, seeing the birds winging low from branch to branch and the turtles slipping from rocks into the water as I approach. The tree has come down right across the river, its foliage spread so wide that it takes me an age to find a way round it, somehow squeezing right up to the bank, where reeds and shrubs a dozen feet high grown thickly. This doesn't bode well, but I imagine it will be easier when I get to the Big River.

Wrong. It's even more frustrating. The Big River keeps dividing around central islands; I try one way round, come across a fallen branch, paddle back and try the other side, only to find its even more completely blocked. Once I have to get out and haul the canoe over the obstruction, and tread on a dead fish.

Then there are the backwaters of thick reed I sometimes manage to find myself in. The only way out is either to back up, or hold the overhanging branches high enough to pass underneath with one hand while paddling with the other.

It seems to be taking for ever. I'm hot, thirsty – my bottle of water long gone – I've got blisters on the palms of my hands and I've been eaten alive by the mozzies. I haven't seen another living soul all day, and I'm just beginning to think I'll never get out of here when I reach what seems to be some sort of civilisation. The river is now straight and wide as far as I can see, and there are gates at intervals along the banks with small private landing stages and boats tied up at them, though still no people. I grit my teeth and paddle on down the river, as direct a course as I can manage, and then – thank God! – I see the log cabins of Simon's Landing.

I make for them, trying to get my mind back on track. For the best part of the day I've thought of nothing but getting myself out of that hell hole that had, at the beginning, seemed like paradise. If Simon isn't here, and I've put myself through all that for nothing, I'll feel like committing hara-kiri. And I have to say, the place looks horribly deserted. No sign of the lad, Dean; no sign of anyone. I try to get out of the canoe and almost fall over – my legs seem to have seized up after sitting in one position for so long. But I manage to pull the canoe up on to the bank, and, awkward as a zombie, head for the office. The door is ajar; I push it open, call out, 'Hello!'

The outer office is empty, but a voice from beyond a beaded curtain calls: 'In here!'

Simon. It's got to be. I mutter a prayer of thanks. I push aside the beaded curtain. There's another small room beyond it, and the man I saw briefly yesterday is sprawled in one of a pair of wicker chairs. On a small table beside him is a tumbler and a bottle of Jack Daniel's.

'You're back, then,' he says. His voice is slightly slurred. 'Enjoy it?'

'Let's say it was an experience.'

He smirks, raises his glass.

'Want one?'

I'm staggered. What is this? What I'd really like is a good long drink of water, but this is too good an opportunity to miss.

'I wouldn't say no.'

Simon swivels in his chair, opens a small cabinet and gets out a plastic beaker that looks as if it belongs in a motel bathroom. He pours a generous measure of Jack Daniel's.

'Here you go. Sit down, do. You're making the place look untidy.'

I sit, and he relaxes back into his chair, staring at me with the peculiar intensity of one who is half cut.

'You're English, Maria tells me. Me too. We don't get many English out here in the wilds.'

Ah, so it's because I'm English that I'm being offered this hospitality! Perhaps the man is homesick.

'Where are you from, then?' he asks.

'I live in Somerset.'

'Well, well. I'm from Bristol. Small world, eh? So, what's it like back home these days?'

A tough one. What does he want to know? That Maggie Thatcher has just completed ten years as prime minister? That unemployment is down to below two million for the first time since 1980? That there have been strikes on the London Underground, and the Ayatollah Khomeini has issued a fatwa against Salman Rushdie for the 'heresy' of his *Satanic Verses*? To be honest, I can't see that he is likely to give a damn about any of that. What about the acid-house culture, with kids turning up en masse to raves that go on for days? I don't think so somehow. It's his old life Simon is hankering after. Falmouth. The sailing crowd. Felicity Penrose, perhaps . . .

It's too soon, though, to broach that subject.

'The girls are still pretty, football's still the national game, and it's still cold and rains a lot,' I say. 'I wouldn't swap it, though. You might have the sunshine, but there are too many damn mozzies here for my liking.'

Simon shrugs. 'You get used to them.'

I scratch ruefully at one of the clutch of bites on my neck.

'Don't think I ever would. And I wouldn't choose this place anyway. Too far from civilisation to suit me. It must get pretty lonely, I'd have thought.'

Simon takes a gulp of his Jack Daniel's.

'You're not wrong there. Bloody place! Can't stand it. Why d'you think I've turned to this?' He waves his glass at me a little unsteadily. 'To make it bloody bearable, that's why.'

'If you dislike it so much, why stay?' I ask.

He snorts. 'Not a lot of option really. When I came here – well, let's just say it seemed a good idea at the time. There were a lot of bridges I wanted to burn.'

Mirroring his body language, I wave my glass back.

'Don't tell me you're a man with a past.'

'Where do I start? Oh, I'm a man with a past all right!'

I have the feeling he's enjoying the notoriety. Plus, the Jack Daniel's is making him garrulous. This is definitely promising.

'I'm guessing there's a woman involved somewhere,' I say, egging him on. 'When things go wrong for us fellas, there's almost always a woman behind it.'

'You wouldn't be wrong there, pal. Bloody women!'

'Life would be a lot simpler without them.'

'Damn right it would. Can't even hit the bottle without them nagging at you to cut it out. Maria – that's my wife – never stops going on at me. Says I'm drinking myself into an early grave. As if I care!'

'And let's face it, if it wasn't for them, we wouldn't need to drink in the first place.'

'Too true. Hey – your glass is empty. Have another, pal. We sure need it!'

'Go on then.' I let him pour me more Jack Daniel's, which I have no intention of drinking. I've got to drive back to Orlando.

'I shouldn't complain about Maria, mind you. If it wasn't for her, God knows where I'd be now. She got her old man to cough up the money to buy us this place when I was in a hell of a bloody mess. Thanks to those other bitches. Between them they ruined my life, those two.'

It's all I can do to hide my astonishment. Two women?

'I wouldn't be in this bloody place now if it weren't for them.' He's staring into his glass, seems almost to have forgotten I'm here. 'Bitches, both of them.'

'What happened, then?' I ask disingenuously.

Simon laughs bitterly, refills his glass, and tells me.

TWENTY

EMMA

I think I can say without fear of contradiction that today has been one of the longest days of my life, even though I overslept, which is very unlike me. I suppose the difference in the time zones has upset my body clock, added to which I'm just plain exhausted. High emotion seems to have sapped all my reserves. It was past nine before I made it down for breakfast, and Mike had already left for Simon's Landing. I've had nothing to do all day but kick my heels and wait for him to get back and hope that the fact that he's been gone so long means he's managed to make progress. I'm afraid to pin too much on it, though.

Around lunchtime – early evening back home – I put in a call to Dad and Maggie. A transatlantic phone call will give my hotel bill an unwelcome hike, but I owe it to them to keep in touch. They must be terribly anxious to know what is going on; this is every bit as bad for them as it is for me – worse, probably. They went through the trauma of Fliss going missing, they grieved for her, a wife and a sister, whereas I was just a little girl who didn't really understand what was going on and whose life continued more or less as normal because everyone was determined to ensure that it did. I was aware that something was terribly wrong, and I missed my mother – of course I did! – but I was quite used to being left with Maggie, and pretty soon life without Fliss became the norm. But Dad and Maggie must have gone through hell.

Now, the suggestion that she may have engineered the whole thing must have left them devastated. Dad is, I know – I've never seen him in such a state – and though Maggie seems to be in denial, I can see she's terribly upset too.

Dad answered the phone and I brought him up to date. He was pretty monosyllabic, which is not entirely unusual – Dad never uses a dozen words where one will do – but the strain in his voice was unmistakable. Maggie was out, he told me, gone to her monthly WI meeting.

'I'm hoping it will take her mind off all this,' he said. 'She's taking it very hard.' It was the most he had said in one sentence throughout the whole conversation.

'Keep me posted, won't you?' he added when I'd finished filling him in.

'Of course I will. Love you, Dad.'

'You too, Emma.'

And then he was gone.

I did wonder if I should ring Philip too. I hadn't seen him since the night I told him what was going on – the night I'd finally realised it was over between us – just left a message on his answering machine to say I was going to America, and I did feel guilty about it. But I couldn't face ringing him now, and I kidded myself that if I did it would only get his hopes up that things were returning to normal as far as our relationship was concerned.

The afternoon dragged interminably. It's seven in the evening now and I'm hanging about outside the hotel, watching the route to and from the car park and getting more and more uptight. I pace, I sit on a low wall beneath a flowering tree, I pace some more. And then at last, when I've reached the stage of thinking he's never going to come back, I spot a figure I recognise heading this way.

'Whew! I'd almost given up on you!' I say by way of greeting.

'Tell me about it! What a day!'

'So – what happened? How did you get on?'

'Give me a chance, can't you? I'm hungry, thirsty, filthy and knackered.'

He looks it.

'Sorry. It's just that . . .'

'I know. I've got to get out of these clothes, though. Come up to my room, why don't you, and when I've had a chance to catch my breath I'll fill you in.'

I'm bursting with the need to know what, if anything, he's found out, but somehow I contain myself. We take the lift. I notice that as well as dirt streaks on his face and arms he's got some nasty red blotches that I guess are mosquito bites, and the stained and crumpled state of his shorts is evidence that he's spent the best part of the day in a canoe.

'You had to make the river trip then,' I say.

''Fraid so. God, I hope there's a bottle of water in the fridge in my room. If there isn't . . .'

'I'll go down to the bar and get you one.' Somehow I don't think this is the sort of place where room service is that brilliant.

Besides the miniatures of spirits, there are only cans of tonic and ginger ale in the fridge. Mike breaks open the tonic and I go back to the bar, where I ask for a litre bottle of still spring water. When I get back with it he's in the shower; I can hear it gushing on the other side of the plywood bathroom door. I wait until it stops, then call: 'I've got your water.'

'Oh, great.' The door opens a crack and an arm emerges. There's another mosquito bite, an angry red swelling, on his wrist, and the band where his watch strap circles it is very marked, lily-white against a mahogany tan. I hand him the bottle of water and the door closes again.

I wander over to the window, resisting the natural urge to pick up the clothes discarded in a heap on the floor. This isn't my room, and Mike is a virtual stranger. It isn't my place to tidy up after him. The odd thing is, though, he doesn't feel like a stranger. I'm very comfortable with him, and something else . . .

235

I don't stop to analyse it, but when he emerges from the bath-room I know what it is all right. Wearing nothing but a pair of faded denim jeans, his hair wet from the shower and smelling of soap, he's a very attractive man. Quite a hunk, actually.

'That's better,' he says, rummaging in his travel bag for a clean white T-shirt and pulling it on. Then he returns to the bathroom for the bottle of water and re-emerges drinking from it. It looks as if it's almost gone – when he said he was thirsty, he wasn't kidding. And those bites look angrier than ever.

'I've got some stuff here that might help,' I say, rummaging in my bag for a tube of antiseptic cream I brought with me in case of just such an occurrence.

He brushes it aside. 'No – no. I'm OK.'

Obviously he is a man who doesn't like being fussed over.

'Well, it's here if you want it. Now, are you going to tell me how you got on with Simon Beacham?'

'Let's go down and get something to eat and drink.'

I get the uneasy feeling he's stalling. Why would he do that?

'Mike, I can't wait any longer!' I explode. 'I have to know! Did you find out if my mother . . .'

He's checking his wallet, sliding it into the back pocket of his jeans.

'Emma . . .'

'Is she alive? Does Simon know where she is?'

Still he doesn't answer. God, he can be stubborn!

'Let's go and find that drink. I need one if you don't. We'll talk then.'

We go down to the same bar as last night; thankfully there are plenty of empty tables. I'm trembling with anticipation – he must have something to tell me, otherwise why would he be so evasive?

Mike orders a beer for himself and a white wine for me and starts tucking into a dish of pretzels.

'So?' I say impatiently.

'Well.' He looks at me levelly. 'I had one hell of a day on the river, but it worked to my advantage. When I got back, Simon was there, alone, waiting for me, and he'd had a skinful. Which is pretty much the norm, I'd say. The man's an alcoholic; he drinks Jack Daniel's as if it were lemonade. But he welcomed me as a bosom buddy just because I happen to be English, and the drink certainly loosened his tongue. If he'd been sober, I'm pretty sure there's no way he would have talked as he did.'

My chest feels tight; I can hardly breathe.

'About my mother.'

'About your mother.'

'And it's true, isn't it, what we thought? She did fake her own death, and he helped her.'

Mike nods.

'I'm sorry, Emma, but yes, that's the way it was.'

I close my eyes briefly, press my knuckles against my mouth so hard that my teeth bite into my lip. The bar, Mike, everything, seems to have gone a very long way away, dissolved into a buzz of voices and clinking glasses and piped music that is no more than a distant backing tape. It's what's inside my head that is centre stage, illuminated by a spotlight, sharp and defined and real.

My mother is alive. She didn't die at sea. It shouldn't be a shock – I'd more or less come to believe it was true, thought I wanted it even. But having it confirmed is quite different to suspecting it. And yes, it is a shock.

'Are you all right, Emma?'

Mike's voice, penetrating the miasma. Mike's hand on my arm. I open my eyes. He's leaning across the table, looking at me intently, anxiously.

I nod. 'Yes. Yes, of course I'm all right.'

But actually I'm not. My mother left my father. Abandoned me. Let us think she was dead. When all the time . . .

'I don't understand!' I say in a dazed sort of voice. 'Why would she leave my father for that horrible, horrible man?'

'I don't think she did. I don't think she ever had any intention of—'

237

'And where is she now?'

'I don't know that yet. Simon doesn't know. He hasn't seen her for years.'

'She left him. Well, I'm not surprised.'

'No, you're not hearing me, Emma. She never was with him. He wasn't the one she ran away to be with. I think she just . . .' He breaks off, unwilling to finish the sentence.

'You mean she used him.'

'It looks like it,' Mike says uncomfortably.

'So who . . .?'

'I have a name, no more than that. But it's a very distinctive name, and I promise you I won't rest till I track him down.'

'Oh my God.' Suddenly the thing that is clearest in my muddled mind is where this is leading. Now that I know my mother didn't die that day, now that it's actually true, not just some implausible suggestion, I'm thinking about Dad and Maggie and what this is going to do to them.

'Poor Dad!' I groan. 'He is going to be devastated.'

Mike says nothing.

'And Maggie! This is going to be terrible for her too.'

Still he says nothing, and in his silence the sounds of the bar, which had seemed so distant just a few minutes ago, seem to be deafening me. I have to get out of here, have to get some fresh air.

'Excuse me . . .' I blurt, getting up, and make a dive for the door.

Outside the air-conditioned hotel the still-hot air hits me, laden with the perfume of flowering shrubs and petrol fumes. I keep on walking. Around the corner of the building is a broad expanse of lawn with clumps of trees dotted about. I start across it, unaware of anything but the need to escape from the dense fog that seems to be suffocating me. Unaware that Mike is following me until he grabs my arm.

'Emma! Where do you think you're going?'

I can't answer him. I don't know, and I don't think I could speak even if I did.

'Come on now. I know you're upset, but . . .'

I turn around, tears bubbling up, tears I'm fighting but can't control. And suddenly, without knowing quite how it's happened, I'm in his arms, my face buried in his shoulder, my hands, balled to fists, pressed against him. For a while he just holds me.

Gradually my world comes back into focus, and as it does, I become aware of things that have nothing to do with the horrendous mess my family is in. The fresh soap smell of Mike's skin. The hard strength of his arms beneath my hands. The closeness of our bodies.

I tip my head back, look up at him. At the lines of his face, where a shadow of stubble is beginning to show dark around his jaw, at his mouth, with its full lower lip, at his crooked nose, and his eyes, narrowed with concern for me. And something stirs deep inside me, a yearning that seems to spring from the very core of me. Something I haven't experienced in a very long time. Something sweet and urgent, powerful enough to wipe everything else from my mind.

We're moving closer so that his face goes out of focus and our mouths are hovering just inches apart. We're going to kiss, and I want − need − that, more than anything else in the world. And then suddenly I remember. Mike is a married man with a young daughter. What the hell am I doing?

I pull back sharply, and though my body is still yearning, the magic is gone.

'I'm sorry,' I say, and I'm not sure whether I'm apologising for my tearful outburst or for almost kissing him.

'No problem.' He smiles crookedly. 'Better now?' I nod. 'Shall we go and find something to eat, then?'

I nod again. He puts his hand under my elbow as we walk back across the lawn, but there's an awkwardness between us now, and I feel as if I'm blushing inside, hot with embarrassment. What must he think of me?

But then again, what does it matter? This is the man who is my best chance of finding my mother. I can't let a moment's madness stand in the way of that.

We eat in the hotel restaurant, pizza with a side order of fries. I haven't much appetite, but Mike is ravenous – he finishes off my pizza as well as his own.

He fills me in on the details of what Simon told him, yet I can't help feeling he's not telling me the whole story. He's keeping something back, I'm sure – it's there in the slight hesitation before he answers some of my questions, and an evasiveness when he does. But at least I have the basic facts. Simon did indeed help my mother to disappear. But it had never been her plan that he would be part of her new life, though it seemed he had hoped he could change that.

The man she wanted to be with so much that she was prepared to fake her own death was an apparently penniless American who had been known to the Falmouth sailing community simply as 'Jeff'. But, Simon had later discovered, his full name was rather more impressive. Jefferson Colville Hewson III. And far from being penniless, his family were well off, something to do with ship-building. Simon had forgotten – or been too drunk to remember – any more than that. But Mike is pretty sure that is enough.

He has contacts, it seems – the same man who found Simon for him – and if he could find a nobody like Simon, Jefferson Colville Hewson III should be no problem at all. Mike has already put in a call to ask him to get on the case, and he thinks he'll have the answer very soon.

'It shouldn't take too long to track him down – twenty-four hours at most, I'd think,' Mike says. 'Are you able to stay on for a couple of days?'

As if I'd miss being there when he finds this man! And possibly my mother too . . .

'Whether or not I should, I'm certainly going to!' I tell him.

In the event, it's much less than twenty-four hours before Mike's private eye gets back with a positive result.

I'm feeling pretty jaded after a restless night when everything kept going around and around inside my head. I still find it hard to believe that my mother could have done what she did, and I honestly can't understand the reason for it. If she had fallen in love with this Jeff, why didn't she just bolt? I suppose things were different back in the fifties, and divorce was less common than it is today, but it was perfectly possible. Why go to the lengths she did?

I don't like that she seemingly used Simon Beacham either. That would be a pretty selfish thing to do. In fact, the whole scenario paints a picture that falls far short of the image of my mother that I've always cherished. But I'll try to reserve judgement. I'm uncomfortable too about the niggling suspicion that Mike is not telling me everything. Why would he do that, unless it was something he thought I wouldn't want to hear? Or something he wants to save for his story, perhaps? I mustn't forget that first and foremost he's a journalist. He's in this for himself, not for me. The whole reason he's allowed me to tag along is to witness the moment if Fliss and I get to meet. The fact that he's friendly and supportive won't actually count for anything when the chips are down.

It's mid-afternoon and we're sitting in the shade of an outsize umbrella in the vicinity of the swimming pool when Mike gets the call from his tame private eye. I've been dozing, trying to catch up on last night's sleep, but when his mobile rings I'm instantly wide awake, every nerve twanging.

'Well?' I ask impatiently as he finishes the call.

'We're in luck. Jefferson lives up in New England, but apparently he also has a condo near Naples, and he's there at the moment.'

'Naples?'

'South Florida. No more than a five- or six-hour drive from here. Pack your bag, Emma. If we get going we can be there by bedtime.'

I pack. And while Mike is phoning ahead to book accommodation for us in Naples, I put in a quick call home. There's no reply, so I leave a message on the answering machine. Then, when we've checked out, we collect Mike's hire car from the parking lot and head down to Naples.

Suddenly everything seems to be moving at breakneck pace. On the drive south Mike fills me in on his plan.

Besides retaining links with the family shipbuilding business, Jefferson has a pet charity; was, in fact, instrumental in setting it up – sailing holidays for disadvantaged children. Mike's idea is that he should use this as the excuse for requesting an interview.

'Sounds a bit like the Jubilee Trust,' I say.

'The Jubilee Trust?' Mike is driving fast, but with a confidence and competence that allow me to feel quite relaxed. 'Have I heard of them?'

'Sailing for the disabled. It's quite a new project, but it's brilliant. I help them out when I can – as watch leader, bosun's mate, whatever. They have a tall ship, the Lord Nelson, specially equipped so that anyone can crew – the blind, the wheelchair-bound . . . anyone.'

'I don't think Jefferson has a tall ship . . .'

'No, but it might be something he'd consider. Just an idea. Another angle, maybe, to get his interest.'

'I'll give it some thought.'

By the time we get to Naples and check in to our hotel, it is, of course, too late to do anything but grab a snack and go to bed. But next morning Mike wastes no time. He's set up a meeting with Jefferson – heaven knows how he managed it, but I suppose journalists are nothing if not inventive – and is to be at Jefferson's condo at three this afternoon.

So once again I'm tight-strung with anticipation. Mike has agreed to let me go with him, ostensibly because I can talk about the Jubilee Sailing Trust, though I can't help wondering if the real reason is because he's hoping he'll witness me coming face to face with my mother.

And perhaps I will. If I do, I honestly don't know how I'll react. And Fliss . . .

I can't think about it. It's just too overwhelming. All I can do is go with the flow and hope for the best. But still it's hammering at me, relentless, unavoidable.

Today is the day I may find my mother.

TWENTY-ONE

JEFF

I've gotta say I'm intrigued. Had a call this morning from a Brit claiming he's interested in my sailing for disadvantaged youngsters, wants to talk to me about it in connection with a feature he's writing. There's a project back home, he said, that caters for the disabled, and he reckons there are parallels to be drawn and ideas to be shared. Well, that's as maybe, but it seems to me it's a heck of a long way to come for a chat we could have had on the telephone. Unless of course he's over here on vacation. Could be that, I suppose. But how did he get a hold of my number – know I'm down here in Florida, even? This is the private side of my life and I like to keep it that way. Hewson Enterprises back home in Maine know I'm here, and how to contact me; same goes for the Sunsail Trust, but they don't give out stuff like that to anyone who asks. Leastways, if they do, heads are gonna roll.

I accepted a long time ago that I couldn't escape Hewson Enterprises, couldn't get away from who I was. God knows, I tried hard enough when I was young. The prospect of being tied to the shipyards that my grandfather, Jefferson Hewson I, built up from nothing scared the hell out of me. I dropped out of Harvard and bummed around for a couple of years. Then life caught up with me, and I figured it was time I grew up and did what was expected of me.

I've been doing it ever since. But every now and then I like to come down here and unwind. Shake off the shackles. Soak up some sun. Do some sailing like I used to. Give some hands-on assistance to the kids on adventure holidays with the Sunsail Trust, rather than just sign cheques to keep them afloat.

Guess that's what I enjoy most of all – seeing those kids blossom, learn to hoist a sail, take the helm, feel good about themselves. It's pretty damn amazing – they arrive from the trailer parks and ghettos, some pasty-faced and troubled, some timid and cowed, some belligerent and aggressive, ready to tell you they've never been in a boat in their lives and sure as hell don't want to start now. A week later that's all changed. The fresh air and good food – my ship's cooks are second to none – the adventure, the learning of new skills, the being part of a team: they can't wait to get the chance to do it all again. I'd like to think I've turned a few lives around, shown them there's more to life than drink and drugs, knives and guns, unemployment benefit and ill-gotten gains, though I can't be sure. For every success I know about – and there are a few notable ones – I dare say there's a failure too, and I wish I could do more.

Which is why I didn't question this guy – Mike Bond, he said his name was – too closely. The Sunsail Trust can do with any exposure he can give it, and I can pick his brains about the sailing-for-the-disabled venture the Brits have set up too. But after I talked to him I got to wondering – and not just how the hell did he know where to find me.

I haven't been in business for more than twenty years without developing a nose for trouble, and though I can't think what it might be, I smell a rat. There's something here that's not quite right. He's using my sailing charity as an excuse. But what's his real reason for wanting to see me? Is there some big story breaking about the shipbuilding industry that I don't know about? We do a lot of government contracts, always have. Back in World War II we were turning out a destroyer every couple of weeks, and though these days things are quieter, the jobs we take on are still massive. Billions of dollars' worth. Though I'm pretty sure my commercial director would have been in touch if a current job had gone wrong, or a controversial new contract was being mooted, I put in a call to the office just to be sure. Nothing. So not the business, then. But what? I can't think of a darned thing that would interest a British journalist. Except . . .

No! Can't be! Not after all these years.

But I've got a bad feeling. And it won't budge from my gut.

My holiday home is on an island, just down the coast from Naples. A low-slung bridge connects the island to the mainland; cross that, cut through the grid of streets on which the town is built, and you reach my condo. It's a good-sized apartment, running the breadth of the building, with the main entrance on the street side and a glass wall on the side that overlooks the ocean. That's where I spend most of my time when I'm not down at the marina or out in a boat – sitting in my leather recliner and watching the sea. I never tire of it – the way the colour changes from aquamarine to midnight blue, the fudge of cloud on the horizon where sea meets deep blue sky. Boats big and small criss-cross my line of vision; the occasional light aircraft or helicopter catches my attention. If there's a thunderstorm, the view from here is spectacular. I can lose myself in the depths of that view, forget everything but nature unfolding herself before my eyes.

Not today, though. Today I'm thinking about this Brit, wondering what the hell he wants.

The bell rings. It's him. I buzz him into the building, then go out into the hallway and wait. I can see the elevator from here, see the doors slide open. The guy I imagine must be this Mike Bond gets out. But he's not alone. There's a woman with him . . .

Shock hits me like a kicking mule, shock like I haven't felt since I don't know when.

Fliss! Oh Christ, Fliss!

As she walks towards me, it's like I'm seeing a ghost. Same dark blond hair, swinging free. Same build. Same casual style, understated yet stunning.

For a moment I'm winded by that initial mind-blowing glimpse, then sweet reason kicks in. It's thirty years since Fliss was a young woman; this sure as heck is not her.

But no matter. I'm no longer a captain of industry, approaching my sixth decade. The years are rolling away as if they've never been, and I'm back in the late fifties, early sixties, just a young guy who can't get a certain woman out of his head or his heart.

I know now what it was the journalist didn't say. The reason he wanted to meet with me.

And I wonder how in hell I am going to deal with this.

Part Four
1959–1961

TWENTY-TWO

'If anything should ever happen to me, you'd look after Emma, wouldn't you, Maggie?' Fliss said.

Maggie, stirring sugar into her tea, looked up sharply.

'What sort of a question is that?'

'You would be there for Emma if she needed you? Oh, Martin would do his best, I know, but he's so tied up with the business, and anyway, it's not the same. A little girl needs a mother figure. You would take care of her?'

'Well of course I would! But this is silly talk, Fliss. Nothing is going to happen to you.'

'You never know. Look at what happened to Jo and me when we did that Fastnet trial. You thought then . . . you told me you were really worried. Suppose we'd never made it back?'

'For heaven's sake, Fliss!'

Maggie was becoming alarmed. She'd been dreadfully worried about Fliss, who had been showing all the signs of sinking back into the terrible depression that Maggie was convinced had been a nervous breakdown, and she'd been surprised when Fliss had turned up this evening out of the blue – it was very unusual for her to pop in for a visit on a weekday evening. There was something really odd about her tonight, too; she was flushed and hyper, which was at odds with the distant flatness that characterised her when she was in the grip of the depression.

251

Fliss leaned forward, her elbows on the table; her eyes were unnaturally bright.

'Promise me, Maggie!'

'Fliss, stop this now! You're really frightening me.'

'I'm only asking, that's all.'

'It's *why* you're asking that's worrying me. You're not thinking . . . you wouldn't . . .'

She broke off. *You're not thinking of doing something stupid, are you?* she'd been going to say. She was remembering how afraid she'd been during Fliss's last spell of depression that she might be suicidal. Martin and Emma would be better off without her, she'd said, the classic *cri de coeur* of someone teetering on the brink. Now Maggie was wondering if Fliss was back in that dark place where her death seemed the only solution to her problems. But putting it into words was beyond her. She couldn't, she simply couldn't, accuse Fliss of thinking of taking her own life; it was hugely insulting, and in any case she didn't want to put ideas in her sister's head if they weren't already there.

'You're got everything going for you, Fliss. A good husband, a lovely daughter, your whole life ahead of you. So let's get off this morbid subject, OK?' she said.

'OK,' Fliss said. But that strange light was still there in her eyes and Maggie knew that however she tried to dismiss it, she wasn't going to be able to stop feeling anxious about her sister.

Ever since the plan had suggested itself to her, Fliss had been in a state of turmoil, one moment believing it was possible and high on euphoria, the next overcome by doubts and racked with guilt that she could be considering it even for a moment. But she was . . . she was. Simply leaving Martin wasn't an option, she'd known that from the start. He'd never willingly give up custody of Emma, she was sure, and no court would take her part. Losing Emma was something Fliss simply couldn't contemplate. But if she was to disappear, if everyone thought she was dead, it would be a different situation entirely.

The idea had come to her like a bolt from the blue and quickly taken shape. She'd fake an accident at sea, make it look as though she had drowned. She couldn't take Emma with her immediately, of course – at least she hadn't yet been able to work out how she could manage that – but once the dust had died down she'd find a way. When she had a new identity, it should be possible to sneak back into the country and kidnap her daughter, whisk her away before anyone realised what was happening. The details of that would have to wait for later, but she'd convinced herself it could be done. In the meantime, Martin and Maggie between them would care for Emma, every bit as well as she could herself, especially if she had another nervous breakdown. And she couldn't live without Jeff, she simply couldn't. It was unthinkable. Unbearable. She missed him so badly the pain had become physical, a constant ache in her stomach as well as her heart, great tearing spasms that left her raw and bleeding. The future without him was a barren wasteland ahead of her that she felt she'd never be able to find a way across; without him nothing had meaning and she had nothing to give.

In a way it reminded her of the way she'd felt in those dreadful weeks when Emma was with her foster mother, an emptiness that swallowed her whole, a despair so black that no chink of light or hope could gain entry, a feeling that she had lost not just a limb but herself. She couldn't go on like this, couldn't live her life without Jeff and all that he was to her. Only now did she fully realise that what they had shared was not just something very special, it was the breath of life to her, and she was ready to do anything necessary to regain what she had lost.

Yet still the guilt tore her apart, and she wondered what sort of a person she could be to do something like this to Martin, who had never been anything but good to her. She thought of the way he had proposed marriage without hesitation when she had gone to him for help; she thought of the life they had built together. Did he love her? She supposed he did, but he wasn't a demonstrative man; he rarely put his feelings into words. In that he was like her father, and her father's emotions had run far deeper than anyone imagined. But Martin had his garage business. He was so wrapped up in that he scarcely had time for anything else. He'd be hurt – no, not hurt; if he thought she was dead he would grieve. But in time the pain would go away. In time he'd find someone to take her place.

Round and round went her chaotic thoughts, and she thought Martin was bound to notice how preoccupied she was. But he seemed not to. And one evening she found out why. Martin's financial problems had worsened; he'd been to see the bank manager and tried to get an extension on the loan – with limited success.

'He's given me another three months to turn things round and that's it,' he told Fliss. 'Three bloody months! It's better than nothing, I suppose, but I can't see that it's going to make a ha'p'orth of difference. He might as well have pulled the rug out from under me today and have done with it. I'm going to go bust, Fliss, and you know what that means. I'll not only lose the business now, I'll be debarred from starting up again unless I can pay off my debts.'

'Oh Martin . . .' Fliss felt sick, not only for him but for herself. How could she possibly leave him when his world was crumbling about him? 'What will you do?'

'God knows. I think I've had it, unless I come into an unexpected fortune, and that's not likely to happen, is it? I don't back the horses, don't even do the pools, and I haven't got any rich relatives to remember me in their will. So . . . there you go. A couple of years' hard work and everything I planned for down the drain.'

An unexpected fortune . . . The breath caught in Fliss's throat as the thought suddenly occurred to her. When Emma was just a baby, Martin had taken out a ridiculously large insurance policy on Fliss's life, and somehow, in spite of their straitened circumstances, he'd kept up the payments. She'd suggested once that he let it go, but he hadn't wanted to. Typical of Martin, really, adhering to the safe and the conventional. Until that moment, Fliss hadn't thought of it; now, suddenly, she realised that if she were 'dead', all Martin's money troubles would be solved.

'Something will turn up, I'm sure,' she said.

And realised she had exactly the excuse she needed to assuage her guilt. Martin might lose his wife and daughter, but at least the business that meant so much to him would be saved.

The euphoria kicked in once more. Though she was, of course, unable to contact Jeff, who would be somewhere in the middle of the Atlantic, Fliss began to make detailed plans, hardly daring to believe they would actually come to fruition, but making them all the same. Which was why she'd decided to call on Maggie. Foolish, really, making Maggie suspicious. And unnecessary – she had no doubt that Maggie would do everthing in her power to make sure Emma was well looked after until Fliss could come back for her. But she'd just had to be sure. Time now to move on to the next step. None of this would work without help – she couldn't achieve it alone. And the first person who had come to mind was, of course, Jo. On her way home, Fliss stopped at the call box at the end of their road and dialled Jo's number. She was shaking all over with the enormity of what she was actually proposing, but when Jo answered, Fliss's voice was steady.

'Jo, there's something I have to talk to you about. Can I come and see you?'

They met as arranged in a pub on the Cornwall/Devon border on the day that Emma was looked after by her childminder, and Jo could see at once that Fliss was in a state of agitation. Her heart sank. Fliss had refused to explain over the telephone why she wanted to meet, and Jo had feared the worst – that Fliss was sinking into depression again. But Fliss didn't seem depressed; though she was certainly tense and nervous, she was also giving off an aura of something like suppressed excitement.

'What's all this about then?' Jo asked when they'd ordered drinks and chicken-in-the-basket.

'I'm leaving Martin.'

'*What!*'

'Well, not just leaving him . . .'

Fliss began to explain, the words tumbling over one another, and Jo listened with growing horror and disbelief.

'What on earth are you thinking of?' she asked when Fliss finished.

'It's the only way I can get to be with Jeff and not lose Emma,' Fliss said. 'I've thought about it and thought about it, and I'm sure it would work. Besides which, the insurance on my life would get Martin out of the hole he's in financially.'

'It's madness!' Jo said bluntly. 'I can understand you're afraid that Martin would get custody of Emma if you ran off with Jeff, and I can understand you can't bear the thought of that. God knows, you lost her once, and that was enough. But this . . . if you're not careful you'll end up losing everything! Is any man worth that?'

'He's not just any man,' Fliss said simply. 'And I can't go on living without him.'

The waitress was at their table with the chicken, unloading the little wicker baskets and the paper-napkin-wrapped cutlery. Jo waited until she'd gone before replying.

'This can't be the answer. There has to be a better way.'

'There isn't. And I want you to help me, Jo. I need someone to take me off the boat and get me away. I thought if you took me to Ireland . . .'

'Oh no, Fliss.' Jo shook her head decisively. 'You can count me out. There is absolutely no way I'm getting involved in something like this.'

Something close to panic crossed Fliss's face.

'But I can't do it on my own! I have to get ashore! If I used the dinghy it would arouse suspicion, and I can hardly swim!'

'Exactly . . . No!' As Fliss opened her mouth to argue, Jo raised a hand like a policeman stopping traffic. 'Please don't ask me again.'

'But . . .'

'I'm always there for you, you know that. I'd do pretty well anything for you. But not this.'

Close to tears, Fliss tried again and again to change Jo's mind, but Jo remained firm – what Fliss was proposing was fraud, and it could only end in tears. Jo wouldn't be party to either.

As they walked out to the car park, leaving their meals almost untouched, a distance that had never been there before yawned between them. Then Jo put her arm around her friend.

'I'm sorry, Fliss. I'm only refusing for your own good.'

'No, I'm sorry. I had no right to ask. But I didn't know what else to do.'

'What you've got to do is forget this whole thing. Look – keep in touch, love. Let me know you're all right. I'm going to be so worried about you.'

Fliss didn't reply. She was fighting back tears, and the despair was closing in once more. But her determination was undented.

She couldn't let this go, she couldn't! If Jo wouldn't help her, she'd have to find someone else who would. And already she had an idea as to who that person might be.

It wasn't ideal – far from it. But Simon Beacham was the one person Fliss knew she could twist round her little finger, the one person who, in his dog-like devotion, would do anything for her. Just so long as he didn't know she intended to be with Jeff. She couldn't imagine Simon would be willing to help her if he knew that.

She spent long sleepless hours wondering how to approach him and what she should say when she did. She could offer him money; the legacy Greta had left her was still more or less intact – Martin had steadfastly refused to accept any of it in spite of his financial worries, and the *Mermaid's Song* hadn't thrown up any big expenses. It wasn't a lot, but she was fairly certain Simon was feeling the pinch too and could do with making a little extra. But alone it wouldn't be enough to buy not only his help but also his silence. She was going to have to dangle another carrot in front of him, and the very thought of it made her recoil in revulsion as well as stirring up feelings of guilt. But she had to do it if she wanted to be with Jeff. She'd do anything, but anything for that.

She went to Falmouth, made her way to the sailmaker's shop. Her stomach was churning, every nerve stretched and jangling, and she felt guilty for what she was about to do. But she had to get Simon onside before she told him the details of her plan – she couldn't risk him talking about it in the bars and cafés – and she could think of only one way to do that.

'Fliss!' Simon's face lit up when he saw her standing in the doorway. 'What are you doing here? The spinnaker hasn't fallen apart again, surely?'

Fliss shook her head.

'I just came to see you, Simon. I *had* to see you.'

His forehead puckered with suspicion, but he also looked pleased.

'That's very nice. But . . .'

'Oh Simon, I'm so unhappy!' she burst out. Tears were filling her eyes, tears that were not part of an act but came all too readily.

'Whatever is the matter?' Simon asked solicitously. 'We can't have this! Come on in and I'll make us a cup of tea.'

Fliss allowed him to lead her into his inner sanctum, where he cleared a chair of a huge pile of what looked like brochures, correspondence and invoices, and helped her into it.

'Now, I'll make the tea and you can tell Uncle Simon all about it.'

Fliss bowed her head.

'I can't! It's too terrible.'

'You can tell *me*, Fliss. You can tell me anything.'

'I can trust you not to tell anyone else?'

'You know you can.'

Fliss gulped. 'Oh Simon, I've made the most awful mistake. I should never have married Martin. You don't know how unhappy I am. I've just got to leave him, but he won't hear of it. I'm trapped. He'll never let me go, not as long as I live.'

'Oh Fliss!' He was gazing at her with those soulful eyes, and she knew she had him hooked.

'Would *you* help me escape, Simon?' she asked. 'If I gave you all the money I have saved, would you help me?'

'I don't want money, Fliss. Any way I can help you, you know I'll do it.'

'But I'd give it to you anyway. And you wouldn't tell a soul, would you? It would be our secret?'

She could see him puffing up with importance at the thought of sharing a secret with her.

'Of course I wouldn't tell anyone if you don't want me to.'

'It's not just that I don't want you to; no one must know – ever! Only you and me . . .'

He squatted down on the floor beside her chair so that their faces were on a level.

'What do you want me to do, Fliss?'

'I hardly like to tell you. But . . .' Steeling herself, she reached out and took his hand. 'I'd be grateful for you for ever and ever.'

'You mean . . .?' Hope was sparking in his eyes.

'I can't promise anything, Simon. Not until I'm free. But when I am . . .'

'Tell me what you want me to do,' he said.

She told him.

When she'd finished, he was pale and shaking.

'But where will you go?'

'Take me to Ireland. I've got friends there,' she lied, a spark of fresh guilt almost stopping the words. But she was too desperate to be deterred for long. 'When I'm settled, I'll get in touch – let you know where I am. But you can see now why you mustn't tell a soul. If you did, you'd be blamed as much as me, and I don't want that. I don't want you getting into trouble with the law because of me . . .'

'Oh, that doesn't bother me,' he swaggered. 'But you know you can trust me.'

'You'll help me, then? And not tell a soul?'

'Oh Fliss,' he said. 'I'd do anything in the world for you.'

Fliss felt as if she was totally divorced from reality. Whilst still going through the motions of everyday life, the essence of her was elsewhere, as if she was existing on another planet, looking in on herself.

The one thing that was real was the overwhelming love she felt for Emma. A dozen times a day, she gathered her daughter to her, hugging her close, breathing in the smell of her, drinking in the warmth of her small, chubby body, storing away memories in her every sense to be taken out and cherished through the long days and months until she could hold her once more.

'We'll be together again soon, my darling,' she whispered into the soft baby hair, knowing that Emma did not understand, but needing to tell her all the same.

When the day of her planned disappearance arrived, Fliss wasn't at all sure she could go through with it. Leaving Emma with Maggie, she felt as if her heart was being torn from her body.

'Mummy will be back soon,' she said, knowing it was a lie. And: 'You'll be fine with Daddy and Auntie Maggie.' That was not a lie, but it brought the tears to her eyes all the same, reliving as she was the terrible moment when she had left Emma as a baby with the foster mother. But she'd got her back then, and she'd do it again.

She kissed her one last time and left the house without so much as a backward glance. If she hesitated, she didn't think she could do this. But it was too late now for second thoughts. Her plans were made, the die was cast.

There could be no going back now.

The *Mermaid's Song* might have been a painted boat on a painted ocean. She rode at anchor five nautical miles off the Cornish coast, sails furled, bobbing lazily with the gentle rise and fall of the tide. On deck, Fliss scanned the empty expanse impatiently. The glare of the sun on the water was hurting her eyes with a brightness her sunglasses could not completely counter; her stomach was churning, her nerves so tight-strung they seemed to twang in her arms and legs and jump in her throat.

Was Simon ever going to come for her? All she wanted now was to get on with it. Anything but this awful enforced inactivity. Anything to take her mind off the terrible physical pain that was her longing for her daughter.

Tears stung Fliss's eyes again as the longing clawed at her and she wrapped her arms around herself, bowing her head for a moment. *Think of the future. Of the new life you can give her in America. Think of Jeff.* But the tears were running down her face again, salty as the sea. She fished a handkerchief out of her pocket, wiping her eyes and blowing her nose, and when she looked up again she saw it.

A flash of white sail against the deep greeny-brown of the sea. Was it Simon? She strained her eyes as the boat came closer, gradually taking shape. It was him – it had to be. But she hardly dared to believe it until it was close enough for her to be sure. Then Simon was calling out to her, throwing her a rope. And Fliss was doing what she had to do, exactly as planned.

'Well I suppose this is it,' she said as they left *Mermaid's Song* behind them, abandoned like a cast-off toy to drift wherever the wind and tides took her.

Then she tipped back her head, feeling the salt spray mingle with the tears on her cheeks, and tried to think only of the future.

TWENTY-THREE

He had to be crazy, Jeff decided. One solo transatlantic crossing should be enough for anybody. When he'd arrived in Falmouth after making the eastbound voyage he'd vowed: never again. But that was sailors all over. When the memories of the discomfort, the loneliness and the fatigue faded, the yearning to do it all again began nibbling away at your resolve until you succumbed. Besides which, he'd made up his mind to go home, and the only way to get the *Jersey Gal* there was to sail her.

He'd hoped, of course, that Fliss would be with him. When she'd told him she wouldn't be, he could have delayed until he found someone else to crew for him. But he hadn't wanted to. He'd wanted to get away, as far as possible from the woman who had come to mean so much to him but who would never be his. Going it alone would be balm for his wounded spirit, he'd thought. The Atlantic gales would blow her out of his head; the rain and the sea spray would wash her out of his blood.

It hadn't worked. Jeff was as wretched at her loss as ever, and now, after more than a month at sea, fighting the elements, living on canned beans, corned beef and chocolate digestives, grappling with sail changes with frozen fingers, thick-headed from lack of sleep, he was cursing himself for putting himself through the whole hellish experience again. He longed for a good night's sleep in a comfortable bed, a decent meal he hadn't had to prepare himself – a T-bone steak and fries would be good – and a hot bath. But most of all he longed for Fliss. God, but he loved her.

It wasn't a word that had been in his vocabulary until he met her – no, actually, until much later than that. He'd been attracted to her, fascinated by her, enjoyed her company and the connection between them. When he'd feared for her safety on that Fastnet trip with Jo, he'd been shocked and scared by the strength of his feelings but he still hadn't acknowledged it as love. Not even when he'd gone away and tried to forget her had he stopped to analyse the compulsion that had drawn him back to her. If he'd thought about it at all, he'd fooled himself into thinking an affair would satisfy him, that if she was no longer forbidden fruit the power of her attraction for him would lose its potency.

But that hadn't happened. Rather than wanting her less, he wanted her more. The little time she was able to spend with him wasn't enough; the fact that she belonged to another man was destroying him. He wanted to share everything with her – his whole life. He wanted a future with her. And he finally acknowledged what he supposed he had known all along – that Fliss and their relationship, the connection between them, was truly special on every possible level.

For the first time in his life, Jeff began to think beyond the here and now, freedom and instant gratification. He realised that he couldn't continue with an affair that was leading nowhere and he couldn't go on bumming around for ever. It was time to begin to plan for the rest of his life – a life he hoped he would share with Fliss. When he went home on the visit to his sick mother he talked to his parents about the possibility of going back to college to finish his studies. They'd been delighted and his father had promised to bring his not inconsiderable influence to bear on those in authority at Harvard. Jeff had no doubt that by the time he reached American soil it would all be arranged and in the fall he would be taking up where he'd left off. And after that he'd be expected to take up a position at Hewson Enterprises. His whole life mapped out for him, as it always had been, but for this brief escape. A secure life. A privileged life. A life that could be, if he put his mind to it, fulfilling.

But nothing of it meant anything without Fliss.

Cold, wet, hungry, exhausted, Jeff opened yet another can of beans, ate them cold with just the flat of his knife to shovel them from can to mouth, and collapsed for a brief sleep on his hard, narrow bunk. But even then, as his thoughts grew fuzzy and he headed towards oblivion, Fliss was there, lying beside him, her hip pressed against his, her breast squashed against his arm, her hair a soft curtain over his shoulder. And when he fell into an exhausted sleep, she haunted his dreams.

The sighting of land after a long voyage is always a moment to be relished. Since leaving England Jeff had steered a south-westerly course as far as was possible, and Nova Scotia and the familiar coast of New England had been too distant – and too shrouded in mist – to be visible as he headed for the Florida Keys. He had, for a little while, been tempted to change his plans and make land in Newport, but Naples was his home port and his friends would be there to greet him. Becalmed for a seemingly endless four days off the coast of the eastern seaboard, he regretted his decision, but once he found the wind again he was glad he'd stuck to his original plan. He was glad too of the extra week or more at sea – it allowed him a little more respite before he had to succumb to the straitjacket of the plans he felt sure had been made for him. But even so, as the Florida coast hove into view, nothing could detract from his feeling of elation.

Done, dusted. He could now almost count off the hours to that hot bath, T-bone steak and a good, uninterrupted sleep. He was talking now to familiar radio stations, names and voices he recognised, old pals urging him on. And then, when he had rounded the Keys and was approaching Naples, the voice on the radio was one that was even more instantly recognisable – Rick Curtis, his oldest friend in the sailing world.

'Hey, buddy, how ya doing?'

'Rick?'

'Sure is! Welcome home, pal! We're on our way out – be with you in five.'

Jeff's spirits rose another notch, but the wind was dropping. He left the radio to go back on deck and put up a spinnaker to catch what was left of it, and just as he was finishing, he heard a yell. He jerked round – a motorboat had come alongside unnoticed by him, and Rick, sitting on the side, was waving wildly, his sun-browned face above a bushy beard split into a wide grin of welcome.

'Jeez, Rick, you sly old coyote! What are you doing here?' Jeff yelled.

'Come to make sure you don't sink Naples' finest on your way in. Hold tight, I'm coming aboard.'

'Like hell you are!'

Rick waved a bottle aloft. 'Still wanna stop me?'

The prospect of an ice-cold beer was more than Jeff could resist.

'OK, pardner. Just this once.'

Rick jumped on board, sure-footed as a cat. The two men embraced, and Rick pulled a couple of bottles out of the pocket of his windjammer, where he'd stowed them to make the leap. A bottle opener followed, and he removed the caps, passing one to Jeff.

'There you go. Don't drink it all at once. Though I gotta say, you look as if you need it.'

'Sure do! It's been one hell of a long time!'

'Tell me about it. It's OK, buddy, if you fall down drunk I'll get the *Jersey Gal* in for you. That's what friends are for!'

It was like old times; for the moment he became the old Jeff.

'Over my dead body,' he said. 'Get out of the way, you useless lump, and let me sail my boat.'

'Yeah? Get on with it then.'

Rick leaned against the cockpit, beer in hand, as Jeff, head spinning from those first greedy gulps, and suddenly feeling every ache and tremor of total exhaustion, did what he had to do.

When the *Jersey Gal* had been towed into her moorings, Jeff took his first unsteady steps on dry land. It never failed to amaze him how, after a long voyage, it was always the ground that seemed to rock far more than the ocean had done, and as he made his way along the wooden jetty he had to concentrate to keep from visibly swaying.

He'd forgotten, too, what a busy harbour Naples was, or perhaps it was busier than usual today. Word that a sailor was coming home after a solo transatlantic crossing had spread and was enough to attract a crowd of well-wishers, old friends and curious strangers. Cheers and yells of congratulation followed him as he staggered along the paved harbour, and every so often he raised a hand in acknowledgement, but the sea of smiling faces, of brightly coloured shirts and shorts, of yachting caps and sunglasses, was little more than a blur to him.

And then quite suddenly one figure detached itself from the melee. A slight figure in narrow white pedal-pushers and a pink gingham shirt, cropped blond hair seeming to reflect the sunlight.

Jeff stopped abruptly, and the ground swayed even more alarmingly beneath him. God, the beer and the exhaustion were having a far greater effect on him than he'd realised. He was hallucinating now! He closed his eyes, covering them with a hand that was inexplicably shaking. When he opened them again, the apparition was just a few feet away.

'Jeff!'

'Fliss?' he said, stunned, disbelieving.

And then she had flung herself at him and the reality was there, in his arms.

She shouldn't have done it, of course, not here, where he was the centre of attention. Even though she wasn't known here, she was taking the most terrible risk. Her intention had been to follow him when he left the marina, and wait for an opportunity to greet him somewhere a lot more private. But she couldn't do it. For one thing she was too afraid she might lose sight of him in the crush, or he'd get into a car and be driven away. For another, the urge to be with him now, this minute, was just too strong. The trauma of leaving Emma, and the loneliness of the past weeks, waiting for him to arrive in Naples, had taken their toll. She needed him more than ever, and she needed him now.

It had to be said, though, that everything had gone a great deal more smoothly than she had dared hope. Simon had taken her to Ireland, and Fliss had made her way to Dublin, where she booked a flight to Florida. She was terrified she might be recognised by emigration officers — she'd had no option but to use her own passport — but they waved her through with no more than a cursory glance. Felicity Penrose's fame obviously did not extend to Ireland, and in any case the passport was in her married name. But nevertheless she was unable to relax until the plane was off the ground, and even then she was looking around at her fellow passengers, fearful that one of them might be regarding her with suspicion.

She felt safer once she had landed in Miami, and stayed there for a few days, but, although common sense was telling her it would be some time yet before Jeff reached Naples, she couldn't rest easy for fear of missing his arrival. She took a flight to Fort Myers and hitched down the coast.

The small amount of cash she'd brought with her, and which she had changed into American dollars at Miami airport, was dwindling fast. Though she had no work permit, and was horribly aware that as an English girl seeking a job here in Florida she would be fairly conspicuous, she really had no choice. She couldn't manage without money. But once again she was lucky. The owner of the little harbourside diner where a card in the window advertised a vacancy for a waitress wasn't one to concern himself with legalities. Only too glad to find an attractive young woman willing to wait tables, he gave her the job on the spot, saying they'd sort out 'all that legal shit' later, and the other waitress, Tami Docherty, offered the use of her sofa bed until Fliss could find somewhere to stay.

It was far from ideal: Tami's apartment was cramped and untidy. That night Fliss had to move a heap of laundry waiting to be ironed – how long it had been there she didn't care to hazard a guess – a clutter of magazines and an empty pizza carton before she could spread out the rug Tami had given her for a blanket. The cushions she was to use as pillows were stained with beer and coffee spills and smelled of stale cigarette smoke. And Tami, generous, friendly soul that she was, barely drew breath between questions. Was Fliss in a relationship? Divorced – married – separated? Where did she come from? Why was she here? How long did she plan to stay?

Fliss felt horribly guilty lying to Tami when she had been so kind, and kept her answers as close as possible to the truth. She had been married, but it hadn't worked out. She'd come to Naples looking for her sailor boyfriend. She wasn't sure when he'd be back, and she didn't know what would happen when he was.

'You're sure he's not just stringing you along, honey?' Tami said. 'That'd be fellas all over.'

She was eating ice cream straight from the tub. She handed Fliss another spoon, none too clean. 'Here you go, dig in like me and you'll feel a whole lot better. Ice cream's better than a no-good guy any day!'

Fliss didn't want ice cream; she didn't want anything but to be with Jeff. She was longing for Emma too, picturing her, soft and rosy from her bath, begging a last bedtime story. As soon as she was alone, she would take out the photographs of Emma that she'd brought with her and pore over them, the only thing she had of her beloved daughter. Looking at them would probably make her cry, but she'd do it all the same.

Fliss dug her spoon into the raspberry ripple because it was expected of her, and it tasted of nothing.

Between waiting tables, fending off the clumsy advances of

red-blooded young sailors, and fielding Tami's increasingly probing questions, Fliss tried to get news of Jeff. It wasn't easy to come by, particularly in the beginning, when he was still far from Florida. There was interest, of course, in the guy who was mad enough to do a second transatlantic crossing, but it was a long while now since Jeff had been part of the Naples scene, and many of his closest buddies had moved on. As he neared home, though, it was easier – talk about his latest position, which radio station he was in contact with, and an estimated date of arrival became more commonplace.

Fliss was at work in the diner when she heard that, with luck and a fair wind, he was expected in the next day. She was serving breakfast when she overheard a couple of young guys in the next booth talking about it. Her heart began thudding, a sledgehammer against her ribs, as delight and terror in equal measures ebbed and flowed. The eagerness to see him, to be with him, was more urgent than ever, but suddenly Fliss was overcome with nervousness too. How would he react to what she had done? He was bound to be shocked, to see her even, let alone when he learned the truth about how she came to be here. Suppose he didn't want her any more – the kind of woman who could do such a thing? Perhaps his feelings had changed anyway; once he'd left England for good he might have forgotten about her, just another girl in another world.

The uncertainty made her feel sick, and for the first time the enormity of what she had done hit her. Ever since she'd abandoned the *Mermaid's Song* she had been living in a vacuum of unreality, geared only to surviving without raising suspicion until she was with Jeff again, when, miraculously, everything would come right. Now, with his arrival imminent, the awful possibility yawned before her – if he turned his back on her, she would be completely alone. She couldn't return to her old life – even if Martin would have her back. Even if she wanted him to. She could never admit to what she'd done; the repercussions didn't bear thinking about. Felicity Penrose didn't exist any more. She was dead.

So who am I? Fliss asked herself. I don't exist. And she shivered, feeling suddenly that she was a wraith, adrift in an alien world.

She and Tami were working different shifts this week – Fliss the early, Tami the late – and when Fliss heard that Jeff was expected the following morning, she asked Tami if they could swap.

'You gotta be joking!' Tami said bluntly. 'I'll be lucky to get home before midnight – you can't seriously expect me to be back in this place at six!'

'What if I came back this evening so you could finish at eight? And I'll do the first couple of hours tomorrow morning if you could relieve me, say, at ten? Carlo won't mind, will he, as long as we've got it covered? Oh Tami, please! Just this once!'

Tami gave her a long, hard look.

'What's going on? Sounds like something pretty important to me.'

'It is. My boyfriend . . .'

'Hey, kid!' Tami had heard the talk about a sailor who was expected after a transatlantic voyage. 'It's not Jeff Hewson, is it?'

'You know him?'

'Not to say know. He used to come in here sometimes, a couple of years ago. Hey, it is him, isn't it? Well you're a dark horse and no mistake!'

'I met him in Cornwall,' Fliss admitted.

'And you've followed him out here? You must be keen! Oh, you don't need to confess – I can see it right there in your face. Well I'll be darned. He's a pretty cool dude, I know, but . . .'

'Will you do it for me, Tami? Please!'

Tami grinned. 'I guess you've got it. And I guess you won't be wanting my sofa tomorrow night.'

Again that leap of the heart. She could think of nothing else now but that tomorrow she would see Jeff again. For the moment there was no room for regrets, guilt, or the shame that sometimes washed over her.

'Oh thank you! Thank you!' She hugged the girl who had befriended her, a stranger. 'Some day I'll do the same for you.'

Hope was buoying her suddenly. Perhaps Felicity Penrose had ceased to exist. But someone new was taking her place. Fliss prayed that that someone would be less likely to screw up her life and the lives of others.

Fliss was at the marina long before the *Jersey Gal* was sighted, stomach tied in knots. She walked from one end to the other, watching, listening, waiting. She'd just begun to give up hope that anything was ever going to happen when the activity began. Two motorboats roared away from the jetty, the men on board waving excitedly to one another. And then . . . oh my God, wasn't that a sail on the horizon? She couldn't identify it yet, didn't know if it was *Jersey Gal* or some other yacht heading for harbour. But the motorboats were heading towards it, and a crowd was beginning to congregate, appearing, it seemed, from nowhere.

'It's him!' she heard someone say.

Oh, if only she could have gone out with the motorboats! If only she could leap on to *Jersey Gal*, throw her arms around him, bury her head in a shirt that would inevitably smell of sweat, taste the salt on his skin, feel his heart beating next to hers . . . But she couldn't. She could only wait.

Until he came ashore, and she could wait no longer.

Fliss pushed her way through the people separating her from Jeff. She saw him stop, and for a dizzying moment he was looking right at her. She ran on, breathless, until she reached him.

'Jeff!'

'Fliss?'

She heard the wonder and disbelief in his voice as if through a raging torrent.

And then she was in his arms.

TWENTY-FOUR

She didn't confess to him that first day the awful thing she had done. To begin with there was no opportunity – Jeff had introduced her to his friends simply as 'my girl from England' and they'd all gone back to Rick's apartment, where the celebrations had continued. Then, when his friends had tactfully allowed them some privacy, she hadn't been able to bring herself to mar the joy of their reunion with explanations she knew, instinctively, would horrify him.

'I can't believe you're here, sweetheart,' he said, and she told herself the truth could wait.

She had wondered if he might have heard via radio contact that she was missing, presumed drowned, but clearly he hadn't, and she didn't think it was the right time to break it to him, with his friends in the next room and him so clearly exhausted. And then it was time for her to go back to the diner to relieve Tami, and she had left Jeff to fall into a deep and much-needed sleep.

It was only as she served meals and cleared tables in the diner that she realised she had actually been putting off telling him because she was scared to death of his reaction.

There was no way she could keep it from him for ever, though. She had to tell him, and in any case she hated secrets coming between them; communication was the bedrock of their relationship. But still the very thought of it made her curl up inside with dread, and when the moment came, Fliss's heart was in her throat.

This was it. No more prevaricating. No more pretence.

'There's something I have to tell you,' she said.

'I can't get my head round this,' Jeff said. He was sitting on the edge of the bunk in the cabin of the *Jersey Gal*, head bowed in his hands. 'What the hell have you done, Fliss?'

'It was the only way,' she said defensively.

'For Christ's sake! You faked your death?' For all that he'd longed for her, for all that he'd wanted her here, sharing his life, this was beyond him. 'Why didn't you just walk out like any normal person?'

'You know why! Martin would never have let me have Emma.'

'And where is she now?'

Fliss's chin wobbled.

'Still in England. But I'm going to get her, just as soon as things have settled down.' She hesitated, fearful suddenly. 'You are happy to take on Emma, aren't you? You said . . .'

'That's hardly the issue here.' Jeff ran his fingers through his hair, much longer now than it had been, long enough to curl over the collar of his polo shirt. 'How the hell do you think you are you going to get her?'

'I don't know yet . . . I haven't worked out all the details . . .'

'Seems to me there's a hell of a lot that you haven't worked out. How you're going to stay in America, for a start, never mind going to England and back again. You're using your own passport, I assume.'

'Well, yes, for the moment . . .'

'And how long will it be before you get caught out? The whole thing's crazy, Fliss. Plum crazy!'

Tears welled in her eyes. 'Don't be cross with me, please! I only did it to be with you.'

'I know that, but . . .' He reached out and took her hand. 'To do something like this . . . It's one hell of a mess. How could you imagine for a moment it could pan out?'

'I thought I could get a new identity – like they do in films. And then I'd be able to sneak back for Emma,' she said wretchedly.

'It didn't occur to you it would arouse suspicion if she were to disappear too? That the insurance company might well refuse to pay out on your life and poor old Martin wouldn't even have that for consolation? And how are you going to get her into America? It's just not going to happen, Fliss.'

'But it has to! I have to get Emma!'

'Truth to tell, I think the only thing you can do is go home and own up – face the music.'

'Oh don't say that, Jeff, please! I can't go home! I can't!' She was crying in earnest now, the full implications of the situation becoming clear to her. 'That's not what you want, is it?'

'Fliss . . . Fliss . . .' He pulled her into his arms. 'Of course it's not what I want. I want you here with me. But not like this. Honey, this is one hell of a shock. Right now I can't think straight.'

'There has to be a way! There has to!'

'Well I sure as heck don't know what it is. You've got me beat here. But . . . Oh hell, Fliss, don't cry. What's done is done, I guess. We'll just have to make the best of it.'

Fliss was shaking, mortified that Jeff was so clearly horrified by what she had done and frightened by his doubts that this could work out. She'd naïvely thought that he would have the answers, that when they were together he'd take charge and make everything all right.

'I'm sorry, Jeff,' she said in a small voice. 'I suppose I have been rather stupid.'

'Understatement of the decade! Shit, Fliss . . .' He broke off. A voice on deck was calling his name.

'Hey, Jeff, you there?' Rick.

'Yeah, down here!' Jeff called back.

A bolt of panic shot through Fliss.

'You won't tell him . . .?'

'You think I'm crazy? This really is something else, Fliss. You gotta give me time to get my head round it . . . Coming, pal!'

And he disappeared through the hatch.

Fliss sat on the hard bunk, knuckles pressed against her mouth, and wept.

She hardly knew Jeff any more. He seemed to have gone away from her. A distance yawned between them; she knew it was because of what she'd done, and she could scarcely bear it. If she had felt alone before, this was much, much worse. Then she had been looking forward to being with him again; now he was here and she was still alone in an isolation of her own making.

She was still living at Tami's. He hadn't suggested she move on to the boat, and she was terrified he might be thinking of taking off without her, that when she went to the marina the berth would be empty and the *Jersey Gal* gone.

And when he said: 'I've got to go home, Fliss,' her stomach turned over and she was filled with sick dread.

'Home,' she repeated dully. 'Why?'

He gave an impatient shake of his head.

'What do you mean, why? For one thing I want to see my mom. She's sick, I told you, really sick if you ask me, though she's trying to keep it from me.'

'Oh Jeff, I'm sorry . . .'

'And there's another reason, too. When I came to England, I'd dropped out of college. Now I'm planning on going back, doing my final year. I spoke to my father on the telephone last night. It's all fixed.'

Her eyes went wide with shock. 'You're going to college?'

'Got to finish my education. Get set up for the future. I can't go on drifting for ever.'

For a moment she was speechless. This wasn't the Jeff she knew. That Jeff stuck two fingers up at the establishment, lived for the day.

'College – where?'

'Harvard.'

'Harvard!' Though she knew next to nothing about American

education, she'd heard of Harvard. Along with Yale it was a name to impress.

He grinned crookedly, but a little self-deprecatingly.

'A family tradition.'

'I don't even know where Harvard it! Is it a long way from here?'

'You could say that. Maybe fifteen hundred miles as the crow flies, give or take a few. I'm going to sail up to New England – I'll be leaving tomorrow or the next day.'

Her heart was sinking; the tears threatened again.

'What about me? What am I going to do?'

'Well,' he said, 'I guess you'll have to come with me.'

The tension was still there between them as they sailed out of Naples, Jeff silent and brooding, Fliss anxious and wretched. He didn't need to reproach her for her to know exactly how he felt about this; it was there in his eyes and his coldness towards her, and she was terribly afraid she had damaged their precious relationship beyond repair.

After a few days' sailing, however, things began to improve. Alone together in a familiar environment he relaxed a little, and though she knew he was still worried, she thought he was beginning to come to terms with the situation.

'We've got to get this mess sorted out,' he said one day as they sat side by side on deck, soaking up the sun. 'Work out just how we're going to get away with it. And I guess the first thing is to organise you a new identity. At some point the authorities are going to start asking questions, and they sure as hell aren't going to like the answers.'

Afraid of saying the wrong thing and shattering this fragile truce, Fliss remained silent.

'Right now I'm not sure how to go about it,' he went on, 'but once we get home I'll do a bit of digging. See if I can find someone who can help us out. They're about, for sure; it's just a matter of getting some names and offering the right price to the right people.'

Fliss shuddered inwardly. The right people. Criminal types, certainly. Mafia possibly! What had she got Jeff into? And of course none of them would fit her up with a new identity out of the goodness of their hearts.

'I don't have any money,' she said in a small voice. 'I've used up what I had, and I only earned peanuts at the diner. Even the tips weren't very good.'

Jeff grinned crookedly. 'No, I bet they weren't. The kind of folk who use that place are pretty hard-up themselves.'

'So what am I going to do?'

'Guess you'll just have to leave it up to me.'

'But you never had any to spare either.'

'Trust me, I can get it. My folks aren't short of a dime.'

The realisation of just how little she knew about Jeff's background – or indeed, his family, whom she was soon to meet – brought her up short.

'Tell me about them,' she said.

He shrugged. 'Not a lot to tell. Anyway, I thought we were discussing your new identity. Like I say, I'll get on to it soon as I can, but until someone comes up with the goods, you're going to have to keep a low profile.'

'I know. How are you going to explain me to your parents?'

'I won't be telling them the truth, that's for sure. No, I reckon I'll just say you're my lady. That's all they need to know.'

The old warmth was there, the old spark, all the more potent for its recent absence. Fliss buried her face in his shoulder, and it was a long time before they gave any more thought to the problems that lay ahead of them.

As they neared New England, and the moment when she would have to meet Jeff's family drew closer, Fliss decided to question him again. Besides her curiosity she was feeling very nervous and wanted to be prepared.

'I don't know a single thing about them apart from the fact that your mother is ill,' she said. 'And I don't know anything about your life before you came to England either. Why don't you ever want to talk about it?'

They were relaxing on deck again, bare sunburned legs touching, smoking cigarettes. Jeff's eyes narrowed behind the curling smoke and for a long moment he was silent.

'I suppose in a funny sort of way I'm ashamed,' he said at last.

'Ashamed – why?' She thought suddenly of the conversation about getting her a new identity, and how he'd said he'd find somebody to fix it. 'Your father isn't a gangster of some kind, is he?'

Jeff laughed aloud.

'Jeez no! Quite the opposite!'

'Then why . . .?'

Jeff inhaled and blew the smoke out in a steady stream.

'It's kind of hard to explain. I had a privileged upbringing, Fliss – never wanted for anything. And I don't just mean the ordinary stuff like good food on the table and a pair of new shoes every time my feet grew a size. Whatever took my fancy, I only had to say the word. "You want a toy car you don't have to pedal, son? An electric one? You got it." "You've outgrown your pony? Well, let's see about getting one to suit your size." "You want to fly the company plane? We'll get you some flying lessons and when you're old enough maybe you can have one of your own."'

'You can fly a plane?' Fliss interrupted, awed and astonished.

'I've got a licence, sure, but I don't fly much any more. It's the sea with me – sailing. I've always had a boat, ever since I was a kid. Never did press for that plane of my own. But if I'd wanted it . . . that's the way it was. And I took it all for granted. A maid to tidy up after me, so I could leave my toys scattered around when I got tired of playing with them, and wet towels on the bathroom floor, and nobody would yell me out. A mom who always looked a million dollars when she stood on the touchline to watch me play ball – freshly coiffed hair, the latest designer fashion, a diamond the size of the Koh-i-Noor on her finger. A father the workers in the shipyard tugged their forelocks to when

278

he passed by. Two whole months' holiday at our summer place on Gull Island, running around with all the other rich kids . . .'

'Gull Island?'

'An island off the coast of Maine. We had a house there – still do as far as I know, though I'm not sure Mom and Dad go there much nowadays. No, back then it never crossed my mind that I was one of the lucky ones. Like I say, it was just what I was used to. Kids don't think too much about things like that. Even when I went to boarding school, most of my classmates came from the same kind of background as me and—'

'They sent you to boarding school?' Fliss said.

'Sure did. A fancy school for fancy families. Mom didn't want me to go – I heard them arguing about it – but Dad got his way. He always did. I was ten years old and I didn't much want to go either, but I didn't get to have a say, and it wasn't so bad once I got used to it. No, I guess it was only once I was thirteen or fourteen that I started thinking how everyone wasn't as lucky as me and feeling guilty that I had everything and they had nothing. And even then it didn't really hit home. Not until I got friendly with Chad.'

'Chad?'

'Yeah.' Jeff took a last pull of his cigarette and tossed it over the rail. 'Like I said, we had this summer place on Gull Island – it's where I first got hooked on sailing. Most of the summer before I went up to Harvard Mom and I spent on the island, and Dad would come over when he could. Chad was employed that year as a lifeguard – with all the swimming and boating and crazy beach parties the families got together and hired him to keep their precious kids from drowning. We were a pretty wild set – all as spoiled as one another, and a lot of them were a darned sight too full of their own importance. They gave Chad a pretty hard time for no other reason than he wasn't one of us. Hadn't been to a fancy school. Was going to the University of Connecticut on a scholarship. Working as a lifeguard to make a few dollars to see him through. Plus for safety reasons they were supposed to do as he told them, and they didn't like that. So they made a sport of taunting him. The guys shut him out, took every chance to show him they were superior; the girls – well, they loved to lead him on, then drop him cold. I didn't like that. It stuck in my gut. Chad and I got to be good friends. The rest of the crowd cut me out of their circle for sticking by him, but I didn't give a damn. He was worth more than the whole lot of them put together.'

He stopped, squinting into the sun, then went on.

'My values changed after that – turned on their head, really. I started hating everything my old life stood for – got to be a rebel. *Rebel Without a Cause* – did you see that film? James Dean? That was me – except that I thought I did have a cause. I even changed my politics. My family are all Republicans – me, I like the Democrats, though I've never yet bothered to use my vote. And I guess that's just about it! I opted out – took off with my boat – and from there on you know.'

Fliss gave her head a small shake, trying to take it all in.

'But now you're going back – picking up where you left off.'

'You could say that. I'd rather call it growing up. I caused Mom and Dad a whole lot of grief, and I'm sorry for that. They only ever did their best for me, I know that now. If Mom is really sick – the big C is what I'm afraid of – I gotta try and make it up to her before it's too late. Go see her as often as I can, make sure she knows . . .' He broke off, turning his head away to hide the sudden rush of emotion, Fliss knew.

'And your father?'

'We won't see eye to eye till hell freezes over. But I guess I can understand now where he's coming from. The business goes back a long way – my grandfather started it, and my father—'

'What is the business?'

'Oh, didn't I say? We build ships. Big time. The whole of our town sprung up round the shipyard – depends on it to this day. One of the reasons I feel obliged to do what's expected of me – finish my education, go into Hewson Enterprises and learn enough about it to keep it running on the right lines when the time comes. A lot of people would lose their livelihoods if Hewson's was no more. But I tell you this, Fliss, things are gonna change. There won't be any tugging of forelocks when I pass by. Hey!' He looked up suddenly at the sail. 'The wind's changing. Time to do some work around here.'

He got up, and Fliss followed suit. But as she went about the familiar routine, she was still reeling from what Jeff had told her. Perhaps his parents would be so glad that the prodigal son had returned that they would accept her. But how in the world was she going to be able to adapt to the lifestyle he had described? And what would it mean for Emma when she eventually managed to get her to America? There would be no boarding school for her, no way would Fliss sanction that. But as for all the rest of it . . .

Fliss's heart lifted as she thought of all the benefits she would be able to give her beloved daughter. Jeff was impatient with those things, didn't think them important, but then Jeff had never had to go without. Easy to be magnanimous when you'd never wanted for anything.

The prospect alleviated some of the guilt she was trying so hard not to think about. She might be taking Emma away from everything that was familiar to her, but she would be bringing her not to a gypsy existence, poverty and hardship, but to a life of luxury. Fliss smiled to herself, and as she coiled the ropes she began to sing – Cliff Richard's 'Travelling Light'. The stiff breeze whisked the sound away, but the words remained in her heart.

TWENTY-FIVE

For all that he had told her about his family, for all that she at least now thought she knew what to expect, Fliss was still totally unprepared for the reality.

Knowing that the town had more or less come into being because of Jeff's family was an awesome experience – Fliss was dazed by its bustling prettiness, sitting as it did on the Kennebec River where it flowed into Merrymack Bay. She loved the unspoiled feel of the area – shipyards there might well be, but there were still peninsulas, bays and beaches that remained as nature had intended, and the land undulated softly away from the sea in a series of rolling hills, farmland and forest. But it was when she and Jeff, in the Pontiac he had hired, turned into a mile-long drive flanked on either side by parkland that the nervousness constricting her chest became pure terror. They drove past a paddock with at least half a dozen horses – sleek bays and a couple of silvery greys – and Fliss had her first glimpse of the house that Jeff called home.

It stood at the end of the drive, a colonial-style mansion. White walls and pillars contrasted sharply with the dark emerald of the evergreens that surrounded it.

'Oh my God,' Fliss said. 'It's like Tara.' He gave her a sidelong glance, amused. 'Tara!' she repeated. 'In *Gone with the Wind*.'

His mouth quirked. 'If you say so.'

But there was no condemnation in his tone now; perhaps, she thought, he was fonder of his family home than he cared to admit, even to himself.

'Welcome home, Scarlett!' he said.

She smiled weakly. 'Jeff, I'm scared!'

'Don't be silly. They'll love you.'

'They wouldn't if they knew . . .'

'But they don't. Relax, Fliss.'

'It's all right for you!'

'It's a long time since I've been home too, remember. Dad may have decided to kill the fatted calf, but not before he's had a few choice words about my misspent years.'

Fliss was too frightened to reply.

'He won't be home this time of day, though,' Jeff went on. 'You'll get the chance to meet my mother without his intimidating presence.'

'No, you're wrong – look . . .' A man had appeared in the doorway of the house.

'That's not my father,' Jeff said, laughing. 'It's Forrester, the butler. He should have been pensioned off long ago, but he thinks the house couldn't run without him.'

'The butler!'

'Old money, Fliss. I did warn you.'

'I had no idea!'

The interior of the house was as impressive as the outside; a wide staircase swept up from an entrance hall larger, Fliss thought, than the whole ground floor of her little home in Cornwall. The butler – Forrester – took their bags.

'Mrs Hewson is in the drawing room.' His tone was formal, then his face broke into a wide smile. 'It's good to see you, Mr Jeff, sir.'

'You too, Forrester.' Jeff touched Fliss's arm. 'Come and meet my mother.'

She followed him across the polished oak block floor and into a large comfortable room. Chocolate-brown leather sofas and armchairs were arranged around a brightly patterned Indian carpet, with occasional tables between. A grand piano was covered with numerous photographs in silver frames, rich red drapes hung at the French windows, and an enormous fireplace took up most of one wall.

'Mom,' Jeff said.

A woman was sitting in one of the armchairs, an elegant figure in a loose sea-green overshirt and navy blue slacks. Her silver-blond hair was an immaculate shining helmet against the dark leather.

'Jeff! Oh, I'm so glad you're here. And you must be Fliss . . . Forgive me if I don't get up. I've not been too well today.'

Fliss's first thought was that Betty Hewson didn't actually look ill at all – in fact she appeared to be glowing with health, a delicate luminescence that made her quite beautiful. It was only when she went closer that she noticed the lines of strain beneath the carefully applied panstick and the reflection of pain in the cornflower-blue eyes. She'd seen that look before, and she didn't like it one bit.

Ovarian cancer. She remembered a woman she'd known in Truro who had died of it, a mother of teenage children. She'd had that same luminescent glow about her the last time Fliss had seen her. She'd thought how bizarre it was that someone who was dying should look so well. She remembered too that Jeff had initially described his mother's illness as 'woman's troubles' and that he'd said he was afraid she was suffering from 'the big C'. Fliss's eyes flicked down to Betty's stomach; it was swollen enough to bulge beneath her overshirt, so that she looked almost as if she might be pregnant. But she wasn't, of course.

Fliss's instinctive reaction was to shrink away, but she knew she mustn't show her horror. She took a step forward, forcing a smile that felt stiff and unnatural, and bent to kiss Betty on the cheek as Jeff had done.

'I'm very pleased to meet you, Mrs Hewson.'

'Please call me Betty. And I'm very pleased to meet you too,

Fliss. I can't tell you how delighted I am that Jeff has finally met a girl who will make him happy.'

A flash of guilt. Make him happy? So far she'd brought him nothing but trouble.

'I'll certainly do my best,' she said.

'Sit down, both of you. I'll have Mimi bring us some tea . . . or . . . Would you mind, Jeff?'

'Bringing the tea?' he said, grinning, but he was already headed towards a bell pull, cunningly concealed in the window drapes. He tugged on it, and a few moments later a uniformed maid appeared in the doorway.

Betty asked her to bring tea, fruit cake and scones, which arrived so promptly that Fliss guessed the kettle had already been boiling and the cake cut and plated the moment they had arrived. She sat down next to Jeff on one of the sofas, nervous that she was going to make some dreadful faux pas.

'So, Mom, how are you doing?' Jeff asked anxiously.

Betty raised a slender hand, waving it dismissively.

'I'm fine.'

'Mom – you're not.'

'Well, maybe not as fine as I'd like, but I have no intention of talking about it right now. I want to hear your news. And I want to get to know Fliss.' She turned to Fliss with a disarming smile. 'You come from Falmouth, England, is that right, Fliss?'

Fliss felt the muscles in her stomach tighten. She'd known the questions would be inevitable, but she was no more prepared for them than she had ever been

'Falmouth, yes,' she said. 'At least, that's where Jeff and I met.'

'My lucky day.' Jeff's hand closed over hers in a gesture of solidarity.

'You sail, then?'

'Yes, I have a boat . . .' *Careful! Careful!*

'That's certainly something you have in common then. Jeff has always been obsessed with boats – to the detriment of everything else, I'm afraid.'

285

'I've come to my senses now, though. Realised I can't go on bumming around for ever.' He was trying to steer the conversation away from her, Fliss knew, and for the moment at any rate he succeeded.

'And thank goodness you have! I can't tell you how pleased your father is that you're going to finish your education, come into the business.'

'It certainly didn't take him long to get me reinstated at Harvard,' Jeff said drily.

'Your father knows how to pull strings.' Betty smiled again, but with more of an effort. She was tiring, Fliss thought, the excitement and the effort of talking taking their toll on her.

'What will you do, Fliss? Are you just here for a holiday, or will you be staying near the college to be with Jeff?'

'I'll be with Jeff.'

They'd talked about it on the voyage north. As a mature student, he didn't think the college would insist on him taking up occupation in one of the male dorms on campus, but they would certainly frown on him living with a woman who wasn't his wife. The best option, they'd decided, was to find rented accommodation nearby for Fliss so that they could be together as often as possible.

'I see.' Betty ran her fingertips, scarlet-painted, over the slight bulge beneath her overshirt and winced. 'And in that case . . . dare I ask? Might we have a wedding to look forward to?'

They'd talked about that too.

'I think we'd better get married once you've got new papers,' Jeff had said, and the enormity of what she had done hit Fliss all over again.

'But that would be bigamy.'

Jeff shook his head; laughed without a trace of humour.

'Hey, what's a little bigamy compared to—'

'Oh don't Jeff, please! I don't want to think about it.'

''Fraid you've got to, hon. Though what you should have done is thought before.'

'I know. I'm sorry.'

'Too late for sorry. We've got to do the best we can now. You'll be a lot safer if you're Mrs Jefferson Hewson, and we'll be able to live together without anyone raising an eyebrow too.'

It struck Fliss that in some ways this would be as much a marriage of convenience as her wedding to Martin had been, as well as illegal. Guilt suffused her, not only for Martin and Emma, but for what she was involving Jeff in too.

'You don't have to marry me,' she said. 'It's wrong of me to get you mixed up in something like this.'

'I am mixed up in it, though, aren't I? If I'd had the first idea what you were planning, I'd have done my best to stop you, even if it meant losing you. But what's done is done.'

Betty Hewson was still waiting expectantly for an answer to her question.

'Yes, Mom,' Jeff said. 'There might be a wedding. Not just yet, though.'

Tears sparkled in her cornflower-blue eyes.

'That is just wonderful! I'm so happy for you both! But . . .' She hesitated. 'Promise me you won't leave it too long. I want to be there . . . it will be here in America, won't it? You're not planning on going back to England? Because I don't know if I . . .'

'We're not planning anything yet, Mom.'

'Oh, I'm sorry. I shouldn't presume.'

'When we set a date, you'll be the first to know. But I warn you, it won't be a big society affair. Just you and Dad and a couple of witnesses.'

'What about Fliss's parents? They'll come over, surely?'

'My parents are both dead,' Fliss said, relieved that that, at least, was the truth.

'Oh my dear! I am so sorry.'

'It's OK,' Fliss said.

'Is it long since you lost them . . .?' She broke off, closing her eyes briefly and screwing up her face into a grimace.

'Mom . . . are you sure you're all right?' Jeff asked anxiously.

'Darling, I'm fine.' But it didn't have the ring of conviction, and her fingers fluttered to her throat. 'But perhaps I ought to go and lie down. Oh what a nuisance! I did so want to talk to you and Fliss.'

'There will be plenty of time to talk later, when you've had a rest. Let's get you up to your room.'

'I'm not upstairs now,' Betty said apologetically. 'I have a bed in the library. And if you could call Mimi . . . I think it's time for my medication.'

'I'll see to that.'

Jeff got up, helped his mother to her feet, and supported her out of the room.

'Mom is a lot sicker than she's letting on,' he said when he returned.

'I can see that. I am so sorry . . .'

'Thank God I've come home.' His face was drawn. He thudded his fist into the back of one of the leather chairs. 'Where the hell is Dad? She shouldn't be left here alone!'

'She's not alone,' Fliss said reasonably. 'She's got the butler and the maid.'

'It's not the same! She needs family. I should have been here for her. I've got to be here for her.'

'You are.'

'Only until I go to Harvard. I don't think I should go.'

'Jeff, you can't not go back to college now.'

'What the hell have I done?' His anger was palpable. Fliss, remembering the way she had felt when her own parents had died, knew it was his way of dealing with the sense of utter helplessness, the first flush of grief.

'It's not your fault, Jeff,' she said, going to put her arms round him. He shrugged her off impatiently.

'How do you know that? I've caused her so much worry! And look what I've brought to her door now. Jeez – if she knew . . .'

'You want me to leave?' Fliss asked in a small voice.

Jeff stood, head bowed, not answering, and a cold place inside her grew and spread. Then, wordlessly, he turned to her, pulling her close, burying his face in her hair.

'No, hon, no. I can't lose you too.'

In that moment Fliss felt the scales tip slightly, the balance between them disturbed, and her self-image, which had taken such a battering in the last weeks, soared. The overwhelming love she felt for him wasn't totally one-sided. Jeff needed her too.

'I'm here for you, my love,' she whispered. 'Just as long as you want me, I'll be here.'

It was well after six before Jefferson Hewson II arrived home. He came into the house on a bluster of self-importance and high dudgeon, a big man who might well once have looked much as Jeff did now, but whose hair had turned grey and thinned so that his scalp shone pink through the combed-over strands, whose nose was red-veined, and whose immaculate white shirt strained over a bulging gut.

'So – you're here then,' he greeted Jeff bad-temperedly. 'Not before time.'

'Good to see you too, Dad,' Jeff returned sarcastically.

'And I suppose you must be Fliss. What in hell is a pretty girl like you doing with a no-good layabout like my son? No, don't answer that. I can take a guess. But at least it seems you've talked some sense into him, and I suppose I should be grateful for that.'

He made for the crystal decanter standing on a silver salver on an occasional table and poured himself a large glass of amber liquid.

'Aren't you two drinking? I thought my bourbon was one of the few things you liked about being home, Jeff.'

'OK, I'll have one, since you're offering. Fliss? What about you? A G and T? I'm sure Dad's got some.'

'Thank you.' Fliss felt horribly awkward. A G and T might help, but she didn't think it would make much difference. It wouldn't make the antagonism between Jeff and his objectionable father disappear, it wouldn't cure his mother's illness, it wouldn't stop either of them from asking questions she couldn't answer, and it wouldn't take away her perpetual longing for Emma.

She had a horrible feeling that the time spent here, in Jeff's home, was going to be something of an ordeal.

Fliss and Jeff weren't sharing a room, of course. That would have been considered highly improper. Fliss had been allocated a guest bedroom at the front of the house with a view over the parkland, the length of the corridor away from Jeff's own room. But that didn't stop him from visiting her at night, when the house was quiet. She was still wide awake when she heard a floorboard creak, the handle of the door turned softly and a shadow slipped inside, dark against the pale green moonlit wall. He crossed the room silently, turned back the covers and slipped under the Egyptian cotton sheet beside her. She snuggled against him, the warmth of his body balm for her bruised senses and tight-strung nerves.

'How are you doing, hon?' he asked, his mouth brushing her ear.

'Oh Jeff . . . I don't know . . .'

'Wishing you'd stayed in England?'

'No, but . . .'

'It's not a barrel of laughs.'

'It certainly isn't that. But what I was going to say is that it's not what I expected. I'm out of my class here! And if they knew . . . they're going to have to know sometime, aren't they? About Emma, at least. And your father is going to hit the roof.'

'Don't worry about my father. He's just a big bully. As for Mom – she'll be tickled pink. All she wants is for me to settle down and have a family – grandchildren she can spoil.'

'Your children. Not mine.'

'I doubt she'll make the distinction for long. She likes you, Fliss, I can see that. Look how she spoke out for you at dinner.'

It was true, she had. Jefferson senior had adopted aggressive tactics to try and draw out some of Fliss's background, and Betty had intervened. 'Leave the poor girl alone, Jefferson,' she had said. 'She's a guest in our home, remember.'

'And your son's intended.'

'All the more reason to stop interrogating her. Don't you trust Jeff to make a wise choice?'

The remark had made Fliss more uncomfortable than ever, and the look on Jefferson senior's face had made it plain that no, he had no faith whatever in his son's judgement. But he had retreated, none the less, not wanting to upset Betty, who was clearly in some pain, Fliss thought.

'She's very sweet,' she said now.

'She's my mom.' His voice was choked, and Fliss's heart ached for him.

His arms enveloped her, and she felt his body stir against hers.

'Do you think we should?' she whispered. All her senses were coming alive with the need of him, but making love here, in his parents' home, seemed wrong somehow.

'Once Dad falls asleep he's dead to the world. And Mom's room is downstairs now – you know that.' He was pushing her night-dress, a froth of pale-blue nylon, up over her thighs, his hand seeking the soft sweet places where his body wanted to be.

'I love you, Fliss.'

'And I love you. I love you so much!'

When it was over they lay entwined, languorous, replete. But as she drifted towards sleep, Fliss's longing for Emma was there, unabated, worming its way to the surface, and she bit her lip, trying hard not to cry.

'Fliss . . . are you still awake?' Jeff's soft voice impinged on her thoughts.

'Mm . . . yes.'

'There's something I'd like you to do for me. It's a really big ask. You can say no if it's too much and I'll understand.'

'Go on.'

'Dad and I had a talk last night after dinner. I was right. Mom does have the big C and there's nothing more they can do for her except make her as comfortable as they can with drugs and more drugs. It's no more than I expected, but . . .' He hesitated. 'I'm really worried about her, Fliss. You've seen what Dad's like. He's too wrapped up in the business to take good care of her. He'll get a nurse in, sure, when she's too ill for Mimi to cope, but it's not the same. And her friends won't want to know. They have their luncheons and their fund-raisers and their shopping trips. While she's part of all that, fine. When she's not . . . I'd bet my bottom dollar she won't see them for dust. They don't do sickbeds for real, just spend their husbands' hard-earned cash pretending they do. I'd be here for her myself, but it would only give her grief thinking I'd missed my chance again because of her, and I was wondering . . .'

Fliss knew what he was going to ask, and her heart sank.

'You want me to stay here with her.'

'That's about it.'

'Do you think she'd really want me here, Jeff?' she asked. 'I'm a stranger, after all. She hardly knows me.'

'But she will. And as my wife, you'll be the closest thing to the daughter she never had as far as she's concerned. Trust me, I know my mom.'

'Oh Jeff . . .' The thought of being left here with a dying woman she scarcely knew was a daunting prospect.

'I'm sorry, I shouldn't have asked. I can't expect you to do it.'

Everything within her was shrinking at the thought of it, but how could she refuse? This was Jeff's mother they were talking about, the woman who had given birth to the man she loved with all her heart. Fliss made up her mind.

'Of course I'll stay with her,' she said. 'If it's what you want, and she wants it too.'

'Oh hon, you don't know what that means to me . . . Thank you.'

He pulled her close again, kissing her, but this time as he loved her, more slowly, more gently, Fliss could feel nothing but a sudden longing for home and all that it entailed. A home she could never return to, a daughter who was growing up, day by day, without her. She had never felt more desolate, and the irony of the fact that she had gone through all this to be with Jeff only to face separation from him again so soon didn't help either.

A tear slid down her cheek; she rubbed it dry with the corner of the sheet and hoped that Jeff had not noticed.

Jeff had been right about Betty's reaction. When he suggested that Fliss should stay on with her when he left for Harvard, she was delighted.

'That would be wonderful!' she exclaimed, hugging Fliss. 'A real chance for me to get to know my future daughter-in-law without you coming between us, Jeff!'

'Well thanks a bunch, Mom!'

'Oh, you know how it is,' Betty said. 'We girls can talk far better when there are no gentlemen around.'

Fliss's heart missed a beat, and Jeff gave her hand a reassuring squeeze.

'I'm sure when you get to know Fliss you'll love her as much as I do,' he said.

Betty smiled, that heartbreakingly dazzling smile that faded now too soon into weariness and pain.

'Darling,' she said, 'I already do.'

He had also been right about the reaction of Betty's friends. Though she had once been part of a vast social circle, as she grew weaker they came to visit less and less often, and always in twos and threes, as if they were afraid to be alone with her. They stayed only a short while, gushing to fill the awkward silences, then escaping on the excuse that they didn't want to tire her.

In a way Fliss could understand. Wasn't it how she had felt in the beginning? But as she and Betty grew closer, she came to despise these shallow women whose only interest in life seemed to be their appearance and whether they could outdo one another in the vast sums their husbands had donated to the latest fund-raiser or bid at a charity auction. Social climbing was their *raison d être* – Jackie Kennedy's name came up a lot, Fliss noticed, and everyone said her husband Jack was going to be the next president.

Fliss heartily disliked all these women, but one in particular she despised.

There was a hardness about Marcia Davenport that somehow went deeper than the brittleness that was the trademark of all of them, a sharpness about her heavily made-up face and a calculation in eyes as green as a cat's. Her voice had a cheese-grater edge to it, even when she gushed sugary-sweet platitudes to Betty, and she treated Fliss with cool disdain. But most of all Fliss disliked her because she suspected that something was going on between her and Jefferson. Of all the women who came to visit, she was the one most likely to choose the evening, when Jefferson was at home, and Fliss had seen the little looks that passed between them. They had history, certainly, she was sure of it, and she suspected Marcia was hoping for a future too – she had been widowed some little while ago when her husband's company plane had crashed in fog into a mountain. She's waiting for Betty to die so that she can move in, Fliss thought furiously. And although she had not one iota of proof, she was sure she was right.

She was proud, though, of the way she was coping. Given her history of emotional breakdown, she had been very afraid it would happen again. But although she missed both Jeff and Emma dread-fully, and knew that for the moment there was nothing she could do to bring Emma to America, she seemed to be managing to take one day at a time, doing what had to be done. The blackness would come when it was all over, she suspected. That was the pattern – strong through the stress, nervous collapse afterwards. But at least this time she had something to look forward to.

Jeff had set things in motion to get her a new identity, he'd told her, and it shouldn't be long before she had her papers. She didn't ask how he had managed this; she didn't think she wanted to know. The idea that her new name would be that of someone who had died, as a child perhaps, was a weird, unsettling thought. But it would mean that she and Jeff would be able to marry, and also that she would be able to go to England and bring Emma to America. She hung on to that thought through the long days and longer nights when her only companion was a dying woman.

So far she had managed to avoid answering too many probing questions about her own real identity, talking in generalisations and veering off into harmless stories about her past. Betty would tire, sometimes even falling asleep as Fliss talked, and as for Jefferson, he scarcely seemed interested at all. Fliss thought she barely registered on his radar.

One evening after dinner Fliss and Betty were sitting in the drawing room watching the sun set scarlet in a sky that had been piercingly blue over trees that had turned to vivid reds, yellows and oranges in the glory of the New England fall.

Betty had had one of her better days, though she was increasingly frail. The almost unnatural bloom had gone now; her cheeks were hollowed, her skin had become grey-tinted and dark circles showed through the foundation she still insisted on applying every day. Jefferson had retired to his den, and the two women were alone.

'You love Jeff very much, don't you?' Betty said out of the blue.

'Very much,' Fliss said, a tad embarrassed.

'That's good.' A small smile lifted Betty's lips. 'And you will be good to him? Take care of him? Oh, it sounds silly, I know, I expect you think he's well able to take care of himself. But most men are little boys underneath those tough fronts they put on. I've always been here for Jeff when he needed me, but I won't be for much longer.'

'Rubbish! You mustn't talk like that!'

'No, Fliss, you and I both know it's the truth,' Betty said, sadly but with resignation. 'And I am so very glad he has you.'

Fliss couldn't help thinking that this conversation was a mirror image of the one she'd had with Jeff when he'd asked her to look after Betty, and sudden tears filled her eyes. He was going to be devastated when the inevitable happened and Betty died.

'You know all about a mother's love for her child, don't you?' Betty said softly into the silence.

Fliss stiffened, startled and dumbstruck.

'You had a little girl, if I'm not much mistaken. A photograph of her fell out of your bag the other day when you were getting a tissue. I slipped it back in again without saying anything. Jefferson was here . . . the time wasn't right. But . . . I'd like you to know that I know – and I am so sorry.'

With a shock Fliss realised that Betty assumed that she had lost Emma.

'It isn't what you think,' she said before she could stop herself.

'My dear, I'm not sitting in judgement. You're not the first girl to have a baby out of wedlock and you won't be the last. What was her name?'

'Emma, but . . .' Just speaking her name brought the tears to Fliss's eyes, and her face felt stiff with the effort of holding them back.

'Oh my dear, don't upset yourself!' Betty reached out a thin, but still beringed hand, and covered Fliss's. 'Do you want to talk about it?'

Fliss closed her eyes, and the hot tears squeezed out and ran down her cheeks. The guilt that came from knowing she was deceiving Betty was overwhelming, especially in the face of her kindness, and she longed to unburden herself, tell Betty everything.

'Emma's not dead,' she said. 'In fact I'm hoping that when Jeff and I are married she'll come to live with us.'

'Oh!' Betty sounded startled. 'He knows about her then?'

'Of course he does. But we thought . . .'

'Jeff thought we'd be shocked, I suppose.'

'No, no – oh, it's so complicated . . .' Fliss broke off, quite unable to confess to something so dreadful. Betty's good opinion was suddenly very important to her.

'It's all right, my dear.' Betty squeezed Fliss's hand again. 'You don't have to say any more now. Just tell me when you're ready. But I really would like to see her picture, if it won't upset you too much.'

Wordlessly Fliss opened her bag and passed Betty the treasured photograph. She gazed at it for a few moments.

'She's beautiful.'

'Yes, she is . . .'

Again the temptation to unburden herself nibbled at her; again she fought it. Somehow she didn't think she would ever be ready to tell Betty the truth; that moment would never come.

She was right; it did not. Just a week later, Betty was dead.

TWENTY-SIX

With Betty's death, Fliss was free to join Jeff. They rented a small apartment and for a little while Fliss simply relished being with him, even striving for the domesticity that had always eluded her. She wasn't a great cook – she never would be – but that didn't stop her trying, buying exotic ingredients she'd never seen in the shops at home and attempting to follow recipes where the quantities were given in confusingly different measures to the ones she was used to. She washed and ironed and cleaned the house – all the things that had made her feel trapped when she was with Martin, but they no longer seemed onorous because she was doing them for Jeff, making a home for him.

But she was missing Emma dreadfully, and the pain seemed only to intensify as the weeks went by – weeks when Jeff was so busy with his studies that she had plenty of time to brood. Her little girl was growing up without her, and for the moment there was nothing she could do about it. There'd been a problem with her new identity – the forger Jeff had been put in touch with had been arrested and was likely to serve a long stretch in gaol; Jeff would have to start all over again trying to find someone who could provide them with the documents they needed, and that was no easy task while he was at Harvard. He'd put out feelers, Fliss knew, but nothing seemed to be happening.

A black fringe of despair began to throw a shadow around her

298

happiness; it was so long now since she'd held her little daughter in her arms, so long since she'd heard her chuckle, smelled her sweet baby smell, and she couldn't see any end to the separation. How could she ever have thought she could bear it? But then she'd been so obsessed with her plans she'd deluded herself into believing they could work out just as she wanted them to, that once she and Jeff were together everything would fall magically into place.

I must have been mad, Fliss thought, and knew it was not far from the truth.

One day when Jeff was at college she'd been poring over her small stash of precious photographs, wondering if Emma's fine, feathery hair had now thickened and grown, if the baby fat was dropping away, how well she was talking, when the need for her suddenly overwhelmed Fliss. She *had* to know that Emma was well and happy, if nothing else. She absolutely had to.

The telephone loomed large in her line of vision and it came to her that all she had to do was to pick it up, call Martin or Maggie, and ask. She stared at the telephone, mesmerised, the link to her beloved daughter, and felt it pull her like an invisible umbilical cord. Her heart began to beat like a drum as the fantasy enveloped her. As if in a dream she got up and crossed the room; her fingers touched the cold Bakelite and grasped it. Emma was almost within her reach, not the warmth of her firm little body or the scent of her hair, but contact none the less. If she was in the room, Fliss might even hear her voice or her laughter. Hardly daring to breathe, she dialled the number for the operator. And then, as it began to ring, panic overcame her all of a rush. She slammed down the receiver, jerking away from it as if it were red hot.

What the hell was she doing?

Trembling from head to foot, Fliss stepped backwards until her shoulders encountered solid wall. She leaned against it for a moment, hands pressed to her burning cheeks, then, like a rag doll, she sagged and slid down the wall until she was sitting in a heap on the floor. The pain came, a cramp in her stomach like the pangs of childbirth, and she doubled over, her face contorted with agony, eyes squeezed tight shut. The tears that escaped ran down her cheeks in a scalding flood.

Oh Emma, Emma! So near and yet so far! Fliss stretched out her arms to emptiness and thought her heart would break.

The telephone tantalised her after that, seemed to mock her, the link to Emma that she could not, must not make. But still she couldn't ignore it – the seed of an idea had been planted in her mind and day by day it grew.

If she were to ring . . . surely she could trust Maggie? She was her sister, for goodness' sake! She'd be shocked, yes, but she wouldn't give her away.

And it wasn't just that Fliss would be able to reassure herself that Emma was well and happy. She could ask Maggie to help her once she had the necessary documentation to get Emma into America. It would make things so much easier – in fact Fliss couldn't actually see now how she could manage it without help. The more she thought about it, the more sense it made. She wouldn't do anything about making contact until she had her new passport – with, hopefully, Emma on it; the less time Maggie had to think about it, the better. But when she was ready she would call her sister and ask for her assistance.

She didn't tell Jeff what she had in mind. She hated having secrets from him, but she didn't want him pouring cold water on her plans, and she rather thought he might. The decision made, Fliss began to feel more positive and much, much happier.

Fliss was not the only one who was not being entirely open about her intentions. Jeff was all too aware that the threat of the draft was still hanging over him. He'd talked to his father about it, and Jefferson senior was of the opinion that he should sign on sooner rather than later.

'It's only a matter of time before your number comes up,' he said. 'Better to volunteer and get it over with. It'll benefit you – you'll have more chance of choosing which branch of the military you want to serve with. And it would make more sense to get it out of the way too, before you come on board Hewson Enterprises.'

Much as he didn't want to leave Fliss at this stage of their relationship, Jeff was inclined to agree with him. But he really did want to settle the matter of her new identity before taking such a drastic step. He redoubled his efforts to find someone in the business of providing false papers, but it was proving difficult, and it occurred to him to wonder if they dared use Fliss's own passport. He couldn't imagine that anyone would pick up on the fact that she was supposed to be dead – after all, the forged papers he had been so set on getting would almost certainly be based on the identity of a person who had died – and besides, her passport, which wouldn't expire for another six years or so, was in her married name, whilst all over the sailing world she had still been known as Felicity Penrose. No pen-pusher or immigration officer was going to pick up on it.

The problem, as he saw it, was Emma. He had no idea how to set about getting her on to Fliss's passport. But then, neither had he any idea how Fliss could ever get her away, let alone on to a plane to America. His opinion hadn't altered since he'd told her it wasn't going to happen, but he didn't tell her that. He was all too aware of how much it meant to her, and how much it would upset her if he voiced his doubts. And he didn't think it would do any good to try again to get her to go home and face the music. Things had gone too far for that. If they were ever to have any kind of a normal life, it was up to him to try to sort out the terrible mess she had got herself into.

He had to talk to her about it all, he knew. But before he had found the right moment he was pre-empted by events. One morning a letter in a plain buff envelope arrived with the mail, a letter from the Selective Service System requiring Jeff to report to his local board. Too late to volunteer – the authorities had got to him first. Too late to try to sort things out so that they could at least be married before he had to begin his army service.

When he told her about it Fliss was horrified.

'Can't you fight it?' she asked, distraught. 'Get an exemption?'

'On what grounds? I'll have finished my studies in a couple of weeks. And in any case, I wouldn't feel right about wriggling out of it. In fact, I'd been thinking of volunteering, getting it out of the way. But I'd hoped to sort out your status first. The fact of the matter is that unless we are married, there's no way you'd be able to join me on a military base.'

'Oh Jeff!' Fliss could hardly believe that they were about to be separated again. She'd given up everything to be with him, and now event after event seemed to be conspiring to keep them apart. 'What am I going to do?'

He took her hand. 'I think you'll be all right here, sweetheart, with your own passport . . .' He explained his reasoning, that really, no one would be any the wiser until the time came when she would need to renew. 'Besides,' he added, 'you've got the backing of my family name. The authorities aren't likely to want to upset the Hewsons. If you're living at Parklands . . .'

'I don't want to go back there!' Fliss said. 'It was different when your mother was alive, but now . . .'

'To be honest, Fliss, I don't think you've got any choice.'

'But what about Emma? What am I going to do about Emma?'

'I don't know, hon.' He braced himself, bit the bullet. 'I think the only way you're going to get her is if you go back, own up to what you've done, and try to persuade Martin to let you have her – or fight him through the courts for custody.'

'I'd never get custody, not in a million years. Not now.'

'No, you're probably right. I guess it would all be down to what you could agree with Martin.'

She shuddered, her whole frame tensing at the thought. 'I can't do it. I just can't.'

'That's that, then.' Even though he'd tried to persuade her to go home and own up to what she'd done, he couldn't help being relieved that she wouldn't do it. If she went back to England, the chances were she'd never come back, and losing her again was something he couldn't bear to think about.

'Isn't there any chance of getting fake papers? With Emma's name on them?' Fliss asked desperately.

Jeff sighed. He hated the thought of leaving her like this, so fragile, so vulnerable, and without hope.

'I'll do what I can.' He was thinking that maybe in the army he'd run up against someone who knew the right person. He'd meet all sorts in the army, he guessed, and the chances of some of them having dubious connections were a good deal more likely than among the scholars at Harvard.

Fliss threw her arms around him, and as he buried his face in her hair, he thought that whatever problems she had brought him, she was more than worth it.

In the two-week break between leaving Harvard and beginning his draft, Jeff took Fliss to Gull Island. For him it was, and always had been, a special place, and he wanted to share it with her, and for her part Fliss was determined to put all her worries to the back of her mind and make the most of the little time they would have together before the inevitable separation that would follow.

As islands go it wasn't large, a mere fifteen miles from end to end. A strip of sandy beach, punctuated by outcrops of rock and hidden coves, encompassed a wild mountainous interior where sheep and goats grazed in the narrow meadows. The Hewson place, one of a dozen houses that had been built by wealthy families as summer retreats, was on the south side, overlooking the harbour where Jeff had learned to sail. Set in ten acres, it was a Victorian-style mansion, and everything about it spoke of old money. When she set eyes on it, Fliss was flabbergasted all over again.

'It's just left empty for when you want to use it?' she said in disbelief.

'That's the general idea. When I was young, Mom and I used

303

to spend most of the summer here, but you wouldn't want to be here in winter. Nobody ever stays here in winter except for the caretaker, and he's a loner anyway.'

'But it's such a waste! All I can say is your father must have money to burn.'

'Anyone who has a house here is seriously rich. If they weren't they wouldn't be allowed to buy in the first place. The islanders are a pretty snobbish lot.'

'So what are we doing here? I thought you hated that sort of thing.'

'We don't have to socialise. It's the place that's special – to me, anyway. I wanted to show it to you.'

A melting sensation warmed Fliss's stomach.

'And I really want to see it,' she said.

The dust covers were off the furniture in readiness for their arrival, the beds aired and made up with fresh linen – Jefferson senior had arranged to borrow the services of a maid who worked for one of the other island families. They unpacked, and then set off for Fliss's first tour of the island.

There was, she had to admit, a magic about the place. Jeff showed her rock pools where he had hunted for crabs, a cave where he'd once hidden out for the best part of a day because he knew he would be in big trouble from his father for some long-forgotten misdemeanour, the beaches where he and the other island youngsters had swum, sunbathed and, when they were older, held wild parties that went on half the night. She was more than fascinated – imagining the young Jeff here started the warm feeling inside again. She wanted to know everything about him, she realised. She wanted to be part of his past, as well as his future, and this was the closest she could come to achieving it.

One day they took a picnic into the interior. Sitting on a boulder with the sun beating down on their bare faces, they ate sandwiches made with the crusty bread that had come in that morning on the schooner that brought supplies once a week, and drank lemonade that Fliss had made from fresh fruit, sugar and water.

'There's a path,' Fliss said, turning her head to follow its narrow, jagged ascent. 'Can we explore it?'

'Not a good idea.'

'Oh come on! I want to see where it goes!'

'The one thing you don't do here is explore mountain paths. At least not if you value your health. They can be real treacherous.'

'That one doesn't look treacherous.'

'Looks can be deceptive, trust me, and you don't want to get caught in a landslide, either, which can happen if the wind gets up.'

'Spoilsport!'

'Say that again, and I'll make you pay!'

'Spoilsport!'

He lunged for her and pulled her, squealing, down on to the scratchy dry grass at the foot of the boulder.

'Now don't tell me that wasn't better than exploring mountain paths,' he said, some time later.

'Mm. Well, maybe. I'll need to think about it.'

She was sun-warmed, drowsy, content. For a little hiatus in time all her problems – even how she was going to get Emma – seemed very distant, as if they weren't actually real at all.

That was how it was for ten glorious days. As the time to leave approached, the world began to creep in once more, a hollow dread in the pit of her stomach, something close to panic at how fast the days and hours were rushing by. But Fliss knew that whatever the future held, this would always be for her, too, a special place.

'I'll never forget, Jeff,' she whispered as she lay in his arms on the last night.

'Good,' was all he said. But without being told, Fliss knew that he felt exactly the same way.

A few days later, Jeff reported to his local draft board along with a dozen other recruits. After a thorough physical examination and a General Classification Test, they travelled by bus to an army base in New Jersey. Some of his fellow inductees were resentful and rebellious – they had done their best to avoid the draft by every means available to them, including, at the last minute, trying to prove they were medically unfit. Others were gung-ho and spoiling for a fight, the sort who either turned into heroes or became trigger-happy liabilities. Almost all were some years younger than Jeff.

Their puppyish attitudes made him feel old, and the things that preoccupied them seemed trivial compared to his concerns. He couldn't get worked up about having his hair shorn into a buzz cut, or having to part with his civilian clothes in exchange for fatigues. He really didn't care about the cold showers, the hard bed and the unappetising food; he was used to living in uncomfortable conditions. But he was worried about Fliss. He knew she wasn't happy about returning to Parklands, and when they left Gull Island she'd become very depressed, flat, listless, tearful even. Jeff had never seen her quite like this before and he didn't like it.

On a practical level she would be fine, he knew. Emotionally, he wasn't so sure. He wondered if he should have tried to get an exemption as Fliss had wanted. There were lawyers who specialised in that sort of thing. But realistically he didn't think he had a leg to stand on, and in any case Jefferson senior wouldn't have put his weight or his money behind an appeal. It was his belief that a man who had done his duty and served his country would be a much greater asset in the long run to Hewson Enterprises than one who had got out of it by means of legal arguments and unfair influence. Actually, Jeff agreed with him; he didn't want to be seen as a draft-shirker or coward, but that didn't mean he was happy about leaving Fliss.

She seemed so vulnerable now, he thought as he stood to attention on the parade ground, and he wished with all his heart that he could be there for her. But he couldn't. He was under the command of the US military and there was not a thing he could do about it.

Fliss hated being at Parklands every bit as much as she had known she would. For days on end she saw no one but Jefferson senior and the domestic staff, and Jefferson was far from being congenial company. Worse, Marcia Davenport was often there too, swanning about as if she was already mistress of the house, which Fliss was sure she would be as soon as a respectable period had elapsed. The prospect was anathema to her, but at least while she was seething with anger and resentment that Betty should be betrayed in this way she wasn't aching with longing for Jeff and Emma. And the temptation to phone Maggie was removed too; she was too afraid of being overheard.

A bright brittle fall gave way to winter, harsh and bitterly cold. The snow came, blanketing the countryside and making her isolation complete. At Christmas Jeff was given a few days' leave and Fliss counted off the hours until his arrival, worried that the roads might be impassable. But this was Maine, not England; they were used to coping with snowfall here. And when he arrived, Jeff had something for her.

As soon as they were alone he handed her an envelope.

'Here you are, hon. Santa's called already.'

'What . . .?' Her eyes went round as she opened it. 'Oh Jeff – my papers!'

'Yep, I managed it. Have a look. See what you think.' The papers looked remarkably genuine, though Fliss was less than impressed with her new name.

'Doris Margharita Ponticano! What sort of a name is that! Do I look like a Doris Margharita?' But she couldn't be annoyed for long. 'Oh Jeff! Emma's on it too! Oh, that is wonderful! I can't believe it!'

'You're pleased?'

'Pleased! I can't tell you! This is my best Christmas present ever! Now at last I'll be able to get Emma! Oh Jeff, I'm so excited!'

'Good.' Nothing pleased Jeff more than to see Fliss happy. But he was worried that she was heading for a fall and he thought it only fair to warn her of his reservations. 'Look, Fliss, I've had them include Emma because I know it's what you wanted. But I have to be honest here. I can't see how the hell you're going to get her.'

Fliss's smile faded. 'What are you talking about?'

'You've got to be realistic, honey. You can't risk going to Cornwall, and in any case, the minute she's reported missing every air- and seaport is going to be on the lookout for her. Even if she's under another name, they're going to be having a close look at any little girl fitting her description. They'll have photographs of her. There's no way you could get her through immigration.'

Though it put a dreadful dampener on her initial excitement, it was only what she'd thought herself, and time and again she'd returned to the idea that had come to her the day she had very nearly picked up the telephone and rung Maggie, worrying at it and moulding it into shape.

'I've thought of that. You're right, I couldn't get back to Heathrow from Cornwall in time – if she's known to be missing. But if I could get Maggie to bring her to London, and give me a head start before she tells anyone, then I could be on a plane home with her before they even begin to start looking for her.'

Her tone was eager, excited, as if she were planning a day trip or a holiday, Jeff thought, and his heart sank. He was already wishing he'd never had the forger include Emma on Fliss's new passport. He'd done it against his better judgement, because he knew how much it meant to her, but he'd thought he could make her see for herself that it just wasn't feasible to snatch Emma – never mind that it was also criminal and, he thought, morally wrong. He should have known that a woman who could go so far as to fake her own death wouldn't be deterred by argument, especially when she was so desperate to be reunited with her daughter; he should have known she wouldn't let it go, that she'd be concentrating all her energies on coming up with a plan that she thought could work. But in her single-minded pursuit of her objective, she'd ignored all the obstacles that common sense should tell her would stand in her way. That was Fliss, the Fliss he loved – impulsive, doggedly determined, passionate. Making her see sense wasn't going to be easy – if he could make her see sense at all!

'Wouldn't you be taking a terrible risk, letting Maggie know you're still alive?' he said reasonably.

'She's my sister! I'm sure I could trust her. In any case, she's a very private person. She's not the sort to blab it out to anyone, and she'd be horrified at the thought of the consequences if the truth came out. No, I'm sure I can trust Maggie.'

She didn't add that in any case she longed to talk to her sister, not just because she wanted news of Emma and to arrange to get her to America, but simply because she wanted to hear her voice. Fliss missed Maggie more than she'd ever imagined she would; though they'd never been particularly close, Maggie was her only family, and the ties were stronger than Fliss had realised.

'OK, so she may not betray you,' Jeff said, 'but to virtually kidnap Emma . . . it's a huge ask, Fliss. From all you've told me about Maggie, I'd imagine she's a pretty law-abiding sort of person. I can't believe she'd implicate herself in something like that.'

A shiver of doubt prickled through Fliss. Jeff was putting his finger on snags to her plans that deep down she'd always known existed but preferred to ignore. Maggie *was* the law-abiding sort. If she inadvertently walked out of a shop with something she'd forgotten to pay for, she'd walk right back. She'd never jump a traffic light – she was always ready to stop the moment it turned amber. She was scrupulously, meticulously, boringly honest and straightforward, and she was respectful of authority. But she was Fliss's only hope. She couldn't ask Jo for help; she remembered all to clearly how adamant Jo had been that she would not assist Fliss with her disappearance. She couldn't call on Simon Beacham again – she didn't want him to know her whereabouts, and he was probably very fed up over her failure to contact him. And she knew Jeff absolutely would not go to England and snatch Emma for her.

That left Maggie.

'And suppose you did manage to get Emma,' Jeff was continuing. 'What then? Are you thinking of bringing her back here to Parklands? Because I don't think my father would be agreeable to that.'

The chasm of despair that was opening inside Fliss yawned a little wider. He was right again; she was only here on sufferance herself. It would have been a different story had Betty still been alive, but Betty was dead. It was Marcia who now had Jefferson's ear, and Marcia wouldn't stand up for her and fight her corner. She didn't like Fliss any more than Fliss liked her.

'Oh – what am I going to do?' she groaned.

He pulled her close, knowing he'd destroyed her hopes and dreams and wanting to comfort her.

'Look, honey, soon as we can we'll get married. Things will be different then. But for goodness' sake put this crazy idea out of your head. There's no way it could work, and you'll end up regretting it.'

She couldn't argue; there was nothing she could say, and his warning was an echo of what Jo had said when she'd told her of her plan to disappear. He was right, just as Jo had been right – the idea had more holes in it than a colander. But she couldn't abandon Emma, and she couldn't abandon her hopes of getting her, Fliss knew she would never rest until she could hold her little daughter in her arms once more.

Jeff's posting to Germany came as a bolt from the blue. When he learned he was to embark on finishing his training, he immediately set about arranging a wedding. Even if they were married there was no possibility of Fliss joining him, for the present at least, but he felt better about leaving her with the protection of his name, and her place at Parklands was assured.

They were married in a brief civil ceremony, attended by only Jefferson, Marcia and two of Jeff's closest friends, during his two-week embarkation leave, and snatched a few days' honeymoon in New York, staying at the grandest hotel Fliss had ever set foot in. All too soon, though, it was over.

Fliss was devastated at being left alone again, and the moment Jeff departed for his base she once again became preoccupied with the compulsion to get Emma. He'd warned her again, before he left, not to do anything rash, and she knew his arguments were valid ones, but she couldn't see that Jefferson would turn her out of Parklands now that she was Jeff's wife, and in any case she hoped it wouldn't be long before she would be able to join him in Germany. The big stumbling block remained, however – getting Emma out of England – and she could still see no way round it but calling on Maggie for help.

With Jeff not there to pour cold water on her idea, the planning began to obsess her. She would fly to London and book a ticket for Emma for the return journey. If Maggie pretended to take the little girl to London for a day trip, she could meet them at Paddington station, whisk Emma away and head straight back for Heathrow. Maggie would need to give her a head start before reporting her missing – saying that she had lost her somewhere really busy, in one of the big department stores perhaps, or whilst feeding the pigeons in Trafalgar Square. It never occured to her that this plan was as outlandish and far-fetched as the one she'd concocted to fake her death, and if it did, she persuaded herself that since that had worked, there was really no reason why this shouldn't too. And if she experienced guilt at the thought of what it would do to Martin if her plan succeeded, she pushed the thought away. Nothing mattered but getting Emma. She couldn't allow herself to be sidetracked for a single second.

The compulsion to speak to Maggie, to get news of Emma and to ask for her help, began to obsess her again. Her nerves jangled, drawn tight as cheese wires. The telephone was mesmerising her once more. Countless times she hesitated, on the brink of picking it up, only to draw back at the last moment. And then one day when she was alone in the house she plucked up the courage to do something about it. When the operator answered, she asked for an international call, and instead of dropping the receiver like a hot coal when the line connected and the telephone began to ring, she remained, motionless, the receiver glued to her ear.

The whole thing seemed unreal somehow, like a particularly vivid dream. It wasn't too late; she could still disconnect and no one would be any the wiser.

And then, echoey and disembodied, she heard her sister's voice.

'Maggie?' she said, tremulously. 'Maggie, is that you?'

There was a long, shocked, crackling silence. Then:

'Fliss?'

She could hear all the shock and bewilderment Maggie must be feeling, the total lack of belief in the evidence of her own ears.

'Yes,' she said. 'Oh Maggie, don't hang up, will you! I have to talk to you!'

TWENTY-SEVEN

'Maggie, is that you?'

Despite the strange echo on the line, despite the fact that she couldn't believe what she was hearing, Maggie recognised the voice instantly. For a moment she couldn't speak, couldn't breathe even.

'Fliss?' she managed at last.

'Yes. Oh Maggie, don't hang up, will you!'

Maggie's knees went weak; the room seemed to be lurching around her, dissolving, while she was caught in a vacuum. Nothing was real; nothing but her sister's voice – a voice she'd never expected to hear again.

'Oh my God . . . Fliss!'

She couldn't take it in, couldn't, for the moment, feel anything but shock and bewilderment, It had never occurred to her that Fliss might not be dead. When the *Mermaid's Song* had been found drifting, from the very beginning she'd feared the worst – in fact, knowing how depressed Fliss had been, and remembering the conversation they'd had that day when Fliss had asked her to take care of Emma should anything ever happen to her, she'd had the most awful feeling that her sister had taken her own life. And the guilt that suspicion had engendered had haunted her ever since. How could she not have recognised how desperately unhappy Fliss was; how could she have let it come to this? She should have known – she *had* known, but she hadn't done anything about it. She'd failed Fliss, and the guilt had compounded her grief; the regret that she hadn't been there for Fliss when she needed her had overwhelmed her. She could take no comfort from the fact that Fliss had died doing something she loved, which was the panacea people kept trotting out. Maggie didn't believe it had been an accident, and the thought of the mental torture Fliss must have suffered that had brought her to the point where she'd decided she could no longer go on tore Maggie apart. But never, never had she considered the possibility that Fliss wasn't dead at all. The thought never once crossed her mind, and if it had she would have dismissed it as impossible.

But the impossible was true.

'Where are you?' she blurted. 'Where have you been?'

'I'm in the States.'

'The States.' Maggie's brain was beginning to function again. Jeff Hewson – the man Fliss had been having an affair with – was American. Somehow, between them, they'd concocted her disappearance so that they could run off together.

'Maggie, I haven't got time to go into it all now. I have to talk to you about Emma.' There was urgency in Fliss's voice. 'How is she?'

A sudden flash of anger penetrated the miasma of Maggie's whirling thoughts and the first disbelieving joy at discovering that Fliss was not dead at all, but alive.

'What do you care?' she demanded.

'Of course I care!' Fliss replied with passion. 'Is she all right?'

'She's fine,' Maggie said harshly. 'No thanks to you. How could you do this to us, Fliss? How could you do it to Emma – just walk away and leave her?'

'I never meant it to be for good,' Fliss said. 'I always intended to come back for her, and now I can. That's why I'm ringing, Maggie. I need your help.'

'What!'

'I've worked out a plan. I want you to bring Emma to London,

314

meet me there. Look, Maggie, I've written you a letter explaining everything and telling you what I need you to do. But I wanted to speak to you first. And I had to know how Emma is! You are telling me the truth, aren't you? She is all right?'

'She's fine and well and happy. Fliss . . . you aren't seriously considering . . .?'

'I can't live without her, Maggie.'

Another flash of anger. 'I thought it was Jeff Hewson you couldn't live without.'

'Oh Maggie, please . . . don't be like this! I thought . . .' The pips sounded; the operator interrupted.

'Your time is up, caller.'

'Can I have another three minutes?' Fliss begged.

'I'm sorry, the lines are booked.' She didn't sound sorry. She sounded smug. 'Try again later.'

'I'll ring again, Maggie,' Fliss said desperately. 'As soon as I can. And you won't tell anyone, will you?'

Before Maggie could reply the line went dead. Fliss had been cut off.

Maggie stood for a moment, the telephone still clamped to her ear, the pounding of her heart throbbing in her ears and punctuating the echoing emptiness of the line. Then the dialling tone cut in and she replaced the receiver, her hand shaking so much that she had difficulty settling it in its rest. Shock had rendered her incapable of coherent thought, her knees, which had almost given way when she heard Fliss's voice, felt insubstantial as lumps of rice pudding, and she grasped the hall table for support. Confused and boiling emotions crashed through her in waves, tumbling one on the other so that she couldn't separate them.

Her first instinct was to ring Martin. She dialled the number of the garage, her fingers fumbling over the digits, but it was Liz, the girl he'd taken on as a secretary/receptionist when the business began to take off, who answered.

'Sorry, Maggie, he's not here at the moment. He's out on a demo run with a client.

Can I give him a message?'

Hysteria bubbled in Maggie's throat. *Tell him his wife's not dead after all; she's just called me from America.* Hardly!

'No, it's all right.'

'I'll get him to ring you when he gets back.'

'No . . .' She shouldn't tell him over the telephone, with Liz in the office and within earshot, she realised. He was going to be as shocked as she was. 'Don't bother him,' she said. 'It's not important.'

She put the phone down, pressed her hands to her cheeks, which felt hot although she was shivering. A cup of tea. Hot, sweet tea. That was what she needed. She dragged herself to the kitchen, set the kettle to boil. Then she thought of Martin's whisky. Maggie rarely drank, and almost never spirits, but perhaps it would steady her. She found the bottle, poured some into a tumbler and sipped it, the glass clinking against her chattering teeth. But the warmth of the whisky was comforting even as it burned her tongue and raked her stomach, and a moment or two later she did indeed begin to feel calmer.

Thank God Emma wasn't here to see her like this! she thought. Emma had started playschool in the village three mornings a week, and Maggie had left her happily sloshing poster paint on to a giant sheet of paper, which would, no doubt, be put up on the kitchen wall when she came home, replacing last week's effort. Maggie's gaze honed in on the picture – great sweeps of green, yellow and blue, and random painty thumbprints.

Emma was such a happy child, sunny-natured and settled, and she'd adapted well to the loss of her mother. They'd done their best, she and Martin, to protect her from their grief, from all the chaos that had followed Fliss's 'death', trying to ensure that the tragedy and the change in circumstances affected her as little as possible, and Maggie thought they'd succeeded. But what now? How was this going to impact on her? On all of them? What was it Fliss had said? That she was going to come to London to get her?

The anger flared in Maggie again. How could Fliss do this to them? How dare she cause all this upset – play such a cruel trick and then think she could simply waltz back and snatch Emma from the safety of her home, from the people she loved, the people who loved her? It was outrageous!

And never mind Emma, what was all this going to do to Martin? He'd been devastated when Fliss had been lost; though he'd tried to hide his grief, keeping it battened down in a way that was typically Martin, she'd known he was heartbroken. He worshipped Fliss, always had, and his pain had been that of a mortally wounded animal. The passage of time had helped him come to terms with his loss, though she knew he still felt it keenly, and for Emma's sake he had rebuilt his shattered life. Learning what Fliss had done would destroy him, and if she tried to take Emma from him too . . .

Maggie began to tremble violently again as the full import of the shocking phone call dawned on her. Fliss was her sister – she loved her, and knowing she was alive was a joy she could not deny. But for all that she couldn't allow her to cause mayhem again. She simply couldn't.

As she thought of the terrible consequences for Emma and for Martin, it came to Maggie that it wasn't only them who would suffer. She was far from immune herself. For in the ashes of the devastation that was the loss of Fliss she had gained everything that had once been so far beyond her reach. Martin, whom she had loved for as long as she could remember. Emma, who was more like a daughter to her than a precious niece. A purpose that drove her every minute of every day from the moment she awoke with a song in her heart until she fell asleep at night, exhausted.

Fliss, her beloved sister, was alive, and it was both a blessing and a curse. If Fliss was alive, if she came back to claim what was hers, Maggie's whole world would come tumbling down around her.

In the terrible aftermath of Fliss's loss, Maggie had given not a single thought to the benefits it might bring her. Her only concern had been Emma. Hadn't she promised Fliss she'd take care of her? And wouldn't she have done it whether she'd promised or not?

She'd taken leave of absence from work – they were very good about it, understanding and sympathetic. Martin needed her help and support – between his grief and his work commitments he couldn't care for Emma alone, and Maggie had stepped into the breach. She collected Emma each day, or Martin dropped her off, and they dispensed with the services of the childminder – better that Emma should be in familiar surroundings with someone she knew, loved and trusted, they reasoned. When she asked for her mother, Maggie would be there to ressure and comfort her.

It was Maggie's employers who eventually suggested she should work from home – an innovative idea, but they couldn't manage without her indefinitely, and were reluctant to appear heartless by replacing her. Now, Maggie went to the office only to pick up files of papers and return them. She missed the company of her colleagues, and often she was still at her desk into the small hours, or rising before dawn in order to get the work done, but having Emma more than compensated for it, and soon she was cooking an evening meal for Martin too, so that he had something substantial to eat before he took Emma home. Arriving in time for breakfast was something else that happened naturally – Martin was struggling to get Emma to have more than her morning milk before leaving home; she wasn't ready to eat so early. So Maggie laid extra places, made porridge and sometimes even bacon and eggs. She did Emma's washing, and told Martin to bring his laundry too – it might as well all go in the twin-tub at the same time, and she'd iron his shirts too.

Martin was working very long hours, especially when the

insurance money for Fliss's life came through and he was able not only to settle his bank loan but also to buy a manufacturer's franchise; often Emma was asleep by the time he arrived for her. Maggie would have her bathed and in her pyjamas, but carrying her out to the car disturbed her, and sometimes it took a long while to get her back to sleep in her own bed.

'Why don't you leave her where she is?' Maggie suggested one night. 'You'll only be bringing her back first thing in the morning, after all.'

From there it was only a short step to Emma staying during the week, and quite often she and Martin spent Sunday with Maggie too.

A year after Fliss's disappearance they moved in. Martin and Maggie had grown close through sharing their grief, Emma loved her as a second mother, and Martin didn't know how he'd have managed without her. He didn't love her the way he'd loved Fliss, Maggie knew, but she didn't expect him to, and she didn't care. As long as he and Emma were there, depending on her, it was enough. She devoted herself to looking after them in every possible way and trying to make up for their loss. Martin was talking about building an extension on the back of the house to make a play-room for Emma. Everything had fallen into place in a way she could never have imagined in her wildest dreams.

Now, in the space of a few short minutes, all that was under threat. Fliss had the power to snatch away everything that Maggie held dear, undermine the stability of Emma's life, break Martin's heart once more. And if the truth came out, Martin would have to pay back the insurance money; he'd lose his business too. The enormity of it all made Maggie's head start spinning again.

She couldn't allow this to happen – she couldn't! How she would stop the house of cards from tumbling down she didn't yet know. But she was ready to fight tooth and nail for the man and the child who were her whole life.

She didn't tell Martin about Fliss's phone call. By the time he arrived home from the garage she had decided to keep it to herself, for the time being at least. She'd have to tell him sooner or later, of course, but she was dreading it, and besides, she wanted to think things through first.

Martin would never agree to letting Emma go, she was sure, but the insurance money was a different matter. He was straightforward and honest to a fault, and when he knew the payout had come as the result of fraud, he'd almost certainly waste no time in returning it, even though it would ruin him.

Was there any need for him to know at all? Maggie wondered. It was her, Maggie, whom Fliss had asked for help, because she knew it was the only way she'd get Emma. She wanted Maggie to spirit her away; she didn't actually want Martin to know she was still alive. Perhaps, if she could keep the truth to herself, she could pull this whole disaster back from the brink. Keeping the secret from Martin made her uncomfortable, but what was a little discomfort compared to the terrible upset that would ensue if she told him that Fliss was still alive?

Maggie was still in turmoil, still turning it all over in her mind, when, a few days later, the letter arrived. She knew it was from Fliss the moment it dropped on to the mat – the distinctive airmail marking around the envelope left her in no doubt – and she scooped it up quickly and hid it in a kitchen drawer, not opening it until she was alone.

The contents confirmed the impression she'd got on the telephone. Fliss was with Jeff Hewson – she'd married him, for goodness' sake! – and she was desperate for Emma to join them. But the plan she laid out read like a crime novel. Maggie was to take Emma to London, hand her over to Fliss at Paddington station and then, when they'd had a head start for Heathrow, pretend she'd lost her in the crowds. Only Fliss could dream up something like this! Maggie thought. Only Fliss could imagine for one moment that Maggie would do as she asked. Didn't she realise the trauma it would cause Emma? Didn't she care what it would do to Martin, believing his daughter had been kidnapped by a stranger – a child trafficker, a paedophile? No way on earth would

Maggie be a part of it. And if Fliss thought she'd do it just because she was her sister, she was very much mistaken. Fliss had forfeited the right to her loyalty when she faked her own death.

Maggie sat down and began writing a letter to Fliss, a letter that she amended and rewrote several times before she'd managed to say all the things she wanted to, but which made it clear she had no intention of complying with Fliss's request. It was not in Emma's best interests, and it would break Martin's heart. She promised she had told no one, not even Martin, that Fliss was still alive, and she wouldn't – to do so would be to destroy the lives that had been rebuilt since Fliss's disappearance. She begged Fliss to forget any thoughts of snatching Emma. 'You made your choice, Fliss. You have to live with it,' she wrote. She finished by wishing Fliss happiness, and signed off with love. As an after-thought, she found some recent photographs of Emma, popped them in the envelope, and wrote a PS on the letter: 'Snaps to show you how settled and happy Emma is.' Then she took it to the post office in the village and mailed it.

The photographs fell out of the pages of Maggie's letter as Fliss unfolded it. She swooped on them hungrily and pored over them, devouring every detail. Emma outside a Wendy house, pretend-ironing on a toy ironing board with handkerchiefs draped over a little airing rack beside her. Emma's third birthday, blowing out the candles on a cake in the shape of a hedgehog, and surrounded by five other little girls. Emma on a boat, snug in a child-size safety harness, and Martin beaming beside her. Emma with Martin again, sitting between his knees to slide down a water chute, laughing and waving at the camera. Fliss went through the little pile one by one, then laid them out on the bed so she could see all of them at the same time. Love welled in her; she stroked the little face with one finger, imagining she was caressing her daughter, and the tears spilled over and ran down her cheeks in scalding rivers.

At last she turned to the letter, nerves jangling with eager anticipation. Moments later she was trembling as she read what Maggie had to say.

> It was wonderful to hear your voice, to know that you are alive and well. But Fliss, darling Fliss, there's no way I can do what you ask . . .

She read on to the end, not really taking it all in the first time, so that she had to go back and reread it, all Maggie's reasoned arguments, how happy and settled Emma was, how wrong of Fliss it would be to whisk her away to an uncertain life in a different world.

> I know this sounds harsh, Fliss, Maggie had written, but the truth is she doesn't even really know you any more. It's getting on for two years since she saw you — that is a very long time for a small child. It's Martin and me who have been there for her all this time. And have you thought about what this will do to Martin? He adores her, he's a wonderful father, losing her would crucify him. Does he really deserve that, Fliss? Don't you think you've hurt him enough already?

The ever-ready guilt pricked at Fliss; she pushed it away. For the moment she could think of nothing but that Maggie was refusing point-blank to help her. Despair filled her, dark and suffocating, and she buried her head in her hands and wept, great racking sobs that felt as if they were tearing the heart out of her. Then, as they subsided, the determination crept in. If Maggie wouldn't help her, she'd have to find another way. She couldn't abandon her daughter, couldn't bear the thought that she might never see her again.

The change of heart came gradually, little seeds of doubt sown, perhaps by Jeff in his replies to her frantically distressed letters.

'Maggie has a point, sweatheart,' he'd written. 'I think you have to bite the bullet and accept it's in Emma's best interests.'

At first Fliss refused to acknowledge it. She couldn't allow herself to think for a single moment that she might be doing the wrong thing in trying to work out a way to get Emma. But they persisted, those seeds – each time she looked at the photographs she could see that Maggie was right – and slowly they began to take root and grow. Emma *was* happy and settled, secure in the only world she had ever known, the family of which Fliss was no longer a part. She had little friends to play with. Her whole life was centred in Porthtowan. And what did Fliss have to offer in return? Not security, certainly. This whole edifice of pretence could come tumbling down at any time. And even if it didn't, she would still be subjecting Emma to an uncertain future. She'd have to get used to first America and then, possibly, Germany, before returning to America again, and all with no one but a mother who was virtually a stranger to her. She'd miss her father, she'd miss Maggie.

She'd have all the things that Hewson money could buy, of course, but none of them would make up for what she had lost – not for years and years, anyway, and perhaps not even then. Jeff had had all those things and they hadn't made him happy. And it was possible that all the upheaval would scar Emma for ever, leave her with an insecurity she'd never be able to overcome completely.

Was she being selfish? Fliss wondered. Perhaps she was. She couldn't wish the terrible longing she was experiencing for Emma on to her beloved child, and it could be that that was exactly what she would be doing. Day after day Fliss agonised, and suddenly she woke one morning and realised: she couldn't do it.

She loved Emma with all her heart. She'd never get over losing her. But somehow, for Emma's sake, she had to find the strength to give up her hopes of being reunited with her daughter. Maggie was right – it was in Emma's best interests to leave her where she was, secure, happy, loved.

Just as long as she never thought that her mother had abandoned her, didn't love her, didn't care. Just as long as she knew that it was because of that love that Fliss had reached this final, heart-rending decision.

She'd write a letter to her, Fliss decided. She'd send it to Maggie, ask her to keep it safely, and then, when Emma was old enough to understand, to give it to her. Perhaps when she read it Emma would come to find her – with all her heart she hoped she would – but it had to be her decision.

With tears streaming down her face she began.

My dearest Emma,
    I don't know how to begin this letter. I don't know how to make you understand. You're only a little girl now, but when you read this you will be grown up. And you will have grown up without me. But I want you to know that I have never stopped loving you, and I never will. That this isn't the way it was meant to be. I can only try to explain and hope that you won't blame me too much . . .

The darkness was back, a pit so deep it seemed bottomless, and Fliss was falling into it. Some days she did nothing but look at the photographs of Emma, gazing at them with tears pouring down her cheeks, the pain inside so sharp it made her double over with it. Some days she couldn't bear to look at them at all, but she could see them still. She couldn't allow herself to weaken, though. She wrote to Jeff, telling him of her decision, and his reply echoed what she knew in her heart: 'You've done the right thing, sweetheart.' Only the thought that soon she would be with him in Germany kept her from slipping completely over the edge. It seemed to offer a fresh start, the one glimmer of hope in a dark world. But even that didn't seem to be happening, and she really couldn't understand why. She'd have thought that even if, as a conscript, he wasn't eligible for married quarters, at least he would be able to find a place to rent or even a hotel where she could stay.

Just to make matters worse, Jefferson and Marcia's wedding day was approaching. It was to be a grand affair, and would be held at the summer house on Gull Island. Fliss had not the slightest interest in the manic planning that was going on, apart from clinging to the hope that Jeff might be given some leave to attend. Marcia, however, was determined to marshal her into line.

'We're going shopping,' she announced. 'You must have something nice to wear.'

Fliss, who hated shopping for clothes at any time, let alone with Marcia, objected.

'Nonsense! You can't possibly be seen in any of your usual things. This will be a very smart occasion, and you are the daughter-in-law of the groom. You'll need at least one new outfit, and possibly two.'

'I don't want a new outfit. I don't actually want to go to the wedding at all.' Never mind the social ordeal, Fliss didn't want to go back to Gull Island, where she and Jeff had been so happy, and tarnish her precious memories.

'This isn't about what you want,' Marcia retorted. 'It's expected of you.'

Fliss had no energy to argue any more and gave in. Marcia took her to New York, to Bloomingdale's, where, in a private fitting room, a fawning personal shopper showed a railful of appropriate dresses and Fliss was bullied into trying them on. A pale-green evening dress was eventually settled upon, suitable, Marcia said, for both the ceremony and the ball that was to follow. She also insisted on buying Fliss a little blue jersey-wool skirt suit with a boxy jacket and a pillbox hat, Jackie Kennedy style, a lilac wool day dress with a wide boat neckline and three-quarter-length sleeves, and a dark-green fake-fur coat. 'Not that I'd dream of wearing fake fur myself,' she sniffed, 'but it is very fashionable and the colour suits you.'

When the boxes were delivered to Parklands, Mimi unpacked them and hung the clothes in the wardrobe. Fliss didn't even look at them, let alone try them on again.

Her hopes that Jeff would be granted some special leave came to nothing, and the wedding was exactly the ordeal she had imagined it would be, lavish and mawkishly sentimental. The house was filled with the sorts of people she was least comfortable with – the rich and self-important, gushing women and powerful men, whose impressive cruisers and yachts filled the little harbour, and in the evening an orchestra played and champagne flowed freely while uniformed waitresses circulated with trays of elaborate canapés. When she could bear it no longer, Fliss slipped away and walked barefoot down to the harbour, carrying her shoes because her stiletto heels were crippling her. There she sat down on the jetty, looking out to sea and remembering that long-ago day when she had done the same thing on the cliffs above Porthtowan after being told she was pregnant with Emma.

'Where on earth have you been?' Marcia hissed at her when she returned. 'There are people who want to talk to you.' And: 'For goodness' sake go and do something about your hair! You look as if you have been dragged through a cactus bush!'

This much was true – the stiff sea breeze had unravelled the once-smooth chignon, but Fliss couldn't care less.

'Go to hell, Marcia,' she muttered under her breath, and if she heard her, Marcia did not respond, but she did glare coldly at Fliss.

'Jeff would be ashamed of you,' she said cuttingly.

Since he had not been granted leave for the wedding, Fliss was delighted but puzzled when, a week or so later, Jeff telephoned to say he was coming home for a few days.

'Why now?' she asked. 'If you were due leave, why didn't they let you have it for the wedding?'

'I can't explain now. I'll tell you when I see you. I thought we could go to Gull Island. Dad and Marcia aren't still there, I take it?'

Fliss laughed. 'No chance! I don't think Marcia likes it very much. It's fine when she wants to show off, have a better wedding venue than anyone else, but it's too far away from all her socialite chums when it comes to her everyday lifestyle.'

'Hmm.' Jeff was no more fond of Marcia than Fliss was, and hated the fact that she'd taken his mother's place so soon after her death. 'You like it there, though, don't you, and it will give us a chance to have some private time.'

'I love it, especially if I'm going to be with you,' Fliss said.

'That's settled, then. Love you, hon.'

'Love you too.'

The darkness had lifted a little; perhaps after all things weren't going to be so bad.

'I miss you so much, Jeff,' she said. They were in bed, limbs entwined. 'When am I going to be able to join you in Germany?'

For a long moment Jeff was silent. He really didn't quite know how he was going to tell Fliss the unexpected turn his military career was taking. It had been a shock to him when he had been called into the office of his commanding officer and informed that he had been chosen for a special assignment; it was going to be a shock – and a blow – to Fliss too, he knew.

'Hon, this is what I wanted to talk to you about. No point you coming to Germany at the moment. I'm not going to be there, for a while at least.'

'Why not? Where are you going to be?' Her heart leapt. 'Are you being posted home?'

''Fraid not. Look, I'm not really supposed to be talking about this, but I'll tell you what I can. Just as long as you keep it absolutely to yourself. A party of advisers are going to Vietnam . . .'

'Vietnam!'

'. . . and I'm going with them.'

'But . . .' She was bemused. 'Why Vietnam?'

'The situation out there is pretty dire, and getting worse. Word has it that before long we are going to have to intervene. It hasn't quite reached that stage yet, but there is a certain amount of high-level involvement.'

'You're not high level!'

He snorted. 'Nor want to be. I guess they just need some

minders who won't let the side down, and I've got the right qualifications.'

'How long will you be gone?'

'At the moment I can't say. Nothing's set in stone.'

Tears were pricking at her eyes.

'Oh, it's just not fair, Jeff! I've given up on getting Emma . . .'

'Which was absolutely the right thing to do, sweetheart.'

'. . . but I haven't got you either. Are we *ever* going to be together? I can't bear to go on like this.'

'You've just got to be brave, honey, and remember it won't be for ever. Another year and I'll be finished with the military. Then we've got the rest of our lives to be together.'

'Oh I hope so! I do hope so!'

'We will be. I promise.'

She curled into his body, feeling his warmth, but it could not reach the cold place inside her. The future together for which she had sacrificed everything seemed as far away as ever.

Just two weeks after Jeff left for Vietnam, a US army officer arrived at Parklands.

Fliss was in the drawing room when the bell rang, reading *Peyton Place*. She'd never been a great reader, but she had to do something to occupy the long, lonely hours, and so she'd gone searching in the library for something that wasn't too demanding. The Grace Metalious was stacked with some other paperbacks on a small side table. It had belonged to Betty, she guessed, and had no place amongst the impressive volumes on the shelves. Now she was actually enjoying the scandalous goings-on in a small American town, and couldn't wait to find out what the colourful characters were going to do next.

When the doorbell interrupted her, she didn't move from her chair. She'd become used to it being answered by one of the staff, and in any case she didn't imagine it would have anything to do with her. So she was surprised when Forrester, the butler, appeared in the doorway. 'Someone to see you, Mrs Hewson.'

The officer was a colonel; tall, distinguished-looking and vaguely familiar. She was to remember later that he had been a guest at Jefferson and Marcia's wedding.

'Please don't get up, Mrs Hewson,' he said. 'This isn't a social call.'

Something about the gravity of his tone and his expression sent a twinge of alarm through Fliss, but she got up anyway.

'I'm sorry . . . I don't understand . . .'

'I'm afraid I'm the bearer of some very serious news concerning your husband. As you know, he is in Vietnam with a party of advisers. But the fact of the matter is that we have lost contact with the helicopter on which he was travelling, and we can only conclude that . . .'

All the blood seemed to drain from Fliss's body in a rush, leaving her icy cold and trembling. She barely heard the rest of what the colonel had to say – she could hear his voice droning on, but it sounded as if he was speaking in an echo chamber.

'I'm very sorry,' he finished. 'If there is any further news, we will of course pass it on to you without delay. But I must stress I am not optimistic.'

The finality of his words chilled her to the core. In that moment it seemed to Fliss that the universe had imploded around her.

Part Five

1989

TWENTY-EIGHT

MIKE

When we get out of the elevator, a man is waiting for us. He's tall, silver-haired, and though he's casually dressed, he still manages to look distinguished. But the moment he sets eyes on Emma, his expression changes to one of shock, and though I take the lead, holding out my hand, introducing myself, it's her he's looking at. He's recognised her, that much is clear, and when I start to introduce her he cuts me off.

'No need. I know who Emma is.' He turns directly to her. 'You're Fliss's daughter, right?'

Though I'd warned her how instantly recognisable she is, I don't think she's believed me until now.

'The last time I saw you, you were just a little girl. In a stroller,' he goes on. 'Now, though . . .'

'You've met me?' Emma sounds startled.

'Just before I left England. You'd have been too young to remember.' He turns back to me. 'I'm guessing this Jubilee Sailing Trust is just an excuse. The real reason you're here is because of Fliss. Am I right?'

'Well . . . yes.' There was no longer any point.

'The reason we're here,' Emma says, jumping right in, 'is because I want to find my mother.'

'Hmm.' A corner of Jeff's mouth quirked, but the bleakness in his eyes was not encouraging. 'You and me both,' he says flatly.

333

Emma deflates like a pricked balloon.

'You don't know where she is?' she said in a small voice.

Jeff shakes his head.

'Honey, I haven't known where she is for the best part of thirty years.'

Emma looks as if she might be going to burst into tears.

'But I thought the reason she ran away was so that she could be with you.'

'Why don't we go in?' He indicates a door, a little way along the corridor, which is standing open. 'I'll get you something to drink – iced coffee, maybe – and then we can talk.'

We follow him into the condo. A spacious lounge area looks out over the sea through a wall of glass; a counter acts as a divider between it and the kitchen, so Jeff is still in full view as he makes the drinks. Emma and I sit side by side on a black leather sofa, and Jeff pulls out a small chrome and glass table to put the drinks on.

'I've got to say this is one hell of a shock,' he says, sitting down too in a director-style chair, also leather and chrome, opposite us.

'Sorry about that,' I say. 'I couldn't warn you, for obvious reasons.'

'You thought you might find Fliss here.'

'It was a possibility, yes. Look, let me explain. It's only a few weeks since Emma found out that Fliss might still be alive, and that is down to me. I am a journalist, and I was following up a lead that came my way. Someone claimed to have seen Fliss here in Naples some time after she was presumed drowned.'

Jeff looks shocked, but says nothing.

'When Emma discovered there was a chance her mother might still be alive, she wanted to be in on my investigation,' I add.

'I need to know the truth,' Emma interposes. 'And I hoped I might find my mother.'

Jeff gives her a long look and his face softens.

'Oh honey, I'm really sorry I can't help you there. I only wish I could. Thirty years on, and I still hope one day she might come back, or I'll spot her in a marina somewhere. I've tried to find her, God knows, but it seems to me she just doesn't want to be found.' He turns back to me. 'When did you say she was supposedly seen?'

'It was soon after she disappeared. Too long ago to be any use, I'm afraid.'

I tell him about Barbara Gooding and he shakes his head.

'Sounds like it might have been the day I arrived back after my transatlantic voyage – there was a pretty fair crowd down at the harbour that day. Is that how you got on to me – this lady saw me with Fliss?'

'No . . .' I'm about to tell him about Simon, but Emma is on the edge of her seat, leaning forward intently.

'My mother sailed the Atlantic with you?'

'No, no. I did it solo. But she was here waiting for me. It blew me away, I can tell you. I'd left her in England – thought I'd lost her. And then, when I landed . . . there she was. At first I thought I was having hallucinations.'

'You didn't plan it together, then?' Emma asks.

'No way.' He's sitting back in his director's chair, one long chino-clad leg crossed over the other. 'I wanted her to come with me, back to the States, but she told me no. She didn't think your father would let her take you with her, Emma, and she wouldn't leave you. But in the time it took me to cross the Atlantic, she must have changed her mind and worked out this crazy plan.'

He gets up, crossing to a built-in dresser that I imagine doubles as a drinks cabinet, and retrieves a packet of cigarettes and a lighter.

'Bad habit – should have given it up years ago. D'you mind?'

We both shake our heads.

'So what happened then?' Emma asks. 'Did you stay here in Naples with her?'

'No.' Jeff lights his cigarette, sits down again. 'I had it fixed to go back to Harvard to finish off the course I'd abandoned some years before. Fliss came with me. Seems like we were fated, though.

335

My mother was dying, and Fliss, bless her, stayed to take care of her. We didn't have more than a few months together all told before I got my draft papers. Selection was pretty random then – it was before Vietnam as you'd think of it got going, but that's where I ended up being sent. On a top-secret mission accompanying what they termed "advisers". Fliss was in one hell of a state about it. Before that I'd been posted to Germany, and we'd been hoping she'd be able to join me there. But Vietnam – no chance. In any case, it wasn't supposed to be for very long. Trouble was, it didn't work out like that. I was on a helicopter that crashed in the jungle and finished up in enemy hands. It was a very long time before I made it back to the States. When I did, Fliss was gone.'

'Gone?' Emma echoes.

'Yep. Can't blame her, I guess. She was staying with my father and Marcia, his wife, while I was out of the picture, and I know she wasn't happy there. She and Marcia didn't get along, so I presume when my helicopter came down she decided she didn't want to stick around any longer. Dad and Marcia had no idea where she'd gone. That's what I never could understand – why she didn't leave them with some way of contacting her, or even get in touch to check whether there was any news. It must have looked pretty bleak to her, I guess, but still, "missing presumed dead" isn't the same as "killed in action".'

He pauses to take a pull of his cigarette and taps ash into a big glass ashtray.

'So – that's about it. I'd spent a couple of weeks' leave with her on Gull Island – that's where my family had a summer place – and then went off to 'Nam. I never saw her again.'

I cover Emma's hand with mine and give it a squeeze.

'You tried to find her, presumably?' I say to Jeff.

'You bet I did! Tried every which way. I looked for her myself in all the places I thought she might have gone, and when I got nowhere I hired private investigators – spent a fortune on them.

It was a risk, too — Fliss was an illegal immigrant, after all, and although she had new papers and we'd got married soon after I was posted to Germany, I was still wary of drawing too much attention to her. Need not have worried, though. We never found hide nor hair of her. Which is why I can't imagine you'll have any more luck.'

'Doesn't sound hopeful,' I admit. Then an idea comes to me.

'There's one thing that might work,' I say tentatively. 'If I could publicise the fact that her daughter is looking for her . . . What was her assumed name?'

'Doris Margharita Ponticano. Well — Hewson after we married.' He grins ruefully. 'Don't ask. She didn't care for being Doris Margharita either. But the publicity . . . well, it could be worth a try, I guess.'

'Hardly. If she could abandon me then, it's not very likely she'll break cover for me now.' The hurt is there in Emma's voice, trembling beneath her brave attempt at insouciance.

'Honey, that's not exactly true,' Jeff says. 'She never meant to abandon you. Her plan was to get you when all the fuss had died down — she was banking on that. She would never have left you otherwise. But it didn't work out. Her sister Maggie thought it wasn't in your best interests to uproot you.'

'Maggie!' Emma looks as shocked as I'd known she would be and I kick myself for not putting her fully in the picture as to what Simon told me. I should have prepared her. 'Maggie knew Fliss was alive!'

Jeff grinds out his cigarette.

'She sure did. Sent Fliss photographs of you. I never did see them myself, but I know from her letters how much they meant to her, more up to date than the ones she'd brought with her, so she could see how you were growing up. And I can vouch for the fact that her plan was always to come back and get you, until Maggie persuaded her it was best to leave things as they were. Take it from me, your mother never meant to lose you for good. Heck, we even had you put on her passport so she could get you.

She missed you like crazy, and when Maggie put her foot down and refused to let you go, it broke her heart.'

He gets up, crosses to the window, staring out across the ocean. This is pretty emotional for him, I imagine, and he needs a moment to collect himself. Then he gets out another cigarette, rolling it between his fingers without lighting it.

'The thing is I've kind of had to get used to the idea that wherever Fliss went she didn't want me to find her,' he says. 'But you, Emma . . . I reckon there's a good chance she'd come out of hiding for you.'

Emma is silent for a long moment, mulling all this over. Then her chin comes up and she gives Jeff a direct look.

'You don't think, do you . . . Well, I know Mum suffered from clinical depression. Dad and Maggie did wonder whether it wasn't an accident at all when she supposedly drowned, if maybe she'd taken her own life. Well, Dad did, anyway,' she amends. 'You don't think it's possible that when she thought you were dead she might have done something like that?'

Jeff shakes his head.

'Possible, I suppose, but I don't think so. She took everything with her, including all her photographs of you. Clothes, her papers, everything was gone and they've never turned up. No, I don't think Fliss took her own life. I think she just wanted to disappear again.'

He pauses to light the cigarette and his eyes are narrowed behind the curl of smoke.

'There was one odd thing, though. I left my boat, the *Jersey Gal*, in Eastville Marina, when I went to 'Nam. When I got home it was missing. Turned up a few hundred miles south. Now whether it was just borrowed by some bum who took a fancy to it, or whether Fliss had anything to do with it, I'll never know. But nobody at the marina where I found it remembered her sailing in, so I just drew another blank.'

I take a moment to digest this. Does it mean something, is it another part of the puzzle? Or was it as he said, just a chance happening? Whichever, there was no point in me following it up. If Jeff had been unable to find out who had moved his boat back then, there was no chance I could learn any more so many years later.

'So would you be happy with me trying to get some newspaper coverage about Emma wanting to find her?' I ask.

'OK by me,' he says.

We talk some more, then Jeff asks if we are going to be staying in Florida.

'Doesn't seem any point at the moment,' I say. 'I can always contact the people I need to from England.'

'I'm going to have to get back,' Emma adds. 'I have work commitments.'

'Pity,' Jeff says. 'I'd have liked the chance to get to know you.'

Emma nods. 'Maybe some other time.'

'I sure hope so. You're welcome any time you care to visit.'

'Thank you. That's kind,' she says.

But I know she's desperately disappointed, as well as shocked to learn of Maggie's involvement.

And I wish, for her sake, it had turned out differently.

TWENTY-NINE

EMMA

'Are you OK?' Mike asks.

We're heading back to our hotel.

'Fine.' It's not true, of course, and Mike knows it.

'It's all right to be upset, you know.'

'I'm not upset. I just don't feel like talking.'

This certainly is true. Normally I can talk for England. Right now there's just too much going on in my head, and none of it good.

'Did you know about Maggie being involved?' I ask suddenly. 'Did Simon Beacham tell you?'

'Actually, yes,' Mike says. 'I'm sorry, Emma.'

'I knew it! I knew you were hiding something!'

'I didn't want to upset you. But I should have told you. I'm sorry.'

'I just can't believe that she knew all the time!' I say. 'How could she keep a secret like that all these years?'

'I don't suppose she had much choice.'

'Oh, don't make excuses for her!' I snap. 'She still wouldn't have it that Mum might not have drowned when I saw her last Sunday. Surely she must have known the truth was bound to come out.'

'She must have been hoping it wouldn't. That it was all too long ago.'

'Well at least I know now why she was so anxious to stop me from getting involved. And why she reacted as she did when I asked her if she'd ever heard of Simon Beacham. Honestly, she looked as if she'd seen a ghost. But even then she covered up.'

I stop talking, replaying the conversation in my mind.

'I'm pretty sure Dad doesn't know anything about it, though,' I say. 'In fact I'm positive he doesn't. He was the one prepared to accept it was possible that Mum faked the drowning, while Maggie wouldn't entertain it for a moment. What's that quotation? "Methinks the lady doth protest too much."? Besides, if he'd known Fliss was still alive, he'd never have married Maggie. It's bigamy, for goodness' sake! Dad is the most law-abiding person I know. He'd never commit bigamy.'

Tears are gathering in my throat suddenly, tears of anger that Maggie could do something like this. I just can't reconcile it with the woman who has always been a mother to me. But I don't doubt for a moment that it's true. Maggie knew that Fliss faked her own death, had conspired in it for all I know, and she's kept it from Dad and me all these years. How could she *do* that?

Then there's Fliss's betrayal. Perhaps Jeff was telling the truth when he said she hadn't meant to abandon me, that she'd desperately wanted me with her, though how she could have been so naïve as to believe it was ever going to happen is beyond me. But certainly she had meant to walk out on my lovely, kind, gentle dad. She hadn't cared how much she was hurting him.

And as if that wasn't enough, it seems she walked out on Jeff too.

'What kind of a fly-by-night was she?' I ask bitterly.

Mike doesn't reply. We've arrived back at our hotel and he's parking the car. 'From what Jeff said, it seems as though she thought he was dead.'

'But why disappear like that? Why not at least check in with his family every so often to see if there was any news? If she'd really cared about him, surely she'd have done that? If you ask

341

me, she went off with somebody else. And I imagine she strung Simon Beacham along, too. What was she like?'

'Come on, Emma, calm down,' Mike says. 'You don't know the full story yet.'

'Nor am I ever likely to,' I say bitterly.

'You never know. An appeal in the press might just work.'

'Do you think so?' My lip is trembling, then the anger is back. 'I'm not actually sure I want it to any more. I've had it with Maggie, and I've had it with Fliss. She didn't want me – why should I want her?'

'You don't mean that,' Mike says.

'Oh, believe me, I do!'

I stare out of the car window, and my eyes are full of a hot haze of tears.

The rest of the day passes in a sort of haze. Mike has booked our tickets back to the UK – we fly out tomorrow at midday. I wonder if I should phone home, but I can't face it, and in any case, it's the middle of the night there. Nobody will thank me for waking them up, except possibly Philip, and I don't want to speak to him anyway, don't want to have to explain what's going on. It's no good; at some point I am going to have to make a decision about him, and I think I already know what it will be. If there was any future for us, I wouldn't get this sinking feeling inside every time I think about him. I'd want him onside, want to confide in him and have him in my corner, and I don't. But I can't think about that now. I'm already on emotional overload.

Mike and I go out for something to eat. We find a little restaurant that has tables set up outside on the pavement – or sidewalk as they call it over here – and Mike orders a steak with mushrooms and fries. I don't think I could manage anything more than an omelette, and even that sticks in my throat, but I manage to put away more wine than is probably good for me.

As we walk back to the hotel I'm ever so slightly woozy, and somehow things don't seem quite so bad. Mike puts his arm round me and I lean into him. What is it about him that makes it feel so right?

We walk in silence. Suddenly I feel little quivers starting inside, and I'm becoming more and more aware of him. His hand resting on my arm, his shoulder beneath my cheek, the hard wall of his chest against my breast. We keep on walking, but I'm savouring the sensations. For the moment they're blotting out all the emotional upheaval of the day; I'm thinking of nothing but how close we are and how much I'm enjoying it. I just want to go on for ever like this, no more, no less.

He bends his head, kisses my cheek. Instinctively I turn towards him and our noses touch. The quivers inside me are sharper now, the awareness more urgent. I can scarcely breathe. And then, quite suddenly, reality kicks in. What am I doing? I pull away, my foot turns on a cobble, and I stumble.

'Careful!' Mike says, steadying me.

And then he's kissing me. And though I know it's wrong, I'm kissing him back. When we stop for breath, he pulls back slightly so we're looking directly into one another's eyes, and I know he's feeling exactly the way I am. It's there between us, crackling like the electricity when two bare wires touch.

'Are you sure you want this?' he says softly, and I know exactly what he means. I nod. I really don't care about anything now – not any of the awful things I've found out today about my family, not the fact that I know Mike is married with a child, not that I'll be cheating on Philip, who is a good man and deserves better. I need Mike, and the need is so powerful I don't even want to fight it.

Arms around one another, staggering like a pair of drunks, we make it back to the hotel, take the elevator. Mike's room is the closest; he has to let go of me to find his room key and open the door, and I drape myself against him, pressing my body into his hip. Then we're inside, the door closed behind us, undressing one another. We scarcely make it to the bed, so crazy are we for each other.

When it's over, we lie entwined, our skin so sticky with perspiration that when we pull apart there's a little sucking sound. It makes me smile.

'Whole new meaning to "stuck on you",' I say.

I'm replete now, still just a little woozy, but there's a lovely languor creeping through my veins.

This, I think drowsily, is what is missing with Philip. I just don't feel this way with him. And a little twinge of sadness pricks my bubble of contentment, though for the moment I can't quite work out what it is, because I am so very nearly asleep, and perhaps, also, because I don't want to.

When I wake a few hours later, though, I can't escape it. I ease out of Mike's embrace and turn over to look at him.

Though it's the middle of the night, there's enough light coming in through the window from the street lights outside for me to see him pretty clearly, and everything about him makes me want him again. But this time it's not purely physical. The yearning is deeper than that – I want him on every level, in every possible way, and there's a tenderness as well as a fierce need in the wanting. To be with him. To know that he's there for me, and to be there for him. To share everything, not just the big things, both good and bad, but the little ordinary everyday things too. I want him to be there when I wake in the night like this; not just on the odd occasion when we've shared the most incredible lovemaking, but always. I want to know his every mood, learn everything there is to know about him. I want to be able to reach out my hand and know that he is there. I want him to love me; I want to love him. Which probably means I already do.

And that is where the dream abruptly ends. There's no way it's going to happen. Last night I was too overwhelmed by the events of the day, too emotional, perhaps even too drunk, to care, but now I'm stone-cold sober I can see things clearly. He's a married man. He has a daughter. And I behaved like a tramp, cheating on Philip, throwing myself at Mike.

344

Shame makes me hot. I'm no better than my mother. In her case, she was the one who was married, but it comes to much the same. Restless dissatisfaction. Desire overcoming all moral scruples. An inability to say no to temptation.

Well, it can't go on. I won't be responsible for tearing another little girl's life apart as mine was torn apart. And I won't be 'the other woman' lurking in the shadows, either. I made a mistake last night, a bad mistake. And if there was an excuse for it then, there's none now, no matter how much I might wish things were different.

Mike stirs in his sleep, reaching out for me, but I wriggle away. Carefully, very carefully so as not to wake him, I slip out from under the covers and climb out of bed. I collect my clothes, scattered over the floor, and my bag – I can't get back into my own room without my room key! In the doorway I stop for just a moment, looking back at Mike. Dark hair against the pillow, strong profile with that crazy boxer's nose, strongly built shoulders, muscled arms, still scarred by mosquito bites. I want him so much, more than I've ever wanted anyone. But it can't happen. Before I can weaken, I open the door stealthily and creep out.

Mike is already in the restaurant having breakfast of ham and eggs when I come down. After I got back to my own room last night I was awake for a very long time while everything went around and around in my head, but I suppose I must have fallen asleep eventually, with the result that it was late before I woke, and by the time I'd showered and dressed it was almost nine o'clock.

I collect a glass of orange juice and a dish of stewed fruit – apricots, prunes, figs – from the breakfast buffet and carry them over to the table where he's sitting. I wish I could avoid him, but I can't. Trying to keep out of his way from now until we get home would be beyond impossible.

He looks up from his ham and eggs.

'Morning.' There's a hint of a smile on his face, a teasing glint in his eye. Unlike me, he doesn't appear in the least ashamed.

I nod coolly. 'Morning.'

'Sleep well?'

'Oh, not too bad – considering.'

'What time did you go back to your own room?'

'I don't know. About four, maybe . . .'

He carries on eating; I pick at my fruit. There's a horrible atmosphere developing. Mike puts down his knife and fork, pours coffee from the cafetière into my cup and his own, then sits back looking at me gravely.

'You're regretting last night, aren't you?'

I don't answer. Part of me doesn't regret it at all.

'I'm sorry,' he says. 'I took advantage of you. Pretty unforgivable, really.'

'You didn't take advantage of me,' I say coolly. 'I don't think I was entirely blameless. But if you don't mind, I'd really rather not talk about it.'

'OK, fine.' He actually has the temerity to look hurt. He's apologised to me, but what about his wife? Surely she's the injured party here.

We finish our coffee in silence. In sharp contrast to how things were before, the atmosphere between us is really tense and awkward. How could I have been so stupid as to get myself into this situation? As if I didn't have enough on my plate already!

'I take it you're packed and ready to go?' Mike says as we leave the restaurant.

'No, but I will be.'

'I think we ought to get going in the next hour or so. We don't know what the traffic is going to be like, and I've got to return the hire car.'

'Is it all right, leaving it at a different place from where we picked it up?' I ask.

'It'll have to be,' Mike says shortly.

Back in my room, I throw the few things I brought with me into my bag, feeling pretty fed up. I'd come here with such high hopes – now I know there's virtually no chance I'll ever find my mother. I've discovered a side to Maggie that I'd really rather not have known about, and it undermines everything that I thought was good and stable in my life. And I've lost the easy friendship that was blossoming between me and Mike and replaced it with painful awkwardness and a stupid, stupid yearning for something that can never happen.

All in all, I feel as if my life has become one horrible mess. And I really can't see any way out of it.

THIRTY

THE LINK

Melanie Thomas is ridiculously excited about her forth-coming trip on the *Lord Nelson*. It's not long now before she'll be setting sail. Her bag is packed with everything she'll need – hat, fleece, sailing gloves, several pairs of thick socks, two pairs of jeans and a pair of shorts, a couple of T-shirts, a sweatshirt and enough changes of underwear to last a week. She's pinned a checklist to the corkboard in the kitchen so as to be sure she doesn't leave anything out when she packs her tote bag: passport – check; sun cream – check; sunglasses, lip balm, shampoo, toothbrush and toothpaste – check. Foreign currency ordered, just in case. New trainers placed tidily in the hall ready to put on. Jubilee Sailing Trust brochure on the kitchen table where she can see the cover picture of the beautiful tall ship with its billowing sails and leaf through the pages while she's eating.

It's all helped to take her mind off Mark. She hasn't seen him again since that day on the Underground, though every time she travels by Tube she keeps a sharp lookout, and once or twice she's thought she spotted him in the street, though of course it wasn't him. But she's trying very hard not to think about him, or at least to keep him compartmentalised so he's just an almost unidentifiable though constant ache rather than a painful obsession.

Everything's arranged for her trip, she's sorted out the required insurance and received her joining instructions, and Anna is going to drive her down to Portsmouth. Mel said there was no need, she'd be fine on the train, but Anna insisted.

'I'd like to wave you off,' she said, 'and I'd like to see the *Lord Nelson* too. They're pretty impressive, those square-rigged barques.'

'Actually *you're* pretty impressive, Mum,' Mel said. 'Square-rigged barque, indeed! You know more about it than I do!'

Anna shrugged. 'I've been reading the literature too.'

'To make sure I'm going to be in safe hands, I suppose,' Mel said. 'Honestly, Mum, you're a real mother hen. I'm a big girl now and quite capable of taking care of myself.'

'I'm sure you are. I'm interested, that's all.'

'Don't worry, I'll take lots of photographs so you'll be able to see exactly what it's like. Ah!' Mel raised a finger. 'Something else to go on my checklist. Camera! And a notebook and pencil. I really ought to keep a diary.'

It's not only Anna who's interested in every detail; the girls at the bank want to know all about it too.

'You are so brave, Mel!' Christine Warren says.

'Brave? Oh, I don't think so!'

'You are! I wouldn't want to do it, and I haven't got the problems you have.'

'Are you really going to climb the rigging?' asks Sarah Pillinger.

'I'm going to try, if I get the chance.'

'What if you're seasick?' Angela Topping.

'I hope I won't be. I've been on a ferry a few times, and I was fine.'

'But ferries have stabilisers, don't they? Does the *Lord Nelson* have stabilisers?'

'I don't know,' Mel admits. 'But once when we went from Holyhead to Ireland it was pretty rough, and I was OK, though Brian . . .' She breaks off. Brian is an episode in her life that she's trying very hard to forget. But she can still see him, deathly pale, staggering from one fixed seat to another in search of a sick bag, and managing to overturn a stainless-steel rubbish bin that was also supposed to be bolted to the floor. She'd been fine then, but it wasn't a very long crossing. A whole six days at sea might be a very different kettle of fish.

Something else to put on her checklist. Seasickness pills. She won't take them unless she absolutely has to, but it would be good to have them by her, just in case.

All this is doing a good job of keeping her mind off Mark, until one day she doesn't just glimpse him but bumps into him, quite literally. She's going down the steps to the Underground at Oxford Circus, he's coming up. Suddenly they're nose to nose and there's no way they can avoid one another.

'Melanie!'

'Mark!'

He's looking as good as ever, better perhaps, because he has something of a permanent tan from living so long in a hot country. She . . . well, she's suddenly acutely conscious of her prosthetic eye; she can see him looking at it, though he's trying not to.

'Not very pretty, is it?' she says defensively before she can stop herself.

'No – no, you just look different and I can't quite work out why . . .'

'I lost my eye,' Mel says. 'It's OK. I'm quite used to it now.'

'Shit! What happened?'

'Life,' Mel says. 'You're back in England, then?'

'Well . . . yes.' People are surging past them like a wave parting over a rock, treating them to dirty looks. 'We're in the way here.'

'Yes. Perhaps we could . . .' She can't believe it – she's on the point of suggesting they should go somewhere for a coffee. But Mark gets in first.

'We must catch up sometime.'

'Yes. I'm still with the bank. Same branch. You can always find me there.'

'Good plan. I'll do that.'

But she knows he won't. If he had the slightest intention of seeing her again he wouldn't let her go now without asking her for an address, a telephone number.

'Got to rush, Mel. Sorry.'

And he's gone, leaving her standing there on the steps, watching him disappear into the surging crowd. Someone collides with her, almost sends her flying, runs on down the steps without so much as a single word of apology. The person she in turn collides with glares at her and rolls his eyes. Mel grips the handrail tightly and goes down the steps. Her heart is pounding, beating out of her chest. She wants to cry.

Forget him. Forget him! But she knows she can't.

Think about your trip on the Lord Nelson. But that will be six days only out of the rest of her life. It isn't going to change a thing. When it's over she'll still be in love with Mark, and he'll still be avoiding her. Mel's excitement has drained away like the water from a bathtub when the plug is pulled out.

She draws a deep breath, desperately trying to regain the state of mind she'd managed before she'd bumped into him. It won't be easy, not now that he has become reality for a few snatched moments rather than just a sad sweet memory. But she'll do it. She has to. What other choice does she have?

THIRTY-ONE

EMMA

There are two things I have to do now I'm back in England, and I'm not looking forward to either of them. I'm going to have to go and see Maggie and have it out with her, and I'm going to have to tell Philip it's over between us. Maybe nothing is going to come out of my sudden and stupid infatuation with Mike – well, it certainly won't; how could it? – but one thing it's shown me very clearly is that I really cannot go on stringing Philip along. I now know I'm capable of feelings very different from the ones I have for him. I can no longer continue to struggle along out of habit and lassitude, settling for OK sex and the convenience of having a partner when I need one, and it's not fair on him either.

He's on the phone more or less as soon as I get home, asking how things went.

'Complicated,' I say. 'I've found out a lot of things I'd rather not have known. But I haven't found my mother, and I'm not likely to any time soon.'

'Ah.' A long pause. 'You want me to come over so you can talk about it?'

Talk, and no doubt end up in bed. That's what he means, and I certainly don't want that.

'Not tonight, Philip.'

'When then?'

'I'm not sure. I've got a hell of a lot of work to do for school.'
That's rubbish of course; it's the end of term and we're winding
down. The fact that I missed most of last week is neither here
nor there – all the hard work was done before then, around the
end of June. I'm just making excuses, putting off what has to be
said. But I can't face it just now. 'I'll be in touch, OK?'

The thing I can't put off is ringing Dad and Maggie.

Maggie answers, and immediately my blood is boiling.

'Maggie. You'll no doubt be pleased to hear that I didn't have
any luck finding Mum.'

'Oh Emma, I can tell how disappointed you are. But . . .'

'You can tell Dad she seems to have disappeared without trace.'

'I'll tell him. He's been wondering why you haven't been in
touch. Did you find out anything at all? Did she really go to
America?'

'You know damn well she did.' Maggie doesn't react, and I
wonder if Dad is within earshot.

'It's just what we were afraid of,' she says, cool as a cucumber.
'Look, dear, can't you come over so we can talk about this
properly?'

'I certainly want to talk about it to *you*, Maggie,' I say. 'Alone.
When Dad's not there. I think you know what I'm saying.'

'Would you like to speak to your dad?' she asks, still keeping
up that front of normality. I really don't know how she can do
it, but I suppose she's had plenty of practice. Much as I would
like to have it out with her now, the last thing I want is for Dad
to overhear the accusations I am dying to yell at her. This is not
the way for him to find out that Maggie has been deceiving him
all these years.

'Yes, I'd like to speak to Dad, please,' I say, controlling my anger.

There's a slight hiatus, then Dad is on the line.

'Emma?'

'Dad.' I'm cracking up a bit suddenly; it's just so good to hear
his voice, and I'm hating what I'm going to have to tell him. 'You'll
have guessed by now from what you've heard of the conversation

what I'm going to say, I expect. I'd have come over to tell you face to face, but I'm up to my eyes here getting ready for school tomorrow, and I thought you ought to know straight away.'

'That's all right, my love. I understand.'

'As long as you do.' I'm feeling guilty now because I could have driven down to Porthtowan – if I'd felt up to facing Maggie. 'Look, Dad, I'm really sorry, but I'm afraid what we thought is true. Mum didn't drown that day. She was helped by a man called Simon Beacham who used to have a sail repair business in Falmouth—'

'Simon Beacham?' Dad interrupts incredulously. 'She wouldn't have run off with him, surely? I can't believe that!'

'No, she didn't run off with him. He just helped her. Picked her up off her boat and took her to Ireland, where she got a flight to America. But there was a man involved, I'm afraid. An American by the name of Jeff Hewson. She met up with him again over there, and they . . .'

I hesitate. I can't bring myself to say that they were married. It seems a step too far. It's pretty irrelevant anyway, so there seems no purpose in telling Dad something that will hurt him even more than he's hurting already.

'. . . they were together for a couple of years,' I say a bit lamely.

'But they're not together now?'

'No. it's a bit of a long story.'

I relate events as Jeff told us – Harvard, 'the draft', as the Americans called it – how he'd left Fliss with his family when he went to Vietnam – how his helicopter had crashed and he'd been pronounced missing, presumed dead. And how, when he finally got home, Fliss had gone, and he'd never been able to trace her.

When I finish, Dad is silent for so long that I wonder if he's still on the line.

'Dad? Are you still there?'

There's a strange, muffled sound that sounds like 'yes' but could well also be a sob.

'Are you all right?' I ask anxiously.

'Yes. Yes!' He sounds impatient now, with himself, not me. Then he sighs deeply. 'Oh, poor Fliss.'

'You're thinking of her, Dad, after what she put you through?' He doesn't answer that.

'She didn't have much luck, did she? It doesn't sound as if anything worked out for her. In fact it sounds like a ruddy disaster.'

'Well, yes, it does really,' I concede.

'It's like the sort of thing that happened in the war,' Dad says. 'Girls got swept off their feet by GIs or American airmen, and when they got over there nothing was what they expected. My mother used to talk about a friend of hers who finished up in a trailer park in the middle of nowhere – no money, no proper home, and the guy a layabout or a no-hoper, maybe even a criminal . . .'

I can't believe he's waffling like this. His way of coping, perhaps.

'Well that didn't happen to Mum,' I say. 'Jeff Hewson seems a very nice man. He has a family shipbuilding business and at least two homes, one in New England and one in Florida. He's beyond rich. And I don't think there's any doubt but that he really loved Mum . . . still does, in my opinion. He spent a small fortune trying to find her.'

'So he says.'

'Actually I believe him. You would too, if you'd talked to him. I'll tell you what I think happened. She didn't get on with his family – or at least not with his stepmother – and there was probably a falling-out. When she thought Jeff was dead, Mum left. Maybe she'd already met somebody else. If they got married, her name would no longer be Hewson . . .' I catch my breath . . . *Careful!* But Dad doesn't seem to have picked up on it. 'America is a very big place,' I rush on. 'They could have gone anywhere from Mexico to the Canadian border or even beyond. But the thing is, Dad, if Jeff couldn't find her, we've got no chance. I'm sorry.'

'Just as long as she's all right,' Dad says. He's still thinking only of Fliss, and it breaks my heart.

'I'm sure she is,' I say, though I'm sure of no such thing.

'So there's nothing more we can do.'

'I don't think there is,' I say. 'And to be honest, I'm not sure we should try. Think of the implications if she's found alive somewhere. You'd have to repay the money the insurance company paid out on her life . . .'

'Oh, hang the money! I just want to know.'

'And you and Maggie – well, you wouldn't be legally married, would you?'

'Maggie and I have been together long enough not to let a scrap of paper, or lack of it, come between us.'

I can't help wondering what Maggie thinks of that, if she's listening. It seems to me that that scrap of paper, as he called it, means a great deal to Maggie. She deceived both Dad and me to ensure she got it.

'This reporter . . . this Mike Bond . . . he thinks he's reached the end of the road too, does he?'

'Pretty much. He's got a couple more angles to try, but he doesn't hold out much hope, and to be honest, neither do I.'

'But you're going to keep in touch?'

Sore point. The flight home was horribly uncomfortable, sitting next to one another in cramped airline seats, studiously taking turns with the shared armrest so as not to touch. And when we parted company we made no plans to meet again, or even to talk on the telephone.

'I'm sure he'll let us know if anything turns up, but I wouldn't hold your breath,' I say.

'Are you OK, Emma?' Dad asks suddenly.

'Me? Yes, fine. Disappointed, of course, but fine.'

'You're a good girl. Your mother would have been proud of you.'

My throat is aching. 'Night, Dad. Take care.'

'Night, my love.'

When he's gone, I put the phone down and imagine him doing the same. Maggie going to him, putting her arms round him, murmuring platitudes, comforting him, kissing him, going to bed with him.

And I feel sick. How can she live with herself? With this charade? How can she carry on as if nothing has happened? I'm so angry I want to hit her. But for Dad's sake I'll have to try to carry on as normal. I really don't know how the hell I'm going to manage it.

Soon after I put the phone down after speaking to Dad, it rings again. I pick it up, half expecting it to be either Maggie or Philip. It's neither.

'Emma! Hi! Sam here.'

Sam – Samantha Becker – one of the girls at the Jubilee Sailing Trust who run the office, sort out the bookings, organise crew. I don't actually know her – she's in Portsmouth, I'm in Cornwall, and I've never sailed with her – but we've spoken on the phone so often I feel as though I do.

'Sam Hi. How are you?'

'In a bit of a hole, actually. That's why I'm ringing you. We've been let down by one of our watch leaders for a sailing next Sunday. Not his fault. He was in a motorcycle accident this morning – came off his bike and broke his collarbone and his leg – and I've got to find somebody to replace him. I know it's short notice, but I don't suppose you'd be able to help me out here?'

'Oh Sam, I don't know . . .' I can do without this. 'When did you say?'

'Sunday. It's only a short voyage – six days, sailing out of Portsmouth. School breaks up this week, doesn't it?'

'Well, yes, but . . .'

'I'd be so grateful. I've already tried a couple of the others I normally call on if I'm stuck, but one's in Portugal and the other is having a hernia op. If you can't do it . . .'

'You'll just have to go yourself,' I say, teasing.

'Ha bloody ha! You think I'll let somebody who doesn't know what they're doing loose on my filing system? Oh please, Emma, help me out here!'

I chew my lip. The prospect is not unattractive. A total break with no time to worry about anything but licking my watch into

357

shape, teaching them the ropes, making sure they're where they should be to do what's required.

'OK,' I say.

'You'll do it?'

'That's what I said.'

'Yes!' Sam hisses triumphantly. 'I owe you one, Emma.'

'Forget it.'

I put the phone down and realise I'm actually glad Sam called. Six days at sea. No pressure to end things with Philip. No upsetting rows with Maggie. No tussling with myself as to whether I should pick up the phone and speak to Mike. It will be hard work – it always is – but just at the moment I think it is exactly what I need.

I can't escape quite that easily, of course. If I simply take off without telling anyone, they'll think I've done a disappearing trick like my mother.

I phone home and am really glad when it's Dad who answers – I couldn't face speaking to Maggie again tonight. When I tell him my plans, he seems pleased for me.

'You go, Emma, and enjoy yourself. It'll do you good.'

That leaves Philip. Predictably – and understandably, actually – his reaction is quite the opposite.

'But you've only just got home. And you said you were up to your eyes this week. How can you just go swanning off again?'

'They're really stuck. And actually it's just what I could do with.'

'If you're desperate for a holiday, I could take some time off . . . we could go somewhere nice.'

'Philip, you're not hearing me. They really need me to help out as watch leader.'

'And what if I really need you? That wouldn't count, I suppose.'

'It's not the same thing at all.'

'No, you're right, it's not. Sailing – well, that's one thing. Me – I'm quite another. I come pretty low down your list of priorities – bottom, probably, actually. And to be honest, I've pretty much had enough of it, Emma.'

I'm quite shocked – Philip is usually a bit of a doormat. He complains and he argues, but he takes it. Perhaps if he didn't, I'd feel differently.

'I'm sorry, Philip, but there's nothing I can do. I've agreed now.'

'Ring them back and tell them you've changed your mind. That I'd fixed a holiday for us that you didn't know about. Look, Emma, I'm quite serious about this. If you choose to go off sailing, then as far as I'm concerned, that's it. You needn't bother coming back. At least not to me.'

Now I really am shocked. This was what I wanted, wasn't it? I've even been worrying about how I'm going to tell him it's over, and now here he is saving me the trouble, and I don't much like it.

'Philip . . .' I protest.

He cuts in. 'No, really, Emma. I'm fed up with you using me. Because that's what you do.'

Can't argue with that.

'So, to be honest, I think we might as well call it a day. Phone me if you change your mind about next week. Otherwise – well, don't bother.'

And he hangs up.

I stare at the receiver and actually feel quite bereft. I hadn't realised until this moment just how much I liked the fact that he was always there, a lifebelt to cling to when things got rough. Or how horrid it would feel to be dumped unceremoniously.

Just how selfish can you be? You take after your mother there all right . . .

It's a sobering thought. I tell myself it's good that Philip got to be the one to end it – that will give him some satisfaction, at least. I tell myself he'll find somebody who'll treat him the way he deserves to be treated. And that perhaps I'll find someone to make me feel the way Mike made me feel. But somehow there's a hollow ring to all of it. I've absolutely had enough. Life sucks.

I go to pour myself a large drink, and I know that I'm going to be crying into it.

THIRTY-TWO

THE LINK

The *Lord Nelson* is every bit as impressive as she looks in the brochure photographs. So beautiful that she brings a lump to Mel's throat. Docked on the Portsmouth waterfront, she's attracting a lot of attention – people, some who have come especially to see her, and some who just happen to be in Portsmouth, are milling about on the harbourside, gazing in admiration and taking pictures, and the cafés and bars on the opposite side of the road are busy.

Anna has managed to find a space outside one of them, though she's not convinced she won't come back to find she's got a parking ticket, but that's a chance she's taking. She's not sure where the car park is in relation to the ship, and she doesn't want Mel to have to walk too far with her bags. Stupid, really – she's going to be tested physically to a far greater degree in the coming days, but even so . . . At the moment Anna feels responsible for her, and she doesn't want her to be tired before she even starts.

They cross the road and are absorbed into the busy hubbub on the quay. It's easy to pick out voyage crew – they're the ones laden down with baggage, and there are at least two wheelchairs being pushed by carers. There's quite a lot of toing and froing on the gangplank, and hugs and kisses as regulars meet up with old friends. Mel's not quite sure what she's supposed to do, but Anna points her in the direction of a grey-haired man in a *Lord Nelson* sweatshirt who's manning the barrier roping off the gangway. He tells her she can come on board and get signed in but then she can go ashore again if she likes, as nothing much will be happening for a couple of hours yet.

'Would you rather go on home?' Mel asks Anna.

'Absolutely not!' Anna says. 'I'm staying to see you off.'

'OK. I'll be back as soon as.'

A plump, motherly-looking woman who apparently is the purser and whose name tag says she is called Sharon asks Mel questions about her medical history and gives her a watch card, which will be her bible for the next few days, detailing where she should be at any given time of the day or night. It might as well be written in double Dutch for all Mel can understand it.

'There'll be a briefing at three. Everything will be explained then,' Sharon tells her breezily. She calls to a youngish chap in shorts and sailing boots who is passing. 'Hey, Barney, could you give Melanie a hand? Help her with her luggage and show her where her berth is?'

'Yep, sure.' He winks at Mel, takes her bag from her and strides off. She follows him down a flight of stairs, flanked by wheelchair ramps, through a spacious room crammed with tables and chairs that he tells her is the mess, along a passage and into a narrow cabin with three tiers of bunk beds on either side. Through a curtain is yet another, identical cabin.

'There you go, that one's yours.' He points to the endmost bottom bunk. 'And that's your locker. The head is there if you need it . . .' He indicates a door at the end of the cabin.

'Thanks,' Mel says. She doesn't need to ask him what the head is – from reading the literature she knows it's sailing speak for bathroom and loo. She knows too that the area she's in is called the fo'c'sle, but she's not about to show off by saying so.

'I'll leave you to it, then. Have you met your buddy yet?'

Her buddy was the person she was to be paired with, who was supposed to keep an eye on her because she was partially disabled.

'No, apparently she's not arrived yet.'

'Oh well, plenty of time yet,' he says cheerily.

Mel makes her way back on deck and heads for the gangway, ducking between myriad groups of sailors. Everyone seems to know everyone else, except for her. She feels a momentary panic, similar to the way she felt on her first day at secondary school, a new girl in a vast unfamiliar building surrounded by hundreds of unknown faces. How ridiculous is that?

Back on dry land, she and Anna cross the road to one of the pubs, where they order scampi and chips and bitter shandy. When it's time for Emma to return to the *Lord Nelson*, Anna is still insisting she's going to stay to see the ship set sail.

'I can have a wander round the marina while I'm waiting,' she says. 'I shall enjoy that. But first I'm going to move my car to a car park. I haven't seen a traffic warden yet, but that's not to say my luck is going to hold much longer.'

Everyone is gathered in the mess for the briefing. Mel finds a seat and squeezes in between a young woman of about her own age and an older man. The young woman appears to be the carer for a teenager in a wheelchair that is parked in the gangway beside her. His hands are clawed around the armrests, his legs, clad in denim jeans, dangle uselessly, but his face is bright with excitement.

'Is this the first time you've done this?' Mel asks the young woman.

'Oh no!' She laughs. 'This is my fourth voyage and Neil's second.' She leans towards the boy in the wheelchair. 'You love it, don't you, Neil?' He nods enthusiastically. 'And so do I! I work in a care home, and any chance I get to be the one to accompany one of our residents, I grab it. You haven't been before, I take it?'

'No. I don't really know what to expect.'

'You'll soon get the hang of it. I'm Brenda, by the way. Ah . . . here's the captain. We'll talk later.'

The briefing begins, although it is, Mel thinks, anything but brief. She's soon lost in a welter of information about the ship, the four watch groups, safety issues, daily timetables. It really is like that first day at school all over again, she thinks, thoroughly confused. The one thing she has grasped is that she is in aft starboard watch – whatever that is – and her first four-hour spell of duty will start at midnight.

The ship's permanent crew are all introduced – bosun, mates, engineer, Sharon the medical purser, even the ship's cook. Next up are the four watch leaders, and Mel sits up and takes notice. According to her bible, her watch leader is also her buddy, and her name is Emma Dunning. When the captain identifies her, she just smiles and raises a hand in acknowledgement, but Mel thinks she looks nice.

When the briefing is over, Emma comes across to her.

'Hi. Sorry I wasn't here to meet you when you arrived. And I'm afraid I'm going to have to dash off now – there's a watch leaders' briefing in five minutes. The first day is always very full-on. You've found your berth, have you?'

Mel nods. 'A man called Barney showed me where it was.'

'Ah, Barney. He's great. He's a fireman in everyday life. That's why they call him Barney. Trumpton, you know? Barney McGrew. Look, we'll catch up very soon. At the drill, if not before. You're in my watch, aren't you? Aft starboard – that's the back of the ship, right-hand side, in case you're wondering.' She glances at her watch anxiously. 'I really must get to that meeting. I'm already out of favour for being late arriving. Will you be OK?'

'Yes, fine,' Mel says.

'It's smoko now anyway – hot drinks and cake on deck, but known as smoko because it was when mariners were allowed a baccy break in the old days. That'll be a good chance for you to meet some of the others. I think you're very brave coming on your own, but you'll find everybody is really friendly. Now – must dash.'

And she's gone.

Watching her disappear up the companionway, Mel doesn't feel brave. She feels lost and very small. But she's here now. She's got to make the best of it. She puts her briefing notes in her bag, a smile on her face, and heads up on deck.

Emma wasn't exaggerating when she said the first day was pretty full-on. There's the emergency drill when everyone goes to their muster stations, and Mel meets the rest of her watch, which, she's pleased to discover, includes Brenda and her charge, Neil. Part of the drill involves manhandling the wheelchairs up the companionway from mess to deck, which Neil seems to thoroughly enjoy. There are six others in her group – 'There should be ten of us,' Emma explains, 'but this voyage isn't up to full strength, so you're all going to have to work that bit harder' – and they couldn't be more different. Besides Brenda and Neil, there's a young man who is totally blind, a married couple in their forties, and a much older man called Leslie, who seems to know exactly what he's doing. He takes Mel under his wing, helping her with her life jacket and the safety belt that must be worn at all times on deck in case of rough seas. There are also harnesses for those who want to climb the rigging. Tim, the blind boy, is at the front of the queue, bursting with enthusiasm, but Mel doesn't feel she's ready to attempt it yet.

'Try on a harness anyway,' Emma says. 'There'll be another opportunity later in the week. It's only these gung-ho types who want to get up there straight away.'

Mel takes a harness. She's not sure if she'll ever be able to get up the courage to actually do it, but she did tell the girls at work she would, and it's all part of the experience after all.

Preparations to set sail are being made now, and Mel is excited all over again to actually be part of them. She really doesn't know what she's doing, but not a lot of skill is called for at this stage – it's simply a matter of doing what she's told, and as the ropes slip through her gloved hands she feels quite the professional.

The Lord Nelson is slipping away from the dock now, a band of clear water opening up between hull and harbour wall. Amongst the watchers on the quayside Mel catches sight of Anna, smiling and waving. Mel waves back, and the excitement ratchets up a notch. Perhaps it's going to be all right after all!

A couple of days and she's really getting into the swing of things. She's learned the different types of square sails – the royal, the T'gallant, the topsail and the course – and that it takes the combined efforts of every available crew member to hoist and lower the royal. She's found out that 'happy hour' is an ironic misnomer – not cheap drinks, but hard, filthy work hosing the decks and washing the paintwork, polishing the brass and scrubbing the heads. She's become used to broken nights – her bunk is directly over the anchor, which clanks loudly and alarmingly, and even if she isn't the one being woken for a turn on watch, there are always others in her cabin who are. Someone creeps in, the thin beam of their torch cutting through the inky darkness; there are whispered words and then the rustling of clothing as someone dresses hastily. Sometimes there's the opening and closing of the door to the head, which is almost immediately behind her bunk.

The head itself is tiny, just a loo, a washbasin and a shower, which cascades everywhere – when Emma tried to use it she managed to soak her towel and clean underwear, and she hasn't tried again. There never seems to be a spare moment anyway. Just as you think you have a free half-hour, the tannoy calls 'all hands on deck'. But it doesn't really matter. Nobody seems too bothered about that sort of thing. It's freedom of a kind Mel has never experienced before, and certainly never thought she'd actually enjoy.

'I haven't changed my socks yet!' she says to Brenda as they sit side by side on deck, enjoying a few minutes' welcome break in the sun.

'Me neither.' Brenda stretches out her legs, looking at her feet critically. 'They'll stand up on their own soon.'

'And besides being smelly, I am going to get so fat!' Mel says. 'I never seem to stop eating! But the food is so good!'

It is. Breakfast, lunch and dinner – all huge meals – cake and biscuits at smoko.

'You won't get fat, trust me,' Brenda says. 'You're working it all off.'

Mel laughs. 'I certainly hope so!'

She's made a lot of friends by now and no longer feels an outsider. In particular she likes Brenda, Tim the blind boy, and helpful, ever-watchful Leslie. She has also developed a soft spot for Barney, the fireman.

She gets on well with Emma Dunning too, though she doesn't see a lot of her except when she's working as part of Emma's watch, and then they're too busy doing what has to be done to chat much.

'I hope I'm not neglecting you,' Emma said on the second day, 'but you seem to be managing well.'

'Yes, I'm fine,' Mel said. Although she's classified as disabled, she really doesn't need nannying; in fact she's actually quite often acted as buddy to Tim, steering him past obstacles – 'The blind leading the blind!' she joked.

The third day is a big one for Mel. She's woken just before 4 a.m. by a shadowy figure who looks like a cat burglar in her well-pulled-down woollen hat, dresses in as many layers of clothes as she can lay hands on, and goes on deck for her four-hour watch. A cup of scalding coffee in the upper mess doesn't do much to alleviate the bitter cold, but she's loving every moment – the companionship, the adventure, the feeling of achievement. She's allowed to take the helm just as dawn begins to break, then she's on lookout. They're approaching Jersey – the winds weren't favourable for Cherbourg as had been planned – and a sharp eye has to be kept out for lobster pots. Gradually the port of St Helier takes shape, and then it's busy, busy again, with barely time to snatch breakfast.

Whilst they're at anchor there is another chance for Mel to climb the rigging, and she's determined that this time she won't chicken out. Some of the voyage crew go ashore, but Mel stays aboard and goes to the foremast, taking her climbing harness with her. A wheelchair is being hoisted up the mainmast – it's Neil, squealing with delight. Mel, though, is shaking with nerves. In order to get on to the rigging, she has to climb on to the ship's rail and swing out over the sea. She doubts she'll even manage that.

'Of course you can do it,' Emma says, helping Mel to secure her climbing harness.

'A sixty-something grandma did it last week, no prob.' That's Barney, grinning encouragement. 'And if you freeze I'll come and get you – carry you down in a fireman's lift.' This is rather tempting, until he adds: 'I'll have to knock you out to do it, though.'

'That wouldn't be much fun,' Mel jokes. 'What's the point of being carried by a hunky fireman if I don't know anything about it?'

'Who's next?' calls Tom, the bosun.

'Me – but I don't think I can.'

'You'll have a line on. There's no way you can fall. And I'll be with you every step of the way.'

'OK, I'll try.' White now, shaking with sheer terror, Mel clambers up on to the rail and takes a first tentative step upward.

'I can't!'

'You can. Don't look down.'

But looking up is bad enough. The first platform seems miles away; the fighting deck – that's where Nelson was when he was shot at Trafalgar, someone has told her – is a tiny speck seemingly miles up into the fierce blue of the sky.

Slowly, slowly, still shaking so much she can scarcely grip the rigging, Mel inches upwards whilst Tom, climbing patiently beside her, keeps up a stream of encouragement. And then, unbelievably, she's reached the first platform. Except that she's afraid she'll never be able to climb off it again, and Barney really will have to come up and get her.

'That's far enough' she says weakly. 'I'm going down again now.'

Slowly, slowly back down until her feet encounter the ship's rail and she swings back on to the deck to congratulatory cheers.

'Told you you could do it!' says Barney.

Mel is laughing, almost hysterical with relief.

'Well done,' Emma says. 'Good girl! We're going ashore tonight for a celebratory meal.'

Good as the food on board is, freely as the drink flows in the bar, the thought of an evening out with her new-found friends is an inviting one.

'Count me in,' says Mel.

It's 1.30 a.m., and Mel is getting dressed ready for her anchor watch. Only two voyage crew need to be on duty, mainly to ensure that no drunken revellers decide to try and board the 'Nelly'. Leslie and Tim had taken the midnight-till-two shift; Emma has teamed Mel with her to cover the next two hours.

'It'll be pretty quiet, I should think,' she had said, but Mel doesn't mind that.

When they relieve Leslie and Tim, Mel boils the kettle in the galley and makes coffee, then carries the mugs up to the chart room, where Emma is filling in the log.

'OK?' asks Emma.

'Yep. Black, no sugar, right?'

'Right.' Emma takes her mug, sips it. 'I needed that! All the wine we had with dinner has given me a raging thirst.'

'Me too.'

'So – what do you think of it so far?' Emma asks.

'Great. I've really enjoyed it.'

'You've done well. Have you never sailed before?'

'No. I've always wanted to, though.'

They've not had the chance of a good chat without interruption before. Now there's just the two of them, sitting on the companionway that leads to the bridge and looking out at the lights of a mostly quiet St Helier. For the first time Emma can ask Mel how she came by her injuries, and Mel finds herself talking with unusual ease about what happened. Generally she's reticent, not wanting to admit to a bullying husband; tonight, here in the quiet darkness, all the horrible details pour out.

'That's just awful!' Emma says. 'Poor you!'

'Well, I've survived,' Mel says, grimly cheerful. 'But that's enough about me. It's your turn now. How come you know so much about sailing? Have you been doing it long?'

Emma stretches her legs and drains the last of her coffee though it has long since gone cold.

She likes Mel, and has the greatest admiration for her. What she's been through! And good for her that she's making the effort to start afresh. The harrowing story has made Emma feel vaguely ashamed of her preoccupation with her own problems.

'I've sailed all my life. It's in my blood. My father taught me to sail, my grandfather built a boat and sailed it to South America, then sold it and crewed home, and my mother . . . well, she was quite well known in her day for her exploits. Not that I ever knew her. She was lost in a sailing accident when I was two years old . . .' She breaks off, realising she's automatically repeating the same old lie.

'That's really sad,' Mel says. 'What happened?'

Emma hesitates. This might be a night for confidences, but she daren't risk telling Mel the truth about Fliss. If the story gets out it will be the talk of the ship, and, worse, the consequences for her father and Maggie will be ghastly. By way of diversion she pulls her wallet out of her jacket pocket. The old newspaper cutting with the photograph of Fliss and Jo Best on the *Pretty's Pickles* is folded inside. She gets it out, flattening out the creases and illuminating it with her torch.

'That's my mother.' She points to Fliss.

'She's very pretty. And you're so much like her.' Mel is studying the photograph, a little frown developing between her eyes. 'But that is really strange . . . Who's the other girl?'

'Mum's sailing partner.'

'Can I have a closer look?'

Puzzled, Emma passes the cutting and torch to Mel, who pores over it.

'This is uncanny. She looks exactly like my mother did when she was younger. But . . . oh, that's ridiculous. It can't be . . . She must have a doppelganger.'

'Jo Best.'

There's a moment's utter silence, then Mel's breath comes out in a little gasp. 'I don't believe this. I've never known my mother to go anywhere near a boat, but . . .' She looks up at Emma, her face the picture of bewilderment. 'It does look just like her, and . . .'

'What?'

'Her name is Anna Payne. But the Anna is short for Joanna. And her maiden name was Best.'

THIRTY-THREE

EMMA

This is absolutely beyond belief. But Mel seems in no doubt at all, and the name and the face both fit. We'd given up hope of finding Jo Best, but now it would appear I'm sitting here with her daughter! I've heard that fate works in strange ways, drawing loose ends together with a sort of electrical magnet; I've heard of the five degrees of separation – or is it six? – but this . . .

'It must be a coincidence, surely!' I say. 'Jo was like Fliss. Sailing was her whole life, and you say your mother has never been near a boat.'

'Not to my knowledge. But she was the one who suggested I came on this voyage, and she was really interested in the *Lord Nelson*. There was a kind of look on her face when she saw it. And she was walking round the marina for hours while she was waiting for us to sail . . .' Mel seems to want to believe it. 'I've always been drawn to the sea too,' she goes on. 'Well – I'm here, aren't I?'

'Jo Best would never have given up sailing,' I say with conviction. 'Believe me, I know. It's a drug.'

'Perhaps she didn't want to sail any more after your mother drowned.'

I chew on my lip. I feel bad about keeping the truth from her, but I'm still not sure that I should share it. After all, I don't actually know for sure that Mel is not mistaken, and even if she's not,

I need to think about this before saying anything. Besides which, it's beginning to get light. I check the time – damn, quarter to four already! We should be waking the next watch.

'Mel, there isn't time to talk any more now,' I say. I find the list of names and bunk numbers for the crew who are to take over from us. 'Can you do the honours? They won't be best pleased if we don't give them a shout pronto. I'll stay here and make up the log.'

'We will talk again, though?' Mel says, taking the paper from me.

'Definitely. But Mel – I'd be really grateful if you'd keep this to yourself. I don't want to be the talk of the ship. Now go! Scoot!'

She disappears into the darkness, which is now more thick grey than black, and I desperately try to get my head round what is required of me. Can't have a watch leader falling apart on the job. But, oh my lord, it's not going to be easy!

Finding a time when Mel and I can talk uninterrupted again isn't easy either. That's the trouble with being a watch leader, it's very full-on. Something or someone is always demanding your attention, and there are frequent briefings to attend. I find myself looking at her, though, as she hauls on a rope or struggles to hold course when she takes the helm, trying to picture in her the woman who was my mother's closest friend. And I know she's looking at me, too, through different eyes, and wondering, as I am.

Is it really possible? It still seems totally incredible. If Anna Payne really is Jo Best, why did she cut herself off from the sailing world? And why change her name? The Payne bit is understandable – presumably it's her married name. But why Anna, when she was always known as Jo? It's as if she didn't want to be found, and I don't understand why that should be. She wasn't involved in Mum's disappearance, if what Jeff Hewson told us is to be believed. She knew about it, yes, but she refused to help. It just doesn't make any sense.

I'm rather anxious, though, that Mel might be tempted to tell someone about this amazing coincidence. I really don't want the entire crew gossiping about it and asking awkward questions. A few of the older sailors know that Fliss was my mother, but it's never mentioned – it is more than thirty years since she disappeared, after all – and I don't suppose the younger ones have ever heard of her. But a story like this would spread like wildfire.

Mel seems quite a private person, though. I'm surprised she opened up to me about her disastrous marriage – I'm pretty sure it's not something she does often, but these lone night watches do invite confidences.

Today she's on messman duty – the only job on board I really hate. Laying up tables and serving the food from the dumbwaiter isn't so bad, but lugging buckets full of dirty plates and cutlery up the companionway to the upper mess isn't a lot of fun, and nor is washing it all up and putting it away. It's a long watch, too, twelve hours, and preparing vegetables is part of a messman's duties. That's what Mel's doing now, sitting on deck with a whole sack of unwashed spuds beside her.

'How are you doing?' I ask, sitting down beside her.

She wipes her nose with the back of her hand, leaving a streak of dirt on her face.

'Coping. This is a bit boring, though, isn't it? Roll on four o'clock!'

'Mel,' I say. 'What we were talking about the other night – are you absolutely sure? It doesn't seem possible.'

'I know. Could I look at the picture again?'

I check to make certain we're alone, take it out of my wallet and hand it to her. She examines it closely and nods.

'It is Mum, I'm certain of it. But why has she never said she used to sail? It's bizarre. But you can be sure I'll be asking her about it.'

This is my opportunity.

'When you have . . . if you're right and she was Fliss's friend . . . I'd really like to meet her,' I say.

'And I'm sure she'd like to meet you. Let me have me your contact details so I know where to find you.'

'I'll write them down for you,' I say. I'm not at all sure Jo will want to meet me. If she's never mentioned her past to her daughter, it seems to me she has something to hide, though what it can be I can't begin to imagine. But I can only hope.

Saturday, the last day, is upon us before I can turn around.

Last night, anchored off Dartmouth, we had an end-of-voyage party, and Mel and I managed another chat. While the punch was flowing freely on the bridge, we found a quiet corner and I told her everything. We'll be going our separate ways tomorrow, so there's no danger of it becoming a nine-day wonder on board, and I actually felt I wanted to tell her. Whether it was the effects of the punch or something else I really don't know, but I did it anyway. Then, as promised, we exchanged addresses and telephone numbers, and I made a photocopy of the newspaper cutting for Mel to keep. I really would like to keep in touch with her — whether or not Jo will actually know any more than I've already learned is somehow neither here nor there. She and Mel are a link to my mother, and I don't want to let it go.

We've docked in Plymouth now and the voyage crew are leaving in dribs and drabs, wheelchairs being pushed down the gangway, groups of friends and relatives waiting on the quayside.

Mel comes to find me to say goodbye, and we hug, not just because we might share a connection, but because it's the done thing. I'm still busy on deck, tidying ropes, stowing gear, but I go to the rail to watch her leave, laden down with her suitcase and tote bag. A tall woman, grey-haired, in tailored jeans and a loose sweater, is walking towards her. They hug; she takes Mel's tote bag. It has to be her mother, who she said was coming to meet her. At this distance it's impossible to see her face clearly, and in any case it's more than thirty years since that photograph of Fliss and Jo together was taken. But certainly the build looks right. And as she gazes longingly towards the *Lord Nelson* for a moment before turning away, a feeling in my gut tells me Mel was right.

My pulse quickens. I have the strangest feeling that for the first time since I was two years old I've been looking at Jo Best. And also that perhaps, at last, I am going to find out what became of my mother.

THIRTY-FOUR

JO

So. The past has caught up with me at last. By the weirdest of coincidences. Little did I think when I encouraged Mel to take the voyage on the *Lord Nelson* that Emma Dunning would be her watch leader and buddy. Or that Emma would show Mel a photograph of Fliss and me together and Mel would recognise me. It must have been a hell of a shock for her. I've kept well away from the sailing world for the best part of thirty years, cut all ties. Mel didn't have the first idea of the life I once led, the person I used to be.

That in itself wouldn't have been enough, though, to bring me to the point of deciding it's time I told the truth. I might well have decided to let sleeping dogs lie, as I have done all these years. In the beginning there were plenty of times when I thought I should come clean about what happened, and my part in it. In the long hours of the night I'd lie awake trying to work out how to go about it, searching for the right words to begin. If only I could find the courage to do that, the rest would come pouring out easily enough. But my resolve always disappeared with the new day. What good would the truth be to anyone? What purpose would it serve? Almost certainly it would destroy Maggie and Martin's marriage. And what about Mel? What would happen to her? It didn't bear thinking about. And so I said nothing, and as the years went by my secret was compounded.

Only two people knew the truth: Yves, the man I was living

with at the time it all happened, and Goff, to whom I was married for fifteen happy years. I told Yves because I had to, and it was the end of us. And I told Goff because in the end I couldn't bear not to and I knew that however shocked he might be – and believe me, he was shocked! – he would let me make the decision as to whether I should tell anyone else. It wasn't a happy time – for a while I thought I was going to lose him as I had lost Yves, but he was stronger than that. We, as a couple, were stronger than that.

As the years went by, I pushed the events of 1962 further and further to the back of my mind until it came to feel like no more than a bad dream. Something that never really happened at all.

Now, that's all changed. Mel has met Emma and between them they've discovered that I was once Jo Best. More. Emma knows that Fliss didn't drown off Falmouth and Martin knows too. And Emma has been desperately seeking her mother.

That really is the clinching factor. I know all about how it feels to be torn apart wondering what has happened to a loved one. In my case it's the baby I had adopted at birth – he's forty-three years old now, but to me he's still a warm, sweet-smelling little body wrapped in a blue blanket. I'd give the world just to see him again, know the man he's grown into, what he's done with his life, whether he's happy. When the law was changed so that adopted children had the right to apply for their original birth certificate, I hoped against hope that he might try to find me. I even wrote to the adoption agency, enclosing a letter to be given to him if he should go to them for information, with details of my whereabouts. But sadly I have never heard from him, and there's nothing I can do to find him – the law doesn't work that way, not yet anyway. So I can well identify with the way Emma feels.

I know the time has come for me to come clean about what happened. And the strange thing is, though I'm dreading it, it is, at the same time, rather a relief. The secret I've kept all these years has been a burden, weighing on my heart and my conscience, surfacing unexpectedly to throw a shadow over what should have been some of the happiest moments of my life.

There's someone else who should be put in the picture too. It came as one hell of a shock to me to learn that Jeff is alive and well. He, of all people, should know the truth.

The scales have tipped; keeping silent is no longer an option. Tomorrow I'll talk to Mel and tell her everything – she came back here with me today and is going to stay the night. Then I'll tell Emma too. But tonight, while London is sleeping under the glowing orange sky that is never completely dark, I'm sitting on the window seat in my bedroom with a cup of tea and a glass of whisky. In the calm before the storm, I'm remembering. Fliss's madcap decision to fake her own death. How she asked me to help her and I refused – something I still regret, because if I'd agreed, things might have turned out very differently. How Fliss went ahead anyway, went to Florida, met up with Jeff. And how things went so terribly wrong – Maggie refusing to let Emma go, Jeff being called up for military service and then being presumed dead in a helicopter crash in Vietnam. I know all this because Fliss and I kept in touch by letter. And I know what happened afterwards because she told me.

All of this leading up to the final act of this tragedy of Greek proportions.

In the very beginning, when Fliss told me what she was planning, I warned her against it and told her it would all end in tears. When she went ahead anyway, I hoped against hope that I was wrong and she'd find happiness. But it wasn't to be.

I'll never forget that late-night transatlantic phone call when she told me of her plight and begged me to help her. Now, in the quiet of the night, I can still hear her voice, shaking with desperation. It's what she told me then, and, even more importantly, what happened later, when I went over to America to be with her, that I have to tell Mel and Emma.

It won't be easy.

But the time for deception is over.

Part Six
1961

THIRTY-FIVE

Fliss was in the darkest of places, and had been ever since the colonel had delivered the terrible news that Jeff was missing, presumed dead, in Vietnam. To begin with she tried to cling to the hope that he might have survived – it was possible, the colonel had said, that the pilot had managed to put down somewhere, but he had added that the helicopter had been over dense jungle when contact was lost, an area that was controlled by the Vietcong, and stressed that she and Jeff's family should prepare themselves for the worst. In those first early days she felt as if she was living a nightmare, a roller-coaster of manic optimism and a despair so deep she felt she was drowning in it. But as time passed with no news it was the despair that enveloped her most often.

And there was no one she could share it with.

Jefferson was, she knew, utterly devastated. She could see it in the droop of his shoulders, the amount of bourbon he was consuming, and the way he seemed to have aged overnight. But Jefferson had never had a great deal to say to her, and now he said nothing at all. He seemed to have shut himself away in a world of his own. As for Marcia, she was cold and contemptuous of Fliss's distress.

'Pull yourself together, for goodness' sake!' she snapped at Fliss when she found her weeping. And: 'If you carry on like this you'll make yourself ill.'

That much was certainly true. Fliss did indeed feel ill, a general malaise that sometimes made her feel very sick. There was a discomfort too in the very deepest part of her, an ache that would not go away. Being in a constant state of anxiety was the cause, she supposed – she wasn't sleeping properly, and she couldn't eat; the very sight of food brought on nausea.

It was only when she actually vomited one morning that she realised her symptoms had a more tangible cause than grief. This had happened to her before, when she'd been expecting Emma. Fliss tried to remember exactly when she'd had her last period – with Jeff missing, it had been the furthest thing from her mind. Now she realised she hadn't had one since he left. That wasn't much more than a month ago, and it was possible that being so stressed could be playing havoc with her monthly cycle. But she didn't think it was just that. Her symptoms were too similar to the ones she'd had before.

Fliss was almost certain she was pregnant.

On the other side of the Atlantic, Simon Beacham was feeling very fed up with life. It wasn't, truth be told, an entirely new experience for him. Beneath the jaunty facade he adopted when he was in the presence of others, envy, resentment and discontent lurked dangerously close to the surface.

Simon was uncomfortably aware that he wasn't liked by his peers – how could he miss the way they excluded him, turning away when he approached, more or less ignoring anything he said, never inviting him to join in whatever they were planning? And the harder he tried to ingratiate himself, it seemed, the more they closed ranks. The only times they were even halfway civil to him were when they wanted a sail repair job on the cheap. In the past he'd fallen into the trap of thinking that if he obliged them they'd be grateful and more accepting of him, but he'd learned the hard way that it didn't work like that. Once they had what they wanted they were soon back to their old ways, shutting him out and, he thought, laughing at him behind his back.

Only one person had made any effort to be nice to him – Felicity Penrose – and that had gone a long way towards making up for the way the others treated him. Fliss was the brightest star in the firmament, beautiful, popular, a brilliant sailor – famous almost! When she smiled at him the hurtful indifference of the others seemed not to matter; when she drew him into a conversation he puffed up with self-importance. If Fliss liked him, the rest of them could go hang. Quite simply, he worshipped her.

More than once he'd tried to capitalise on the attention she paid him, but nothing had ever come of it. She always let him down gently, though. He took heart from that, running over and over both the excuses she had made and the ones he invented himself to explain why she had rejected him, and though the spark of hope that one day she might throw him more than a crumb might sometimes flicker and dim, it was never quite extinguished.

Even when she married Martin Dunning he'd refused to give up entirely. She'd had no choice, he told himself. She'd never have done it if she hadn't had to. It rankled that she'd allowed Martin to make her pregnant in the first place when she'd never let Simon so much as kiss her, but he could imagine Martin forcing himself on her. He was a big bloke; Fliss wouldn't stand a chance against him. Simon's initial disappointment and disgust quickly changed to a feeling of protectiveness. In his mind she was his Fliss; he still adored her.

When she began coming to Falmouth again he was pleased and excited. For a while just seeing her was enough, and he chose to ignore the fact that she seemed very friendly with the Yank. He was jealous, of course, but he didn't see Jeff as a real threat. Jeff was a womaniser who'd chatted up half the girls in Falmouth, and probably slept with them too. If Fliss was friendly with him it was probably his boat that was the attraction. Simon remembered how she'd remarked on it that first day she'd seen it, the same day she'd brought her spinnaker to him for repair. He burned with resentment – if he had a boat like that, he'd be able to take her out on it as Jeff did. But he didn't, and he had to console himself that it wouldn't be long before Jeff moved on. Chaps like him never stuck around for long.

And of course he hadn't. He'd gone off first on a refitting job in Hayling Island, and then to sail the Atlantic, and Simon had been working on ideas for trying to worm his way into Fliss's favour when, out of the blue, she'd come to him to ask for his help in escaping her loveless marriage.

It was more than he could ever have hoped for in his wildest dreams. She wasn't happy with Martin. She wanted to escape. And he was the one she'd confided in! He had a nasty suspicion that maybe she was going to chase the Yank across the Atlantic, but he couldn't see that working out. She'd promised to keep in touch; said he was the only one she could trust. If he did this, and if things didn't work out as she planned, he would be the one she would turn to. 'I'd be grateful to you for ever and ever . . . I can't promise anything until I'm free. But when I am . . .' Her words were burned into his memory.

Simon waited with growing impatience to hear from her, just a brief message to let him know where she was, how she was. When it didn't come, he started making some enquiries of his own, asking anyone and everyone what they knew about Jeff Hewson, and what he found out disturbed him. Far from being the penniless sailor he'd pretended to be, Jeff came from a wealthy and influential family. So if she was with him, as Simon was becoming increasingly convinced, she wouldn't be struggling at all – she'd be living in the lap of luxury. His disappointment was festering now, turning to bitterness and resentment. She'd used him. Fliss, his adored Fliss, was no better than all the others.

Just to rub salt in the wound, Martin Dunning seemed to be doing very well – the garage was thriving, and Simon guessed it was as a result of the injection of cash he'd received from the insurance company. Everybody seemed to be profiting from the risk he'd taken in helping Fliss – everyone but him.

It was this realisation that gave him the idea. Blackmail. He didn't call it that, of course; he preferred to think of it as payment for his services and his silence. Martin Dunning could well afford it. Trouble was, he didn't fancy approaching Martin. Maggie would be a far easier option. She was living with Martin now – someone else who'd benefited from Fliss's disappearance. He'd start with her. If he asked for only small amounts at a time, she could surely find a way of paying him, and it would provide a modest but regular income. The idea of such easy money excited him, as did the feeling of power. It didn't make up for knowing that Fliss had used him, but it certainly went some way.

One Saturday morning when he was fairly sure Martin would be at the garage, he paid a visit to Porthtowan.

Maggie was in the garden, hanging out washing, while Emma propelled herself up and down the path on a toy car. Simon's heart was in his mouth as he pushed open the gate and approached her, but he still managed a smile of greeting.

'Morning, Maggie.'

She whirled round, a shirt of Martin's dangling from her hands.

'Simon! What on earth are you doing here?'

'Come to see you. I think it's time we had little talk.'

Maggie had begun to tremble the moment she turned and saw Simon standing there grinning at her, that horrible, smug grin that had always made her skin crawl.

Simon was the one person who could blast Fliss's deception to smithereens, the one person – apart from her and, she rather thought, Jo – who knew for certain that Fliss was not dead. Because as Fliss had explained in one of her letters, Simon was the one who had helped her. Maggie had never been able to understand why Fliss had gone to him for assistance, or why she'd trusted him, but then Fliss had always had the capacity to believe what she wanted to believe, close her eyes to what she didn't want to see. Ever since Fliss had told her how she'd stage-managed her 'death', Maggie had been afraid of what Simon might do or

385

say when he realised she'd taken advantage of his infatuation for her. When the gilt came off the gingerbread of feeling important and special because he knew something no one else did. Until now her fears had not been justified. Now, as he grinned at her conspiratorially, her heart came into her mouth with a sickening thud and she had the most terrible feeling that chickens were about to come home to roost.

'What do you want?' she asked sharply.

'Oh, don't be like that, Maggie. It's in both our interests that we remain friends. I just wanted to talk to you about Fliss.'

The lump in her throat jolted again.

'What about Fliss?'

There was no point trying to pretend she didn't know the truth. She'd bumped into Simon in Truro not so long after she'd first heard from Fliss, and, flustered by his innuendo and snide questioning, had let the cat out of the bag. Since then he'd phoned a few times, asking for any news she might have, and she'd done her best to satisfy him with half-truths. But worried as she had been as to what might happen if he became dissatisfied and disillusioned, at least it had concentrated her mind and given her the chance to mull things over and gather some ammunition, which she'd hoped she wouldn't have to use.

'There's nothing I can tell you,' she said now, and her aggressive tone didn't betray the turmoil inside. 'And I'd really rather you didn't come here unannounced.'

Simon was not to be put off so easily.

'She's still with Hank the Yank?'

'As far as I know. Now, will you please go?'

He made no move.

'We still haven't talked properly. The thing is, Maggie, I'm a tad financially embarrassed at the moment. Now you and I both know a way I could make enough to put me right – I'm pretty sure there are newspapers that would pay me handsomely for the story I could tell them. But I didn't think you'd want that to happen. If you were to see me right, I'd have no need to look for a buyer for my story.'

It was no more or less than she'd expected – sooner or later. She'd known he wasn't to be trusted, and she had been right. But at least she was ready for him. She tossed the shirt she was holding back into the laundry basket.

'Are you trying to blackmail me, Simon? Because if you are, I'm afraid it's not going to work.'

He held her gaze. 'So I'm going to have to take my story to the papers, am I?'

She snorted. 'If you dare! Let me remind you, Simon, you are hardly the innocent in all this. You're the one who spirited Fliss to Ireland. You were complicit in a fraud that could never have happened but for you. Do you really think you'd escape criminal charges?'

Simon was looking less confident suddenly.

'I think you'll find you wouldn't,' Maggie went on. 'You'd be looking at a lengthy prison sentence, I'd say, for aiding and abetting fraud.'

That set him back on his heels, just as she'd known it would.

'And if you manage to wriggle out of that, I can assure you I'll make certain the Inland Revenue catch up with you. You've been cheating them for years. Then there's the benefits you've been falsely claiming.' All this was a stab in the dark; she had no shred of proof that he was a tax and benefits cheat, but the look on his face told her she wasn't far from the truth.

'You forget I work for a firm of accountants,' she added for good measure. 'I know about these things. No, I wouldn't go to the papers if I were you, Simon.'

'You wouldn't dare say anything!' He was still trying to bluster.

'Try me,' Maggie said grimly, thrusting the pegs she was still holding into the pocket of her apron. 'I'll tell you what I will do, though. I'll give you enough for you to make a fresh start somewhere as far from here as you can go. I don't want to see you or hear from you ever again. If I do, I will tell the Inland Revenue and the benefits people what I know. Wait here.'

She started towards the back door. He made to follow and she wheeled round.

'Wait here, I said. I don't want you in my house.'

Emma had scooted up the path on her ride-on car; she was looking at them curiously.

'Inside, Emma, there's a good girl,' Maggie said, unwilling to leave her outside with Simon. 'You haven't played with that new bubble tub we bought this morning yet, have you? Come on, I'll open it for you.'

She found it, still in her basket, unscrewed the lid and gave it to Emma.

'Here you are. See how many bubbles you can blow while I'm upstairs.'

In the spare room she reached up to the top shelf of the built-in wardrobe and took down an old handbag. Inside was a wad of notes – money she'd been saving to buy Martin a new cine camera for his birthday; his old one was too heavy and out of date, he had said. Giving it to Simon stuck in her craw, but the important thing was getting rid of him, and she couldn't risk him turning up here again demanding money when, perhaps, Martin might be at home. She replaced the bag on the wardrobe shelf, ran back downstairs and out into the garden.

Simon was pacing and glowering.

'Here you are.' She thrust the money at him. 'But that's it. If I ever see you again . . .'

He was counting the money, still not ready to give up.

'How far is this likely to take me?'

'It's all you're getting.'

Emma had appeared in the doorway, bubble wand in one hand, dangerously tilting pot in the other. There was a large wet patch on the bib of her dress.

'Auntie Maggie – I spilled it. It's all gone!' Her lip was quivering.

'Just wait, Emma . . .' Maggie turned back to Simon. 'Get out of here before I change my mind and make a few phone calls right this minute.'

She went back into the house, taking Emma with her, and slammed the door. She was shaking all over, but she crouched down to Emma, struggling not to let it show.

'Let's get you out of that wet dress, my love.'

'Who was that man?' Emma asked.

'No one. No one at all.' She took the half-empty bubble tub and wand from her. 'Hands up, hands up, the robber cried . . .'

The irony of it struck her suddenly. She was always quoting that silly verse when she wanted to undress Emma, but it had never seemed more apt. For once she was quite unable to finish it.

On the other side of the closed door Simon Beacham stood for a moment, glowering. How dare Maggie treat him like this after what he'd done for Fliss? But he wasn't finished yet. Maybe Maggie wouldn't play ball – she was a hard nut – but he was fairly sure Fliss would. Always a softer touch than her sister, as an illegal immigrant in the States she was the one with the most to lose. Plus she was still with Hank the Yank, whose family were rolling in money.

Simon's scowl faded as he looked down at the wad of notes, which he thought should be enough to take him to America. He'd approached Maggie first because it had been the easy option, but the one that really appealed to him was finding Fliss. Who knew – if things weren't working out for her, perhaps he was still in with a chance. And if not . . .

His lip curled. If not, Hank the Yank was the golden goose who could provide him with a life of luxury, unless he was prepared to run the risk of his precious Fliss being exposed and deported.

He stuffed the wad of notes into the top pocket of his shirt and walked towards the road, where his old rattletrap of a car was parked.

Those snooty Penrose girls might think they'd got the better of him, but they were in for a shock.

Fliss really did not want to tell Jefferson or Marcia about her pregnancy. Perhaps it was because she wanted Jeff to be the first to know – anything else seemed wrong somehow, an admission that he never would. Perhaps it was because she didn't want them organising her life as she felt certain they would once they knew. Whichever, she shrank inside at the very thought of sharing her secret. But for how long could she hide it? Probably not as long as she had with Emma – she understood that a second baby showed more quickly. And they would have to know sooner or later. She was going to have to stay at Parklands for the time being; she had nowhere else to go, and besides, she needed to be here in case there was any news of Jeff. But as the weeks passed with no word, she felt herself sinking into the familiar abyss.

Desperately, Fliss fought it. Somehow she must remain strong. She was carrying Jeff's baby. It was the one good thing she could cling to.

Marcia might be a self-obsessed harridan, but she was not blind or stupid.

'Is there something you'd like to share with us?' she asked archly one day when she and Fliss were alone.

'What do you mean?' Fliss asked, though in truth she already knew. Her waistline was spreading and her breasts were swollen – wand-thin and fashion-conscious Marcia could hardly have failed to notice.

Marcia smiled slightly, as if humouring a rather dense child.

'You're pregnant, aren't you? There's no point denying it – it's perfectly obvious. Have you consulted a doctor?' Fliss shook her head. 'I thought not. Well, that will have to be remedied. I know an excellent obstetrician. You've left it a little late, but I'm sure he will agree that a termination would be by far the best option under the circumstances.'

Fliss stared at her, shocked, and Marcia raised a plucked and pencilled eyebrow.

'You're not considering having this child, surely? Your husband is dead.'

'We don't know that!' Fliss retorted.

Marcia patted her hair into place.

'I'm afraid it is time to face facts. Bob – Colonel Davidson – has told Jefferson there is absolutely no hope that Jeff could have survived,' she said flatly.

Fliss gasped, horrified, though it was exactly what she had begun to realise must be the truth. But to have her deepest fears confirmed was to make them real

'Colonel Davidson said that?' she whispered, her lip trembling.

'I'm afraid so. We've kept it from you so as not to upset you any more than you already are. But I think the time has come for absolute honesty. Jeff is not coming back. I know that and so do you. So let's be sensible here. You can't possibly bring up a child alone in a strange country. And Jefferson and I certainly couldn't entertain having a mewling infant here at Parklands. Really, a termination is your only option.'

Fliss could scarcely believe what she was hearing. She'd always known Marcia was an absolute bitch, but this . . .

'How dare you!' she exploded. 'How dare you suggest that I abort my baby! I know you don't like me, and you don't want me here, and I might as well tell you that the feeling is mutual. But I am absolutely not going to pay a visit to your tame obstetrician. I would never get rid of Jeff's baby – never – and I can't believe it's what Jefferson would want either. It's his grandchild, remember.'

Marcia shrugged carelessly.

'Take a sensible decision and there is absolutely no need for Jefferson to know anything about it.'

'Oh, he'll know about it all right!' Fliss flared. 'If you think you can bully me into playing your game, you're very much mistaken.'

For a moment Marcia stared at Fliss with undisguised hatred.

'You,' she said coldly, 'are a foolish and very selfish woman.'

'Maybe,' Fliss shot back, 'but don't you think that is very much a case of the pot calling the kettle black?'

When Jefferson returned home from the shipyard that evening, Marcia made certain that it was she, not Fliss, who broke the news. But Jefferson's reaction was exactly as Fliss had predicted.

'You'll stay here with us, of course,' he said. 'I've lost my son, but at least I'll have his child.'

In the background Marcia glowered helplessly.

She was beaten and she knew it.

But Fliss knew she had made a very dangerous enemy.

THIRTY-SIX

Simon Beacham pulled his hire car in to the side of the road outside the gated entrance to Parklands and pursed his lips in a silent whistle. He'd been told that the Hewsons were wealthy and influential, but this was something else. He should have guessed, of course, when he'd had no difficulty in locating them. Hewson Enterprises was well known in America as a huge shipbuilding concern, but even so, this was beyond anything he had envisaged, and it threw a spanner in his plans. There was no way he could simply walk up to the front door and confront Fliss. What was more, it dashed his hopes of getting together with her again. When he'd asked around in Eastville – where he'd booked himself into a motel – and learned that Jeff was missing, presumed dead, he'd been elated. Surely, alone in a strange country, she'd be only too pleased to see a familiar face. Now, he doubted it. He couldn't imagine her giving up the life of luxury she'd apparently landed up in to take off with a nobody like him.

But did he really want her, after the way she'd used him and let him down? Though she still fascinated and excited him, he also burned with anger and resentment, the adoration he'd once felt for her soured so that it curdled in his stomach. Better to play the cards he held and set himself up for a new life in a new country – America, the land of the free and the home of the brave. And the unbelievable wealth of the Hewsons promised rich pickings indeed. A family like this would almost certainly want to avoid any hint of scandal, and they could well afford to pay for his silence.

For a long while Simon sat in his car watching the gates and hoping Fliss might emerge. If she did, he'd follow her and wait for a chance to approach her, he decided. But the only traffic in and out of the gates was a Chevrolet driven by a glamorous woman with a headscarf tied over her head Jackie Kennedy style, and an assortment of delivery vans. It gave him plenty of time to think, though, and decide on an alternative plan.

Soon after five in the afternoon a black Cadillac driven by a silver-haired man swept up to the gates – Jefferson Hewson II, he presumed. Simon decided it was pointless to wait any longer. Besides, he was warming to his latest idea, which he thought might well be preferable to confronting Fliss. It was, after all, Hewson senior who would be providing him with his pay-off – why not go straight to the horse's mouth?

Simon drove back into town, where he stopped off at a stationery store and bought writing paper and envelopes. In one of the restaurants, he treated himself to a T-bone steak with fries and all the trimmings, and a slice of apple pie with ice cream, followed by a liqueur coffee – he'd be able to afford to eat like this every day soon, he reasoned. Then he went back to his hotel.

Fortified by a miniature of whisky from the small fridge in his room, he sat down at the little writing desk, only to realise he didn't have the paper and envelopes he'd bought. He'd put them down beside him on the banquette in the restaurant and must have forgotten to pick them up. Well, no matter, there was a stack of headed notepaper on the desk ready for the use of guests, and he couldn't see that it mattered that the Hewsons would know where he was staying. He'd have to give them contact details sooner or later if he was to collect what was due to him.

Simon uncapped his fountain pen and began to write the letter that he was sure was going to transform his life.

The day's mail was waiting for Jefferson when he returned from the shipyard, stacked in a neat pile on the hall table. He took it into the drawing room, as he invariably did, to enjoy a pre-dinner drink whilst opening it. The handwritten envelope was on the top – a begging letter requesting a donation to some charity or other, he supposed. He poured his drink, took a seat in his usual chair, and opened it.

At first he assumed the contents were some kind of hoax, but as he reread the letter he realised that too much of it fitted with the pertinent facts of Fliss's arrival in their lives to have been written by someone unfamiliar with the details.

'Holy fucking shit!' he said.

Marcia, who was leafing through the latest edition of *Vogue*, looked up, startled. Jefferson rarely, if ever, swore. His father, Jefferson I, had been known for his ripe choice of epithets, particularly when he was dealing with some crisis at the shipyard, but her husband was far more restrained. Marcia didn't think she'd ever heard him use such language in all the time she'd known him.

'Jefferson? What on earth is the matter?' she asked.

'If this is some arsehole's idea of a joke . . .' He crossed to the drinks table, refilled his glass, and drank the bourbon straight down. Then he picked up the letter and read it again, shaking his head and uttering more swear words as he did so.

Marcia closed her *Vogue* and got up.

'Really, darling! Must you use such disgusting language? Frankly, I'm shocked and I don't think I want to stay here and listen to it.'

She moved towards the door, but Jefferson held out the letter, waving it under her nose.

'Have a look at this, *then* you can tell me you're shocked.'

Much as she wanted to show her displeasure by ignoring him,

curiosity got the better of Marcia. She took the letter, and as she read it her scarlet-painted mouth fell open.

'But this is . . . this is unbelievable . . . Can there possibly be any truth in it? Oh surely not . . .'

Jefferson's face was like thunder.

'I've no idea, Marcia. We shall just have to ask her, won't we?'

'It's terrible! Terrible! Oh, I've never liked her. Never trusted her. I've always thought she was a gold-digger. But this . . .'

'Where is she?' Jefferson demanded.

'In her room, I suppose. Moping as usual.' It wasn't only shock at the contents of the letter that Marcia was feeling now. An edge of something like sly triumph was beginning to creep in. 'Shall I have Forrester call her?'

Jefferson thumped the drinks table with his fist so hard that the glasses and decanter shook.

'Yes, dammit! Get her down here now. And let's see what she has to say for herself.'

The words on the page were blurring before Fliss's eyes, dancing a macabre jig, fading and taking shape again, and the room was going away from her. She grasped the back of one of the solid leather armchairs, afraid she was going to faint, and the letter fluttered to the floor. Jefferson retrieved it, waving it at her furiously.

'Well? Is any of this true?'

For a moment Fliss stared at him, speechless with horror. Then she buried her face in her hands, gasping.

'I think we can take it the answer is yes,' Marcia said unpleasantly.

'Oh, please . . .' It was a small, heartbroken sob.

'So it is true!' Jefferson thundered. 'You faked your own death, followed my son to America and married him? You've got a husband and a child back home in England? Jesus H Christ!'

'Jefferson!' Even in this moment of high drama, Marcia couldn't bring herself to let his blasphemy pass.

'But why the hell would you do such a thing?' Jefferson's fury was giving way to total incomprehension.

'For Jeff,' Fliss whispered. The tears were beginning to ache in her throat; she could hardly breathe for them. 'I did it for Jeff.'

'Don't dare to try to put the blame for this on my son!' Jefferson warned, outraged.

'I'm not! It wasn't his idea . . . he didn't even know . . .'

'You tricked him!' Marcia accused. 'You knew a good thing when you saw it and you tricked him into marrying you! Why, you little tramp!'

'I didn't trick him . . .'

'You expect us to believe that?' Marcia was thoroughly enjoying the moral high ground here. 'Jeff was a good man. An honourable man. He would never—'

'Oh, I don't care what you believe!' Fliss was sobbing now. 'What does it matter now? What does any of it matter?'

'It matters a great deal,' Marcia snapped. 'How dare you lie and deceive and take advantage of our kindness to you?'

You've never been kind to me, Fliss wanted to say. *You've been an absolute bitch.* But she was crying too hard.

'I'm sorry. I'm so sorry . . .' was all she could manage.

'I should hope you are! What on earth can you have been thinking of?' Marcia turned to Jefferson. 'This is appalling, Jefferson. What are we going to *do*?'

Jefferson paced the room, then wheeled round, waving the letter in Fliss's direction.

'How many people besides this criminal know the truth?'

Fliss gulped, wiping the tears from her cheeks with her fingers.

'Just my sister, Maggie. She wouldn't say anything – ever!' The very thought of Maggie was enough to start the tears flowing again. Never before had Fliss felt quite so alone as she did at that moment; never had she needed someone in her corner so much. She pressed her hands to her mouth as the full horror of what had happened washed over her in waves. 'You want me to go?' she whispered.

Jefferson shook his head, but his face was hard, the face of a seasoned businessman planning his next move.

'For the moment I think it's best you stay here. This problem has to be contained, and the less in evidence you are, the better. As for this . . .' he crumpled Simon's letter into a ball within his fist, 'you will leave me to deal with it.'

'You're going to give him what he's asking for?' Fliss asked, surprised.

Jefferson snorted. 'Hardly! I don't take kindly to being blackmailed.'

'Then what . . .?'

'I really don't think I care to discuss it with you. But rest assured your friend will wish he'd never had the temerity to threaten me.' He glared at her. 'Neither, I might add, do I take kindly to being made a fool of. I can't tell you how disappointed I am in you. As Marcia said, we have wondered about you, but we were glad, for Jeff's sake, that it appeared he had found someone to bring him to his senses, settle him down. He seemed happy with you, and that was enough for me. And I was grateful to you, too, for what you did for Betty. Now . . . well, I'm beginning to think that was all just a part of your plan.'

'No!' Fliss interrupted. 'Of course it wasn't! I loved Betty! You can't think . . .'

Jefferson sighed heavily. 'Truth to tell, I don't know what to think. I only know you've landed yourself in one hell of a mess, and it's going to be up to me to get you out of it. Now . . . do me a favour, lady – get out of my sight.'

Jefferson wasted no time in speaking to his chief of police. Eastville was his town, Eastville paid the wages of the police department, and besides, the two men were old friends. That evening, when Simon emerged from the restaurant where he had enjoyed another lavish meal, he was startled to be accosted by a uniformed officer, who took him to a car where an older, and obviously far more senior, officer was waiting. The older man invited him into the car politely enough, but when Simon was sitting beside him on the rear seat the gloves came off. Simon was told in no uncertain terms that he should get out of town if he knew what was good for him, and if he ever made mention to anyone of the events he'd described in his letter to Jefferson, he would not only be charged with attempted blackmail, but the English police would be made aware of his part in what had happened.

'They'll be told where you can be found too,' the chief warned, 'and don't think we won't know that. You might run, son, but you can't hide.'

Shaken to the core, Simon didn't even try his usual bluster. He'd seen American cops in films; he didn't want to tangle with any of them. Defeated, not knowing what the hell he was going to do next, he went back to his hotel, packed his bags, and left town as he had been instructed.

'You do realise that we can't allow you to stay here indefinitely, don't you?' Marcia said.

Fliss, wretched, groggy from lack of sleep, and still in such a state of distress that she could barely comprehend, stared blankly at Marcia.

'Jefferson has dealt with your friend – this Simon Beacham,' Marcia went on. 'It's highly unlikely we'll be hearing from him again, but we have no way of knowing if he mentioned this dreadful business to anyone else, or whether he will at some time in the future. We've talked it over, and it's not a risk we're prepared to take, I'm afraid. We want no part of this. Besides,' she added acidly, 'Jefferson can't bear to look at you, let alone have you living under his roof.'

She might also have said, though she did not, that neither had Jefferson wanted to be the one to tell Fliss of the decision they'd reached. That in fact it had been she who had insisted Fliss should leave, while Jefferson, though beside himself with anger, still felt a responsibility for the woman his son loved. His deepest gut instinct was that it would be a betrayal of Jeff to turn her out, not to mention the fact that she was carrying Jeff's child. A child who was, essentially, a Hewson, a son perhaps, to carry on the family business one day. Jefferson's grandchild, the only one he would ever have now, with Jeff gone. While Marcia had been all for showing Fliss the door right away, he wouldn't have it. And so they had eventually reached a compromise, one that Marcia was about to outline to Fliss now, revelling in every minute of it.

'I understand,' Fliss said woodenly. 'I'll go and pack my things.'

'And go where?' Marcia raised a finely arched eyebrow. 'In your condition, my dear, I really don't think you are in a position to be on the streets. We aren't quite the monsters you seem to think us. No, Jefferson would like you to remain here until the baby is born. Afterwards, though, we want you to leave as soon as possible.'

'With a newborn baby. Surely . . .'

'No, not with the baby.' Marcia's lips were a tight line. 'It's perfectly obvious that you will be in no position to care for a child, and Jefferson is not prepared for his grandson to be dragged around the country from one seedy ghetto to another. Our decision is that you will leave the child with us; we shall raise him here, as the next generation of Hewsons, in his father's home.'

Fliss gasped.

'You can't be serious!'

'Jeff's child will want for nothing. You can be sure Jefferson will see to that.'

'But you said you didn't want a baby here . . .'

'Jefferson is insistent – he won't let his grandchild go. We shall hire a live-in nanny for him, and he'll have all the advantages that being a Hewson can bring. But you, I'm afraid . . . there is no place for you in our lives or his. All connection must be severed if your baby's future is not to be jeopardised. You will leave him here with us, and you will never see him again.'

Fliss was shaking from head to foot.

'I won't do it! You can't make me do it!'

'Why not?' Marcia sneered. 'You've already left one child – why wouldn't you leave another? And to be honest, I don't think you are in any position to argue. Jefferson has made his decision, and the sooner you accept it, the better. And now . . .' she patted her heavily lacquered hair and smoothed into place what she perceived to be a wayward end, 'now I really must go and change. I'm due at a luncheon in just over an hour. I'll leave you to think about what I've said.'

Fliss was beside herself. She didn't blame Jefferson and Marcia for wanting her out of their lives; given what had happened, that was understandable. But how dare they think they could steal her child? There was absolutely no way she would let that happen. She'd lost Emma; she hadn't the slightest intention of losing this child too. But how could she fight them? Jefferson was the most powerful man she'd ever met; Marcia the most ruthless woman. If she didn't do as they said, they might well expose her in order to gain custody of her baby. Jeff's baby. A Hewson. There was no doubt in Fliss's mind as to who the courts would favour if it came to that. And in any case, if the truth came out she would probably be extradited back to Britain, where she would face heaven only knew what charges.

Distraught, Fliss paced the huge, empty house desperately trying to work out what she should do.

Perhaps the best option would be to go home of her own accord, own up and face the music. After all, the reason for her disappearance no longer existed. Jeff was dead, and she was all alone in a country where she knew no one, really, but his family. And if she went home she'd see Emma again. Even if she was sent to prison for what she had done, it wouldn't be for ever. When she was released she could set up home with Emma and the new baby. Martin wouldn't want her back, of course – she couldn't imagine he'd ever forgive her for what she'd done – and it seemed he was settled now with Maggie. But Fliss was reluctant to do something so drastic simply as a knee-jerk reaction to Marcia's threats, and she was all too aware of the repercussions such a course of action would have on Maggie, Martin and even

401

Emma. She needed time to think it all through if she was not to make yet another stupid decision that could end in disaster, and she needed to get away from this house. But where could she go?

The idea came to her in a lightning flash: Gull Island.

The summer was coming to an end; the families who spent long vacations there would have gone home to New York and Boston, Philadelphia and Washington. The Hewson house would be locked up and empty; there was no way Jefferson and Marcia would be using it again this year, and Marcia hated it on the island anyway. And she, Fliss, still had a set of keys from when she and Jeff had gone there for their idyllic break before he left for Vietnam, those few magical days when she was sure her baby had been conceived. Was there a more fitting place on earth for her to flee to now?

Suddenly the island was calling to her. The cliffs and the sandy beach with its outcrops of rock and hidden coves. The mountainous interior where they had picnicked in a picturesque valley. The harbour where Jeff had learned to sail, the rock pools where he had hunted for crabs. For a few brief moments she was reliving the glory of the days they had spent there, the peace and the ecstasy, the love and the longing, the hope and the promise of a future together when Jeff had served his draft, and it was where she longed to be.

It wouldn't be without its problems, of course. Winter was coming, and Jeff had told her Gull Island was a bleak place in winter. And she didn't suppose there would be a doctor to continue the regular antenatal checks that she had been having. But since the first months, when she had suffered from dreadful sickness, Fliss was feeling perfectly fit physically, and she couldn't see that the checks were necessary. She'd have to get back to the mainland in time for the birth, of course, but she'd find a hospital some- where where the Hewsons weren't known, and then, when the baby was born, she could disappear again. The solitary months on the island would give her space to work out a plan.

Now that her mind was made up, Fliss was reluctant to delay.

She didn't want to face Jefferson, and she certainly didn't want to see Marcia again. She packed her belongings into the bag she'd arrived with and called a taxi. She had it drop her in Eastville, near the train station, where she bought some provisions, then she took another taxi out to the marina. The *Jersey Gal* was still moored here; Fliss boarded her.

She slept that night in the narrow bunk where she and Jeff had made wonderful love, both passionate and tender. Next morning she manoeuvred her way out of the river and set sail for Gull Island.

There were no boats in the harbour; as Fliss had guessed, the summer folk had all gone now. The only person left on the island was Fletch Myers, the caretaker, who lived there all year round with his ill-tempered dog, Caesar. Even he wasn't in evidence as she moored the boat and lugged her belongings up to the house on the cliff; he was probably somewhere in the interior tending to his sheep and goats. He'd know someone was in residence when he saw the boat, of course, and she wouldn't be able to get fresh provisions without his knowledge, but Fletch wasn't going to tell anyone about it. He was a morose man who kept himself to himself and never spoke a single sentence when a grunt would do. According to Jeff, he never left the island, and since the only person he was likely to see for the entire winter was the captain of the boat that brought provisions and mail once a week, Fliss was confident no one would ever know that she was there.

The house had been shut up for winter, the furniture covered with dust sheets, and already it had a dank, unlived-in feel. Fliss lugged in kerosene stoves from one of the outhouses and got them going in the living room, and the smell brought on the nausea that she had been free of the last months. She was worried too about how long the kerosene would last – if the house was this cold already, what was it going to be like in winter? And what about the electricity supply? Keeping it up and running in summer was part of Fletch Myers' brief, but would he have turned it off now that the houses were shut up? For the first time Fliss felt a niggle of doubt. What had seemed like the perfect solution back on the mainland now seemed like yet another foolish decision taken too hastily. Would she never learn?

It wasn't long before Fliss was in no doubt that once again she had done something very stupid. The isolation that had seemed to be the answer to her problems was, in fact, a prison; the island was no longer the idyllic haven where she and Jeff had been so happy, but an outpost of a frozen hell. Fliss was lonely, frightened and cold, and things could only get worse. Snow was threatening; the sky was heavy with it, the quality of the light had altered and she could smell it in the air. Fliss found some warm clothing left by Betty and layered it on, but still she was chilled to the bone, and though she moved from the main house to the servants' quarters over the garage things were not much better.

She wasn't sure how much longer she could stand it, but what alternative did she have? She couldn't return to the mainland; the prospect of Jefferson and Marcia finding her and taking her baby the moment it was born was more than she could bear. She'd lost Emma and she'd lost Jeff; she couldn't risk losing her unborn child too.

The grief for both of them that was still raw overwhelmed her, and she huddled in a ball of despair, weeping helplessly.

Oh Jeff, Jeff . . . I can't do this on my own, but there's no one I can turn to . . . No one . . .

Jo. The vision of her friend was suddenly there before her eyes as if she had somehow summoned it by magic. Jo, who had refused to help her, who had so rightly predicted that the whole messy business would end in tears, but whose last words to Fliss had been: 'I'm always there for you, you know that.'

Would Jo come here to be with her? It was an awful lot to ask, but Fliss had a gut feeling that she would. They had always been close, so close; Jo had been more like a sister than a friend. Longing for someone who cared about her, someone she could talk things over with, consumed her. She'd get in touch with Jo, ask – no, beg – her to come. Thank goodness there were now telephones on the island – Jeff had told her that until a couple of years ago there had been none.

She went into the hall and picked up the heavy Bakelite handset, praying that it hadn't been disconnected. But to her enormous relief, after what seemed like a lifetime, the operator was on the line. Fliss gave her Jo's number, waited with bated breath.

When she ansered, Jo sounded startled and a bit woozy, and Fliss realised what she had forgotten until now, that in England it would be past midnight.

'Jo,' she said, 'it's me.'

'Fliss? Oh my God, Fliss! Where are you?'

'On an island off the coast of Maine. All by myself. I had to get away. Oh, it's a long story but . . . Jeff's dead, Jo. And I'm pregnant. Oh Jo, please! Will you come out? Please, Jo – I really need you.'

THIRTY-SEVEN

Jo arrived on Gull Island on a bitterly cold afternoon in late October, brought by the schooner that delivered the mail once a week. The three days she'd had to wait for it after reaching Maine had seemed endless, but at least it had given her plenty of time to shop for warm clothes and food supplies – in that desperate late-night phone call Fliss had told her she was bitterly cold – freezing – and the canned food she'd found in the larder was fast running out. She also bought baby clothes, diapers, as they were called here, and some packets of infant feed and bottles. She wasn't sure how far advanced Fliss's pregnancy was and she didn't want to be caught out if the arrival of the baby was imminent. She'd tried several times to ring Fliss but had been unable to get a connection – unsurprising, the receptionist at the motel where she was staying, had told her. Lines very often came down at this time of year in remote spots, victims of the high winds and early snow.

Jo was dreadfully concerned for her friend and had hoped, too, to be able to talk to her again about her cover story as to why she wanted to go out to the island. It was, apparently, almost unheard of at this time of year. The only resident was an old man who acted as caretaker for the properties, and Jo's first suggestion had been that she should pretend to be a relative of his visiting, a niece perhaps, but Fliss hadn't been happy with that.

'He's not the sort of man anyone would visit,' she'd said. 'Couldn't you pretend to be a naturalist of some kind? Writing a thesis or something?'

So that had been agreed upon, but not knowing the first thing about the island, Jo was worried she'd be less than convincing if the captain of the schooner should ask her questions.

In the event she need not have worried. The captain and his brother, who acted as mate, were men of few words and seemed ready to accept her story. The fact that she was both English and – as they'd been led to believe – an academic was explanation enough for what they thought was utter madness.

'Good luck t'ya,' Todd Barrowman, the skipper, said as Jo climbed out on to the wharf, and his brother, tossing a mostly empty mailbag ashore, echoed him.

'Reckon y'll need it.'

The old caretaker, who had come down to meet the mail boat with his dog straining and barking on the end of a leash, was even more silent.

'Up thataways,' he grunted when Jo asked directions to the Hewson house, jerking his thumb in the direction of a rough road leading up a hill.

'I'm a friend . . .'

'Don't matter to me who you are, gal, just so long as you keep outa my way.'

He made no attempt to help Jo with her bags, stumping off in the opposite direction, his dog still turning periodically to snarl at her. She started up the steep road, shivering as the icy wind threw snow flurries at her. They stung her cheeks, clung to her eyelashes and lodged in her fringe, which peeped out from beneath her woollen cap.

No wonder Fliss was desperate, she thought, alone in this godforsaken place, with just that evil-looking old man and his even more evil dog for company. There had to be a better solution to her problems.

The road was flanked by pines, shivering and creaking in the howling wind. Then, as she rounded a bend, the house came into sight, a solid, impressive mansion that would have been better suited to a country estate than this bleak place. And standing uncertainly in the road a few yards from the entrance was a slight figure wrapped up in a full-length fur coat and with a twenties-style cloche hat pulled well down on her head. As Jo hove into view, the uncertainly became purpose, and she began to run towards her.

'Oh Jo! You came! You're here!'

Jo dropped her bags, held out her arms, and Fliss ran into them, sobbing with joy and relief.

'For goodness' sake, Fliss, just look at you!' Jo held her at arm's length, looking her up and down and laughing because laughter was the only antidote to the tears that were welling in her eyes. 'What in the world are you wearing?'

Fliss looked down too at the fur coat, which fell almost to her ankles, with her sturdy trainers peeping out beneath.

'It was in a wardrobe. It must have been Betty's. It was the warmest thing I could find.'

'It smells terrible!'

'I know. It's the mothballs. Awful, isn't it?' Then: 'I'm so glad you're here!'

'And not before time, by the looks of it. Oh Fliss, what sort of a mess have you got yourself into this time?'

The wind gusted again, blowing a fresh flurry of snow at the two girls.

'Let's get inside,' Jo said. 'This is shit.'

'We've been through worse together.'

'Really?' Jo said grimly. 'You could have fooled me.'

'Come on then. I've moved into the servants' quarters over the garage. It's easier to keep warm – the house is like a mausoleum.'

Fliss led the way up a flight of steps to a wide veranda and into a poky room that smelled so strongly of kerosene that it quite masked the camphor of the mothballs that had impregnated the fur coat.

'Home!' she said, smiling grimly. 'The only one I've got now.'

Jo shook her head in disbelief.

'This is crazy. You can't stay here!'

'What else do you suggest? I'm an illegal immigrant, persona non gratis. I'm expecting my dead lover's child, and his parents want to take the baby away from me. I'm an absolute, total mess. And I don't know what the hell I'm going to do.'

Jo put her arms around her friend.

'Oh Fliss, Fliss . . . I don't know. But we'll think of something.'

That, however, was easier said than done. Unsatisfactory as conditions might be on Gull Island, at least as a place to hide away it had its advantages until they could come up with an alternative. No one but Fletch Myers knew that Fliss was here, and he wouldn't be saying anything to anyone any time soon, if ever. If Jefferson chose to try and find Fliss in order to claim her unborn child, it would never occur to him that she might be living in his empty house on the island in the dead of a New England winter. But they couldn't stay here for much longer. Conditions were becoming unbearable, and besides, Jo was increasingly worried for Fliss. She should be checked out by a doctor, and she would soon need to decide on a hospital for the birth.

'OK, here's the plan,' Jo said. She'd been awake most of the previous night thinking about it, though truth to tell the bitter cold would have kept her awake even if her overworked brain had not.

'We'll take the boat and head south, more or less following the coast so that we can make for land if there's any sign of you going into labour. Chances are we can get as far as Florida. You know people there, don't you?'

'In Naples, yes. Jeff had friends there, and there was Tami, the girl I stayed with while I was working at the diner.'

'Would she help you?'

'I'm sure she would.' Fliss didn't know why she hadn't thought of Tami before; Tami had a huge heart and, better yet, she was American and would know how to play the system. Fliss rather thought that Rick Curtis and Jeff's other sailing friends would help too if she asked them. But the sailing fraternity were as transient as they were unorthodox, and Fliss wasn't at all sure they'd still be in Naples.

'We won't need accommodation,' Jo went on. 'If we can get a mooring we can live on the boat. I might even be able to find some kind of job to help with the finances. Then, when you've had the baby, we'll think again. With your American passport you can go just about anywhere in the world and make a fresh start.'

'Anywhere but home,' Fliss said bleakly.

'Well, yes. Unless you're prepared to face the music.'

'I did think about it,' Fliss admitted. 'I miss Emma so much! Did you know I was going to go to London to get her? I was going to meet her and Maggie at Paddington. But Maggie wouldn't do it.' Her eyes filled with tears. 'She said it wasn't in Emma's best interests. That she was settled with her and Martin.'

'She's probably right,' Jo said flatly.

'I know. My head tells me that she is. But it doesn't alter the way I feel. I can't bear being separated from her. Well, you know how it feels, don't you? We've been here before.'

'Yep.' The sadness was there in Jo's eyes, as it always was when she thought of the son she had given up for adoption.

'It was bad enough when I had to give her up as a baby,' Fliss said. 'But it's even worse now. She's my little girl! I had her for two years, Jo. Loved her, looked after her, knew her little ways. Does she remember me, do you think? And if she does, does it make her sad? I don't want her to be sad! And I don't want her to think I didn't love her.'

'Why would she think that if she believes you drowned accidentally?' Jo reasoned.

'Well she wouldn't, I suppose. But if it should ever come out . . . I wrote a letter to her and sent it to Maggie to keep for her, just in case. And I promised to keep in touch so she'd know where to find me. Do you think she might one day? Come and find me?'

'I'm sure she will.' Jo was not sure of anything of the sort, but she wasn't about to say so. 'In the meantime you've got to think about the baby you're carrying now. Jeff's baby.'

Fliss sighed. 'You're right.' Her hands went protectively to the swell of her stomach.

'So we'll head down to Florida then, shall we?'

'Yes. We'll do that. It's strange, you know,' Fliss went on reflectively. 'I came to the island because Jeff and I were so happy here. But he's not here any more, is he, and we were together in Florida too. I think he'd like me to take the *Jersey Gal* home.'

Jo took her hand.

'So you shall. And the sooner we can get out of this hellhole the better.'

Was nothing ever to go right for Fliss? Jo wondered. Had there been an evil fairy at her cradle who'd put a spell on her so that everything she touched turned to dust? What had happened to the golden girl Jo had known in the days when they had first started sailing together? To her dreams, to her shining promise? Fliss was impulsive, yes, she was reckless and naïve. But she was also kind and loving. She didn't deserve this. She didn't deserve to be thwarted at every turn.

And it was happening again.

When they went down to the harbour to prepare the *Jersey Gal* for sailing to Florida, they found her damaged – the recent high winds were probably to blame. There was no way they could leave until repairs had been made.

Of the two of them, Jo was the more practical, but even with

411

her expertise it took a week or more to make the boat seaworthy. The girls could only work on her for an hour or so at a stretch before frozen fingers forced them to abandon what they were doing and return to the servants' quarters to thaw out. Then first Jo and then Fliss came down with a flu virus – hardly surprising, given the conditions under which they were living – and it wouldn't have been wise to set sail until they were both fully fit.

Best to play a waiting game, Jo thought. There was still time to reach Florida before Fliss's baby was born.

They slipped out of the harbour early one November morning, the bows breaking a thin covering of ice, with only the howling of Fletch Myers' dog to bid them farewell.

In the grey light of the breaking dawn Fliss looked back at the island where she and Jeff had been so happy and wept silent tears for a lost dream. The past was a distant country now, and she must leave it behind. It was time to look to the future.

In some ways it was like old times, sailing together, though Fliss was now more a passenger than an equal partner. She was struggling under the weight of her advanced pregnancy and Jo took on the heavy work whenever she could, calling on Fliss only when she really needed a second pair of hands, which wasn't too often. The *Jersey Gal* was equipped to be sailed single-handed – after all, Jeff had crossed the Atlantic twice all alone, and this was a walk in the park by comparison.

Or it should have been.

When the storm blew up and fast became a howling gale, there was nothing to be done but sit tight and ride it out. But they were being blown off course, Jo knew, and it concerned her. Though Fliss never complained, Jo had seen her holding her stomach, supporting the precious bundle with both hands; she'd seen her rubbing the small of her back and gritting her teeth as she climbed from the cabin on to the deck. What the hell would she do if the baby came early? It didn't bear thinking about. Best to concentrate on doing all she could to get to Florida before anything happened, or, failing that, at least to some place where medical attention could be had.

The trouble was that after the storm the winds died completely, as if they'd expended every last breath, and when Jo tried to start the outboard motor it refused to so much as turn over. It was the one thing she hadn't checked thoroughly – no self-respecting sailor likes to use a motor, and she'd not anticipated trouble on what had promised to be a fairly easy voyage. Now she cursed the oversight. Time was running out, and being becalmed was a nightmare she could have done without.

Fliss, however, seemed to have found a new serenity, and when at last the first breeze stirred in the canvas she helped Jo set the sails with surprising energy.

'Florida here we come!' Jo leaned against the rail, judging their work with a practised eye.

'Calls for a cup of tea, I'd say,' Fliss said gaily. 'I'll make it.'

'No way! Your tea is disgusting! You never let it stand long enough.'

'And you do? Beggars can't be choosers, my dear.' Fliss, at the head of the companionway to the cabin, turned to grin at Jo.

And lost her footing.

Her scream and the awful clatter as she fell against the wooden ladder alerted Jo and she raced down the companionway.

'Fliss! Fliss – are you all right?'

Fliss was lying in a heap on the floor of the cabin. For what seemed like endless moments she neither moved nor spoke, then her breath came out on a groan.

'What happened?'

'You fell, that's what! Can you get up? Here, let me help you . . .'

She raised Fliss into a sitting position, then supported her as she struggled to her feet, dazed and shaken.

'Come on, lie down on the bunk.'

'No, no – I'm fine . . .'

'For once in your life, Felicity Penrose, do as you are told!'

413

For once in her life, Fliss did.

'Fancy giving me a fright like that!' Jo said. 'Are you sure you're all right?'

'Yes . . . actually . . . no. I do feel very peculiar . . .' She broke off as the first pain contracted her stomach, gasping at the sudden intensity of it. Then, as it receded, she looked up at Jo, her eyes full of panic.

'Oh my God, Jo! I think I've started!'

'No way! Don't frighten me like that! It's the fall, that's all . . .'

'You think so?' Fliss desperately wanted to believe Jo was right, that though she'd recognised the merciless hand tightening around the deepest part of her as a contraction, it would be just the one.

A few minutes later, however, as another pain consumed her, there was no getting away from the awful certainty.

'No, Jo, I really think this is it,' she gasped after she had ridden it out. 'The baby's coming! Oh my God, what are we going to do?'

'Shit!' But Jo knew she had to keep calm. 'OK, hang in there, kid. How long do you think . . .?'

'I don't know. Emma took for ever, but second babies can be really quick . . . A couple of hours maybe?'

'I'm going to have another go at that bloody engine.' It was, Jo knew, their only hope. With power there was just a chance they might make landfall before the baby was born. Without it she would have to deliver it herself. Jo, intrepid in the face of most things life could throw at her, had never been so afraid.

For an hour she battled with the engine, trying every which way she knew to coax it into life and stopping now and then to check on Fliss, whose contractions were now coming strongly every minute or so. Suddenly, to her enormous surprise and relief – success! The engine coughed, and though it died again almost immediately, Jo was heartened by that first erratic sound of life. She tried again, and glory be, it fired!

'We have lift-off!' she called to Fliss. 'I'm setting a westerly course. We should—'

'Jo!' Fliss's response was an anguished cry, the urgency of it unmistakable.

Jo rushed back to the cabin. Fliss was on her hands and knees on the floor.

'I need to push!'

'Oh no, Fliss. You can't!'

'I have to!'

For a moment white-hot panic engulfed her, and then, quite suddenly, she was the old, calm, efficient Jo, who could cope with any crisis. 'Hang in there.'

The first thing to do was to shut off the engine again and hope against hope that she'd be able to start it again later. She couldn't risk powering shorewards when she wasn't on deck to keep a sharp lookout for other shipping. The next thing was to spread a tarpaulin topped with a clean sheet on the floor for Fliss to lie on, set water to boil and collect towels and linen and a knife and a couple of lengths of twine to enable her to cut and tie the cord. By the time she had done all this, the baby's head was just visible. Twenty minutes and a last enormous effort later, the newborn slithered into Jo's welcoming hands.

'Oh my God, Fliss,' gasped Jo, overawed and jubilant. 'It's girl! You have a little girl!'

The baby uttered her first complaining wail, and Jo wrapped her in a clean towel and placed her in Fliss's arms. Oh, she was so beautiful! Her puckered face, with button nose and little pursed mouth, was topped with thick, glistening hair, her ears pinned tight against her head. One little hand had escaped Jo's inept swaddling, and she gazed in awe at the tiny fingers, each capped with a pearly nail. Jo had never cared much for babies – apart from her own – but now she felt her heart swell as if it would burst. That this perfect little human being could have emerged unscathed was cause for such wonder that Jo knew she would never be the same again, and she didn't know how to tear herself away.

But there were things to be done. Presently, she supposed, she must wash the little mite, though the thought of handling her scared Jo to death; then she would have to clean the cabin and make Fliss comfortable. But first and foremost she needed to go on deck and check that they were still well clear of other shipping.

'Stay still and rest,' she said to Fliss. 'I'll be back in a minute.'

The sky was clear and blue as Jo emerged from the cabin, the sun warm on her face, the sea a millpond, broken only by long white furrows in the gentle swell, as empty as it had been before the momentous events of the previous half-hour.

I delivered Fliss's daughter, she thought, pride and joy lifting her to a new plateau. *All by myself. At sea.* And that seemed very right too. Now all she had to do was get mother and daughter safely to land. What would happen then she hadn't the first idea, but for the moment that didn't seem to matter. If she could do what she had just done, she could do anything.

It was only when she returned to the cabin that Jo realised something was terribly wrong. The sheet she'd put under Fliss was soaked with blood, the tarpaulin beneath awash with it. It had even swum upwards, towards Fliss's head, so that her hair, tangled loosely about her white face, was crusted with it.

'Fliss!' she shrieked. 'What's happening?'

'I think I'm bleeding.' Fliss sounded very frightened.

'Is it the afterbirth?' Jo asked, trying to keep the panic she was feeling out of her voice.

'I don't know . . . I think it's more than that . . .'

Jo thought so too, and the panic twisted another notch tighter. She'd heard of women haemorrhaging after giving birth but it had never occurred to her that it might happen to Fliss.

'How do I stop it?' she asked, her voice rising despite her best efforts to keep it level.

'I don't know . . . oh Jo, I'm sorry . . .'

'Don't be silly! It's not your fault.'

The bleeding was showing no signs of abating, and Fliss had begun to tremble violently.

'Oh Jo . . .' Her voice was faint, now, and shaky. 'Am I going to die?'

'Of course you're not! You're going to be fine.'

But Jo was all too aware that unless she could stop this bleeding, there was no way Fliss could survive.

Something she'd heard, or read, somewhere popped into her mind. She pressed on Jo's stomach, which felt flabby beneath her hands, trying to massage her friend's womb.

'Jo!' Faint as it was, there was a deep urgency in Fliss's voice as she struggled to muster her remaining strength. 'Take my baby!'

'In a minute . . .'

'No, take her to England. Don't let Jefferson and Marcia have her! Promise me!' Her breathing was shallow and laboured; she struggled to finish. 'Promise me you'll take care of her . . .'

'Don't say such things, Fliss!'

Fliss's fingers closed over Jo's wrist.

'Promise!'

'Oh, of course I promise.'

Fliss's hand fell onto her flabby stomach, exhausted by the effort, but satisfied to have Jo's promise. Her eyes were unfocused now, she was drifting away.

'Fliss, stay with me! Please stay with me!' Jo begged.

'Melanie,' Fliss whispered.

'What?' At first she didn't understand what Fliss was saying, but as her lips moved again, slowly, deliberately she realised.

'You want to call her Melanie?'

The merest nod of Fliss's head, and again the desperate struggle to form words. 'Take me . . . England . . . look . . . after . . . her . . . please . . .'

Tears were streaming down Jo's cheeks now.

'I will, Fliss, I will.'

Fliss's eyelids fluttered, her head lolled to one side.

'I love you, Fliss,' Jo said.

Fliss did not reply. With shaking hands Jo checked her pulse – nothing. She brushed the bright gold hair from the pale, clammy face with the utmost tenderness. Then she lifted the baby, cradling her close. She smelled of Fliss, of Fliss's blood, and Jo's tears fell on to the little red, screwed-up face.

'Oh Fliss!' she whispered. And then: 'Oh Melanie! What am I going to do with you?'

It was a question that needed no answer, but for the details. There was no way on earth that Jo would break her promise. She would get Melanie back to England. And she would raise her herself, as Fliss had asked.

In that moment the promise she had made to Fliss became a sacred oath. And Jo knew that her own life would be changed for ever.

Part Seven

1989

THIRTY-EIGHT

Jo and Mel sit at the kitchen table, a pot of coffee, long gone cold, between them. Late morning sun slants in at the window; it had been raining earlier but the sky has cleared while Jo talked, though neither of them noticed it. As she comes to the end of the story Jo raises her eyes, meeting Melanie's. The shock on the face of the girl she has raised as her own daughter is palpable; throughout the telling of the story Jo has avoided looking at her, staring instead at her hands, knotted on the table in front of her.

'I'm sorry,' she says weakly. 'I should have told you a long time ago.'

'Yes,' Mel says, 'you should. I knew – I think I've always known – that there was something you were hiding. I told myself I was imagining things, but I knew, deep down, that there was something. I used to wonder if perhaps I was adopted. I mean – I don't look at all like you and Dad, do I? I thought a lot about it when I was what – thirteen or fourteen. I asked to see my birth certificate – do you remember? Said it was for a project at school. It was a proper birth certificate, though it gave my father's name as Yves something-or-other, and you said you'd had me before you were married, and my real father had died in an accident. And I believed you, thought that I must have taken after him in appearance. I really don't understand. How could you do that? How could you lie to me about something like that?'

'I thought it was for the best,' Jo says wretchedly. 'You were just a child.'

'I was fourteen!'

'A really vulnerable age. I didn't think you could cope with it then.'

'Well I haven't been fourteen for a very long time! I can understand – sort of – why you kept it a secret in the beginning. But all these years . . . You should have told me.'

'I know.' Jo bows her head, then reaches for Mel's hands across the table. 'Can you ever forgive me? I am so sorry, darling.'

For a moment Mel leaves her hands in Jo's, then she pulls away.

'It's such a shock. I can't get my head around it. Would you ever have told me if I hadn't met Emma? If she hadn't shown me that photograph of you and Fliss?' She breaks off as realisation dawns. Until now the terrible story has been so overwhelming she hasn't thought beyond it; now the full implications confront her head on.

'If she's Fliss's daughter and I'm Fliss's daughter, then she's my sister!' The word is imbued with a sort of awed reverence.

Jo nods.

'I have a sister! A whole family I don't know, who don't know about me! A whole family!'

'Well, strictly speaking, they're not your family. Apart from Maggie.'

'And what about my father?' Mel's voice is rising, shock giving way to anger that she should have been kept in the dark in this way.

'I thought I'd explained that,' Jo says, anxious to make Mel understand.

'Fliss was desperate they shouldn't get control of you. It would have been different if Jeff's mother, Betty, had still been alive. Fliss was very fond of her. But she hated Marcia, the second wife. According to Fliss she was a shallow, self-obsessed bitch, and Jefferson had no time for anything but his business. That was why he was so determined to have you – if you'd been a boy you would have been able to carry on the family name, step into the

422

business as Jeff was supposed to be going to do. It wasn't about love, it was about inheritance. Fliss knew that. It's why she made me promise to take you as far away from them as possible.'

Mel laughs mirthlessly.

'Well there's a thing! I'm an heiress and I never knew it.'

'You'd have wanted for nothing, I'm sure. But you'd have been raised by a succession of nannies. You'd have had no proper family life. At least I've given you that, even if we have had to struggle sometimes. Fliss thought that was more important than a life of luxury, and funnily enough, so did I.'

'This isn't about money – I couldn't care less about that!' Mel flashes. 'It's much deeper. It's about my roots. Who I am.'

'I know. And I know too that you are going to want to go to America and meet your father. It's only right that you should. What you do then . . . well, that's up to you.' She sighs, shifts in her chair. 'Do you want another cup of coffee?'

Mel snorts. 'Believe me, I could do with something a whole lot stronger. I don't suppose you've got anything, though.'

Jo isn't really a drinker, never has been.

'I think there's some Bacardi left from Christmas. But isn't it a bit early?'

'Who cares!'

'Well, you know where it is.'

Mel disappears, returns with a glass of Bacardi, topped up with Coca-Cola, Jo guesses.

'I've put the kettle on for you, Mum.'

'Actually,' Jo says, 'if you haven't emptied the bottle, I think I could do with a Bacardi too.' She goes to get up; Mel stops her.

'It's all right. I'll get it for you.'

'So,' she says when she comes back with Jo's drink, 'what happened to my mother?'

'I told you, darling. She died.'

'Well, yes, but . . . what happened to her body?' Mel's voice is curiously flat, emotionless, but Jo knows what she's thinking. Is there a grave somewhere she can visit?

She closes her eyes briefly, trying to shut out the images that have haunted her down the years. How she had wrapped Fliss's lifeless body in the tarpaulin, trussed it, somehow manhandled it on deck. But when she speaks, her voice is as devoid of emotion as Mel's.

'I buried her at sea,' she says simply.

'You threw her overboard?' Mel is horrified.

'It wasn't like that,' Jo protests. 'I could hardly leave her there in the cabin, could I? When someone dies at sea, that's what happens. It's what she would have wanted.'

'All the same . . .' Mel takes a gulp of her Bacardi and Coke.

'It was done with love,' Jo says quietly. 'And it was respectful. I said some of the prayers from the service for burial at sea before I . . . did what I had to do.'

'And then?'

'And then I . . .' *Cleared up*, she was going to say, but that was too brutally graphic. Mel didn't need it in glorious Technicolor. 'I had to think of you,' she says instead. 'Somehow I managed to look after you as well as sailing the boat. Luckily you were an easy baby – you took to the bottle very quickly. If you hadn't, I don't know what I would have done.'

'So how did you get me back to England? You didn't sail across the Atlantic with me, surely?'

Jo shakes her head, smiling faintly.

'Hardly! A single-handed transatlantic crossing is enough of a challenge under normal circumstances. No, I headed for shore – which was actually a lot closer than we'd realised. I'd cleaned up the *Jersey Gal*, disposed of all Fliss's things so that whoever was next on board would have no idea what had happened. When I landed, I took a flight home.'

Mel is shaking her head in disbelief.

'Didn't anyone question the fact that you had a young baby with you?'

'No. I was afraid they might, but they didn't. Things were much more lax in those days. There wasn't all the red tape and security that there is now.'

'And when you got back to England?'

Jo sips her drink, makes a face, but takes another sip anyway.

'That was the most difficult part. I couldn't risk going home to Plymouth, or anywhere I was known. So I came to London. I figured that was the best place to become invisible. I hoped Yves might join me . . .'

'Yves? The man you told me was my real father?'

'Yes. We'd been together for a long time and I hoped he might understand. But he didn't. It was the end of us.'

'I'm not surprised!'

'No, me neither, looking back at it. But it would never have worked anyway. Yves was a sailor through and through. He couldn't have been happy away from the sea.'

'And have you? Been happy away from the sea, I mean? Emma said . . .'

'I've missed it, of course,' Jo admits. 'If Yves had been more understanding, we could have moved back to the coast, I expect – somewhere different, where we weren't known. But as it was, I had to find a job, earn enough to support us, and again, London was a good option. There was plenty of temping work in those days. And then I met your father – well, Goff – and the rest you know. We got married and he brought you up as his own.'

'Did he know?' Mel asks. 'That I wasn't really yours?'

Jo nods. 'I told him, eventually.'

'So he kept it from me too.'

'He left it up to me as to whether or not you should be told.'

'Great.'

'Mel, you must not blame Goff,' Jo says sharply. 'He was a wonderful father to you. He just didn't think it was his place to tell you the truth. Blame me if you like. But don't blame him.'

Mel is silent. Just now she feels as if the whole of her world has collapsed around her.

'If it's any consolation,' Jo says, 'I have never for one moment regretted the promise I made to Fliss. You've been nothing but a joy to me, the most precious daughter. I suppose over the years

I've almost forgotten I didn't give birth to you – I came to think of you as mine. I delivered you, remember. I heard your first cry. It was me who fed you, changed you, did everything for you. I couldn't have loved you more if you had been my own baby. And I suppose . . . I suppose it went some way to making up for . . .'

She breaks off. There's a very faraway look in her eyes.

'There's something else I ought to tell you,' she says after a moment.

Mel groans. 'Oh Mum – no! Does it have anything to do with Fliss and me?'

'Not really, but . . .'

'Then don't, please. Not now. I'm already on overload. I don't think I can take any more.'

Jo nods. 'Very well. But I do want to tell you when you're ready. I've had enough of keeping secrets.'

'Another time, yes?'

'All right. Another time. Oh Mel . . .'

Mel sighs. 'Oh Mum.' She laughs bitterly. 'I suppose I can still call you that.'

'I certainly hope so.' Jo holds out her hands again, and this time Mel takes them. 'Please, darling, I know this changes everything. But there's one thing it doesn't change. I love you very much. I always have and I always will.'

Mel's eyes fill with tears.

'And I love you. You've been a great mum – I couldn't have asked for better. I just wish you'd told me before.'

'So do I. But at least you know now. And whatever you decide to do about it, you know I'll always be here for you.'

It's an echo of the words she spoke to Fliss all those years ago, words that had such life-changing consequences.

With all her heart Jo hopes they won't come back to haunt her now as they did then. But somehow she doesn't think so. Mel might be Fliss's daughter, but she isn't Fliss. She's much more level-headed, much more balanced. A trait inherited from Jeff, perhaps? Or a result of the secure upbringing Jo was able to give her? Jo doesn't know, and it doesn't matter.

Once she's got over the first shock, Mel will deal with all this as she deals with everything, pragmatically, sensibly, bravely.

As for herself . . . the telling at last has been an ordeal. But now that it's done, Jo feels lighter, the weight of the secrets she has kept all these years removed from her shoulders and her heart.

For the moment it's the most she can hope for.

Since she arrived home yesterday Emma feels strangely disorientated. Ever since Mike Bond first arrived on the scene with his devastating suggestion that Fliss faked her own death, it's as if everything that was comfortably solid in her life has been broken apart, thrown in the air like the pieces of a jigsaw puzzle and come down in a confusing, random heap. Until now she's been scrabbling around trying to fit them together, but now she can do nothing but wait. To see if anything comes of Mike's press appeal, to hear from Mel. It's inactivity on a grand scale, and the one thing Emma hates is inactivity.

On top of all this, her emotional life is in turmoil. Though she's sure it's for the best, she still feels dreadfully guilty about hurting Philip and wishes she could speak to him again and explain that he just isn't the one for her and she doesn't want to make the same mistake as her mother and settle for a man she can't commit to body and soul. But how would that help? It might salve her conscience, but raking over the coals won't help Philip.

Then there's Mike. She absolutely can't get him out of her head. And quite apart from the ache of longing to hear his voice, she's really anxious to know if he's made any progress with his press appeal to Fliss. But feeling the way she does about him, she knows that the safest thing is to keep her distance. No way is she going to do anything that might contribute to the break-up of his marriage – she feels guilty enough already, knowing she crossed the boundaries by making love to him. Presumably he'll contact her if there's any news.

The one thing she can do – must do – is speak to her father and Maggie. She really should have phoned them last night, but by the time she'd finished up on the Lord Nelson and driven back from Plymouth, all she wanted to do was have a long soak in a hot bath and catch up on some much-needed sleep. It never fails to amaze her how the unflagging energy she musters while on board becomes utter exhaustion the minute she sets foot back on dry land, just as the perfectly steady sea legs turn to a peculiar loss of balance, with the solid ground beneath her feet seeming to sway far more than the decks of an ocean-going sailing ship ever do.

Now, though, she absolutely must tell them that she has met Jo Best's daughter. Things are moving fast, and she has to keep them up to speed. She's dreading it, though, shrinking inside as she thinks of how upset her father is going to be, and still angry with Maggie that she could have known all these years that Fliss was alive and kept it secret from both her father and her.

She's about to pick up the phone when it rings. Maybe they've beaten her to it. Or could it be Mike? Her heart lifts treacherously. Or Philip? A corresponding downward lurch.

She lifts the receiver. 'Hello?'

'Is that Emma?'

She recognises the voice immediately.

'Yes, Emma here. That's Mel, isn't it?'

'Yes.' There's a pause, then Mel says: 'I've spoken to Jo. About Fliss.'

Emma catches her breath.

'And?'

'It's a very long story,' Mel says. 'I can't go into it over the phone.' She sounds awkward somehow, not the easy-to-talk-to girl Emma knew on the Lord Nelson.

'I take it that means she is who we thought she might be? The same Jo Best who was Fliss's sailing partner?' Emma says.

'Yes. She is.' A small pause. 'Look, Emma, you will want to see her, I know, and she wants to meet you. But . . . I want to tell you first what she told me.'

'What . . .?' Emma is mystified.

428

'I don't want to go into it over the phone. I was wondering if we could meet – somewhere sort of midway for both of us, perhaps? The only thing is, I can't make it until next weekend – I'm back at work tomorrow.'

'Could you manage an evening?' Emma is tingling all over. No way can she wait a whole week to find out what Mel has to tell her.

'Well, yes, but . . .'

'Then why don't I come up to London? I'm on holiday now, so my time is my own, and I haven't been to London for ages.'

'If you're sure . . .'

'I'm sure. I wouldn't suggest it otherwise. When shall we say . . . Tuesday evening? How would that suit you?'

'Fine, I think. Look – where will you stay? You're welcome to come to me if you'd like to. I've got a spare bed. It's not exactly luxury, but . . .'

'After the *Lord Nelson*, anything is luxury!'

Mel laughs, the first time in the entire conversation that she has sounded completely natural.

'You're telling me! I slept like a log last night. And it's so nice to be clean again.'

'That's shipboard life. Pretty basic.'

'Yes.' Mel goes quiet again, and Emma has no way of knowing it's because she's thinking of Fliss, giving birth to her in a tiny cabin.

'What time will you arrive?' she asks.

'Not sure yet. I'll let you know. And thanks, Mel.'

A pause, then Mel says: 'Don't get your hopes up, Emma.'

Emma's heart sinks. 'Jo doesn't know what happened to my mother?'

Another pause. Then: 'She does know, yes. But it's not good news. Look – I really don't want to tell you over the phone. We'll talk on Tuesday.'

Emma can feel her nerves jangling. But she can't press Mel. It wouldn't be right.

'I'll be in touch as soon as I've sorted out train or coach times.'

She disconnects, stands for a moment wondering what it is that Mel has to tell her. *Not good news.* Something she didn't want to say over the phone. It's pointless to waste time speculating, but Emma has a bad feeling about it.

She goes to the kitchen, makes herself a coffee, knowing all the while that she's delaying the moment when she must ring home. But she can't put it off for ever – now that she knows for sure she's found Jo Best, it's become more important than ever. Steeling herself, she dials.

It's Maggie who answers.

'Emma! You're back. Did you have a nice time?'

Incredible! Emma thinks.

'I always enjoy the *Lord Nelson*,' she says. 'But something pretty unbelievable happened, given that I've been trying to find out what became of my mother. I met a girl called Melanie Thomas. And it turns out she is Jo Best's daughter.'

She hears the sharp intake of breath at the other end of the line, and it's not difficult to imagine just how shocked Maggie must be.

'Small world, isn't it?' she says harshly. 'Anyway, I'm going up to London on Tuesday to see her. Apparently she's talked to Jo since she got back, and she has something she wants to tell me. About Fliss, presumably. I think we might be on the point of finding her.'

The silence at the other end of the line speaks volumes. It's just as she thought – Maggie doesn't want Fliss found. Her anger bubbles up again.

'How could you do it, Maggie?' she asks furiously. 'How could you know all the time that Mum was alive and keep it from Dad and me?'

'Emma, please . . .'

'Don't pretend you don't know what I'm talking about. I know that not only were you perfectly well aware that she was alive, you were in contact with her. She wanted me back and you talked her out of it. And you never told Dad, and you've never told me. How could you do that, Maggie?'

'It was for the best, Emma! I was only thinking of you . . .'

'That's what you probably kidded yourself into believing. It couldn't have been, I suppose, that you didn't want your own cosy life to fall apart?'

'Oh Emma . . .' Maggie's distress is becoming more and more evident. 'Darling, please, why don't you come over and we can talk about it.'

'Have you told Dad yet? That you've known all along? Because I think you'd better, before I come along and put my four penn'orth in. It should come from you, don't you think? And I'll leave you to tell him about Jo Best, too. But for goodness' sake do it soon, Maggie. Like now. He's got to be fully in the picture before I hit him with whatever it is Mel has to say.'

'I know.' Maggie's voice is shaking. 'And Emma . . . I am so sorry. But you must believe me . . . I thought it was for the best . . .'

'So you said before.'

'You will . . . let us know what Jo says? If she knows where Fliss is now?'

'You're sure you don't already know?'

'No . . . I haven't heard anything from her for years. The last lot of photographs of you that I sent her were returned "not known at this address". That was when you were about five . . .'

'Oh Maggie, Maggie.'

Unable to continue the conversation, Emma hangs up.

There's someone else she should ring, though. Mike. It is really only right that she should fill him in. She dials his number, and there's no way she can escape the racing of her pulse as she listens to the bell ringing at the other end.

It's not Mike who answers, though. It's a small, quite prim voice.

'Hello? This is Daisy Bond. Who's there, please?'

For a moment Emma is completely flummoxed.

'Hello, Daisy,' she says. 'I'm called Emma Dunning and I'm a friend of your daddy. Is he there?'

'He's in his office. I'll just get him.'

Footsteps, the same childish voice calling, 'Daddy – Daddy! Phone! For you!' More footsteps. And then Mike is on the line.

'Emma?' He sounds eager, the same sort of eager she'd felt a few moments ago, but hearing his daughter's voice has completely dampened that now. Instead she's angry with him. What sort of a man is he to betray his family for the sake of a cheap affair?

'Mike. I just thought I should put you in the picture . . .' She tells him about Mel and Jo.

'That's amazing!' he says.

'I didn't want you going to a lot of trouble sorting out contacts in the American press when I might be able to find the answer a lot closer to home. Especially since I'm hoping you'll drop the story altogether. I know it meant a lot to you, but I really, really don't want it all to come out.'

'I know. I've already decided this isn't one I'm going to write. I'm not in the business of wrecking the lives of ordinary decent people to make a few bucks.' He sounds affronted. 'The only reason I was going to place the story was because I knew how much you wanted to find your mother. But if you've got another lead, that's fine by me.'

'Thank you. I'll make sure you're reimbursed your expenses for the trip to America.'

'There's no need for that. I'm doing a feature about canoeing in Florida, with maybe the Simon Beacham story to follow. Not involving your mother – just the story he told me about how he fetched up in that backwater along with a feisty Italian woman who was also anxious to hide away. I can write the whole lot off against tax, no problem. Plus another story has dropped into my lap – a holiday timeshare scam. So you see, I'm pretty busy right now. Funny how it all seems to come at once.'

That easy way of Mike's is getting to Emma again. She hardens her heart.

'That's about it, then. I don't want to waste any more of your time.'

'Emma,' he says, 'that's the last thing you've done.'

Her face is burning, the blood singing in her ears.

'Bye, Mike,' she says.

She hangs up, and it's all she can do not to burst into tears.

Maggie goes out into the garden, where Martin has been mowing the lawn. He's finished now and is sitting on the rustic bench beneath the apple tree where Emma once had her swing. His head is tipped back so as to catch the sun on his face, hands lying loosely over his jean-clad knees. But there is a sad, reflective look on his face, the same look he's worn ever since he learned that Fliss might have disappeared of her own volition rather than drowned. Love wells in Maggie, as it always has when she looks at Martin, but this time it is tempered with dread.

It's all going to come out – that she has known all these years that Fliss was alive – and Martin will never forgive her. Nothing they have shared will make up for it. Fliss was the great love of his life. She, Maggie, is second best. She's always known that. But second best has been good enough for her. She settled for it because having Martin and Emma was all she ever wanted. Being second best was better than coming nowhere. Without Fliss here to outshine her, second best has been fine. She's been happy knowing she's been a good wife to Martin, a good mother to Emma, and she thinks she's made Martin happy too. But now everything is going wrong. She's already lost Emma – the coldness in her voice when she speaks on the phone cuts Maggie to the quick. But the really terrible, unbearable thing will be losing Martin too. And she will lose him, she is under no illusion about that.

But she has to tell him first, before Emma does. She honestly doesn't know how she's going to do it, but do it she will. It has to come from her, in her words. And it has to be done now.

Maggie sits down on the seat beside Martin.

'The lawn's looking nice.' What stupid, mundane words, when her world is about to come to an end.

'Yes. It grows so fast this time of year I can't keep up with it.'

433

'The roses are doing well too.'

'They're your department, though.'

Maggie knots her hands around the edge of the seat, holding the warmed wood so tightly her knuckles turn white.

'Martin, I have to talk to you.' He glances at her, puzzled by the sudden seriousness of her tone. 'About Fliss,' she says.

She sees the way the muscles in his neck tense, the tightening of his jaw.

'What about Fliss? Emma hasn't found out where she is, has she?'

'No. Not yet, as far as I know.' She gives him a sideways glance. 'Do you want to know where she is?'

Martin huffs breath over his bottom lip.

'Well of course I do. Don't you?'

'I suppose. And there's a chance we might. By the strangest coincidence . . .' She tells him how Emma has met Mel, how she is going to London to see her. 'If anyone knows anything it will be Jo,' she says. 'They were always very close. It could be they kept in touch.'

Martin says nothing. He's gone back into his cave again.

'That's not what I want to talk about, though,' Maggie says. 'There's something I have to tell you — about her disappearance. And I honestly don't know how. You are going to hate me so much . . .' Her voice cracks. 'I'm so ashamed.' She breaks off, biting her lip. She can't look at him.

'You've known all along that she isn't dead,' Martin says flatly.

Maggie's head snaps up; her expression is startled and her voice, when she speaks, breathless with astonishment.

'You know?'

'I guessed. As soon as we found out the whole thing was a set-up, I guessed. Did you help her arrange it? She couldn't have done it on her own.'

'No! No, of course I didn't!' Maggie is shocked that he should think such a thing for a moment. 'I knew nothing about it until she phoned me from America.'

'And when was that?'

'Oh . . . I don't know. About a year after she disappeared, maybe a bit more. She wanted Emma, Martin! I couldn't allow that!'

'But why didn't you tell me?'

Maggie bows her head. 'It's all so complicated. I didn't want to hurt you. I thought it would be better if you thought she was dead than that she'd gone to those lengths to leave you. And then there was the insurance money. Your business had been in such dire straits, if you remember, and the payout on Fliss's life put you right. I had this awful feeling that if you knew that she wasn't dead at all, you'd feel you had to repay it . . .'

'Which I will, of course.'

'Martin, you can't! That would be to admit—'

'I'm not entitled to it, Maggie. End of story.' He slaps the bench with the flat of his hand, making it clear this is not up for discussion. Then he sighs. 'OK, I suppose you've put your case for not telling me at the time Fliss got in touch, but what about when Simon Beacham turned up here? Didn't you think I should know then?'

'What do you know about that?' Maggie asks, staggered.

A muscle tightens at the corner of Martin's mouth.

'So I was right,' he says grimly. 'I thought as much. Did he try to blackmail you? Am I right there, too?'

Her face was telling him that he was. 'Thought so. You see, when I discovered that Simon Beacham was involved in Fliss's disappearance, I remembered something. Something I'd totally forgotten about. Years ago, when Emma was just a little girl, she told me that a man had come here when I was at work. "A funny man, Daddy," she said. "I didn't like him, and neither did Maggie. She was shouting at him. But she went upstairs and got something and gave it to him and then he went away." I would have asked you about it, but you were out – it was your night for WI – and I thought it must have been one of those door-to-door salesmen selling tea towels out of a holdall and I forgot all about it. But it wasn't, was it? I reckon it was Simon Beacham.'

'Yes,' Maggie says softly, thinking it's no wonder Martin has been so quiet. He's been thinking all this through and has actually come up with the right answers. 'It was Simon. He came here asking for money, threatening to go to the newspapers with his story. But I got rid of him . . .' She breaks off, covering his hand with hers. 'Oh Martin, I should have told you, I know, and I am so, so sorry . . . What must you think of me?'

Martin removes his hand. He doesn't look at her.

'Truth to tell, I'm disappointed, Maggie. Fliss had her secrets – I always knew that. But you . . .' He shakes his head, gets up. 'I've got to get on. I have a load of lettuce plants to prick out.'

'Martin . . .' Maggie is utterly floored. 'You can't just . . .'

'Can't just what?'

'Leave it like this. We need to talk!'

'What else is there to say?'

He turns his back on her and walks away across the newly mown lawn towards the vegetable patch. Maggie starts after him, then stops. She knows him too well, knows his every mood. There's no point going after him now; she has to leave it until he's good and ready. It's how she's kept things so harmonious all these years, anticipating his reaction to any given situation, knowing when to make a fuss of him and when to leave him alone. But she also knows that this is far more serious than any of the minor domestic problems she's smoothed over in the past. She's wounded him very deeply, and she's terribly afraid that that wound will fester, and nothing will ever be the same again.

And besides . . . Now that he knows there is a very real chance that Fliss is still alive, he won't rest until he finds her. His heart belongs to her still; he'd forgive her anything. Maggie watches the man she loves with the whole of her being, the man who has been, and always will be, the only one for her, disappear into the greenhouse, a stiff, lonely figure, and she feels as if her heart will break.

THIRTY-NINE

It's just before 6 p.m. on Tuesday evening when Emma's National Express coach pulls into Victoria coach station. She'd decided that since Mel would not be free until the evening, she might as well go by road. It was a good deal cheaper than the train, and she didn't especially want to be hanging about in London for too long. The shops don't draw her – they never have – and she has no great desire to sit in cafés drinking endless cups of coffee while she waits for Mel. But the journey has been a long one, she's been hot, tired and bored, and once they hit the capital the traffic seemed to be one solid jam. Who'd live in London? Certainly not her!

She unloads her small overnight bag from the luggage rack, disembarks and looks around the echoing, grimy expanse that resembles a warehouse. The floor is covered with cigarette butts and droppings from the dozens of pigeons that swoop and flutter between the roof space and the daylight beyond the exhaust-stained walls. Mel had said she'd be waiting in the cafeteria; Emma locates it in a far corner and goes inside, hoping very much that Mel hasn't been detained. The cafeteria throngs with fed-up-looking travellers, drinking coffee from cardboard beakers and leaving half-eaten packets of sandwiches on plastic trays. A child in a pushchair is screaming blue murder. And then Emma sees a hand shoot up in greeting – Mel, getting up from one of the tables and coming towards her.

'Hi! You're here, then! Was it an awful journey?'

'Not a bundle of fun. But never mind.'

'Let's get out of here.' Mel turns, cannoning into a chair, which reminds Emma that she is only partially sighted; most of the time she manages so well, it's easy to forget. She rights the chair now, and Emma doesn't mention it or do anything to help her. Mel wouldn't appreciate it; she's trying very hard to be independent, and making a pretty good job of it.

'I thought we'd eat out,' Mel says. 'I know a nice little Italian not far from here. Are you OK with Italian?'

'I love it,' Emma says.

Mel leads the way, and again Emma is struck by how totally proficient she is at negotiating every obstacle, from lagging pedestrians to pelican crossings. They exchange a few words as they walk, but it's small talk only. The main business will wait until they're somewhere more private – the restaurant, Emma assumes. When they're seated at a table, their meals ordered and a bottle of red wine opened and poured, she looks at Mel expectantly. But Mel shakes her head.

'I think it might be better if we wait until we get home before I tell you what Mum told me,' she says.

Emma's having none of it. She feels she's waited long enough.

'It's all right, I know it's not good news. You already told me that. I've never known my mother, remember. I've lived my life thinking she died when I was just a little girl. OK, since Mike broke the news that she might not be dead, I have been hoping I might find her, meet her, but if you're going to tell me that's not going to happen, I'm not going to fall apart.'

Mel looks at her uncertainly.

'It's a pretty harrowing story.'

'And I'm a big girl. I just really, really want to know what happened to her.'

'Are you sure?'

'Absolutely.' Emma takes a gulp of her wine. 'See – a good Chianti and I'm ready for anything.'

'Well, for now I'll stick to the bare bones. I'm sorry, Emma, but yes, I'm afraid Fliss is dead. A long time ago.'

Though it is exactly what she was expecting, it's still a huge shock to Emma. She hadn't realised until this moment just how much she had wanted Fliss alive and well, a real living person, albeit much older than the fairy-tale princess of her vague memories. She hadn't realised that on an almost subconscious level she had dreamed of a tearful reconciliation. In rational moments she had known such a thing was highly unlikely, even given that she could discover Fliss's whereabouts. A mother who could abandon her, albeit unintentionally if Jeff was to be believed, and never come back to look for her in thirty years was hardly likely to welcome her with open arms now. But deep down she had cherished that little shard of hope. Which had now been utterly dashed.

'How did she die?' she asks, trying to hide the fact that a huge void has opened up inside her, a sense of loss out of all proportion really, given that she has, in her own words, lived her life believing her mother dead. 'Was it an accident? Or was she ill?'

Mel cradles her wine glass in her hands, twisting the stem between her fingers.

'That's the thing, Emma. The really remarkable, unbelievable thing.'

'She drowned for real,' Emma says. 'A sort of poetic justice.'

'No.' Still Mel hesitates, and Emma has no way of knowing it's not just that she's reluctant to describe the manner of Fliss's death; that she's afraid of rejection.

'What then?'

'You remember telling me that Jeff said he was in a helicopter crash in Vietnam?'

'Yes, and when he got back, Fliss had gone.'

'She thought he was dead. Everyone did – in fact Mum was really shocked to discover that he wasn't actually killed in the crash. But there was another reason why Fliss fled. She was pregnant. Jeff's father and stepmother had made it clear she was to leave their home once the baby was born. But they intended to keep the baby – Jefferson's grandchild. You have to understand – they were a very influential family. Fliss, as an illegal immigrant, wouldn't have stood a chance against them. She ran away to an island off the coast of Maine where she thought they'd never find her, and when things got tough, she sent for Mum. And Mum went over to America to be with her.'

Emma is having difficulty following all this. The details are coming too thick and fast.

'Sorry, you're losing me.'

'I'll fill you in later. You asked me how Fliss died, and that really is the crux of what I've got to tell you.'

Emma frowns, sensing that something important is coming. 'What happened?'

Mel stops fiddling with her glass, meets Emma's eyes across the table.

'She died in childbirth.'

Emma closes her eyes briefly.

'That's awful! Oh poor Fliss!'

'I know. She haemorrhaged, I think. Mum couldn't do anything to stop the bleeding – they were all alone at sea in Jeff's boat, heading for Florida, when it happened. But the baby was fine. And when she was dying, Fliss made Mum promise . . .' She falters.

'Promise what?' Emma asks urgently, though she actually already has an inkling where this is going.

Mel, with whom she had bonded on sight. Mel, who had taken to sailing as if she'd been born to it. Mel, who actually isn't so different to her physically. Fair hair. Pert nose. Same build . . .

'Promise what?'

'That she would bring the baby home to England. Take care of her. Can you guess what I'm going to say, Emma? That baby was me. I'm Fliss's daughter too, though I never knew it.' She smiles, almost apologetically. 'I'm your sister.'

If the coach journey to London had seemed endless, the journey home bears no relation to real time at all. Emma sits staring out of the window as London mutates into countryside and sees nothing at all.

They'd talked late into the night, she and Mel, and she'd barely slept, but she's still wide awake, every brain cell in overdrive. This is beyond belief. Melanie Thomas is her sister.

When she gets home, she's going to have to break it to her father and Maggie. She's going to have to get in touch with Jeff Hewson and tell him he has a daughter – she and Mel had decided that since she had met Jeff, she should be the one to make the initial contact. And she supposes she really should fill Mike in on the end of the story; she owes him that much – or is that just her way of finding yet another excuse to speak to him again?

Really, though, she can't concentrate on any of that at the moment. It's the details of the story Mel told her that are going round and round in her head. *Oh Mum, Mum, how frightened you must have been. How alone. Why did you do it – any of it? Why?*

But she knows. If Fliss felt about Jeff the way she feels about Mike, it's entirely understandable. Right now she'd give up everything just to see him, hear his voice. Oh shit, shit, is it a curse on the Penrose women, to love where they have no business to love? But she's not her mother. She won't make the same mistakes.

It's getting dark by the time the National Express pulls into the bus station. Emma collects her car and drives home. The answering machine is flashing as she lets herself into the hall, a winking red eye in the semi-dark. She dumps her bag, switches on some lights, puts the kettle on and goes back into the hall to see who's been leaving her messages.

The first is her dentist's receptionist, informing her rather curtly that she was expected for a check-up at ten thirty this morning, and that she will be liable for a fine for missing it. Emma curses. The dental appointment had completely slipped her mind.

The second is her father, and he sounds anxious.

'Emma – sorry to bother you, love, but is Maggie with you? Can you give me a call when you get in?'

A prickle of alarm. Emma picks up the phone and dials her

441

father's number. He answers immediately, as if he was waiting beside it.

'Dad? What's this about Maggie?'

'It's probably nothing, but . . . She's not with you, I take it?'

'No, I've been to London. I've only just this minute got back. Isn't Maggie at home, then?'

'She's not, no. She wasn't here when I got back from work. I don't know where in the world she can be. I'm a bit worried, Emma. It's not like her.'

It's certainly not. Maggie is such a homebody. Apart from her WI, she rarely goes anywhere.

'She's not visiting a friend?' But it's highly unlikely, Emma knows. In the morning for coffee, possibly. In the afternoon for a cup of tea, perhaps. But she's always home by five, making a start on Martin's dinner.

'It's very strange, Dad.'

'I suppose it's too early to be really concerned. She's taken this business about Fliss very hard; she probably just wants a bit of time to herself, to think things through. But all the same . . .'

Emma knows what he's thinking. She's thinking the same. If Maggie disappears as Fliss did, the nightmare is far from over.

'Keep me in the picture, Dad.'

'Will do. Oh . . . how did you get on in London, by the way?'

'It'll keep, Dad.'

There's no way she's going to add to his troubles by telling him the whole story just now.

Tired as she is, Emma decides she'll make the telephone call to Jeff and get it over and done with. If she leaves it until morning, it will be the middle of the night in America, and she has no idea how the rest of her day will pan out. If Maggie still hasn't come home, she may have to go out with Martin looking for her. Trouble is, she doesn't have Jeff's contact details. To get them she'll have to ring Mike.

Her stomach knots at the prospect, but there's no way round

it. She half wonders if perhaps his wife will answer the phone; half hopes she will. If she hears her voice, as she heard Daisy's, it will make her a real person. Perhaps that will make it easier for her to forget Mike.

But it's Mike himself who answers.

'Sorry to ring so late,' Emma says, 'but something has come up and I really need to speak to Jeff Hewson.'

'Ah. Right. And there was I thinking perhaps you were missing me.'

Bastard! she thinks. He wouldn't be saying that if his wife was within earshot.

'You do have his number, don't you?'

'I do.' The teasing has gone out of his voice now. 'Hang on, I'll just get it.' After a few moments, he's back. 'Here we are. Ready?' He dictates two telephone numbers, one for the Florida condo, one for Eastville, Maine, and Emma writes them down.

'Am I allowed to ask what this is about?' he says.

Emma hesitates. He assured her he won't be using the story, that he's now busy with another project, but all the same she's wary. This whole thing has become so newsworthy, will he be able to resist?

'I really don't know that I should tell you,' she says. 'At least not before I've spoken to Jeff Hewson. He has to hear it first. Whether or not he wants to tell you is up to him.'

'OK.' There's a small silence, then Mike says: 'But I really would like to see you again, Emma. And not just because of the story. I think you know what I'm saying.'

Her heart leaps treacherously. Oh, how she wants to see him again too! But it's not going to happen.

'I don't think that's a good idea, Mike,' she says. And slams down the telephone before she can weaken.

She sinks into a chair, her head in her hands. What a mess! She's been on emotional overload ever since Mike appeared on the scene, and it's just getting worse. More and more complicated, more and more draining. And now, on top of it all, Maggie seems to have gone missing, and Emma realises just how worried about her she is. It is so unlike Maggie to go off without telling Martin, and to have failed to come home at this time of night . . .

Anxiety makes a hard knot in Emma's throat. This whole business must have upset Maggie dreadfully, particularly since she must feel really guilty about the secret she's kept all these years. She must be beside herself with worry as to the consequences of it all coming out. Emma has been so angry with her she hasn't really stopped to wonder how Maggie is feeling; now, for the first time, she can almost, if not quite, see just how devastating it must be for her; almost, if not quite, understand. She should have told them, of course she should, but Emma is in no doubt that Maggie was telling the truth when she said she had thought it was for the best. That was Maggie all over, a little bit controlling, a little bit too sure that she knew best, but kind, loving, self-sacrificing even.

She finds herself thinking not of the Maggie who has become a stranger to her in these last weeks, but of the Maggie who has always been a mother to her.

That Maggie was always first in line to collect her from play-school so that Emma wouldn't think she'd been forgotten – she could still remember how, when the doors opened, Maggie would be there, perhaps holding Emma's little umbrella, the pink one decorated with ladybirds, if it was raining, or with her tricycle if it was fine. Emma would run to her, wrapping her arms around her, feeling safe, so safe.

That same Maggie bought all her clothes and shoes – always Clarks, because the Clarks shop measured her feet properly with a sliding scale. She was the one who baked fairy cakes, letting Emma help, and lick the spoon afterwards. Who was always there at school concerts and prizegivings and sports days, who taught her to play card games like Newmarket and sevens, who made clothes for her doll, Arabella. The one who told her the facts of life and was always awake when Emma came home from her first dates, though she pretended not to be. The Maggie who was always there for her, through sunshine and showers.

Now Maggie's world has fallen apart, and has Emma been there for her? Not a bit of it. She's been too busy being angry. And a part of her still is. But she also knows she does care about Maggie, her distress, and now her whereabouts. Where the hell can she be? Is she all right?

The doorbell rings, making her jump. She goes to answer it, slightly apprehensive and wondering who it can be at this time of night. It would be sensible to have a spyhole or a chain, but she has neither. She's never been the cautious type.

She opens the door, and relief floods through her.

Standing on the doorstep is Maggie.

'Maggie!'

'Oh Emma, I'm sorry turning up like this, but I didn't know where else to go.'

Emma has never seen Maggie look, or sound, so helpless. Maggie the strong, the controlled, who always has a solution for everything, stands there in her lightweight poplin shower coat, clutching her oversized handbag to her chest, looking utterly lost.

'Come in, for goodness' sake! What are you *doing*? Dad's out of his mind with worry about you.'

'I shouldn't think so.'

'He is! And so was I. Sit down, let me make you a cup of tea, and then I must ring him, let him know you're safe.'

'No, don't do that, please. I don't want him to know where I am. If I could just stay here tonight, I'll be gone in the morning.'

'Of course you can stay. But you're not going anywhere. This is madness, Maggie!'

'It's for the best.'

'Oh don't be so silly! Look, I'm going to ring Dad now, this minute. Just sit there. You look absolutely awful.'

This much is true. Maggie is very pale and drawn, her normally immaculate hair is untidy, and mascara smudged underneath her eyes gives away the fact that she's been crying. Emma leaves her in the living room and goes into the hall to telephone Martin. There's no reply.

'He's not answering,' she says, going back to Maggie.

'He's probably in bed and asleep.'

'I doubt it. More likely he's out scouring the streets looking for you. Whatever are you thinking of, Maggie? Have you two had a row or something?'

It's a pretty unlikely scenario – Emma can't ever remember Maggie and Martin rowing – but these are unlikely times.

'We haven't had a row, no,' Maggie says. 'He just won't talk to me. I don't think he can even bear to look at me. Hardly surprising, really.' She fishes in her bag for a handkerchief, wiping the palms of her hands with it as if she can somehow wipe away her guilt. 'To be honest, I wasn't sure if you'd let me in. You must hate me.'

'Of course I don't hate you, Maggie,' Emma says. 'I was angry that you should keep something like that secret all these years. Hurt too. And I'm sure Dad feels the same. You just have to give him time.'

Maggie shakes her head.

'Things can never be the same. That's why I think it's best if I just go.'

'Oh don't be so silly!'

'It's not silly. It's facing facts at last. I've only ever been second best to your dad. It was always Fliss with him. And now, if he finds her – well, I don't want to be around, and I don't suppose they'd want me either.'

Emma takes a deep breath.

'Maggie – Fliss isn't coming back,' she says.

'How can you possibly know that?'

Emma can hear the kettle boiling in the kitchen. 'I'll make the tea. Have you had anything to eat today?'

'No, but I don't want anything.'

'I'll make you a sandwich anyway. And then I think it's time we sat down and had a good talk.'

* * *

They do talk, long into the night, Emma telling Maggie all that Mel told her, and there are a lot of tears and deep emotion. Eventually Emma is able to get hold of Martin, who had, as she thought, been out looking any- and everywhere for Maggie. When at last they go to bed, both sleep late, and are woken only when Martin arrives. Emma tactfully leaves them alone.

'What on earth possessed you, going off like that?' he asks Maggie.

'I didn't think you wanted me around,' Maggie says simply.

'You silly, silly girl. Of course I want you around.'

'After what I did? I can't blame you if you never want to see me again. I know it's always been Fliss with you.'

'Maggie,' Martin says, 'I did love Fliss, very much. Still do, I suppose. But I'd have thought you and I have been together long enough for you to know I love you too. You've been everything to me these last thirty years. I don't know what I'd have done without you. And I don't know what I'd do without you now. So let's not have any more talk of you leaving.'

He puts his arm round her; she buries her face in his shoulder for a moment. Then: 'Martin, there's something you should know,' she says. 'Something Emma has found out.' She hesitates, then calls to Emma. 'Are you there, darling?'

Emma, who has been hovering, comes back in.

'Emma – will you tell your dad what you told me? About what happened to poor Fliss?'

Emma does.

When they've gone, Emma feels drained, but relieved. At least there are no more secrets within their immediate family. And she's pretty sure, too, that things are going to be OK between Maggie and Martin. His anxiety when he thought she had disappeared too had broken down the barriers, and there's no doubt in Emma's mind that he does love Maggie, and has done for a very long time, even if she hadn't been able to bring herself to believe it. Emma thinks that her father has probably been far happier with

Maggie than he ever could have been with Fliss, and in the end the bond of the years, and all they have shared, is strong enough to withstand the shock revelations of the past weeks.

She hopes very much that she will find a love like that, but she's not holding her breath.

What she must do, however, as soon as America is awake, is put in a call to Jeff.

Jeff Hewson is back in Maine, back in the driving seat at Hewson Enterprises. This morning he was up at the crack of dawn for a breakfast meeting; he knows he'll still be at his desk come late evening. The business is his life – that and the Sunsail Trust, his charity for disadvantaged youngsters to experience the joys of sailing – and has been for so long now he can't imagine anything different. Perhaps that was the reason he'd kicked so hard against it when he was young – he'd known the business would devour him whole. But it has been his saviour, too. When he was buried deep in keeping Hewson Enterprises at the forefront of the ship-building industry, there was less time to think about Fliss, to miss her and mourn her. The business had gone some way to filling the vast empty hole she had left in his life and in his heart.

He'd never married again; never wanted to. There had been other women, but they'd never lasted long. No one had ever come close to matching up to her, and in any case, as far as he was concerned Fliss was still his wife. He'd never quite let go of the hope that one day he'd find her again, though he'd thought that he'd come to accept at last that it wasn't going to happen.

And then, out of the blue, her daughter Emma and the reporter investigating her original disappearance had turned up, and suddenly she was at the forefront of his consciousness once more. Just as in the early years, after he returned from captivity in Vietnam to find her gone, he could think of nothing else. Try as he might to concentrate on the business in hand, his mind kept wandering back to the unexpected visitors to his condo in Florida.

It wasn't that he was expecting them to have any more success in finding Fliss than he had done, more that they had stirred up the past. Fliss's daughter was so like her mother had been the last time he'd seen her, it was almost as if he'd been visited by a ghost, and it had revived all his precious memories of her and the time they'd shared.

He wondered too how his life might have been different had she not disappeared. Whether they'd have gone on to have a family of their own, who would, by now, be grown up themselves. One thing was for sure, he'd never have become so centred on the business – if he'd been able to find her, he'd never have left her alone again.

He thought too of how ecstatic she'd have been when Emma walked through the door, remembering her heartbreak when she'd come to the decision that she must, for Emma's own good, leave her with her father in England. He was surprised, actually, that she hadn't made contact with her daughter in the intervening years. He'd have thought that in the end, the pull of the maternal bond would prove too strong to resist. But it seemed she hadn't, and now the fact is filling him with deep foreboding.

Back at his desk, he's trying to put Fliss and Emma out of his mind. He buzzes Julie, his secretary, to bring him a fresh coffee and opens the file that was the subject of the breakfast meeting, and which has the makings of another lucrative contract. He's just dragging his attention back to where it belongs when the telephone on his desk buzzes.

'Mr Hewson.' It's Julie. 'I'm sorry to interrupt you, but I have a call on the line from England. A young lady who's insisting on speaking with you. She's giving her name as Emma Dunning.'

Jeff's pulse quickens; he pushes the file to one side. Million-dollar deals? They can wait!

'Put her through, Julie,' he says.

Ten minutes – fifteen? Really he has no idea – later, Jeff is pouring himself a stiff drink from the fridge in his office. Not something he usually does at this time of day, but then, nothing about today is usual.

He's in total shock – although so far he knows only the bare bones of the story, it's enough to send him reeling. Fliss, his beloved Fliss, is dead, and has been all the years he's been searching for her. But he has a daughter. A daughter! Jeff empties his glass in one swallow and refills it, the questions coming thick and fast.

Did his father and Marcia know that Fliss was pregnant? They must have done, surely. But he can't ask them about it. His father has been dead now getting on for ten years, and Marcia suffers from Alzheimer's. He'll have to go to England if he wants to know everything Jo Best can tell him, and he will. Soon as he can book a flight. And he'll meet the daughter he never knew he had too.

For the first time in thirty-odd years he has something other than the business and his charity in his life. Jeff had almost forgotten how good it could feel.

Emma rings Mel.

'I've spoken to Jeff,' she says without preamble.

She hears Mel take a deep breath. This is huge for her, Emma knows.

'And?'

'As you can imagine, he was staggered.'

'But pleased?'

'Definitely that. He wants to meet you. I took the liberty of giving him your phone number, so – expect a call.'

'Oh my goodness! I just don't believe this – any of it! First a sister, now a father!'

'It is pretty amazing, I must agree. Anyway, it's over to you, Mel, on the Jeff front. But actually, I'd like to meet him again if he comes to England – or if you're going to America and want some company. If I won't be intruding, that is.'

'Of course you wouldn't. Though maybe not the first time . . .'

'I understand. It's just that . . . well, he was the man my mother fell in love with, the reason all this happened . . .'

'Absolutely. Your mother, my mother – our mother!'

When she puts the phone down, Mel is so excited she feels quite sick. And wishes desperately there was someone she could share it with. There's Jo, of course; she's pretty sure Jo will be delighted for her. But the person she really wants to tell is Mark.

Stupid, stupid. He doesn't want her, he's made that perfectly plain, and yet still she can't forget him. But she has to. She must count herself lucky to have found a sister and a father she never knew she had. Anything else is a dream too far.

FORTY

I t's thirty-odd years since Jeff has been to England. He remem-
bers it as being quiet and peaceful – uncluttered roads, midweek
half-day closing for the shops, and nothing at all open on a Sunday.
Country pubs where the landlords called time in the early afternoon and again in the evening, cinemas showing two films back
to back, the main feature and a black-and-white 'B' movie, plus
Pathé News. Scooters and bubble cars, fish and chips wrapped in
newspaper, and prawns and cockles in soggy paper twists. He
wonders how much it will have changed, become more like
America, and hopes it hasn't. He'd like the England of his youth
to be exactly as it was then, preserved, along with his special
memories, for all time.

It's a vain hope, of course, he knows. As impossible as that
his beloved Fliss will be there in her pedal-pushers and gingham.
That Fliss would have disappeared long ago, even if she were
still alive. She'd have been in her sixties by now, like him, the
bright gold of her hair flecked with grey, her face showing the
signs of too much exposure to wind and sun. But essentially
she'd still be the same Fliss – he can't imagine her ever changing
inside. And his heart aches that they have not been able to grow
old together. But at least he has the consolation of knowing
that she didn't choose to disappear again. At least his memories
of what they shared are unsullied by doubt. They remain as

pure as they are precious. A bright shining love in the summer of his life.

And she has left him the gift of a daughter.

Jeff doesn't want to to think about how Fliss must have suffered. Not now, coming in to land at Heathrow. He's agonised enough over that since learning the truth, cursing himself for not being there when she needed him most, even though he knows there was nothing he could have done to change that. It's not in his nature to blame fate for his misfortunes; he likes to feel he's in control. But on that occasion he wasn't. As a soldier in the US army, he had no free will.

They've landed now. Jeff retrieves his bag from the overhead locker and is glad he hasn't brought any hold luggage with him. This bag might be pigskin with a designer logo rather than the holdall he used to carry, but he can still travel light. A change of shirt and underwear, a toothbrush, shaving kit and comb, a pair of crease-resistant pants and a jumper for the cool English evenings – what more does he need?

Melanie is coming to the airport to meet him. He'd said not to, that they could meet at the Savoy, where he is staying, but she was insistent. He wonders if he'll recognise her; if she'll recognise him. Perhaps she'll have one of those boards with his name on. Or hers.

Melanie. He likes the sound it makes on his tongue. Fliss chose it, apparently, before she died, and Jo Best stuck with it.

He doesn't quite know what he thinks of Jo; he's grateful to her, of course, for being there for Fliss when he couldn't be, but he can't help feeling angry that she has deprived him of all his daughter's growing-up years. He can understand that Fliss would have wanted her baby kept out of his family's hands if she believed he was dead; he can't blame her for that. His father was work-obsessed and Marcia was a prize bitch – still is, by all accounts. Giving the staff at her luxury care home one hell of a time of it. But Melanie would have been fine when he came home. He'd have given her the world . . .

No sense thinking that way now, though. He's through immigration and customs, walking towards the arrivals hall, scanning the faces of the crowd, three deep, on the other side of the barrier.

And there she is. Somehow, without a shred of doubt, he knows it's her. Not because she's the image of Fliss, as Emma is, though there are similarities in build and hair colour, but from some deep instinct. Later, he'll notice things about her that are very like his mother – Betty's smile, some of her mannerisms – and even something of himself. But it's not that yet. It's just an invisible connection, a deep knowing that he doesn't stop to question. He starts towards her; she sees him and knows him too. He can see the tears sparkling in her eyes, the tremor of her mouth.

'Melanie?' he says.

She nods. Throws her arms round him. Buries her face in his shoulder.

And a wave of emotion more powerful than anything he has felt in more than thirty years sweeps over him.

His daughter. His and Fliss's. Jeff holds her, and feels he will never want to let her go again.

'Daddy,' Daisy says, 'why are you always so miserable these days?'

'Miserable? I'm not miserable!'

'You are too.' Daisy stands defiantly in the doorway of Mike's study, hands on hips, small face pursed up in a scowl. 'You've been in my room, haven't you? The stuff from my secrets box is all mixed up. I was sorting it out and now I'm going to have to start all over again.'

'Your room was a tip, Daisy. I tidied it up, that's all.'

'I was tidying it up! I knew where everything was and now I don't.'

'Well I'm sorry, but I don't see why that makes me miserable.'

'It's not just that. It's everything. You made meatballs for tea, and you know I hate them.'

'Rubbish. All children love meatballs.'

'I don't. They're yuck. And you made me eat them. And you wouldn't let me watch *Grange Hill* . . .'

'Because you watch too much TV.'

'Hmm!' Daisy snorts. 'It's that lady, isn't it? You've been cross ever since you went to America with her. Don't you like her?'

Mike sighs, switches off his word processor. Clearly he's going to get no peace until she's had her say. Just like her mother. Just like Bev.

'I don't not like her, sweetheart. The trouble is I like her too much, but she doesn't like me.'

'How can she not like you?'

'Hard to believe, eh? Now, will you please find something to do until bedtime so I can get some work done?'

'I've got loads to do sorting out all my stuff that you messed up.'

'That's OK, then.'

Daisy huffs, and departs. But she's too busy thinking about what Mike said to concentrate on sorting her spy box. And she comes to a decision. Checking that Mike is still busy on his word processor, she goes to the hall, checks the address book that lives on the table there, picks up the telephone and dials.

It's about time somebody did something to lift Daddy out of his foul mood. And it seems like she's the one who's going to have to do it.

The phone rings in Emma's flat. What now? she wonders. She's beginning to get used to shocks. But even so, she's totally unprepared for this one.

A child's voice. Very prim, very determined.

'This is Daisy Bond.'

'Daisy?'

'Yes. I'm just ringing to ask you something. Will you please, please be nice to my daddy? You're making him miserable, and I'm the one he takes it out on. That's really all I wanted to say.'

For a moment Emma is too taken by surprise to reply.

'Please?' Daisy reiterates.

'Well, it's nice to speak to you, Daisy,' Emma stalls, 'but I really don't understand. Why . . .?'

'It's easy. He likes you and you don't like him and I wish you did.'

Emma gives her head a little shake.

'I do like him, Daisy. But that's neither here nor there. What would your mummy say if she knew you were ringing me?'

There's a silence; Emma imagines Daisy is chagrined. Then she says:

'I don't have a mummy.'

'I'm sorry . . .?'

'I don't have a mummy. She died. And that made Daddy miserable. And then he was kind of OK when he met you. And now he's not,' Daisy says matter-of-factly. 'So will you please, please talk to him again, because if you don't, he's going to drive me mad.'

Emma doesn't know whether to laugh or cry.

'Is he there now?' she asks.

'Well of course he is! He doesn't leave me on my own!' Daisy sounds outraged. 'If he has to go away, Granny and Grandpa look after me.'

'So do you think I could speak to him now?'

'I suppose. As long as you don't tell him I phoned you. I think he might be cross with me.'

'I won't tell him. We'll pretend I'm the one who made the call and you answered it.'

'OK.'

In the ensuing silence, Emma thinks she can hear the beating of her own heart. Then Mike is on the line.

'Emma?'

'Mike,' she says. 'I was just wondering . . . I've got quite a lot to tell you. Do you think we could meet? I know I've been a bit off lately, but you'll have to put it down to emotional overload. I'm sorry.'

'No apology necessary. When . . .?'

Now! she wanted to say. *Tonight! This minute!*

'As soon as you can make it, really.'

'Tomorrow? I can come down to you, or . . .'

'Meet you halfway.'

'Great,' she says.

She wants to dance and sing; it's crazy, unbelievable. How could she have got it so wrong when it had felt so right? How could she have thought for a single moment that he was the sort of man to cheat on a wife? No wonder he'd been so hurt when she'd cut him after the night they'd spent together, after the closeness they'd achieved. She can only suppose that with everything else that had been going on she just hadn't been thinking straight. Now . . . it's early days, of course. But Emma feels instinctively that this is the start of something wonderful.

FORTY-ONE

THE LINK

Mark Moss has spent the last few years trying to forget Melanie Thomas, or Melanie Payne as she was when they were an item. He'd thought that taking the job in Singapore would be the answer; at least if he was on the other side of the world there would be no danger of bumping into her. It had been a golden opportunity in any case, one that he'd intended her to share in. He'd been going to ask her to marry him, had even bought the engagement ring, a single diamond set in white gold. But that was before he'd found out the awful truth. After that, all he could do was cut loose. He hadn't told her the reason, didn't want to inflict on her the same torment that he was suffering. He'd simply said that it was over, and left the country. But the miles between them hadn't helped; he still couldn't get her out of his head or his heart, and it had hurt that she'd married, quite soon after their break-up, though he'd told himself it was good she'd recovered so quickly.

Back in England, the danger of meeting Mel was ever-present. You'd think – wouldn't you? – that in a city the size of London it was highly unlikely. But no, he'd run into her, literally, on the steps leading down to Oxford Circus Underground. That in itself would have been had enough, but worse, something dreadful had happened to her since he'd last seen her. She'd lost an eye. Shocked, he made enquiries of mutual friends and learned that she'd been

458

involved in an accident following a bust-up with her husband, and that since then he'd divorced her – because he couldn't come to terms with her injury, he was told.

Mark had flamed with fury. He wanted to kill the bastard, or at least beat seven bells out of him. And he wanted to comfort Mel, tell her that to him she was still every bit as beautiful as she had been before. That he'd take care of her, make sure nobody ever hurt her again. But he couldn't. He had to keep his distance.

The best option would be to go abroad again. There was another posting coming up, this time in Hong Kong; his boss had already made noises about it, suggesting that Mark would be just the man for the job, and he rather thought he would take it. Anything to get him out of London, and well away from Melanie.

His friends are concerned about him, he knows. Can't understand why he's still footloose and fancy-free when they have all settled down to family life, married and even divorced again, some of them. They're forever trying to fix him up with one girl or another. Tonight is just another instance. Dan Collier, one of the lads he shared a bachelor pad with in the old days, has arranged a foursome, himself and his wife Fiona, and a blind date for Mark. They've been to a show and now they're eating in an upmarket West End restaurant. It's been a pleasant enough evening, and his date, whose name is Louise, is a very attractive girl – pretty face, long dark hair worn loose and the kind of figure that makes men's eyes stand out on stalks. But Mark can't work up any enthusiasm for her, though Dan is clearly hopeful, giving him sly winks, and Fiona, whose friend Louise is, is also going at the matchmaking none too subtly.

'Well?' Dan says when the girls pop out to the ladies' room between courses. 'What do you think? She's a right little cracker, isn't she?'

'Yes, I suppose she is,' Mark says non-committally.

'Oh mate, what is the matter with you? She's drop-dead

gorgeous! Could be the next Julia Roberts with that hair and those eyes, not to mention all her other attributes . . .'

'I'd noticed. I'd have a job not to,' Mark says drily. He has, after all, been sitting opposite a cleavage to rival the Grand Canyon throughout the meal.

'How can you not fancy her?' Dan says. 'If I wasn't a married man I'd be after her myself.'

'Well I'm not you.'

'And she's not Melanie.' Dan sighs, shakes his head, empties the wine bottle between their glasses and signals to the waiter for more. 'I don't know why the hell you two broke up. You always seemed so right together. Why don't you look her up? Give it another go? She's had a pretty rough time of it since you've been gone. She could do with a bit of spoiling. Still, I suppose that's on the cards anyway, the way things have panned out.'

Mark's eyes narrow. 'What do you mean?'

Dan guffaws. 'She's a bloody heiress, isn't she? Turns out her real father is an American who owns a shipbuilding company and Christ knows what else besides. He's been over here to meet her, and the word on the block is it's only a matter of time before she heads off to America. Startling stuff, eh?'

Mark is staring at his friend incredulously. 'Her real father? Are you saying Goff wasn't her father?'

'Certainly wasn't. And her mother wasn't her mother either, if you get my meaning. According to what Mel told Fiona, her *real* mother was the woman her *other* mother used to sail with. Anna must have adopted her or something, though Fiona didn't seem to think it was that straightforward. Oh, I don't suppose I'm making a lot of sense, but you can take it from me, it's true.'

Mark sits forward, elbows on the table. His head is spinning.

'Let's get this straight. You're saying Anna and Goff aren't Mel's real parents?'

'That's what I'm saying. Where are those girls? How can they take so long powdering their noses or whatever it is they do? And what the hell is up with you, mate? Anybody would think I'd just told you her ma and pa are bloody aliens from Mars.'

Mark is certainly visibly shaken. In fact, he's gone into a world of his own.

'What?' Dan asks, genuinely puzzled.

Mark pulls himself together with an effort.

'Nothing.'

From where he's sitting, he can see the staircase leading up to the cloakrooms; the girls are coming back, taking the stairs slowly, chatting as they go, little, round Fiona, tall, slender Louise with hair falling all the way down to her cleavage. A beautiful girl certainly. But not Mel. Never Mel. The only woman he's ever wanted.

And now, by some miracle, it seems there's not a single reason why he can't be with her. All that heartache. All that guilt. All that wasted time. And all unnecessary.

'Do you have a phone number for her?' he asks urgently.

'For who? Louise?'

'No – Melanie.'

Dan looks staggered.

'I haven't, no. Fiona will have. But . . .'

'Can you get it for me?'

'I suppose so – but not now. You can't ask for another woman's phone number when you're on a date with—'

'I know that. I'll give you a bell tomorrow.'

Dan shakes his head again. This is all quite beyond him, particularly in his inebriated state. But he's sober enough to realise one thing. This blind date is not going to be the success he and Fiona had hoped. In fact, from here on in, it's going to be tough going.

When he's back in his flat, having said good night to a disappointed Louise with a chaste peck on the cheek, Mark pours himself a large whisky and put a tape in the deck – the Last Night of the Proms. It's a long time since he's played it – it reminded him too much of Mel. They bought it after that fantastic night when they went to the Albert Hall, gloried in the music and the atmosphere, sang along with the sea shanties, waved their flags for 'Land of Hope and Glory'. Tonight, though, it's exactly what he wants – to remember how good they were together, the sound of her voice, the sweet scent of her perfume, the softness of her body in his arms. All the things that have disgusted him these last years, all the things that have torn him apart since he found out . . .

Mark had always known he was adopted. His parents, bless them, had never made any secret of it. And they'd raised no objection, either, when he told them he'd like to try to find his real mother. All they had been able to tell him about her was that she was very young when she had him, a single girl with no means of keeping him. He'd never expected to know more than that, but when the law was changed to allow adopted children to access their original birth certificate, he'd done just that.

Joanna Best, that was his mother's name. The space where his father's details should have been was blank. He'd tried the address at which she had been living at the time of his birth, but no one there knew her or what had become of her, and he'd decided not to pursue it. All very well for his mother to say she was cool with what he'd intended to do; he couldn't help feeling that deep down she'd be hurt, and he didn't want that. She'd been a fantastic mother – she *was* his mother – and he didn't want her to feel that he wanted more.

It was only after he met Mel and knew that he wanted to marry her that he thought about it again. His adoptive mother was dead now, and somehow it had suddenly seemed important that he should know more about who he was, what traits or weaknesses he carried in his genes. He went back to square one with his investigations, this time pursuing them more thoroughly, and what he found out shocked him to the core.

Joanna Best had become Anna Payne. Which meant that Melanie was his sister.

The shame and disgust that Mark felt then was indescribable. He ended the relationship without explanation and left for Singapore to put as much distance as possible between them. But still he hadn't been able to get Mel out of his head or his heart, and he had castigated himself for being a sick pervert. It had played its part in his inability to engage with anyone else – quite apart from the fact that none of them measured up to Mel, he felt like a leper, and no longer trusted his own judgement.

But now . . . now suddenly the instruments of torture have been whisked away. He feels euphoric in a way he'd never have dreamed could be possible ever again. It's all he can do not to phone Dan now, this minute, and ask for Mel's number. But that will have to wait for morning.

A cold blade of doubt suddenly pierces the euphoria. Suppose she doesn't feel the same way? She's not the girl he left; she's been married and divorced, discovered a new, wealthy family in America. She may well have put him, and all they shared, firmly behind her.

That's something he must be prepared for. But the joy, the lightness of spirit, refuses to be quelled for long.

Tomorrow promises to be the first day of the rest of his life.

'This is beyond belief,' Mel says.

It had been startling enough to find Mark on her doorstep – a Mark who was obviously very worried that she wouldn't want to see him, let alone talk to him – but what he's told her is more incredible yet. She's listened in astonishment to what he had to tell her, but now, at last, it's beginning to sink in. He didn't leave her because he didn't want her any more. From what he's saying, he's never stopped loving her. And the real reason he cut her out of his life is the thing she simply cannot get her head around.

Mark is Jo's son, placed for adoption at birth. In a heart-to-heart since all the secrets of the past have come out, Jo had told Mel about him, and Mel had seen for herself the pain and regret Jo had lived with for most of her life, the longing to find him again. But that the lost child would turn out to be Mark – her Mark – is, as she says, simply beyond belief. Beyond belief, confusing, but also rather wonderful.

'I don't know what to say,' she whispers, but already the happiness is beginning to swell, a flood tide of emotion that needs no explanation.

'Me neither.'

For a long time neither of them say anything at all.

Jo – Anna – is shaking with nervousness. It's not like her – normally she takes everything in her stride. But this is different. This is huge. She is about to be reunited with the son she gave up as a baby. With the added pressure that he is the man Mel is in love with.

Jo never met Mark when he and Mel were an item. Strange, really, since she had had a nodding acquaintance at least with most of Mel's boyfriends. But that was just it, of course. They had been *boys*, the ones Mel had gone out with when she had been a teenager, living at home. They'd called in for coffee, sprawled on Jo's tiny back lawn with their ghetto blasters, even stayed for supper, or tea on a Sunday. But by the time Mel met Mark, she was living in the city, in a shared bedsit, and things had not become serious enough to warrant introducing him to her mother before Jo had taken off on her year's sabbatical, or 'wrinkly's gap year', as Mel had teasingly called it.

She'd completely missed out on Mark, and had formed an active dislike of him for making Mel so unhappy. Now, it seems, it was entirely her fault that it had all gone wrong. If she'd told Mel the truth long ago, Mel would surely have told Mark and the dreadful misunderstanding would never have arisen. It followed that Mel would never have married Brian, and the accident that had cost her her eye would never have happened. Besides which, Jo would have met her son long ago.

Jo feels thoroughly chastened, and her nervousness at meeting Mark is made worse by the fact that she thinks he's bound to blame her for all that has happened. She desperately wants to see him, hold him in her arms, but she's also very, very afraid of what he will think of her.

They're due any minute, Mark and Mel. Jo has made a huge effort – she's bought fresh cream cakes and a bottle of sparkling wine – champagne seemed a bit over-the-top and presumptuous. She's tidied all the clutter away from the living room and cut enough roses to fill a vase. And she's even put on some lipstick, almost unheard of for her, and some mascara from a wand that Mel had left on her dressing table.

She thinks she hears a car door slam and rushes to the window. They're coming up the path, Mel leading the way. Jo's heart gives a tremendous leap into her throat. Oh my God, he is so tall, so handsome! She can't equate him at all with the baby in the blue blanket she was forced to give away. It can't be him – can it?

She hurries out to open the door, but she's too late. Mel has already used her own key, and they're coming in. Jo stands for a moment, hands pressed to her mouth, tears filling her eyes as she just stares at him.

'Mum – this is Mark . . .' Mel says, but really there is no need.

'Mark . . . Oh Mark!'

He's staring at her too, so that their eyes are locked. And suddenly she's not afraid any more. There's no condemnation in his gaze, not for giving him up, nor for keeping Mel's true identity secret. Nothing but a reflection of the overwhelming emotion she's feeling.

She holds out her arms, and he goes into them, a grown man, all hard muscle, not a tiny soft baby any more. But he's still her son. Whom she had never expected to see again.

Joy overwhelms Jo, and her tears soak a wet patch on to the front of his shirt.

EPILOGUE

It's a perfect day for a winter wedding – crisp and clear, with a pale sun shining in a sky the colour of bluebells. The bride – Mel – looks beautiful, as all brides should, in a silvery-grey coat dress and fascinator, but it's the glow of happiness that truly shines out as Jeff leads her into the flower-bedecked room and towards Mark, who is waiting for her. Man of the world though Jeff is, he is so overwhelmed by emotion he can feel tears gathering in his eyes. To be able to give away the daughter who was born of the love he and Fliss shared is both a joy and a privilege. He only wishes Fliss could be here now to see it.

He's not the only one. Jo – also brimming with pride and tears that she's not even trying to hide – is remembering her friend with love. For a moment she wrenches her gaze away from Mark and Mel, now standing together in front of the registrar, and glances at Emma.

Oh how like her mother she is! It could be Fliss sitting there beside her – if only it were! But perhaps Fliss is here, sharing in this very special occasion with her two precious daughters. Jo has never been one for indulging fantasies, but as dust motes dance in the winter sun that slants in through the arched windows of the register office, it seems to her that Fliss is indeed here. The poignancy is almost unbearable, made more so by her own joy. How very lucky she is – the son she had thought was lost to her for ever marrying Fliss's daughter, whom she had raised as her own. It defies belief.

It's quite a small gathering – just family and close friends. Mel wanted it that way. She'd had her big white wedding first time around, and that had been nothing but a charade. But everyone who matters to her is here, and the intimacy of it lends meaning to the vows she and Mark are making. This time it is so right; this time she means every word.

Maggie and Martin are among the guests. They had taken some persuading to attend, but Emma managed it. Both girls felt very strongly that they should be here. Maggie is, after all, Mel's aunt, and the family has been split apart for far too long. It's time to try to bring it together. They've all met a few times now, and the first awkwardness is beginning to fade a little. There's still some way to go, but it's a start.

As Mark and Mel are pronounced man and wife, Emma glances at Mike, and as they exchange a look Emma feels as if she will burst with joy. She can still scarcely believe her luck – that not only should she have found someone who feels exactly like her soulmate, but also that he is free. Though both of them are absolutely sure they want to spend the rest of their lives together, they haven't rushed into anything; they want Daisy to be comfortable with the inevitable changes that will follow. Not much worry there, though – after all, it was Daisy who was instrumental in bringing them together, and since Mel and Mark's wedding invitation arrived she has been asking when they are going to get married, and please can she be bridesmaid?

At last the ceremony is over and bride and groom emerge on to the street, posing for photographs at the top of the impressive flight of steps. Emma reaches into her bag for the confetti she's stowed there, and her fingers touch a folded sheet of paper. The letter Fliss wrote to her when she knew she had lost her for ever, the letter Maggie has given her since all this came out. It's incredibly precious to Emma; she carries it everywhere with her, and often reads it, though she now knows it off by heart. Not so long ago she would have found it difficult, if not impossible, to understand the love Fliss spoke of, but now she does. It's the difference between the way she felt about Philip and the way she feels about Mike. A very special love. And she has been lucky enough to find it at just the right moment in her life.

'I'm so sorry, Mum, that things didn't work out for you,' she whispers. 'And I'm sorry too that I never got to find you.'

For a moment tears sparkle in her eyes, then she pulls out the confetti and closes her bag. The past is over, done with. Though Fliss will never be forgotten, it's time to move on.

But you left me a very precious gift, she adds silently. *My lovely sister.*

And she tosses a handful of confetti, which lands in Mel's hair and fascinator and clings like a blessing.

THE LETTER

My dearest Emma,

    I don't know how to begin this letter. I don't know how to make you understand. You're only a little girl now, but when you read this you will be grown up. And you will have grown up without me. But I want you to know I have never stopped loving you, and I never will. That this isn't the way it was meant to be. I can only try to explain and hope that you won't blame me too much.

    You'll wonder, I expect, why I did what I did. How I could have left you and your daddy, who I'm sure you love very much. And so you should! He is the kindest, sweetest, most honourable man I have ever known, and I loved him too. But not in the right way. Not the way I should have loved him. And then I met someone else, who was the very breath of life to me.

    It's hard to explain that sort of love. Unless you have experienced it for yourself, it's impossible to know what it feels like. I hope and pray you <u>will</u> experience it — it is the most precious rare gift, to be with someone who feels like another part of yourself, the part that makes you whole and complete. And I hope and pray that you won't be in the terrible place I was in when it happened to me — already married to someone else, someone good and kind but who can never be that special person, the love of your life. I don't want you to have to experience that kind of torment. Don't ever marry, Emma, unless you are absolutely, totally sure that you simply cannot live without your husband-to-be, whatever the pressures, whatever the circumstances. If you do, you too will risk finding that special person when it is too late, with all the heartache that will bring.

As for you, my darling, it was always my intention to come back for you. I couldn't contemplate a life without you — I love you so much. But in the end I came to realise that I just couldn't do it. Couldn't uproot you from your home, everything that was familiar, the people you loved and who loved you. Who knew what damage it might do? As things are, I know you are well and happy, and that must be enough.

I do cling, though, to the hope that one day you will come and find me. To think that I may never see you again is a pain I can hardly bear.

Please try to understand, my darling. Please don't judge me too harshly. I've done some foolish things in my life, but one thing I can never regret, and that is giving birth to you.

I'm sure you will grow up to be wiser and stronger than I ever was, and, I hope, luckier. But perhaps we make our own luck. If we do, I know you'll be just fine.

With all my love for ever.

Your loving mother,

Fliss